GHETTO GAMES

"G-Prince"

Author 2013

G. Prince author

 Ghetto Theory Publishing

ISBN: 978-0-9897486-0-5

Synopsis

G-Fly, Ty and Julian are three of the ghetto's most finest breed of youngsters to ever play and become exposed to the game.

Survival was a constant hustle that justified the means of everyday life and age was no exception to the rule.

Destiny meets fate through the sinful hands of coincidence which united these three youngsters with the real and undisputed "Game", better known as one of the most vicious west coast kingpins.

Game introduced the three youngsters to the dope game and problems couldn't ask for more trouble as the three youngsters become the coldest west coast dons to ever embrace the dope game.

Money, sex, murder, betrayal, drugs, and revenge only spell one thing, "*Ghetto Games*!"

This urban street novel is action-packed from beginning to end and guaranteed to keep the reader captivated with excitement while lost in the treacherous and scandalous world of the street games.

ABOUT THE AUTHOR

G. Prince was born in California. He found a profound love for creative writing and storytelling during his incarceration in federal prison.

He was crowned the Ghetto Prince for his explicit and realistic depiction of his ghetto tales.

His characters come alive in every story and he has a way of keeping his readers emotionally lost and captivated in each plot as if the story was being played out in front of them on the big screen.

G. Prince is one of the best authors yet to come and an urban bestseller.

Dedication

This book is dedicated to my two divine guardian angels:
My father and brother, thanks for always watching my back.
"I'll mourn you until I join you"! To my mother and sister, . .
"Thanks for loving me and believing in me."
To my three sons and ghetto seeds:
Xavier, Tyquoine and Bryan Jr.,
"Keep it GP 4 Life."
To my daughter and princess, Brynelle -
"Time or location can never change dedication."
To the real, I give a toast! And to them sucka's, tricks
and fakes. . . "I devotedly give you the finger."
"Don't hate the player, hate the game and feel the pain
that pertains, because all niggas ain't created the same."

TABLE OF CONTENTS

TABLE OF CONTENTS (continued)

Chapter 1
California Bread

It was the last day of school and the school parking lot was packed with kids from the high school cheering on as Tyquoine, aka "Ty," was having a fight with Wheels, a local gang member and the high school varsity wide receiver and track star.

The reason why this physical confrontation was taking place was because Xavier, aka G-Fly and Ty were in the school bathroom trimming their normal vic's in a casual game of dice when Wheels jumped his ass in the game as if he had some game and G-Fly trimmed him for his little $15 as quick as he can drop it.

Being the sore loser that he was, and being a junior surrounded by freshmen, he tried to put his buffalo hand down. But little did he know, Ty and G-Fly were two out of three that vowed "Death before dishonor."

Their third party Bryan, aka Julian, was in class at the time but he supported every thought or act that his two comrades Ty and G-Fly endured.

Wheels said, "Nigga, you're not going to ever get away with beating me outta mine!"

Ty said, "That's a done deal so what's next?"

And G-Fly said, "Yeah, make it light on yourself, nigga."

Wheels knew that he was outnumbered and didn't anticipate these young niggas challenging him. The lookout said, "Man, here come Big Max," and everybody ran toward the urinal, sink and mirrors and played it off as if they were just handling their common needs.

Big Max was an ex-amateur boxer who was 45 years old and in tip-top condition. He got into a fight at a club when he was in his prime and got shot 8 times with a 9 mm which put an end to his boxing career. Now he just do a little sparring on the side. Rumor has it that he's crazier then a road lizard.

Big Max said, "I guess you niggas think that ya'll got

all the got damn game. Now, I've watched about 10 of you muthafuckas come in here 20 minutes ago, and ain't no one came out. I don't see no girls in here and I hate to think otherwise, so I'm going to do you a favor and give you shady niggas one minute to get your asses up out of here and find your class or I'm going to take your asses to the principal office and let you explain your bladder problems!"

Everyone started breaking for the door as Big Max started busting up. Wheels looked over at Ty and said, "I'll see you after school."

And Ty started laughing and said, "Nigga, I can't wait!"

Big Max grabbed G-Fly by the arm and said "hold up a minute playa! You know that gambling on school grounds is a felony, and I'll bet a hundred dollars to a bucket of shit that you got two pair of dice in your pocket. One for the game and the other one's for the lames! Now, game recognize game all over the world and you know that the house must get its cut in order for the game to be real."

G-Fly reached into his pocket and pulled out a couple of bills and handed Big Max a $10 bill and said, "You're one big ugly scandalous muthafucka, but I ain't mad at you!"

Ty was standing there watching and started laughing and said, "Don't drink it all in one place nigga!"

And Big Max started smiling at the two youngsters as they all walked out and Big Max said, "Now take your bad asses to class, you only got a couple of more hours until school is over and you two niggas is out here playing hooky."

Ty was in the middle of the circle of kids doing what he enjoyed doing best, "Kicking ass!"

G-Fly was on the side taking bets and Julian was coaching his homie. Ty was working his job like a professional boxer and Wheels was swinging wild and trying to find a punch that would help his situation. Ty seen that he had Wheels swinging wild and timed it just as Wheels threw a wild right hook. Ty ducked it and stepped in with a strong overhand right that sent Wheels to the pavement for the second time. But this time, it was obvious that Wheels didn't have a chance to recoup, because Ty squatted over him and started putting the finishing touches on Wheels' ass whoopin'.

After Ty socked Wheels in the face a half dozen more times, Julian grabbed him and said, "Come on 'rade before you catch a hot one on this buster."

Ty looked down at Wheels as Wheels was curled up like a bitch semi-conscious and said, "Nigga, you better watch who the fuck you disrespect round here. My name is Ty not 'cry,' nigga, ain't nothing soft about me!"

G-Fly said, "Fools you know what time it is, kick mine in" and started collecting his winnings from the niggas who bet on Wheels.

As they walked away, they saw Big Max and Roger the gym teacher, standing in the back of a pickup truck and Roger handed Big Max a stack of bills as Big Max was smiling at the youngsters and gave Ty a victory shout and thumbs up.

Ty smiled as he threw his hands up displaying his victory as the undisputed champion.

As they were walking home from school caught up in their excitement, G-Fly said, "man we made $66 dollars today as he gave Ty and Julian both $22 dollars a piece. Ty said "Nigga, you better not ever let me find out that you're trying to get one over on us!"

G-Fly said, "Man what kind of shit you on? We're brothers in this struggle my nigga! Ya'll all I got and care about.

You know that I wouldn't do no scandalous shit like that with ya'll. I rather starve to death then to put money over our bond. I don't see how you can even say some shit like that or even think some shit like that."

Julian said, "Yeah nigga, you know that we vowed death before dishonor when it comes to our brotherhood."

Ty said, "Ya'll right. I apologize G-Fly. I'm just still hyped about that ass whoopin' that I put down on that busta, that's all!"

G-Fly said, "Well, don't let that be the reason that you get knocked the fuck out today," and socked Ty in the chest.

Ty grabbed his chest as everyone started laughing and said, "Okay, you got that one off, I deserve that one," as they turned down the alley that was a short cut through their neighborhood.

As they were walking down the alley on their way to the supermarket by their house, G-Fly said "look" and as Ty and Julian turned and looked they saw Rider, a known gang member slumped up against a fence next to a trash can with a bullet hole through his forehead and two through his shirt in his chest area.

Ty said, "Damn, looks like Rider has seen a bad day!" Julian said, "Yeah, his last day!"

"No more riding for his ass," G-Fly added. Then he said, "I wonder do he got any money on him?" and went over and patted his pockets.

Julian said, "G-Fly, let the dead rest in peace, man!"

G-Fly said, "I ain't gonna' disturb his rest, but he don't need this where he's about to go," and pulled out a miniature wad and then closed Rider's eyes and said, "Keep it 'G' gangsta!"

And they walked away as G-Fly counted out $300. Julian said, "Man you're a cold hearted muthafucka!"

G-Fly laughed and said, "What you don't want your cut?"

"I didn't say that! I just said you're a cold hearted nigga" and everybody started laughing as Julian snatched the hundred dollars from G-Fly's hand.

Chapter 2
Young & Polished

While at the supermarket Ty and Julian was stuffing their book bags full of food items. They was grabbing stuff like lunch meat, cheese, steaks, roast, pork chops, cookies, mayo and candy bars. G-Fly took a couple of items like bread, fruit, potatoes, milk, cereal and eggs to the counter. After the cashier rang up the items and gave G-Fly his change, G-Fly said, "It must be some sort of misunderstanding. I gave you a $20 bill, not a $10 bill."

The cashier said, "Sir, you must be mistaken. I'm sure that you gave me a ten dollar bill."

G-Fly went into his performance and said, "What you think that I can't count? Do I look like a fool to you or something? Or maybe you're trying to short change people and make you some extra money on the side? Well, I'm not going for it. I want to talk to the manager!"

About this time a small crowd was gathering around the cashier check stand and the manager ran over with the security guard to see what the big commotion was all about. The white manager said, "Excuse me sir, is there a problem?"

G-Fly said, "Yep, it's a problem, this lady (and pointed at the cashier) is trying to beat me! I gave her a twenty dollar bill and she gave me change for a ten dollar bill. How many people a day do she beat like this?"

And the crowd started whispering and making noises displaying their shock and surprise. The manager looked over at the older white woman who was the cashier and she said, "Jim, I'm pretty certain that this young man only gave me a 10 dollar bill."

G-Fly saw Ty and Julian laughing as they walked out. G-Fly said, "Look here lady, I know what I had. I had three twenty's in my pocket," and pulled out his wad of bills which displayed three twenty dollar bills in plan sight and he looked up at the woman with a surprised look on his face and said, "Ma'am, I am so sorry! I don't know where my mind is today. I lost my father to a car accident a couple of days ago and I just haven't been able to think straight."

She smiled as the crowd looked on sympathetically and the cashier said, "It's quite alright, sir, I understand!" And handed him his groceries and said, "My condolences to you for the loss of your father."

G-Fly looked up at her and said, "No need for sympathy; he wasn't shit anyway", and smiled and walked out as the cashier, manager and security guard's eyes all displayed shock.

The three youngsters laughed all the way home as they made it to their club house that they referred to as "The shack".

The shack was a vacant house in the hood that the youngsters converted into their club house. Ty had to whoop on a couple of smokers to mark their territory but after that was established, they hired some smokers to clean up the place, paint the walls, clean the carpet and tile, and scrub the bathroom and kitchen down and it was considered a home away from home.

The old lady next door to the shack charged the youngsters $20 a month to run an extension cord from her house to the shack and use her electricity. Really, she was glad that the youngsters ran all of the base heads and smokers out of the house. The youngsters had the locks changed and boarded up the broken windows so now they're the only ones who have access to the house "illegally".

The base heads and smokers brought old beds and furniture over and sold it to the youngsters and they even got a microwave, stereo system, and two TV's in the shack. So all and all, this is where all three of them consider home, that is, when they could get away from the chaos and confusion of their so-called family matters.

It seemed like they all had a typical ghetto family upbringing that cultivated the strength of their ghetto characteristics. G-Fly was only 14 years old but well laced in various aspects of the street hustle. G-Fly's mother got turned out on crack cocaine when he was only 11 years old but from then on, so much game had been exposed to his mind and character. He had seen his mother turn tricks numerous times for dope and money. She used to take him boosting with her and her smoker friends, show him how to play con games, and her old smoker boy friend was an old-school pick pocket who used to do everything from hot wiring cars, petty con, to burglarizing houses.

So, G-Fly was surely a young seasoned vet whose game was above average. He was a light brown skinned brother with an innocent face, and he wore his course hair short and waved up.

He stood six feet, pretty tall for a young man his age with a healthy slim physique. He didn't mind fighting, but was more of the type that would bust a person upside the head with something or stab him.

Ty, on the other hand was the aggressor of the three. He loved to fight and was pretty good at it. He wasn't the bully type, but he didn't believe in backing down and if you had a beef with the three, then he would most likely be the one that you would end up fighting. Ty grew up in a household as a single child with an alcoholic father who tended to always get drunk and whoop on him and his mother. Although his mother was also a tough one to match up with, Ty always took it upon himself to start the confrontation once his father got drunk to take the ass whoopin' off his mother.

Ty's father Eddie, used to enjoy this entertainment until Ty reached the age of 13 and started winning a lot of their fights. After Ty sent Eddie to the hospital for the second time in two weeks, Eddie stopped drinking as much and started respecting Ty and his mother Ruby more. Ty grew up to be a young stocky brother with a strong definition. He stood 5'10" and weighed in at 180 lbs, with a build like a running back. Ty was the second oldest of the three and would be 15 years old in three months. Ty was a dark-skinned brother who was average looking except for his pretty dark brown eyes that all of the ladies seemed to compliment him on.

But out of the three man crew, Julian was the one that

they both looked up to as the big brother and the thinker. He was the smartest of the crew in various aspects but always valued his comrades' thoughts and feelings. He kept them both on an equal level and called themselves "The Three Generals."

Julian was raised by his mother in a single parent home. His mother was a real pretty and thick light-skinned sista with hazel eyes and long wavy hair. She's the type of sista that's very educated and street wise and although she is on the county and Section 8, she still worked at a strip club on the side as a stripper to overcome her struggles and in the mornings, she attends nursing school so she can get her nursing license.

Niggas be jockin' her hard but she's the type that only fuck with men who's already married and got money because they can afford to trick and ain't looking for no commitment.

Julian is her pride and joy and she did everything possible to lace him on women, suckas, the game, and how to be a strong and real man from a woman's prospective. Also, she kept him in them books and taught him how to think on a profound level.

Julian was surely a cut above the rest in the way he embraced and perceived life. Also, he was considered a pretty boy by every woman's standard.

He's a light skinned brother with hazel eyes and long jet black wavy hair that he wear in a pony tail. He stands around 5'11" and weighed 165 lbs., with a nice slim physique.

Truthfully, he is also more aggressive then both of his comrades, but you will never be able to tell by his demeanor. Because he didn't seem like the type that would be violent, but he was a mastermind who enjoyed the games that trouble and problems brought.

His mom also used to take him over to his uncle's house who used to be a boxer. And his uncle taught him the fundamentals of how to box and Julian was becoming pretty good until his uncle died of an overdose of heroin. Nevertheless, his uncle was also an old-school ex-black gorilla family lieutenant who used to lace Julian with the codes and ethics of being a true gangsta.

Julian's heart embraced these teachings and learned how to represent it to the fullest. Also, he motivated his comrades to also embrace and live by these standards.

Back at the shack, they were stuffing their stomachs with sandwiches, chips and soda and talking about the party that Janet was throwing tonight. Janet had the hot's for Julian, but Julian played her off like a sister because he wasn't really feeling her style or promiscuous ways. She was a bona fide hoodrat, and although she was really cute and had a nice body, she still wasn't nothing but a nut to a hard-up fuck.

G-Fly said, "Man, we need to hit the mall and grab some gear for the party tonight."

Ty said, "Man, my pockets ain't fat like that."

G-Fly said, "Mine ain't either, that's why I said 'grab' something from the mall. You know, that ten finger discount!" and they started rolling.

Julian said, "Well, we need to make a move before it gets too late" and they all agreed as they headed out the door.

It was 6 o'clock when they reached the mall and everybody already knew the game plan. They walked into Bullocks separately and once G-Fly saw his comrades in position, he fell out and started faking a seizure. Everyone ran over to see what was going on as the store clerks started trying to assist the matter. Julian and Ty were already on point and were stuffing their book bags to capacity. They grabbed Fila sweaters, Fila shirts, Guess pants and coat jean outfits and Julian grabbed a few different colognes on the way out.

G-Fly kept track of time in his head and calming down like he was coming out of it. He looked up in the pretty blue eyes of the store clerk that had him cuddled in her arms and she said, "You just had a seizure, you'll be alright."

G-Fly said "My pills are in my right pocket" and she reached into his pocket and retrieved a fake Medical bottle that had aspirin in it, and took one out and put it in G-Fly's mouth, as G-Fly thanked her and struggled to get to his feet. He played like he was embarrassed and checked his wrist for his fake epilepsy bracelet and to allow everyone to catch a glimpse of it, and then he gave the pretty blue eyed white girl who helped him a big hug and kiss on the check and said, "Thank you very much, pretty lady. You are an angel," and she blushed as he turned and walked away, rubbing his arm as if he hurt it.

Once he got down the way and met up with his comrades, Julian looked at him and shook his head and said, "Man, you should try to become an actor, because you'll give Denzel Washington a run for his money," and they started laughing as Ty said, "And that's real!"

Julian handed him an orange bang and a bag of Famous Amos home made chocolate chip and walnut cookies from the Cookie Bakery.

G-Fly said, "I'm trying to go buy me some of them new Fila tennis shoes to go with this outfit."

Ty said, "Yeah, I'm feeling that," as they walked down to the Foot Locker shoe store. After they left the Foot Locker, G-Fly stopped and glanced at this sophisticated men's clothing store at this silk short pants and shirt set, and noticed this older white man in his 40's putting a fat wad of money back in his right pocket. G-Fly casually walked away and called his two comrades and said, "Peep ya'll, I just spotted a lick! This older white man just put a fat ass wad in his pocket and I'm going to dip on him." Julian said, "Man, do you think that you can get him?"

"It's worth a try!"

"Man, let's just knock him out and take it," Ty stated.

"It carries damn near the same amount of time!"

G-Fly said, "Look here Brutus, you got to learn how to have some finesse with shit."

Julian laughed and said, "How are you going to do it G-Fly?"

"Man, just bump into the dude on his left side and I got this! There he is!"

As the older white man was walking out carrying his

brand new suits covered in plastic, Ty moved quickly with G-Fly and got into position.

Once G-Fly gave the nod, Ty bumped the man with a pretty hard and solid collision, and as the man went to catch his balance, G-Fly grabbed him and held him up while Ty said "Excuse me, Sir," and bent down to pick up the suits that the man dropped. G-Fly shoved the man back aggressively and said, "You need to watch where you going, punk."

The older man said, "Excuse me, son, it was an accident; he ran into me."

G-Fly started rubbing his chest like he was hurt and walked away.

Ty handed the man back his bag and said, "I apologize; I was looking at that pretty girl over there" and pointed at a cute sista with some tight jeans on and the older man said, "I probably would have lost control too," and they laughed and parted. G-Fly and Julian met Ty outside the mall at the corner liquor store. Ty walked up and said, "Did you get it?"

"What you think nigga? I told you to stick with me and I'll take you places." And he handed Ty a small bank roll of $230.

Ty said, "I got to hand it to you G, you're the flyest nigga I know!" And he gave his comrade dap.

Julian said, "I agree. I almost fell out when I saw him put it down. You should've seen him push the man and tell him to watch where he was going. I almost fell out on that one," Ty said.

An older brother walked out the store and gave G-Fly a bag and held up his bottle of wine and said, "Good looking young bro," and held out the two dollars in change and G-Fly said keep it OG, put it on your next one!

The bum said, "That's love youngster!"

And they parted as the three youngsters headed back to the shack sipping on the six pack of Miller Genuine Draft that the bum just bought for them.

When they got back to the shack, they started ironing their outfits and took a quick shower. After they all were dressed to impress, they left out at 9:30, stopped by their parents' houses and headed to the party. G-Fly gave his mom $50 and told her to go and get her something to eat before she went on her smoking spree. She agreed and walked down to the hamburger fast food spot and grabbed a hamburger, fries and coke and stopped by the dope spot and got her a fat $30 rock and went back to her little two bedroom apartment and partied.

Ty stopped by his house to basically go check on his mother. Eddie was drinking but they were laying up in their freaky mood like love birds so Ty just slid $50 in the old pan where his mother keep her stash at and left.

Julian's mother was gone as usual so Julian just put a $50 dollar bill in his mother's panty drawer and left.

It was 10:45 when they arrived at the party and the party was jumping. Janet's mother was selling chicken plates for 5 dollars a pop, beers were $2, and hard liquor, gin, and E & J was both $4 a pop and Janet's older brother James was selling the fat Indo sacks. There was wall-to-wall honeys and all of them was looking sexy and flied up. School was officially out and everybody celebrated summer like a legal holiday to get wild and freaky.

Ty tapped G-Fly on the arm and said, "Look at that bad bitch over there. I ain't never seen her."

"Me either," G-Fly admitted. "And you're not lying, she's a bad muthafucka! Are you going to holler at her, or just gonna' stand here staring all night?"

Ty said, "Oh man, I was just putting you up on her. You know, just in case you wanted to get at her."

G-Fly said, "What nigga? Let me find out your game, shy?

Ain't this a bitch? I can't believe you're a scary cat. As much ass as you whoop around town; I thought that you'll be an animal on a bitch."

"Man, fuck you! I ain't scared of nothing nigga! I just ain't tripping off no bitch right now."

G-Fly started busting up and Julian walked up with two Miller beers and handed them to his two comrades.

G-Fly said, "Julian guess what?"

Julian looked at them both and said, "What?"

"Your general over here is game shy."

"You're bullshitting!"

"Man, I'm dead serious. See that little pretty dime piece over there.

Julian looked and said "Damn, she's right! Yeah your boy here is fending for her attention, but scared to go holla."

"Man I ain't scared, I just ain't tripping!" Julian said.

"Listen Ty, we're all mac's by law, it's in our blood. When you're down with us, you represent the best so don't ever be scared to go and holla at a woman. All she can say is 'no,' but if you don't try then you'll never know so do us all a favor and go and represent for your 'rades. Here, and Julian gave Ty his beer and said, "go over there and give her this beer and introduce yourself, and tell her that you love her profile and was hoping that you could get to know her better. If she accepts the beer, then she's interested, and just mac on her like you know I would and I guarantee, she'll be given up the snatch by the end of the night."

Okay, you know that I'm going to rep for my 'rade!" And he looked at them and said, "You ain't said nothing" and he started walking over toward the cute thick sista.

G-Fly said, "Man, you pumped that nigga up to get his feelings hurt. He's a straight square to the mac game!"

"What you mean nigga, he's been hanging around us long enough to know by now, he just ain't use to spittin' it."

They looked on as Ty walked up and handed the girl the beer and the girl took it and smiled, and wet her lips and said thank you.

Julian smiled and said, "Man, I told you."

And G-Fly said, "If that lame ass game worked, then I'm going to get a 6-pack" and they both started smiling.

As Ty nervously walked up to the cute thick sista, he gave her the cold beer and said "How you doing? My name is Ty. I couldn't help myself. I had to come over here and introduce myself in hopes that I could have the pleasure of getting to know you better."

She said, "Thank you! My name is "Dezae."

"That's a very lovely name. Here, let me open that for you." And he twisted the top off of the cold beer and she said "Thank you."

Ty said, "Are you enjoying the party?"

"Yeah, it's nice."

"Who did you come with?"

"Oh, I'm here with my cousin Fay, but she ran off with her boyfriend about 30 minutes ago and I was just enjoying the music."

"Are you from out this way?" Ty asked.

"No, I'm from Pasadena."

"Oh, yeah? I heard that Pasadena had a lot of beautiful ladies, and I see that it wasn't a lie" and he smiled at her.

She said "You got some pretty eyes" and Ty blushed.

Ty said, "Listen baby, since you came without a date and I came without a date, how about we make the best of it and go and turn this party out?"

She said "I'm feeling that" and they went out on the dance floor and started partying.

G-Fly went over to the bar and said "Let me have some of that E&J and coke."

Janet's uncle said "Are you 21?"

"Man, everyone in here is 21" and G-Fly pulled out his wad of bills and gave the bartender a five dollar bill. The uncle leaned over and said, "You know that it's a private dice game in the back room, $10 admission."

G-Fly said, "For real? Quit playing!"

"What you trying to do?" Janet's uncle asked.

"I'll be right back!"

G-Fly walked up to Julian who was on the dance floor getting his freak on with Janet's thick hot ass. "Peep this out, 'rade!

"Hi, G-Fly," Janet said.

"What's up girl, you keep throwing that ass on my nigga like that he's going to give you what you're begging for!"

"I wish he would."

Julian just smiled, knowing that his 'rade just set him

up with some for sure pussy tonight.

"Listen J, I'm about to go in the back room and trim these fools in some of these rocks."

"Oh yeah, Janet throwing a party like that?"

"Baby, you know I ain't no square bitch. I just need a real and down nigga in my life."

G-Fly said, "Ain't nothing better than a down bitch, but you know if you're down with one of us then you got to be down with us all!"

"As long as ya'll know how to keep it real with a bitch."

"Yeah, we need to give you a personal interview and see if you qualify."

"Whenever you ready, Fly."

G-Fly looked at Julian and said, "We might need to recruit her and she smiled and shook her big sexy ass against Julian's crouch. Julian's eyes gave that expression like you may be right. G-Fly looked over at Ty who was getting his ultimate party on with the cute thick broad he was digging on.

G-Fly said, "I'll be damned. Remind me to get a 6-pack before we leave." Julian looked over at Ty and started busting up.

G-Fly said "You know where I'll be."

And Julian shook his head and said, "Aye," and gave G-Fly a hundred and said "let me get a piece of that!"

G-Fly looked at Julian and smiled and said "Smart man! Let Ty know where I am in case he's trying to come up."

And he walked over to Janet's uncle and gave him $10 and Janet's uncle opened up the door and said "Have fun."

G-Fly walked in the bedroom and another old man was in the room over seeing the dice game. He said "Welcome, young playa.

The rules are simple. You can roll your roll. The house cut 5 dollars off 6 and 8 once only on every point, once we cut on a point on a 6 and 8, then we don't cut again until the next point. Bet what you want to, money on wood and no tee's or juice allowed!"

G-Fly said, "That sounds good to me" and saw that it was only two young dudes in the room and the rest was old heads and they had big money in the game. It was 8 people altogether in the room and a cool 20 g's laying around. G-Fly peep the old man in front of him roll, and knew that he knew a little something so he said, "I got 20 saying he hit," and two people gave him a fade and the old man hit his point. G-Fly said, "Bet back; I'm going to give you action, bet the whole $40 to both of you."

He got the fade and the old man came out with a 7! G-Fly said, "Let it ride" and both of his vics faded the $80 and the old man came out with another 7. G-Fly picked up $80 from both stacks and said "Let it ride" and his vic said, "Let him catch a point."

"Man, don't get paranoid, now! The old man came out with a 4 little Joe! Both of the vics wanted the fade now. G-Fly said, "Ah, ya'll like that point, huh? Bet!" And the old man shot 8 times before he hit little Joe! G-Fly said "Quit playing with them and let's get this money."

G-Fly said, "Can I get a fade?"

"Let him catch a point first!"

The old man rolled and hit a 6 and nobody wanted to really bet. G-Fly said "Can I get a fade for a dub or something" and one of the vics threw a $20 out there. And the old man came out with 7 and crapped out. G-Fly's dice were next and one of the vics said "What you going to do with them and how much you betting on yourself?"

G-Fly said "I got a hundred to one and all!"

Three of the vics dropped a hundred dollar bill and G-Fly took the fades. The old man dropped a $50 riding with G-Fly.

G-Fly hit 7 three times in a row in all different ways.

One vic said, "I got $500 saying that you do come out with another 7."

G-Fly said "I'll put up $250 to your $500!"

The vic said "Bet" and another one said "Can I get the same bet?"

G-Fly said, "I really don't want to, but I'm not going to deprive you!"

And the vic dropped the $500 and G-Fly met the fade and came out with 4-3 and picked up his money. One of the vic said one more time give me the same bet and G-Fly dropped $250 and looked at the other vic and he said, "Hell yeah," and dropped $500.

The other vic said "I want some too" and dropped $500 and G-Fly dropped another $250 and he looked at the old man on side of him and the old man said, "I believe in you youngster," and G-Fly came out with 5-2 and picked up his money.

He said "Can I get a fade" and one of the vic said, "Hell, you might as well pass the dice now cause ain't nobody going to challenge your stroke after hitting 5 licks back to back."

G-Fly said, "Okay hustler, shoot your shot, I got your fade" and the man picked up the dice and said "I'm shooting $50 a roll. G-Fly took the fifty and put up a hundred and said, "You got a fade!" and the man started trying to shoot his shot, but did have one and fell right off.

After G-Fly left Julian and Janet on the dance floor, Janet turned toward Julian and said, "Let's go to my bedroom so we can have some privacy."

Julian said "Lead the way," and Janet escorted Julian to her upstairs bedroom and once they got there, Janet locked the door and pulled her one piece mini dress over her head and stood there in her sexy black lace panties and bra set and black high heel suede pumps.

Julian said, "Damn baby, I knew you was stacked, but I didn't know that you had it that good!"

She unhooked her bra and pulled her panties off. Julian was undressed in twenty seconds flat; he reached into his wallet and grabbed his condoms and it was on.

Julian was wearing Janet's thick light-skinned ass out for an hour straight. He must've hit that pussy ten difference ways. After they finally satisfied their sexual appetite she said, "Did you enjoy it?"

"Baby if I knew that pussy was that good, I would've been hitting that thang on a regular."

"So do I qualify?"

"Well baby, I can't make that decision alone. Like G-Fly said, you got to be down and devoted to all of us. And we don't play that jealousy shit, so you got to know and recognize your position as a thorough bitch in our lives and play your role to the fullest."

"Baby you know that I'm down, and I'll do what needs to be done to prove to ya'll that I'm down and real to ya'll."

"Well, you can start by showing me how good that head of yours is!"

"You know that I got the bom!"

And she smiled and went down on him and started giving him some of that bom ghetto head. "Yeah baby, you're the bom."

Now put this condom on and show me how good you can ride this dick!"

She smiled and put the condom on him and straddled him and rode him like a veteran. Julian said, "Damn baby, you got that chronic!"

"You like it?"

"Hell yeah."

Then he turned her over and put her legs on his shoulders and started fucking the mess out of her. And she loved every bit of it. She dreamed of the day that Julian would give her some dick and now her deepest fantasy was becoming a reality.

Ty was sweating as him and Dezae walked off the dance floor and Ty led her over to the bar and grabbed two gin and 7 Ups.

Dezae said, "Ty, I got to use the restroom. Can you go with me because I don't know nobody?"

Ty said, "Yeah come on, I got to go too!"

As they walked up to the bathroom, a boy and girl just walked out together and was laughing. Dezae grabbed Ty by the hand and said, "Come on, you can come in with me."

They went inside of the bathroom and she locked the door and pulled up her mini skirt over her ass and squatted over the toilet and peed. Ty said, "Damn, I didn't know that women can piss standing up."

"Look at you getting you an eye full, huh? Do you like what you see?"

"Yeah, you got a pretty pussy."

She wiped herself and he walked and pulled out his dick and started pissing. The alcohol was taking effect now and Ty was getting bolder by the minute. She looked over at Ty's dick and said, "Damn, you got a nice big one."

Ty smiled and said "Do you like it?"

She said, "Maybe."

She walked over and grabbed it after he got through pissing and wiped off the head with a wet piece of toilet paper and Ty started getting rock hard as she played with it and she started tongue kissing him.

She said, "If you had a condom, I'd give you some of this bom pussy."

Ty said, "You ain't said nothing," and reached into his wallet and pulled out a Magnum. She took it and put it on his big 9 inch dick and bent over the sink and let Ty hit it from the back. Ty was stuffing her full of his manhood and thought back to what Julian told him about how easy it was to mac a bitch down and get the pussy. Julian told me that I'll be hitting this pussy tonight if I mac'ed her down right.

Ty pulled out and laid her on the bathroom floor and started kissing her to stop her from moaning so loud and she was hot as a fire and coming back to back as Ty deep-stroked her.

She put her legs around his back and he started power driving her as he felt his nut coming, and a minute later they were locked up in ecstasy as they let go and released a profound orgasm.

She said, "Did you like it?"

Ty said, "Baby you got the bom."

And she started smiling as she gave him a deep satisfying kiss. They washed up and walked out and another couple was patiently waiting and Ty recognized the dude from school and the dude said "What's up Ty? I see you enjoying the party" and smiled.

Ty said, "But of course, and I hope you do the same!"

"You're reading my mind" and he walked into the

restroom with a fat white girl.

Ty walked over where G-Fly, Julian and Janet was standing and G-Fly and Julian was eating some chicken dinners and Ty said, "What's up 'rades, this is Dezae, a very good friend and companion of mine."

G-Fly looked at Julian then back at Ty and said, "It's a pleasure to meet you Dezae."

And Julian said, "Yeah," and reached out his hand and shook hers and said "This is our close companion Janet" and Janet shook her hand as Ty looked at his two comrades for some sort of understanding and Julian said, "Baby why don't you take Dezae and grab her and Ty a dinner and a couple of beers?"

She said, "Okay baby, come on Dezae" and the girls went to get the food.

Ty said, "What's this 'our companion' shit?"

Julian said Janet want to be on our team and we told her, come one, come all!" and she said she'll be down for all of us, as long as we accept her and be down and keep it real with her."

"Is that right?"

"Yeah, she got that chronic too."

Ty looked at G-Fly and said, "Did you hit it too?"

"Not yet, but it's on my agenda for what I got plans to do tonight. What about you and that cute thick thang?"

"Oh yeah, I just got through tearing that up and it's fire!"

"For real?"

Julian said and gave his homie dap and said, "I told you that you was a true mac, you just got to believe in yourself!

G-Fly said, "Nigga, I'm proud of you. Now I know that you're a true 'G'!" and they laughed and gave each other dap.

G-Fly said, "Guess what else?"

"What?"

"They had a dice game in the back room and I went in there and hit for 4 g's."

"You're bullshitting!"

"Man don't worry" G-Fly said, you know that you got a cut coming! I told you man, I'll never leave my niggas out of a good lick. We're brothers man!"

Ty said, much love my nigga," as he received the fat roll of bills from his comrade. "How much is this?"

"It's $1,200" G-Fly said.

Ty looked at both of his comrades and said, "You know that I love you, right?" And they both shook their heads, as Ty put the wad of bills in his pocket and gave them both a ghetto embrace. The girls came back with beers and chicken dinners and Dezae gave Ty a piece of paper with her phone number on it.

"I see that you read minds too," Ty said. And Dezae started giggling as they dug into the chicken dinners. Ten minutes later, Wheels and two of his homeboys walked into Janet's party. One of Ty's young admirers said, "Hey Ty, heads up man. That nigga Wheels and two of his homeboys just hit the door."

Ty, G-Fly, and Julian all looked up and saw Wheels standing by the door with two other niggas from his gang. G-Fly said, "I had a feeling that these niggas was going to show up" and pulled out his buck knife nonchalantly.

"Ain't nothing better than a good fight" Ty said.

Julian said, "We hit them hard and quick and 'G' it's too many witnesses around so make sure you don't hit no vital spots with your Jason act."

"Got you," G-Fly said. Janet and Dezae just watched in surprise as they saw the three young playas instantly flip into gangsta mode. Julian led the pack as they quickly walked up to Wheels and his homeboys and when Julian got 8 feet away from Wheels biggest homeboy, he just ran over like a lion on his prey and started beating the shit out of him. Wheels and his other homeboy was caught off guard and once they realized what was going down, it was too late. Ty caught Wheels with a right hook that broke his jaw and knocked him unconscious.

G-Fly took on a different approach and bust the other gang banger over the head with a Miller bottle that sent the gang banger to the floor and then he started kicking and stomping the dude in the face.

Ty said, “G-Fly, G-Fly, that’s enough G!”

And G-Fly looked up at his two comrades and took his buck knife and stabbed the dude twice in the arm.

Julian said “Let’s roll my niggas” and looked over at Janet and gave her a hundred dollar bill off of his bank roll and said “Nice party baby girl,” as him and his comrades ran out the party and made their get away.

Chapter 3
A Dream Come True

As they were on their way back home laughing and talking about their current events, G-Fly looked over at his two comrades and said, "Peep my niggas, this shit got to come to an end."

"What?" Ty said.

"How in the hell are we going to be trying to make a quick get away on foot? We need to all put up like $500 and buy us a cool bucket!"

Julian said, "I'm feeling that!"

"Yeah, that's a good idea!" Ty said.

"And also that way we can take our little hustle act on the road," said G-Fly.

"Listen man, I was thinking that we need to invest our money in a dope sack and really put our hustle down. It ain't like we don't know the game. And truthfully, we know all of the smokers in the hood. And all the illegal shit we be doing, we're facing the same consequences," Julian said.

G-Fly said, "Man, you know I'm down."

Ty said, "Me too."

G-Fly said, "Man, fuck this shit. I'm tired of walking."

"Man what you about to do?"

"I'm about to hotwire this bucket so we can get back to the hood quicker."

Julian said, "Man, you should have been did with that shit!"

"I didn't think about it until now."

G-Fly slid into the driver's set and started looking for the right wires so he can cut. Julian and Ty was so caught up trying to see how G-Fly was going to hotwire the car that they didn't see the man that was creeping up behind them.

Game said, "You niggas got to be out of your got damn minds!"

The youngsters all looked up and saw the presence of a stocky built tall dark-skinned brother, who was holding a big fat 357 magnum with an 8" barrel. "Get the fuck up out of my shit!"

G-Fly stepped out of the car and Game said "Drop the muthafucken knife nigga! Did you cut any of them wires?"

G-Fly dropped the knife and said "Naw man, I didn't get a chance to!"

"What the hell are ya'll doing in my shit?"

Julian answered, "Man don't shot us! We was just trying to steal a ride home!"

"Yeah man, we're coming from this house party and we're tired of walking, so I was trying to put my lick down so we can get a ride back to my crib," G-Fly said.

Game said, "Nigga, how old are ya'll?"

Julian said, "I'm 15 and both of my comrades is 14!"

Ty said "Man if you're going to shoot us then go ahead and bust, but my arms is getting tired of being held up like this and my feet is tired too!"

Game started laughing and said, "Man put your hands down. You! Pick up your knife and put it in your pocket, ya'll smoke weed?"

G-Fly said, "That's what I'm talking about, put it in the air!" And everyone started laughing. Game put his gun in his pants and said, "Come on" and they followed Game up to Game's nice little two bedroom apartment.

"Have a seat!"

"This is a nice place," Julian said!

"Yea, this is the kind of shit I need," G-Fly said.

Game laughed and replied, "What's ya'll names?" as he put a cigar box full of that purple hair indo on the living room table in front of Ty and said, "Roll us some up."

Ty opened up the cigar box and said "Daaamn! Not the Icky Sticky!"

Julian said, "My name is Julian and these are my two comrades. That's G-Fly and this is my nigga, Ty."

"Oh yeah? Well, my name is Game. How the hell did you learn to hotwire a car?"

"Man, we're not lames to the game and I seriously doubt that it's not too much that we don't know about!"

Game said, "Is that right, well what you know about

this?" and he pulled out a brown paper bag and poured out like 20 ounces of rock cocaine.

G-Fly said, "Man, who don't know what that is? My mom is fucked up off that shit right now!"

Julian said, "Listen Game, me and my comrades was just talking about investing our money in some of this shit, so we can come up. We've been petty hustling and it's about time that we advance to a higher level of the game."

"Is that right?" Game said. "How much money are ya'll trying to invest?"

"Well, my nigga over there just came up on a cool lick on a dice game and we all came up with a cool $1,500 apiece, but we want to buy us a cool bucket too, so we won't be walking, so we probably can come up with about $1,500 to invest."

Game was captivated by the way these young niggas carried it and wondered if they would be a blessing in disguise. "So, what are ya'll affiliated with a gang or something?"

"Naw man, we don't get down with that crazy unnecessary shit. We're just comrades in the struggle, the three generals of the ghetto!"

Game laughed and said, "So all three of ya'll stick together like brothers, huh?"

"Yea ride together, hustle together, and will die together," Ty said and passed Game a fat joint and put two more on the table in front of them.

"What if ya'll get busted and go to jail and the police tell ya'll, that ya'll can go home or get out, if ya'll show them who you cop from?"

Julian said, "Hold up nigga! We don't believe in no snitching! We live by the code 'Death before dishonor,' and we're true to this gangsta shit!"

"G-Fly, put that up!"

And Game glanced over and saw G-Fly close his buck knife and realized that these young niggas had a lot of heart and were some pretty down young niggas.

Game said, "Hold up youngstas, I was just trying to see what type of time you young niggas was on, because I need some young soldiers on my team and I got to make sure that I don't mistake the fake for the real. You feel me?"

Julian said, "We're trying to, but why don't you be a little more specific?"

"Listen, I'm looking for some real down niggas to put on my team. I got a lot of dope spots that I push and I got an escort service that needs a little more security placed on it. I'm allergic to suckas, tricks, vics and bustas!"

G-Fly passed the joint back to Game and let out a cloud of smoke and said "We are too!"

Ty said, "For real!"

Game said "Listen here. Instead of investing your money in a sack, how about coming to work for me? Ya'll will oversee all my houses and make the drop off and pick up to each one, and handle some of my other clientele and the security over my escort service. I'm talking about becoming my three gangsta generals and I'll pay each one of you a thousand dollars a week, hook you guys up with a cool apartment and some nice bucket so ya'll can handle our business appropriately. What do you guys think about that?"

Julian looked at both of his comrades and could easily read their minds and he said, "I think fate has brought us together!"

G-Fly said, "You ain't lying, because I just fell in love with this nigga." And everybody started busting up.

Game said "Listen ya'll loyalty and devotion is a must. If you guys ever try to deceive me, betray me or disrespect me, then I will kill you with no hesitation. When you represent me, you represent the best, and ain't nothing supposed to ever come before us or between us. And I expect you guys to always keep our business between us. Do you understand where I'm coming from?"

Julian said, "Yeah big bro, we live by the code and ethics of silent and secrecy and we're going to be down for you and have your back to the fullest!"

"Good, good. I believe you too."

Game looked at his watch and said, "It's 2:40 a.m. Come on ya'll, I got to make a run!" And he picked up the ounces of dope and the joints and they headed out the door.

Game took the youngsters with him to deliver his dope to his dope spots and then he stopped at a hamburger fast-food spot that stays open all night. They all ordered them something and after receiving their order, they all went back to the car and Game said, "Ain't this a bitch" and jumped out of his bucket and ran over to another older heavyset dude's car who stood about 5'10" and weighted about 210 lbs. The dude just pulled up and was getting out of his car when he looked up and saw Game pointing a big fat 357 at his head.

Game said, "Get out of the car nigga!"

Big Mike said, "Hold up Game, don't shoot me man."

And the youngsters walked up as Game reached down in Big Mike's waistband and pulled out Big Mike's 9 mm automatic and handed it to Julian.

Game said, "Nigga where is my got-damn money?"

"Man, I've been trying to come up, but I've been taking some losses. You know as soon as I come up I got you!"

"Muthafucka, do you think that you can just run off with my shit and act like I don't exist?" Game slapped Big Mike with the 357 magnum across the head and Big Mike fell to the ground as Game slapped him a couple of more times and started kicking him and Ty and G-Fly joined in and started helping Game stomp Big Mike out.

Game stopped the ghetto soccer game and told Big Mike, "Nigga you got a week to get my money to me or I ain't going to be playing with you next time I see you. Let's roll!" And they all went and jumped in the car and left.

Game looked over at his new comrades and handed G-Fly a joint and said "Put some fire to this 'rade." And G-Fly said "Put it in the air then!" And everyone started laughing.

Ty said "Man, it seems like I've been fighting all day. I kicked a nigga's ass after school, and then knocked the same nigga out at the party three hours ago, and now we had to stomp this fool out."

Game said, "Damn nigga, you've been getting down

like that?"

"Yea man, it seems like I can't duck a fight tonight."

"Yea, but my nigga got a cool vicious fight game," G-Fly said.

"What about you?"

"Oh, I'll get down in a heartbeat, but I'll put something in a nigga!"

"What about Julian?"

"Oh, he's a straight animal! But I'll kick both of their asses truth be told, but I just give them passes because they're my comrades!"

And everybody started laughing and Ty said "Yeah right, let you tell it!"

They pulled back up at Game's apartment and went upstairs and started smashing their food. Game said, "ya'll can kick it here tonight and tomorrow we'll go and get ya'll situated."

Julian said, "Game can I have this 9mm that you took off that fool tonight?"

Game said, "Naw that damn thang could be dirty. I got some new heat that I'm going to give you. Don't worry my nigga, I'm going to get you right! You guys are going to have everything that you ever wanted as long as you keep it real and be down for the cause. This ain't no bullshit game that you're getting involved in everything from this point on in your life will become a very serious matter. So don't ever take nothing for granted. The only reason why that fool tonight is still breathing is because it was too many witnesses around and even sometimes that don't make a difference. When you enter this game your very soul becomes your collateral and if you fuck up or get caught slipping then you will find yourself dead or imprisoned or sometimes both.

I've been in this game for a while and not only am I pretty successful, but I also master this shit. Therefore, you guys are fortunate enough to be learning from one of the best who ever played in this ghetto game. If you got a conscience then you better abandon it now, and if you're scared to pop that pistol on a nigga, bitch or police, then this game ain't right for you. My word and thoughts is law and I expect ya'll to enforce it by all means and in everyway. Together we will always rule and succeed, but if ever your brother should try to betray the family and foundation that we're building, then it's your sworn duty to punish him or kill him, as the problems see fit. And never show weakness. If you got to die then always die a man, not a coward. You feel me?"

"Hell yeah, we feel you," Julian said.

"We all going to die anyway, so we might as well die for a cause that's worth dying for! We ain't trying dying in this world broke without a chance to enjoy life, or have nothing in life. That shit is for them cowards and suckas! We're trying to at least live before we got to die. And if anyone get in our way or try to oppose our cause, then they will be dealt with like they supposed to get dealt with. Ain't that right ya'll?"

"You're muthafuckas right!" G-Fly answered.

"Man, we don't duck no rec!" Ty said.

Game smiled and said "That's right!"

"Man, it's us against the world and we're down for you in everyway and to the fullest," Julian added.

* * * *

They all stayed up 'til 5 a.m. before they dozed off. Julian took the extra bedroom and G-Fly took the couch, while Ty went hard on the carpet.

Game woke them up at 11 a.m. and Lady-G already had lunch cooked. She cooked up a country breakfast with the eggs, sausage, bacon, hash browns, and pancakes. Game introduced everyone to his bottom lady, Lady-G and the youngsters instantly fell in love with her like a big sister. She was real down, thick and very attractive! She stood 5'6", weighed 125 lbs., all in the right places. She was a beautiful brown complexion, with long pretty hair and had that sexy innocent features that would deceive any man. She was a bona fide hoe, and ran the escort service and was as down as they came.

G-Fly said, "When I seen Lady-G walk in the house

this morning I thought she was an angel, so I just rolled over and went back to sleep because I knew regardless of where I was heaven or hell, I was in the right place!"

Everybody started laughing and Lady-G blushed at the compliment. After they got through eating, Game took the youngsters with him as he went to make his deliveries and pick ups and he introduced the youngsters to the worker who was running his dope spots and told his worker that the youngsters would have power and authority over the dope spots and they should be given the utmost respect. His workers were kind of doubtful, but knew better then to try to question Game's authority. Game took the youngsters by the shack to change their clothes and was tripping off the balls of these young niggas. The shack looked like an old run down vacant house from the outside, the windows were boarded up and everything. But on the inside the house was clean and slightly fixed up.

Game said, "Man ya'll crazy. What if the owner comes around here?"

G-Fly said "Man, fuck the owner. I'm the new owner now!" And everyone started laughing.

They left and Game took his young comrades to the Fox Hills Mall and spent $1,500 a piece on them and got them all a cool wardrobe. They all got the latest Fila, Guess and Nike outfits and tennis shoes. And grabbed some khaki outfits, 501's, boxer drawers, and white t-shirts. It was the summer of 1987 and the beginning of a new life for the youngsters.

After they left the mall, Game took them over to their new apartment. It was a nice 3 bedroom townhouse built apartment, with 8 apartment complexes total on the property. And the apartment was just as fixed up and nice looking as Game's other apartment. Game gave them keys to three nice buckets that were parked out front. One was a '77 Cutlass, the other was a '76 Malibu, and the other was a '75 Monte Carlo. And all of them was in tip top condition. Game gave them a duffle bag full of guns that had a 45 automatic that G-Fly grabbed and instantly fell in love with, two 9 mm automatics, one 380 automatic, and two 357's, one with a 4 inch barrel and the other with the 8 inch barrel. Julian grabbed a 9mm and a 3.80, and Ty grabbed the 357 with the 8 inch barrel and the other 9 mm.

G-Fly looked at the other 357 magnum with the 4 inch barrel and said, "Come here baby, don't worry I won't leave you behind." And everybody started laughing.

Game gave them all pagers and gave them 100 ounces already cooked. "Listen," Game said, "Once you get down to your last 10 ounces, then call me and let me know and I'll bring you a hundred more. After you pick up the money for the day, then call me, so me or Lady-G can pick it up. Now, this is you guys home and security. But it's not a place where you bring people to kick it at. The only one that should know about this place is you three, me and Lady-G, anybody else becomes a possible threat.

Bitches will set you up and have niggas run in your spot to try to jack you, and them niggas that you think is your so-called friends would eventually become jealous of you and tell on you to the police or other envious niggas, or plot to jack you, so keep this spot as your secret hide away, because this is where you lay your head at and keep your money and dope. It ain't good to sleep on your dope like this, but since this is a new spot and you won't be moving nothing out of it, it's acceptable for the time being. Now, if you want a spot to entertain your little girl friends at, then set one up for that purpose or take them to the motel. Either or, you guys got enough money to do both! Keep a bitch out of your business and never trust anyone outside of our circle. Here's your first week payment" (and he gave them all a thousand dollars).

"One thing I want you to learn and to practice and that's how to stack your money. This is your first lesson in the game!

Once you master this lesson, then you will become rich! Lady-G is cooking dinner for us over at my main house, so after you guys finish your deliveries and pick ups this afternoon, then stop through. Here's the address" and he gave them a piece of paper with his address and home phone and pager number. "Once you remember it, then burn the paper. Also, Lady-G got an appointment for you guys at the DMV to hook you up with some fake ID's! You know that you got to be 21 years old to really be able to have fun. And, also we don't need the police pulling you over and searching and find the dope, or money, because you ain't got no license to drive. Is it anyone who don't know how to drive? Good! Lady-G would lace you guys on the functions of the escort services tonight. The refrigerator and cabinets are full and there's a ounce of that indo under the couch. Any questions?"

Julian said, "Naw man, this is the realest shit a nigga ever been exposed to!"

"Yeah, I keep hoping that I'm not dreaming," G-Fly said. And everybody laughed as Game said "Believe me 'rades, this is only the beginning. I just want to make sure that you guys is right for the position. If I gave it to you all at once, you would probably go crazy!"

"Shit, you ain't lying, because my thoughts is spinning a thousand miles per hour right now," Ty said. And everyone started rolling.

Game said, "I know that ya'll got a lot to talk about and digest, so I'll catch back up with ya'll tonight. If you need me, page me."

Everybody gave Game a ghetto embrace and Game left out the door.

Ty turned to his comrades and said, "Man, can you believe this shit? This is the best thing that ever happened to me in my life!"

G-Fly said, "I know man! The game lord is truly watching over us!"

Julian said, "Peep, this ain't nothing to take for granted. Game is a real nigga and we got to accept him in our heart and life as our comrade and be totally devoted and loyal to him and this game. Either you're in or you're not; it ain't no half stepping at this stage of the game. Call it?

G-Fly said, "Man, I've been born for this kind of shit, you know that I'm down!"

Ty said, "My nigga, I'm ready to kill or die for this cause and you know I'm down for my 'rades to the fullest."

Julian said “Well, it’s official then, we roll with Game to death do us part.”

Game was about to walk back in the apartment to ask them a question when he overheard his young comrades discussing their decision on whether they were going to be down and devoted to the cause. And smiled and just walked away after hearing them express their hidden devotion to die for the cause. Game knew that these three youngsters were thorough and a blessing to the Game and he looked forward to lacing them and having them on his team.

Chapter 4
Blessed by Game... Baptized Into Sin

After the youngsters made the afternoon deliveries and pickups, they counted the money and made sure that the full 20 g's was there and then they headed to Game's main house that was located in the Hollywood Hills. Julian pulled up in the '77 Cutlass and G-Fly asked "Man, are you sure that this is the right address?"

"Yep! That's what it says on this paper," Ty replied.

There was a 560 convertible SEC Benz, a 300E Benz, a Vet and a black Chevy Blazer, all parked in the front yard and driveway, as Game opened up his front door with a welcoming smile. The youngsters got out of the car and Game welcomed them all with a warm ghetto embrace. G-Fly said, "Man, is this your tilt?"

"What you thought, I was faking with you? I told you that I've mastered this game in a major way! Don't worry, stick with me and you'll have one too," Game said, as he led the youngsters into his 7 bedroom baby mansion. Julian handed him the big brown paper bag with the 20g's in it as Game showed his comrades around his plush tilt. Lady-G walked out of the kitchen and said, "What's up. I hope ya'll are hungry, because I cooked a royal feast for ya'll."

Ty said, "Yeah, we're starving! I've been thinking about this meal all day and it smells like the bom!"

Game said, "Oh, ya'll ain't had a good meal until you've tasted Lady-G's southern comfort this woman is a master in that kitchen."

Lady-G blushed as Game gave her a gentle kiss on the forehead and handed her the bag of money and said "Here, put this up baby."

"Ya'll come on in the family room, the Lakers is whoppin' on the Suns."

They walked in the family room and Game poured everyone a double shot of Louis XIII Hennessy and blazed a fat joint. G-Fly took a sip of the Hennessy and said, "Man, this is the bom, what is it?"

"It's called Louis XIII it's an expensive kind of Hennessey, it cost $2,500 a bottle!"

"Damn, now this is what I call living good," Julian said, "And that ain't no lie" as he hit the indo joint and passed it to Ty.

"Man, I don't mean to be all up in your business, but I'm curious as to how much a house like this cost" G-Fly asked. Game said, "Oh, I paid three and a half million for this one."

Ty almost choked on his Hennessy and said "Three and a half million? You ain't lying you've mastered the game!" And everyone started laughing.

Game said, "This is my main house, but I got 3 more mansions that my girls stay at. I got an 8 bedroom mansion in Westwood, a 7 bedroom mansion in Altadena, and another 7 bedroom mansion close to the Marina. We got around 20 women who occupy them spots, and they all work for our escort service. Also, I got a couple of apartment complexes, a beauty salon and a couple of other investments that's doing pretty good. See, this dope game isn't nothing if you don't invest your money in some legitimate investments. Because you can have 5 million dollars dirty in a wall safe, and 1 million dollars in the bank, and the 1 million dollars would be worth more than the 5 million. Simply because you can properly invest the 1 million dollar in a legitimate business venture and the 5 million is only good for small and foolish shit, like clothes, jewelry, tricking and shit like that.

The object of the game is to take your dirty money and clean it, and invest it in good investments to make it grow on paper legitimately, so when them people look at you, you look like a legitimate businessman instead of a dope dealer.

Also, you need to focus on secure investments and I'll teach you this, and how to start corporations in fictitious names to hide your investments so if ever you get popped, then they won't be able to find and take all of your property and business investments away from you. The best lie is always the one that's hiding behind a gang of other lies.

Remember that!

Lady-G peeped in the family room and said, “Time to eat!”

Game looked around and saw that his three comrades were in a trance by the jewels that he was dropping on them and he smiled and said, “Ya’ll digest that in your heads while we go stuff our stomachs with this blessed meal that Lady-G has put down for us. You guys can use the restroom down the hall to wash up.”

They all stood up and Game held up his Hennessy glass and said “To us and the blessings that our future holds.” And all of them held up their glasses and downed their Hennessey.

Ty said, “I’m starving and that Indo didn’t do nothing but make it worse.”

Everyone laughed as they walked out. Everybody sat down at the table and it was obvious by the looks on their faces that they were deeply captivated by the assortment of food. Lady G cooked some fried pork chops, fried turkey wings, ham-hocks and oxtails, greens, macaroni and cheese, yams and some chicken fried rice. And for dessert, she brought a German Chocolate Cake and pecan pie.

Game said, “Lord, thank you for this wonderful meal that you have provided for me, my new comrades and lovely family and the many blessings you have given us! Amen.”

And everyone said, “Amen” and Lady-G said “Well, don’t just look at it, help yourself” and everyone started digging in. The door bell rang and Lady-G said, “Oh, that must be the girls” an she went to open up the door and four of Game’s ladies that work for his escort service came walking in and said “Daddy, we apologize for being late, we got stuck in traffic, but you know that we had to come when we herd that Lady-G was throwing down,” and they all kissed Game on the cheek.

Game said “Ladies, these are my three god brothers and comrades. They will also be providing security for you girls.

That’s G-Fly, Ty and this is Julian. Gentlemen, this is

Peaches, Precious, Unique and Star."

Everyone gave their greetings and Lady-G said, "Ya'll go and wash ya'll hands and come and eat," and the four ladies disappeared into the bathroom.

G-Fly said, "Now, that's what I call a vicious stable."

Ty said, "Man you ain't lying."

Lady G looked at them and said, "You ain't seen nothing yet. They ain't even considered the pretty ones."

G-Fly said, "You're bullshitting?"

Julian said, "Don't be swearing at the table nigga!"

"My bad, but that was like a brain shocker" and everyone started laughing as the ladies came and sat down at the table and started fixing their food. Star was a cute blonde haired white girl with a body like a sista and Peaches and Precious both were dark skinned sistas with big hips and asses. Peaches was 5'8" and Precious was 5'2" and both had nice bobbed hair cuts. And unique was a cute Mexican young lady with a nice full breast and wide hips with an acceptable ass. She was 5'4", had long pretty jet black curly hair that complimented her beauty.

Precious said, "So how old are ya'll" and everyone looked up at her with surprise.

G-Fly said, "However old you need us to be!" and everyone started laughing.

She said "I only asked because ya'll look kind of young."

G-Fly said "Can you keep a secret?" and she looked at him in a confused way and shook her head as everyone got quiet and was listening attentively. G-Fly said, "We got this old lady in our neighborhood who's Haitian and she gave us all some youth serum 20 years ago and this is the result." And everyone started dying laughing.

She said "You're crazy boy!"

"Baby, you don't know the half of it, but for real, you're worried about the wrong things" and he looked over at Julian and said, "A lot of these women are so used to messing with these suckas, and they don't even know how to act when they're in the presence of real men. Listen, sweetheart, a man's a man, and age is irrelevant to that fact.

You just need to be happy that some of us still exist."

Game said, "That's right, check her crazy fickle minded ass man." And everybody started busting up as Game and G-Fly gave each other dap.

Precious said, "You're right; I'll give you that!"

"Naw baby, I took that and I appreciate it if you think before speaking to me from now on."

Lady-G said "I guess that you didn't understand what Game meant when he said that these were his god brothers and comrades. Now you know!" And everyone started busting up.

Ty said, "Lady-G, I got to compliment you on this beautiful meal that you prepared for us, it's for sure one of the best tasting and fulfilling meals that I ever had in my life."

"Man you ain't lying" Julian added.

Lady-G said "Thank you very much, you know I had to put together something special for my god brothers."

Julian said "I'm surprised Game isn't fat from eating all this good food"

"You know I'd be working out trying to keep the cheat off me plus, we be on the move so much she very seldom has the time to put it down like this. Only on holidays and special occasions."

And the three youngsters blushed as Star said, "So, what's the special occasion?"

Game said, "You're looking at them!" And the four ladies knew right then that these three youngsters would become the next ghetto kingpins.

"Desert anyone?" Lady-G asked? The youngsters all had a slice of both the German chocolate cake and pecan pie. Star and Peaches had a slice of pie. Lady-G and Game got a piece of the cake and Unique and Precious both passed in fear of loosing their nicely toned bodies. After desert, Lady-G took the youngsters in the den and gave them the run down on how the escort service was operated.

"When the girls have dates with new and unfamiliar clients, then I would page one of ya'll to accompany them. If the girl don't come out of the motel room, or page you on the hour, then whoever's their security should go and check up on them to make sure that they're alright. Now, every time ya'll get called to go on security watch for one of the girls, then ya'll will get paid $20 an hour. And believe me, you guys will be called anywhere from 5 to 20 times a day and this can be at any time. So, don't be surprised if you get a call at 2 to 3 o'clock in the morning to go and watch one of the girl's back.

Also, it should be obvious that the girls are questioning you guys' abilities to play this part as their security, so don't get upset if they be acting kind of funny until they get to know you. Also, I ain't got to tell you that these women specialize in playing on a man's sexual weaknesses and if they see any trick characteristics in you, then they're going to loose a lot of respect for you. So my advice to you is, to play them with a pimp dick and if you do fuck them, make sure that they be the one's who pay for it. Other than, just remember that Game respects and appreciates all of his girls like his wives, and expects you to protect them the same as his money. So, always understand your obligations.

Any questions? Okay, if you guys need any advice or have any questions then I'm here for you, and I'll take you guys to the DMV tomorrow morning at 9:30 a.m. so be up and ready to go. I'll come pick you guys up."

"Thanks sis," Julian said, as all of them kissed her on the cheek and they all left the den together. Lady-G and the youngsters went back into the family room, where Game and the four girls were kicking back and having a drink. Lady-G fixed her and the youngsters a drink as Game's pager went off. Game walked into the other room to make a call while the youngster's grabbed a seat on the big, soft burgundy leather corner group. Julian said, "So ladies, which house do you girls live at?"

"Oh, we stay at the house in Westwood," Peaches said.

"Is all of our girls super fine like ya'll?"

They blushed and said, "But of course, all our sista's is top notch."

G-Fly looked over at Lady-G and said, "Sis, do we

have any vacancies at any of the houses?"

"Yeah, we just got a vacancy at the Westwood house! One of our sisters just got married to this rich white man, who is a real estate developer. It's been vacant for a month now. But vacancies are very uncommon in our family. Our ladies are spoiled to death and if a man ain't a millionaire, then they're not thinking about leaving!"

"So basically, you're saying that all of our ladies is game orientated?"

"Yep, very!"

G-Fly looked over at the four ladies and said "I guess you are my type of ladies."

And Star said, "And what type is that?"

"The type that's down, devoted to the cause and know the meaning of a hustle." Game walked back into the family room and looked at the youngsters and said "Come and roll with me ya'll!"

The youngsters stood up and downed their drinks and Ty looked over at the ladies and said, "We'll see ya'll later" and everybody said their goodbyes as Game and the youngsters walked out.

When they got outside of the house, Game said, "I got to go and make a big delivery around the way and I want ya'll to roll with me and watch my back." Game jumped in the Blazer with Julian, as G-Fly and Ty followed him in the Cutlass. Game stopped at another one of his safe houses and ran in and grabbed 20 keys of cocaine. He put them in a duffle bag and took it and put it in the trunk of the Cutlass and looked at G-Fly and Ty and said "Are ya'll strapped?"

G-Fly said, "It's part of our religious belief now!"

"Good! Follow me and I want you guys to stay in the car. Me and Julian are going to go in and make sure everything is cool. If it is, then one of us would come and get the dope out of the trunk, okay?"

"Got you!"

And they followed Game to an apartment on the eastside. Game and Julian got out of the car and walked into the second apartment. Ty watched them to see what apartment they went into and then went to sit back in the

Cutlass with G-Fly. G-Fly said, "I got a funny feeling about this" and took out his 45 automatic and took it off safety.

Ty said, "Is that right?" and pulled out his 357 magnum and said "Talk to me."

"Just play it by ear and keep your eyes and ears open."

Game and Julian stepped into the apartment and two men and a woman was in the house. Game said, "What's up Black?"

"Hey, what's up Game? Who's your young friend?"

"That's not important! Do you got the money?"

Black pulled out his 38 and said "It ain't no sense in play. Hell naw I ain't got the money," and Black's partner pulled out a 9mm.

Game looked at them and said "Damn, is this the way ya'll getting down?"

"You got damn right nigga, now put your muthafucken hands up!"

"You got that off man. Just don't shoot. We're not trippin' on this small shit."

Black looked over at the lady and said "Jan, go grab their guns."

Jan walked up and took Game's 9mm out of his waistband and went over to Julian and grabbed his 9mm out of his waistband too. Black said, "Go sit your ass down on the floor over there."

They both complied and Black said, "Now where's the dope at?"

Game said, "I didn't bring it because I wanted to make sure that you had the money first."

"Nigga, you think that I'm playing with you" and he pointed the gun and Julian said "Hold up man! Game, it ain't but some got damn dope. Just don't hurt us and I'll tell you." Game looked at Julian with an angry expression. Black said "At least someone is smart. Where is it then?"

"My homeboys are outside in the car with it."

"What kind of car and how many homeboys?"

"It's a beige '77 Cutlass and it's two homeboys of mine."

Game said "Man, if I would've have known that you was this scary, I wouldn't have never fucked with you."

"Man, fuck that shit, I'm not going to die over that shit.

That's your shit, not mine!"

Game seen a strange look in Julian's eyes as Game turned away and just shook his head as if he was disgusted. Black and his homeboy and home girl started laughing and Black looked at his homeboy and said "Go tell them that Game said to bring the dope in. And try not to make a big scene out there."

"Got you," the short man said as he put his 9mm in his waistband and walked out. Black looked at Julian and said, "Smart move, kid, you saved yourself some abuse."

Julian said "Man, I ain't trying to go through all that. I'm only 14 years old. I got my whole life ahead of me."

Game didn't peep his comrade's play and didn't know that Julian carried two guns on him and still had his 3.80 in his back. Also, Julian knew the type of comrades he had in Ty and G-Fly and that G-Fly can smell a set-up a mile away and would never allow a sucka to trick them that easily.

The short man was walking up to the Cutlass and G-Fly said, "This nigga must be on dope or something."

The short man walked up to the car and said "Game said bring the stuff in!"

G-Fly and Ty raised their guns at the same time and said "Nigga, put your damn hands on your chest!"

The short man said, "Why you trippin'?

"Nigga, you heard what I said. If I ask you again, I'ma blow your fuckin' back out!"

"Okay man, okay, don't shoot."

Ty walked around the car and behind the short man and reached around his belt and pulled his 9mm out as G-Fly stepped out of the car. G-Fly said "You better talk quick but don't talk slick."

The short man said, "Man, ya'll trippin" and Ty slapped him in the back of the head with the 357 magnum and said, "Nigga, we ain't started tripping' yet."

"Okay, okay, it was Black's idea, he set up the lick and told me to have ya'll bring the dope in."

"How many people in the house?"

"Just Black and his bitch."

"Where's my homeboys?"

"They're in there. Black made them sit on the floor in the corner."

G-Fly went and popped the trunk and grabbed the duffle bag and grabbed the little man by the back of his pants on his waist band and said, "If you try something stupid I'ma cripple you for life."

"Man I'm cool, just don't shoot me!"

G-Fly looked at Ty and said, "Let's do it Rider style!"

Ty reflected back to the picture of Rider dead in the alley with a bullet in his head and knew where his comrade's thoughts were. As they were walking up to the apartment door, G-Fly said, "I want you to open it and act like everything is cool. If you do something stupid, then you're dead. We just want to get our homeboys."

"I got you man."

G-Fly said, as he was walking up on the door. "Oh yeah, today was a nice day. I was thinking about pulling the barbecue pit out."

The little man turned the knob to open the door and as the door was swinging open, G-Fly pushed the short man in the apartment full force and started bussing at the same time. The short man took three in his back and Julian made his move as soon as the door opened. Black was taken off guard at Julian's fast and unexpected move. When he looked up, Julian shot him twice in the side. He turned to look at Julian as Ty unloaded both the 357 and the short man's 9mm all up in Black's face and body. The lady was in shock at the scene that was going down in front of her and when she looked up, G-Fly had his 45 pointed in her face. She said, "No please," and G-Fly shot her twice in the face and then once in the chest. Ty said "Are ya'll alright?"

Game said, "We are now."

And he ran over and grabbed the two 9mm that the lady took off of them. The short man was on his back looking at the sky paralyzed and Game walked over to him and shot him three times in the head and said, “Let’s roll.”

They ran out and jumped in the cars and Game led them over to another spot of his and parked the cars in the back yard. They showered and changed clothes and they all went and wiped down the cars as Game’s homeboy came and got the cars and drove to a junkyard to have the cars stripped down.

Lady-G pulled up and after cleaning the guns, Game gave them the keys to another bucket, a blue 84 Nissan Maxima and told them that he’ll catch up with them later. “I’m about to go out to Santa Monica Pier to get rid of these guns. When I get back, I’ll give ya’ll a call.” The youngsters agreed and they parted.

Chapter 5
Don't Test Me

Once back at their apartment, the youngsters were charged up and full of excitement. Ty said, "We need to smoke a fat one to that!"

"Put it in the air my nigga," G-Fly said.

Julian said, "Man, you should've seen me. I put the G-Fly con game down vicious. Game was looking at me like I was crazy, but I was just trying to buy time to get to my spare gun, so I could lay some shit down and I knew that ya'll wasn't going for the okie dokie, so I said in my head, 'When my 'rades come through that door, it's on,' so I was waiting for your queue and when I heard you talking and laughing, I knew that you was acting and on point."

"Man, I told Ty that I felt that strange feeling that I be getting, didn't I Ty?"

"Yep, that nigga sure did and you know me, I just pulled my heat out because I know that G-Fly's in tune with that psychic shit."

G-Fly said, "Yeah man, that little short smoked out lookin' muthafucka come walking up smiling talking bout Game said bring the stuff, and me and Ty draw our guns on him together, huh Ty?"

"Yep, and I got out and asked him what the fuck was going on and he started stuttering and talking like ain't nothing was wrong, so I slapped his ass in the head with that 357 and he told everything, huh G-Fly?"

G-Fly took another hit of the joint and passed to Ty and said, "Hell yeah, like a snitch in church giving confession!"

And everyone started busting up. "I just told Ty let's do it Rider style, so he would know that it's going down and as we walked in the apartment, I just pushed that smoked out nigga in and started bustin' at him as he was falling forward and the rest was uncensored."

Julian said, "Man, as soon as I saw the door open, I

went for my 3.80 and got a couple of shots off of that fool that Ty punished!"

"Yeah, man, I just got busy on the first nigga that I seen."

"Yeah, you tore his ass up, I thought he was 'pop locking'," G-Fly said, as he laughed.

Julian said, "You wasn't playing no games either the way you dealt with that scandalous bitch.

Listen man, when it comes to my comrades, it ain't no sympathy or rules. They're going to kill me or I'ma kill them."

Julian said, "That real my nigga."

"Hey Ty, cut on the news and see if they're talking about it."

Ty hit the TV remote control and yep, the police was at the scene with the apartment taped off. G-Fly saw an older lady who was standing in the doorway of her apartment building, #4, as they was escorting the smoker dude into the apartment right before the shootout began. And said, "Look Ty, that's that older bitch that was standing in her doorway when we was walking dude in."

"It sure is. What she saying?"

The lady was getting interviewed by the news anchor and said, "Yep, I was standing in my doorway when I seen two young Mexican mans, walk another older short light skin black man in the apartment and once they walked in, all hell broke loose, all you heard was gun fire and about 30 seconds later four Mexican mans ran out."

Ty said, "You hear that? She said that it was Mexicans that did it!"

Julian said, "She must've known that ya'll seen her and wanted to let ya'll know that she wasn't going to tell on ya'll."

G-Fly said, "Now, that's a smart ghetto bitch for you. After this shit is over, I'm going to have to shoot her a couple of g's."

An hour later, Game and Lady-G came in the door. The youngsters had showered again and was just laying back kicking it. Ty looked up and said, "Hey, big bro!

What took ya'll so long?"

"What's up ya'll? You know I had to make sure that everything was disposed of."

That's right."

G-Fly said, "Hey sis, can you do us a favor?"

Lady-G said, "Sure, what's up?"

"Can you run to the store and get us something to drink, you know, we got to celebrate."

"Okay, what ya'll want?"

"We want a bottle of Hennessy, and a 12 pack of Miller Genuine Draft." G-Fly tried to hand her $50 and she said, "No, keep that, this one's on me!" And smiled as she kissed Game and walked out.

Game said, "Did you do that to get rid of her, or did you really want something to drink?"

"Both" and they all started laughing. Game said, "Is ya'll cool?"

"Of course my nigga, we live for this kind of shit" G-Fly said. Game said, "Man ya'll are the coldest young niggas that I ever met and I love ya'll."

Man, you're our comrade. We'll go to hell to get you if we had to," Ty said.

Game looked over at Julian and said, "That's my bad for doubting you, 'rade, but how did you know that Ty and G-Fly would come in shooting?"

"Man, these are my soul-mates and I know that they would do the same thing that I would do, plus I had my 3.80 in my back, so I knew if I can delay them long enough, then I can possibly gain the upper hand, so I pushed the con game. Acting tough ain't going to do nothing but get us killed, so I had to try to stop you from trying to provoke the situation long enough to get to my heat. But, as you see, my nigga's was on point."

G-Fly said, "Man, did you tell Lady-G about it?"

"Yeah, but believe me, she's just as crazy as ya'll and have put her work in before, too. So, don't get it twisted. She's my bottom lady for a reason!"

"What she say?"

"She was proud of ya'll. She believed in ya'll's ability

to deal with problems more than me and you know that I've always had faith in ya'll."

"For real?"

"Yeah, she already told the girls that they had three new men!"

"Is that right?" Ty said with a grin.

"Hey big bro, you know that we made the news per se."

"What do you mean, 'per se?'"

"Well, the bitch who lives in the building seen everything. Well, she seen us escort dude in and then all shit broke loose and she seen us run out. But, on the news, she made it clear that it was four Mexicans who was involved instead of us!"

"Is that right?"

"See for yourself" and turned back up the news as they showed the part of the woman's interview again. Lady-G walked in with the bag of liquor and set it down on the table. G-Fly said, "Good looking out baby" and kissed her on the cheek as he went to get five glasses. Ty patted the seat on the couch next to him and Lady-G went to sit down next to him. He said "Listen sis, when you come to pick us up in the morning, bring us some of them leftovers, okay?"

She smiled and said, "You really like my cooking, huh?"

"Baby, you cook better than my moms, so you can imagine how I feel about it!"

She smiled happily. G-Fly passed around drinks and looked at Game and said, "Julian thinks that after seeing our work, she wanted to make it clear to us that she wasn't going to tell on us because she knows that we saw her and knows where she lives.

I was thinking about hitting her off with a couple of g's after the smoke clears and that way she would know that we know her and we appreciate her thoroughness."

"Good idea! But peep, I'm curious, how did you two know that we was in trouble?"

Well, I got this gangster instinct right. Similar to Spider Man's spider senses!" and everyone started laughing and Ty said, "That nigga's for real!

"Anyway, as I was saying, I got this gut feeling that trouble was close and then this short ugly smoked out ass nigga came to the car talking about you said bring in the stuff!

Automatically me and Ty draw down on him and after Ty slapped him cross the head with that big ass .357, he told us what was going on and the rest played out in front of you. Yeah also, we need some more guns and you know that I got to have another 45!"

"Don't worry, I got you," Lady-G got a page and went to use the phone. She came back five minutes later and said "Nina and China got a double date and need security. Who wants to go watch their back?"

"Fuck it, I'll go," Julian said. "What time is it?"

"11:45 p.m. They live in the house in Altadena. Here's the address and phone number."

"Got you"

"And Julian, remember my ladies is your ladies also, so don't hesitate to check them if they get out of line. I got confidence in your respect and characteristics as a man as well as a player. You feel me?"

"Yeah, I feel you 'rade."

Ty reached in his waistband and pulled out his 9mm and said, "Here, take care of her."

Julian grabbed the gun and said, "Of course I will and if she get's horny, I'll finger fuck her for you!"

Everybody laughed and Ty said, "You better" as he gave his comrade a ghetto embrace. Game said, "I'm out of here too ya'll. I'll get back at ya'll tomorrow."

Lady G said "Bye, ya'll, see you guys in the morning and no Ty, I won't forget your leftovers."

"Thank you sis!"

Game, Lady-G and Julian all left out of the door. G-Fly looked over at Ty and said, "You know, I love you right?"

"Yeah I know."

"Then why don't you love me back and twist us up one! Put it in the air!"

Chapter 6
Always Keeping It Real

The next day, Lady-G picked up the youngsters in the morning and took them to get their new fake driver licenses.

She also gave them a bag full of guns and an envelope with 5 g's a piece in it from Game. G-Fly said, "Sis, we're not trippin' off no money for what we did. It's the way we get down for each other."

"Well, I guess that you can understand the way Game get down for his comrades! Believe me, you guys will be rich very soon. You see, your big brother ain't hurting at all. He just wants to make sure that ya'll can handle the game before he give it all to ya'll. To be a gangsta is one thing, but to know how to hustle and manage money is totally different. Some people ain't made to have and know how to deal with having or making big money. And if you force it upon them, then they would go crazy with it and possibly get everybody caught up. So, he's just testing ya'll."

Julian said, "If that's true, then why are you telling us this?"

"Let's just say that, I want to see ya'll succeed and I believe the more you know, then the better your understanding is and the better chance you have at knowing how to play your position in life. Remember this, just because you're born with a dick don't mean that you're going to grow up to become a man.

A male is not born to be a man; he's taught how to be a man."

"Now that was some deep shit," G-Fly said.

"Anyway, I know that ya'll got a lot to do, so I'll get back with ya'll later."

"Bye sis, and tell Game that we said good looking out on the extra chips," Ty said and kissed Lady-G on the cheek. Lady-G said, "Oh Julian, I forgot to tell you, the girls at the Altadena house liked the way you carried yourself. I don't know what he did but it gained some stripes."

And she smiled and kissed him and G-Fly on the cheek and left. Ty said, "Now that's a down and real sista."

"I agree with you on that" G-Fly said and then he said,

"Man, what did you do so fly to gain all them ladies respect?"

"I just kept it real. When I got there, I was greeted at the door by this big booty red bone named 'Mimi' and she had on this red see-through baby doll lingerie that wasn't hiding too much of nothing. I looked her up and down as she gave her little pose and I said "Nice" and she blushed and introduced me to these other two ladies. One was a beautiful chocolate Amazon named Del that I gave the new nickname 'Egypt'! She was 5'10" and thick all in the right places with a short bob and slanted eyes. She had on a black silk short t-shirt lingerie and some sexy black silk lace panties. And the other girl's name was Diamond and she was mixed with black and white with pretty hazel eyes and a honey complexion. She had sandy brown wavy hair and a nice body. She had on a short woman's sport's top and some sexy sport's panties. I called her 'Pretty Eyes.' Then, Nina and China came down and both of them is superfly. Nina is a Puerto Rican honey, 5'2" and stacked like a sista with light brown eyes and a olive tan complexion and she wears her hair in this sexy short wavy hair style that makes her look even more beautiful than the eyes can argue. And China was black and Chinese. A body like a sista and features like an Asian with the tight eyes and a sexy brown complexion with a flipped out bob. The other two ladies was asleep, so I didn't get to meet them. Anyway, I just kicked it with them for a minute and didn't act like I was stuck on their looks. I asked Nina and China how did they meet these guys and what age and race were they. I told them that I'll knock on the door on the hour and I wanted them to come and open up the door to let me see that they were okay and if something was wrong, then just say that you're fine through the door and count to ten and hit the floor. The girl's laughed but liked my strategy and we left. They stayed for two hours and I took them back home and we made $80 that I put in the Fila shoe box under the bed in my room. Them ladies all got expensive cars and fly jewelry. Believe me, we got some of the baddest hoes in the game. Whatever ya'll do, never pay for it, never fall in love with it and if you do hit it, then make sure that the second time them hoes is paying you. The first one's a treat, but the second one's a profit. Always fuck with a pimp's dick!"

For two week's straight, the youngsters was picking the money up and delivering the dope to all of the dope spots and running 10 to 20 ladies daily on their dates. It was Friday, at noon time and Ty was at the motel playing security for this conceited thick pretty high yellow bitch named Jewel and it was on the hour but Jewel hadn't come out of the room yet, so Ty creeps up to the window and peeps in and Jewel was tied to the bed and the white man was pacing back and forth with a belt in one hand and a knife in the other. Ty didn't hesitate. He kicked in the door and when the man turned around and saw Ty, he swung the knife wildly. Ty went back just in time to duck it and kicked the big tall, 6'6", 300 lbs white man in his 4 inch dick and sent him to his knees in pain as Ty slapped him in the face with the fat short barrel 357 magnum and knocked the man unconscious on the rug. Ty picked up the knife and went to untie Jewel and take the gag out of her mouth. Ty said, "Are you alright?"

"She said, "I am now."

"Did he hurt you?"

"He hit me in the face and knocked me unconscious and when I woke up, I was tied to the bed and he was using that dildo to fuck me and whipping me with that belt, then he said that he was going to cut my body up because I didn't deserve to look this good."

"Oh, he wanted to disrespect one of my girls like that? Get dressed baby!" And she started getting dressed as she watched Ty tie the big man up on the floor with his legs spread wide apart tied against the legs of the motel room table. The man was lying on his stomach and chest and hands was behind his back. Jewel was standing there watching and confused and said, "What are you doing?"

Ty looked at her and said, "Ain't no one going to disrespect one of my girls like that and get away with it!" And she started smiling with pride and admiration.

Ty said, "Go and wash your juices off of that dildo and bring it back" and she ran and did what he said and when she came back, the big white man was gagged and waking up. He looked up and Ty had the knife and the belt and said "What up, you sick son of a bitch? You like to play crazy games, huh?" And the white man started shaking his head no and trying to talk. "No need to try to thank me, it's my pleasure. We're going to enjoy this moment together" and then he slapped the man hard in the face with the belt and said "How does that feel? Do you like it?"

The man shook his head "No."

"Oh, you don't like to receive it, but you like to inflict it?" And he slapped him across the face again with the belt. And said, "Well, maybe you will like this better. Baby, would you show him how it feels to be fucked by a big black dick?"

Jewel said, "It would be my pleasure" and the man started trying to squirm and Ty put that big knife on his cheek and said, "If you do that again, then I'm going to start cutting your sick ass up, do you hear me?" And the man shook his head 'yes.' Ty said "Now take it like the bitch you are" and he looked at Jewel and Jewel started forcing the big fat 11" dildo up his ass. The white man started weeping as Jewel had the dildo halfway up his asshole. Ty looked down at him and said "Oh, you're a virgin, huh?" And the man shook his head, 'yes."

Ty said, "I want you to remember how good a big black dick is going to feel inside that little tight pussy of yours. You hear me?"

And the white man shook his head 'yes.' Ty looked at Jewel and said "What? Are you a soft sympathetic bitch or something?

Fuck him with it like he was fucking you!" And you

can see the hate in Jewel's eyes as she started ramming the big fat dildo all the way up in the white man's ass without mercy. The white man was crying in agony as Ty started whipping him on his back leaving big red whip marks all over his back and Ty looked down at the man and said, "You're my bitch now, you hear?" and the man shook his head, 'yes' and was moaning like he was enjoying it. Ty said, "Hey baby, cut on that vibrator for a minute" and Jewel did it, but kept up her hard stroke and the white man started trying to hump the dildo back.

Jewel looked up at Ty and said, "I think he likes it" and Ty started hitting him with the belt again and the man started humping faster and let out a loud moan and Ty stood back and said "This sick ass muthafucka really enjoyed this shit."

He looked at Jewel and said "Go and wash that shit off and clean yourself and wrap that thing in a towel so we can get rid of it!"

Ty looked down at the man and said "You like big fat dicks up in your tight little ass, huh?"

And the man shook his head in a convincing manner. "You know that we got to charge you for your services" and the man shook his head as Ty went into his pants pocket and pulled out a fat wad of 20's and 50's. Ty counted it and it was $460 and then Ty looked into his wallet as Jewel walked back into the room and Ty saw a stack of hundred and removed them and counted it. It was $7,200 and Ty pocked it and said, "This gay boy got paper, who is he?"

"Oh, Doctor James L. Smith, neurosurgeon."

"No wonder why you're crazy!"

Ty slid his two gold cards out of his wallet and his certified doctor's ID card because it didn't have a picture.

Then he wrote down the doctor's address to his house and his work place. And said, "Listen here gay boy, I got your address to your work and home so if you try to call the police or call my escort service again, then I promise you that I will kill you. Today never happened and I don't want to ever see you again, do I make myself clear?"

Ty removed the gag and the white man said, "I understand and I'm sorry, I didn't mean to hurt anyone and thank you for the very fulfilling experience. I really enjoyed it! You can have the money; I won't tell, just don't hurt me and I would love to pay you again if you will satisfy me like this again."

Ty looked at Jewel and Jewel was smiling. Ty said, "I turned you out, but you got to get someone else to turn you on!

"Here's $10 and I'm sure that you will be able to get yourself loose eventually." Ty said, "do you got everything?"

Jewel said, "Yes" and Ty went into the bathroom and wiped down the top of the table and rolled up the bed spread and took the belt and knife with him and said, "It's been fun but we got to run! Don't forget, I know who you are, fuck boy" and him and Jewel laughed as they walked out the motel room.

They got into the Malibu and Ty started driving away and said "Are you alright?"

Jewel said, "Yeah, I'm fine now and thank you for watching my back like that."

"What you mean? You're my girl so I'm obligated to you and your sisters."

And Ty pulled up in a 7-11 and jumped out and threw the blanket and dildo, knife and belt away. Then he ran in and grabbed two sodas and two bags of Doritos and jumped back in the car and said, "Now, let's go and spend this crazy fool's money" and pulled out the two credit cards. She said "Oh no you didn't!"

"Oh, yes I did! You down or what?"

"Hell yeah, you know I'm down!"

Ty ran straight to the jewelry store in the mall and bought two men's Presidential Rolexes, three women's gold Rolexes, three pretty diamond ankle bracelets, three fat Turkish chains and four proper men's diamond rings and three women's diamond rings. The lady looked over at him like he was crazy and Ty said, my company just completed a multimillion dollar contract and I'm handing out presents. The lady said, “I see; that would be $78,000.”

Ty handed her the Gold Visa card and his ID and she said “Oh Dr. Smith, It’s a pleasure to meet you.”

“No ma’am, the pleasure’s mine! Wow! I forgot about Ed and Ron, my public reps. You know what, give me two more of those gold Presidential Rolex watches.”

“No problem sir. That would be $98,000. Okay, that should do it and here’s your receipt and thank you for shopping at Exotic Jewelers.”

“Thank you.” And Jewel watched Ty walk out and was excited. They hit all of the expensive clothing stores and Ty was shopping for him and all of his comrades. Also Ty had Jewel grab Lady-G some nice expensive outfits and perfumes. Ty said “Come on baby let’s roll” and they made a quick dash up out of there.

Ty took her back home to the Marina Del Rey mansion and all of the ladies was envious of all of Jewel’s fly clothes.

Jewel’s had around $5,000 worth of clothes, not including her new $4,000 brown mink ¾ length coat. Then Ty gave her a gold Rolex watch and a diamond ankle bracelet that together cost $9,500 and she was in love with his down ass. Ty kissed her on the cheek and said, “We hit a nice lick, huh?”

She said, “Yeah, you’re the best!”

Ty said, “What kind of nigga would I be if I didn’t look out for my crimee?”

And she smiled and gave him a big hug and kiss. Ty smiled and walked away and said, “I’ll see you later baby,” and went and jumped in his car and headed home.

Jewel jumped on the phone and called Lady-G and told her what just transpired. And Lady-G knew that Jewel would be forever devoted and in love with Ty. After Jewel told Lady-G, she told her sisters who were wondering how she came up with all that fly shit and they all were surprised and captivated by the story and the story spread house to house like a wild fire.

Ty got home and his brothers were gone so he brought in all of the shopping bags and separated everything. He brought Game two fly ass leather Fila sweat suits with the Fila shoes to match. A ¾ length black mink coat and a gold Presidential Rolex watch and a nice diamond ring. He got Lady G a matching mink coat and a gold ladies Rolex watch and a diamond ring and ankle bracelet and two nice $800 Gucci dresses and two pairs of $1,000 Gucci boots and purses to match. And he got him and his comrades everything from fly clothes to jewelry. About $20,000 on each one of them. They all had a gold Presidential Rolex watch, a nice diamond ring, a fat Turkish chain and six pairs of tennis shoes a piece, 8 fly ass sweat suits a piece, 5 Fila sweaters a piece, 3 bomber jackets a piece, 5 pairs of leather Guess pants. All kinds of colognes and five packs of drawers, t-shirts and socks. After Ty put everybody's stuff up on their bed in their bedrooms, he put Games and Lady-G's stuff to the side and counted his money that he came up on and went to put the $7,600 in the Fila shoe box so he can properly split it with his homies. He rolled a joint and then called Game up.

Game answered the phone and said, "I heard about your little situation. All of the girls is in love with some Ty. You know that you got you a fan base now!"

Ty said, "Man, you know that I was just keeping it real."

"I see, well you know all of the girls is wondering why you spent all that money on her."

"Shit, she was my crimee and considering the circumstances, she deserved every bit of it. I got you and Lady G some fly shit, too."

"Is that right?"

"Yep, ya'll need to come on through and pick it up."

"Lady-G, your brother said he got us some fly stuff over there and we need to stop through there and get it. Okay 'rade, we're on our way, in a minute."

Julian and G-Fly pulled up at the seventh house where they pick up the money and dropped off the dope at. Julian was about to get out of the Maxima and G-Fly grabbed his arm and said "Hold up."

"What's up 'rade?"

"I got a fucked up vibe! Trouble is somewhere close by."

Julian said, "Well let's go and creep around the back way and we'll leave the dope in the car until we make sure everything is cool."

They got out of the car and crept around the back and when they got to Jack's bedroom window, they saw Jack and his girlfriend tied up on the floor and two niggas in ski masks was in his bedroom looking around. Julian said, "I'll be damn!"

G-Fly whispered, "What I tell you? Let's go and see if the back door is open."

And they crept around to the back door and the window was cracked and the door was opened a little bit. "This must've been where they came in at." Julian said "Listen, keep your head down and only shoot if you have to 'cause if we kill one of them, then we got to kill Jack and his bitch too."

G-Fly said, "Damn I kind of like Jack too!"

They crept in, one of the robbers said, "Nigga you think that we're playing with you. I know that you got more money then this! Maybe we ought to fuck his bitch and see if he would tell us then. She is a thick muthafucka too!"

"Please don't hurt me. I'll do whatever you want, just don't hurt us."

"Pull her panties down man. Damn, she got a fat hairy pussy man."

"Why you doing us like this? We ain't got no more money man."

"Shut the fuck up before we fuck you next nigga!"

"Open up your legs bitch!"

"Nigga if you put your dick in her, I'll blow your fucking head off," Julian said, as both robbers were caught with their pants down and dick in hand. The one standing up still had his 38 in his hand, but he saw that 9mm that Julian had and that big ass 45 that G-Fly had pointed at his chest and head and knew that he didn't have a chance. G-Fly said "You got a couple of seconds left to drop your gun or I'ma empty this clip up in your punk ass."

The robber dropped his gun. "Get off her, you sick muthafucka," and Julian kicked the robber who was between Missy's legs in the face and he hurried up and crawled off of her. Julian picked up the two robbers' guns and put them in his belt and searched them and found the keys to the handcuffs and gave it to G-Fly and G-Fly unlocked the handcuffs from Missy and said "Damn girl, you do have a fat hairy pussy!"

"Oh, my bad Jack" and then he removed Jack's handcuffs. Julian took the handcuffs and handcuffed both of the robbers and pulled off their ski masks. "Do you know them, Jack?

I've seen them around before." And then Jack looked at Missy and said, "Did he penetrate you baby?"

"No, they stopped them just in time, thank you," and Missy kissed Julian on the cheek and went over and kissed G-Fly, but more erotically and on the neck and said, "I owe you one" and gave him a seductive smile. Jack was talking to Julian and didn't see Missy give G-Fly her sexual hint. And G-Fly just smiled knowing that Missy probably would've enjoyed the little rape that was about to go down. Jack stood 6'3" and was every bit of 260 lbs. He gave Julian the money and said "I'll get the work tomorrow."

"Cool man here, you can have these guns too" and gave him the robbers' guns. Julian, G-Fly and Ty all carried brown gloves in their back pocket so they stayed ready for drama.

Jack said, "Can you guys drop Missy off at her sister's house for me? Certain things she shouldn't see!"

"I got you man and I hope that me and my nigga won't have no problems from these two niggas later."

"I seriously don't think that that shit would be possible."

"We're out!"

"Missy, come on baby, we're going to drop you off at your sister's so you can stay with her for a couple of days."

"Okay, call me baby" and she went over and kissed Jack and kicked one of the robbers in the face and said,

"You sick muthafucka." Julian said "Come on girl, let's roll." And all three of them left. Julian said, "Missy this ain't nobody else's business. If you go around and run your mouth then you can get yourself and your man in trouble, so please keep your mouth shut about this, okay?"

"Don't worry, I won't say nothing, I know how to keep a secret" and smiled at G-Fly. They dropped her off and finished their route and headed back to their apartment.

Chapter 7
It's On and Poppin'

As Julian and G-Fly walked into the door of their apartment, Ty was sitting on the couch smoking a joint and said, "Man where ya'll been?" You wouldn't believe what happened today."

"No, you wouldn't believe what happened to us," Julian said.

"Wait, man, let me tell you first!"

G-Fly saw the gold Rolex watch, the proper diamond ring and the fat Turkish rope necklace that Ty had on and he hit the joint and said, "Man, let Ty speak!"

Ty read his comrade's thoughts and said, "Oh, you like the new fly pieces, huh? Don't trip, you know that I wouldn't even feel right if my comrades ain't rolling fly too. And he told his comrades what happened and escorted them into their bedrooms and told them "I put all ya'll stuff on your beds."

They looked at all their stuff on their beds and gave Ty a big hug and then went into their rooms and started checking out all their fly shit. G-Fly put on his Rolex watch, diamond ring and Turkish rope necklace and said "Now, this is GP my nigga" and Ty just smiled. Julian walked out his room draped with his jewelry on too and said "This is the best gift that anyone ever gave me." G-Fly said "Me too" as Julian and G-Fly grabbed Ty and wrestled him to the ground.

"A'ight, you guys win. Ya'll going to break my necklace!"

They laughed and let him up. Ty said, "I put $7,600 in the shoe box too."

"Man, that was a cool lick," G-Fly said.

"Is Jewel okay?" Julian replied.

"Hell yeah, after we went shopping, she forgot about all of that crazy shit."

G-Fly said, "Ain't that the light skinned pretty bitch

who be acting all conceited and shit?"

"Yep, but I think that our little experience changed her whole little attitude. She was holding my hand and kicking it with me at the mall like I was her man and she was in love with my dirty draws."

"Man of course, how else is she supposed to act at the mall with a nigga blessing her with a gang of fly shit?"

"Yeah, I considered that too, but I caught a different type of vibe. Anyway, being that she was my crimee, it's only right that she should benefit too!"

Julian said, "That right, you got to keep it real!"

"I brought Game and Lady-G some fly shit too, come and check it out."

Julian said, "My nigga got class"

"And is true to the game," G-Fly added.

They heard the door open and Ty said, "That must be Game and Lady-G, they said that they were on their way.

As Game and Lady-G walked in, the three youngsters walked downstairs to meet them and they were carrying all of the bags that Ty had for them. Game saw his three comrades come downstairs with a gang of shopping bags with their new pieces on looking fly. Game said "Look at my niggas looking all draped and shit."

Everybody smiled and Ty said "Here, ya'll know, this is from us to ya'll. Ya'll know we love ya'll right?"

Lady-G said, "Of course we do" and Game and her started pulling their clothes out of the shopping bags. They both pulled out their his and hers black ¾ length mink coats and Game said "Damn, my nigga got that fly exquisite taste."

Lady-G said, "Yeah baby, this is beautiful" and ran over and gave the youngsters all a big hug and kiss.

Ty said "Oh, it gets better than that" and Lady-G looked at Ty and ran back over to her bags excitedly and started pulling out her other stuff. She pulled out the two Gucci dresses and said "Damn, my little brother got good taste" and then pulled out the Gucci boots and purse that matched. She said "This is beautiful little bro."

"You might want to check inside of your purse," Ty

said.

Lady-G pulled out a jewelry bag and looked up at Ty and Ty smiled as Lady-G pulled out the first jewelry box and when she opened it, it displayed a gold Presidential Additional Rolex watch. She said "Oh, this is all that" and looked up at Ty.

Ty said "Keep going" and she smiled excitedly and pulled out another jewelry box that had a diamond ankle bracelet and then she pulled out the other one and opened it and it had a flat 4 carat diamond ring in it. She put on her ring and watch and walked over to Ty and gave him the ankle bracelet and asked, "Will you put it on for me?"

"Of course sis" and Ty bent down and clipped it on her right ankle and said "Now that's GP" and Lady-G gave Ty a big hug and said "I love you little bro. Thank you."

Ty said "You know I got to look out for our princess."

Game pulled out his Gold Presidential Addition Rolex and said "Now, this is proper and he pulled his other jewelry box out and opened it and saw a fly 3-1/2 carat diamond ring.

"Man, I don't know what to say."

"What you mean man? We're comrades. You're a part of us now, so it don't make no sense in trying to understand the love."

"It's us against the muthafucken world!" G-Fly said, and everyone started laughing.

Julian said, "I don't mean to cast stones at your party, but me and G-Fly just ran into a little problem at your spot that we had to regulate."

Game looked curiously as his facial expression changed.

Everyone looked at Julian as he told them what happened and how they dealt with the situation.

Game said, "I'm proud of ya'll! That was very wise the way you guys handled the situation. I've been knowing Jack for a long time and I'm sure that he's going to handle it appropriately. Is Missy alright?"

G-Fly said "Yeah, her freaky ass is alright. She tried to throw me some pussy after that, she's a cold freak. I think that she was getting off with the thought of getting raped like that."

Lady-G said, "Possibly, you know a lot of women get off on things like that and even more, when they see a man display a show of power or security. Your brother Ty got all the ladies jockin' ya'll now. They know that ya'll are real and down for them, about your money, and don't possess sucka characteristics.

In other words, they are down for accepting ya'll in their lives as their men too."

Game said, "That's good because they are wearing my black ass out."

"You were having sex with all those women?" Ty said.

"Of course! They're my ladies. But I try to keep them on a strict dick diet."

Lady-G is the only one who be getting it the most. Lady-G smiled and said, "Now I can get it even more now that ya'll are a part of our family."

"Wait a minute! I thought that we're not supposed to fuck' em," Ty said.

"Ya'll can fuck them, they are ya'll ladies, but don't fall in love and always remember that they are career hoes and that a hoe's job is to pay and cater to a pimp and never let them dictate nothing or accept one of them as your one and only. Maybe your bottom lady but never your one and only!"

"Damn, that sound kind of strange coming from you Lady-G, especially spoken in the presence of Game," Julian said.

"Listen baby, a real lady is going to always keep it real with her man and around her man. If a woman's down for you and real with you, then her actions are going to reflect her heart and mind. I'm all of ya'll's bottom lady, and it's my obligation to make sure all ya'll's game is tight, and that you know what you need to know in this game dealing with these bitches, because they will take advantage of you if they catch you slipping. Why do you think pimps have bottom ladies? A bitch can see through another bitch's game better than a man!

We got special powers too, similar to G-Fly's gut feelings."

"Well in that case, I might need to get me two bottom ladies," G-Fly said.

Game looked over at him and said "Why two?"

"Shit, so one can watch the other one!"

And everyone started busting-up. Julian said, "Yeah baby, I feel you and I'm blessed to have you in my life. And she smiled as she gave him a big hug.

Ty said, "I don't know about them but before I choose me a bottom lady, I'm gonna to for sure let Lady-G lace them."

G-Fly said "I heard that" and Lady-G just blushed.

Game said "Listen 'rades, we need to go and recoup tomorrow and I'm introducing ya'll to my connection. His name is Hector, and he's a Mexican that been supplying me for a long time. We're going to take three cars and follow Lady-G from a distance and make sure that she makes it back safely. I'll come and get ya'll at 9:30 a.m. and we'll roll out then. Ya'll stay away from Jack's spot until further notice."

Lady-G said "I'll page ya'll if the girls need your assistance. If ya'll need me, I'll be at the main spot, okay?"

"A'ight!"

They all embraced as Game and Lady-G left out with a hand full of shopping bags.

After Game and Lady-G left, Julian said, "Lady-G is a real and down sista!"

"I know, and she fine and sexy too. That's the type of lady that I need by my side," Ty said.

"Not me, I need two of them! Because I'ma keep it fly until I die" G-Fly said with assurance.

Ty said "Man, I don't know about ya'll, but I'ma about to call that little cute thick bitch that I met at the party and see if she's trying to finish what we started."

"I ain't mad at you player. I got a full clip that I need to empty, too!"

Julian why don't you call up the home girl and see if she's trying to get her brains fucked out? We can hit her with that train. Julian looked at G-Fly and said "Good idea."

"Or we can tell her to call up one of her home girls and switch it up."

"Yeah, I'm feeling that, tell her to call up Little Tish! That little small big butt girl got it good."

Ty got off the phone and said it's going down. I'ma grab a motel room out there in Pasadena, so if you need me, then page me!"

Yeah cool, but peep ya'll, I was thinking that we should also stop by that lady's apartment that threw the police off our scent and bless her with a couple of g's" G-Fly suggested.

"That's a good idea," Julian and Ty agreed.

"Julian said "Let's call Game and make sure that he's cool with it before we do it, to make sure that he's with it."

"Good idea," Ty said, "Ya'll want me to roll over there with ya'll?"

"Naw man, go and get your freak on. I know how hard it is being around all them pretty half naked hoes and trying to hide your desire."

Ty looked at Julian and said, "Man, I feel like my nuts about to explode!"

And they started laughing as Ty rolled up two joints and left. Julian called Janet and Janet was more than happy to hook up with them, and she called Little Tish on the three way and Little Tish was game to kick it with them too. Julian told Little Tish that him and his comrade wanted to have an orgy and she was all for it. Julian hung up and called Game and told him that they wanted to give the lady some money and Game agreed and said, "But be careful."

Then Julian told Game about their plans for a night of fun and told Game to page them if he needed them. Game agreed and they hung up. Julian said "It's all good!"

G-Fly said "How much should we give her?"

"I think 3 g's should be a blessing for her."

G-Fly went to grab the money out of the stash and Julian rolled up 4 fat indo joints and they was out.

Julian and G-Fly pulled up at the spot on the eastside

where they had to lay them niggas down at and Julia looked over at G-Fly and asked his psychic comrade “Is it cool?”

“Yea, we’re cool!”

It was 8 o’clock at night and only the moon and street lights was illuminating the darkness. Julian and G-Fly walked into the apartment building and as they walked up to the lady’s apartment, G-Fly noticed that the door was open and music was playing at a nice mellow level. G-Fly knocked on the screen door and the older thick big boned lady walked to the door and recognized G-Fly and Julian and said, “Baby didn’t say nothing, I swear.”

G-Fly said, “We know baby, but can we holla at you for a minute?”

She hesitated for a minute and then opened up the screen door. As G-Fly and Julian walked in, they noticed a little boy who was around 4 years old sitting at the table and eating some Top Ramen soup. Julian said, “Is that your baby boy?”

She shook her head, yes. G-Fly realized that the brown skin sista was pretty attractive with a full thick physique and fat in all the right places. She stood around 5’2” and looked around 23 years old. The only thing that took away from her appearance was the nappy braids that she wore and old cheap clothes. She said “I told the police the people that I saw was Mexicans.

I swear that I didn’t tell them about ya’ll! I put that on my only son. Please don’t hurt us!”

G-Fly said, “Baby, we believe you and we respect and appreciate the fact that you kept it ghetto. Here,” and gave her the 3 g’s that was rolled up in a fat wad of 10’s and 20’s.

She took the money and said “What’s this for? I can’t accept this. I didn’t do it to get paid for it. I did it because that’s the way that I was raised to keep my mouth shut and never snitch on no one! I knew that you seen me and I didn’t want ya’ll to do the same thing to me and mine, so I told the police it was Mexicans to throw them off your tracks.

Why you did what you did, ain’t none of my business, and I don’t want to know. I appreciate the offer, but I can’t accept it."

G-Fly said, "Girl don't be silly. I love me a thorough and real bitch like you. You're a rare breed and hard to come by, and being the real niggas that we are, it's only right that we show you our love and appreciation for watching our backs. Now, I want you to take them tired ass braids out of your nappy ass head and go get you one of those fly ass silky bob hair cuts to show off those beautiful African features of yours" and he lifted up her chin as she blushed. And go and get you some nice clothes that show off that killer body that you're hiding and get some 'got damned food in here' before that little nigga's eyes get tight from eating all that Chinese shit!"

Julian and the lady was busting up, "And if you ain't got a car, then go and get a bucket. But, if your man ask tell him that you found the money."

"I ain't got no man."

"What? A sista as fine as you ain't got a man? It's probably them tired ass braids messing up your play!"

And everyone started busting up. She slapped G-Fly gently on the arm and said "Fuck you nigga, you're crazy, but I like the way that you keep it real. Do you got a lady?"

"Baby, I'm a different breed of man. I believe in companionship, good sex and keeping it real. Anything more or less then that will only confuse and stagnate the situation."

"Well, if you ever need a special friend then stop by and see me."

"That sounds very tempting."

"Let me give you my number" and she walked to the kitchen and wrote it down and said, "I'ma make sure that I go to the beauty salon and get me some nice sexy clothes just for you."

And walked over and gave G-Fly a hug and seductive kiss on the lips and said, "Thank you."

G-Fly caressed her big butt and said, "Later for all that!"

"I'll be waiting."

She gave him her number and G-Fly said, "Doni,

huh?

"Yep!"

"How about I call you Daja!

"Daja?"

"Yeah, short for Dajavoo!"

"Yeah, I kind of like that! And what should I call you?

"Just call me your man for right now. You got notches, but you ain't earned stripes yet!"

She laughed and gave Julian a hug and said, "Thank you too. When I earn my stripes then you can tell me your name too!

"Baby, we got to go. I'll see you soon."

"I hope so!"

"Bye ya'll."

"Bye."

As they walked out Julian said, "Man, you're crazy!"

G-Fly said, "I got a good feeling about her and if she tries to cross me then I know and she knows that y'all going to kill her" and he started laughing! Julian just shook his head.

* * * *

Ty was in the motel room with Dezae drenched in sweat and pulling in work, and Dezae was coming like crazy and loving every bit of Ty's performance. She said, "Oh baby, you got that bom dick. You make me feel so good."

Ty put her legs on his shoulders and started power-driving her pussy and she was crying and moaning like a freak in heat.

Ty busted his second nut and rolled off her exhausted. Dazae said that was the bom and gave Ty a deep passionate kiss. She said, "Let's go get in the Jacuzzi, so I can wash you up, and then I'ma give you some bom head and fuck your brains out. Ty looked down at her and she smiled at him seductively.

"I love a lady who knows how to satisfy her man. You keep that type of ambition up. We're going to fuck all night!"

She smiled and got up and went to fill up the Jacuzzi. Ty smiled as he looked at his reflection on the wall mirror next to the bed and he poured them both a cup of Hennessy and blazed the joint as he watched Dazae's sexy thick flawless body entice his thoughts from across the room.

* * * *

Julian and G-Fly picked up Janet and little Tish and stopped at the liquor store to grab some drink and needed necessities. They grabbed a 12-pack of Miller Genuine Draft, two pints of Hennessy, some Coke and cranberry juice, some Doritos and barbecue chips, candy bars, gum, certs, baby oil, Listerine, four toothbrushes, toothpaste, two kinds of deodorants, two 12-pack of Magnum condoms, and a bag of ice.

Before they got to the motel, they went to grab a bucket of Kentucky Fried Chicken. They went to the Snooty Fox on Western and got the motel room that had the Jacuzzi and see-through shower with the double twin-size bed. Once they got into the motel room, G-Fly fixed the drinks and Julian blazed the indo.

Everybody was catching a good buzz and G-Fly cut on the TV to the porno station and looked at the ladies and said, "I'm trying to see them sexy bodies that ya'll hiding in them clothes."

Janet said, "You ain't said nothing. Come on Little Tish, let's give them a strip tease."

"I'll go for the strip, but you can keep the tease," G-Fly said as everyone started laughing. The girls started getting undressed in a slow and seductive way. Janet was a show piece with a perfect thick well-developed body. But Little Tish was only five feet tall and weighed about 110 pounds with big hips, ass, and thighs, with a small waist and small sexy tittys that was perfect for her small frame and set up perfect. She was light skinned with light brown eyes and long wavy hair. They both got naked and then started undressing them. Little Tish was undressing G-Fly and Janet was undressing Julian. Once they all was undressed, the men put on condoms and it was on and popping. From the looks of the scene, you would think that everyone was competing. Julian and G-Fly were trying to show their skills and both of the ladies were trying to prove that they can fuck better than the other. Julian put Janet's legs on his shoulders and Janet wasn't holding her sounds of pleasure back.

G-Fly told Tish to get on her hands and knees and toot her big ass up in the air and started banging her from the back and spanking her big yellow ass. Tish was talking nasty to him and backing that ass up and working her pussy muscles. G-Fly said, "I knew that you had that snapper with your little sexy ass."

She pulled out and said, "Lay down. I want to ride that bom dick of yours." She straddled him with her ass pointed to his face and started fucking him while her pussy was sucking on his dick like a mouth.

He said, "You freaky little heffa. Damn that pussy fire!"

Janet put Julian in the chair and squatted down in the chair over him with her feet standing in the chair and started jumping her ass up and down like she had hydraulics in her ass.

G-Fly said, "Damn Janet, I see you girl. I knew you was a cold freak, but I did know that you was that vicious!"

Tish looked over and saw Janet and turned her body around so she would be facing him and said, "Tell me if you like this" and she squatted with her feet on one side of him and held on to his shoulders and started hitting her hydraulics and making her pussy squeeze his dick while she was bouncing. "Oooooh damn baby, you know that you're one of a kind."

They both started feeling their orgasm coming and started fucking like rabbits in heat, and they both looked up in a ball of pleasure. At the same time Julian and Janet was hugged up and shaking a deep orgasm loose from their lustful desires.

Tish went to dispose of the condom and got a towel and cleaned them up and Janet did the same. G-Fly was looking at the man and lady fucking in the porno flick and automatically got back hard. He went over to Janet and said, "You know I got to hit some of that too!"

Julian got up and walked over to Tish and said, "I heard you had that fire!"

She smiled and said, "Yep, and I heard that you got it good too," and giggled. Julian put on another rubber and said, "Let me hit that thang from the back," and Tish got in a doggy position and said, "You can have it however you want it!"

G-Fly had Janet on her knees in the chair hitting her from the back and spanking her as she was moaning and backing that ass up on him. Tish always wanted to fuck Julian's fine ass, but knew that her home-girl Janet had a crazy crush on him, so she kept her secret to herself. But now that she finally had the opportunity, she was set on making an everlasting impression and try to keep him coming back for more. Julian was hitting Tish from the back and Tish started making her pussy lock up tight around his dick, and Julian said, "Damn baby, you got that snapper!"

"Yeah baby you like it?"

"Hell yeah, it's the bom!"

And he pulled out and turned her around and put her legs on his shoulders and said, "Let me give you what you really want" and started power-driving her. Tish was loving it and putting on her best performance.

G-Fly had Janet sitting on the table with her legs on his shoulders and banging her hard and deep.

Janet said, "Do you like this pussy baby?"

"Oh yeah, you got that chronic for real!"

"I want to be down for ya'll. You know that I'm down and I'll be loyal and devoted to only ya'll. And you know that I got down bitches on my team like Little Tish, Dee-Dee, and Gwen that's down too and would like to be down for ya'll too! I'll keep them in check and we can always get together and keep each other satisfied."

G-Fly took her to the bed and slid up in her missionary style and said, "It sounds good, but what kind of hustle are ya'll down with?"

"Whatever. Dee-Dee and Gwen both be selling rocks, and me and Tish sell a little weed and boost."

"Have you ever sold some pussy?"

"I've fucked niggas for money and played suckas out of money before. All my girls will trick with a sucka, but we don't stand on no corners or nothing."

"Have you ever used a gun?"

"No, but I will if need be. You know I'm a ghetto bitch, so I'm down for my man like that!"

"If I told you to crawl under a baller and set him up so we can jack him, would you be down?"

"Of course. As long as you're my man, then I'm down with ya'll to the grave!"

"Can you handle us all?"

"I'll die trying!" And she giggled.

"Okay, I'll holla at my 'rade and suggest that we let you have a chance to prove your loyalty and devotion to us."

"Oh, thank you baby, you won't be disappointed, I promise.

Now fuck me good baby!"

Julian and G-Fly dropped the girls off at 3:30 a.m. and promised to hook up again soon. On the way home G-Fly told Julian about his conversation with Janet and Julian agreed that it would be a pretty good move. Julian said, "We'll run it by Ty and see what he thinks."

Chapter 8
Steal Sharpen Steal

Julian woke up at 8:00 a.m. and went to do the deliveries and pick-ups by himself. He made it back at 9:10 and Ty and G-Fly were already woke and smoking a joint so they can begin the day right. Ty said, "Why didn't you wake us so we could have rolled with you?"

"Man, I wasn't tripping. You know I had it. Hey Julian, I told Ty about what we were discussing regarding making Janet our bottom hood-rat and he like the idea. He said we should go and get us another apartment and let her fill it up with down bitches for us, and we be the only niggas living there and who can go there. That way we won't be so horny working around these other bitches, and we can conduct or game better. I can't lie. I be wanting to just get butt ass naked and run through the mansion fucking everything up in there." And everyone started busting up.

Julian said, "Yeah, I feel you. Me too! But we got to find a good hustle to occupy them girls and keep them making money for us, because tricking is against my religion, you dig."

"Of course my nigga," G-Fly reassured his comrade that they were cut from the same thought.

Game and Lady Fly would be here at 10:30," Julian said, "so we better get ready and it will be best if we dressed regular and didn't wear our jewelry. We don't want to attract the wrong attention."

"We feel you on that, 'rade!"

Julian went and started cooking them some breakfast while Ty and G-Fly showered and got dressed. At 10:20 a.m., they all were fully dressed in old clothes. Jeans, polo dress shirts and old tennis shoes. Game and Lady-G walked in the door at 10:25 a.m. and Game saw his young comrades dressed like nerds and started laughing to himself, knowing that his comrades was on top of their game.

They left the apartment in three cars, Lady-G and Game was in a rental car, Julian was in the Maxima, and Ty and G-Fly were trailing in the Monte Carlo. They drove to San Diego and pulled up in front of a big house in a nice area. Hector walked out and greeted Game and Lady-G with a warm embrace.

Game motioned for the youngsters to get out of the cars and join them. Game said, "Hector, I want you to meet my generals and god-brothers. This is Julian, that's Ty, and that's G-Fly. Gentlemen, this is Hector, a very good friend of mine. Everyone greeted Hector with a respectful handshake.

Hector said, "So young and strong looking, that's a good combination. Always good to get them and teach them while they're young. It breeds them well. Come, I'm barbecuing for you guys and Maria is cooking a nice meal for you too."

They walked through the house and met his wife Maria and then went to the backyard and met his son Juan, 16, and bodyguard Big Frank. Hector was a short man, 5'4", and kind of heavy built for his stature but not fat. Real nice and respectful, but you could tell that he had power, influence, and big money.

Juan was quiet and stood around 5'5" with a slim build. He was respectful but not quick to open up. Frank, on the other hand, stood 6'4" and weighed 280 pounds and looked like a wrestler. He was friendly but you could tell that he would kill at the drop of a dime. Juan had a kennel with six pit-bulls, all fighter, and the two female pit-bulls were pregnant and expected to drop their litters within the month. They also had eight fighting cocks and put on a little exhibition of a small fight.

They ate then Game pulled the car in the garage and Frank and Juan were counting the money on the four electric money counting machines, as Hector and Game loaded the trunk of the rental car with two suitcases full of cocaine in airproof suitcases. Hector looked at the youngsters and said, "I' got a gift for ya'll," then said something to Juan in Spanish. Juan brought back another suitcase and gave it to his father. Hector opened it and it displayed pounds of indo. Hector said, “This is 20 pounds, a gift from me to you! If you like it and want to get more, then I’ll sell it to you guys for $500 a pound.”

Julian said, “That’s love. Gracias my brother.”

The youngsters all thanked Hector and he put the suitcase in the trunk of the rental with the cocaine. Game and Hector spoke in private for about thirty minutes, then embraced and they departed.

It was 5:00 p.m. when they left Hector’s house. Lady-G was driving the rental in the lead, and Julian and Game were trailing her in the Maxima. Ty and G-Fly were following them a half block behind in the Monte Carlo. The drive went smoothly and they made it back at the safe house at 6:40 p.m. They unloaded the suitcases and took them into the house, and Lady-G ran to the store to grab some items, came back, and took ten kilos out and started cooking them. Game told the youngsters to help her and she started teaching them how to dry cook. After cooking the first ten with them, she took ten more kilos and made them cook all of them while she just watched and gave them the appropriate instructions. After doing the first five with her watching over them, they did the other five like professionals. A kilo is 36 ounces, but the way she taught them how to dry cook it into crack, they were turning 36 ounces into 47 to 48 ounces on each kilo. It was 9:30 when they finished and everyone was exhausted.

Julian said, “Game, me and our ‘rades want to rent another house so we can put some of our down young ladies in. We’re going to let them move this weed for us and that way we won’t be so horny around the other ladies that work the escort service.

We got a down bitch that we believe got the qualities to satisfy our expectations and we would like to put her down.”

“Well, if that’s what you feel that you want to do, then I have Lady-G go look for you something tomorrow. How many bedrooms do you want?”

“Three at the least!”

"Will this place be a hustlin' spot or a hideaway?"

"A hideaway spot. Only the girls and us would know about it, and only the ladies who would be staying there would know about it."

"What you want…a house or apartment?"

"Either or, but I think a house would be better. Okay, I'll have Lady-G get right on it."

"But you know that it's all right for ya'll to fuck the ladies that work at the escort service. They're nothing but a gang of freaky ladies anyway."

"Hell, I be wanting to get butt naked and go room to room and fuck everything in there."

Game started laughing and said, "What's wrong with that? I do it!"

"You do?" Ty said in a surprised voice.

"Hell yeah, but I could never make it pass four of them."

"Damn," G-Fly said, "it's on now! I've been dreaming about a gang of them bad ass bitches. My dick stay hard when I sleep!"

And everybody started rolling and Lady-G said, "Ya'll are meant for each other because all ya'll are crazy."

Two days later Lady-G rented them a four-bedroom house with a pool in West Los Angeles. The rent was a thousand dollars per month and Game paid the first, last, and deposit for them. The youngsters spent $12,000 plushin' it out. Three bedrooms had king-sized beds. The living room and family room were both leathered out, and the family room had a 60" big-screen TV.

They also bought two more buckets—a '79 Cutlass and a '77 Toyota Corola.

Each pound of indo could make 10g's selling $20 a bag, so the youngsters decided to give it to the girls for $6,000, and let them profit $4,000 off every pound. They all went to pick up Janet who was glad to see them and even more glad that they wanted to kick it with her. She thought that they just wanted to pull a train on her to see if she would be down, and really she wouldn't mind because she really liked all of them. They was down and real niggas and she knew that they all was good lovers—at least two of them she knew for sure. She wore a sexy mini-skirt outfit that showed off her nice curves and some open-toe high heels. She sat in the back seat with G-Fly as Julian drove and Ty sat in the passenger seat.

G-Fly said, "You look nice baby."

"Thank you. You know that I got to look nice for my men."

"Listen baby, we all sat down and discussed the situation of having your presence in our lives as our bottom gangsta bitch, and we all believe that you can fulfill this position in our lives and that you will be totally devoted and loyal to your obligations to us."

She said, "I will. I promise!"

"We expect you to bring only the downest and finest bitches into our stable, and they got to be hustlers because our money is our primary interest. We can get sex anywhere, but we giving you this position to fulfill as well, and any ladies that you bring into our family got to be down and devoted to us like you. If they running around fucking with other niggas without our permission, then they get the boot! We're going to provide y'all with a comfortable hustle so ya'll can live fly. But if you ever try to cross us or deceive us, then I'll personally put you to sleep. Do you hear me?"

"I understand, baby. I'll always be real and down with only ya'll. You can believe that, and if any of the ladies that I bring into our family try to do some scandalous shit, then I'll deal with it myself!"

Julian pulled into the driveway to their new house and G-Fly looked at Janet and said, "You better. I went to bat for you and I hope that you don't prove me wrong."

"I won't baby. You'll see!"

"Okay then, give me a kiss then."

Janet gave him a deep passionate kiss and they all got out of the car and followed Julian into the house. G-Fly handed Janet a pair of keys and said, "Welcome home Princess!"

She looked at the keys and at all of them and said,

"Quit playing!"

Ty said, "Baby, you said that you wanted to be down with the real. Now represent!"

She gave a big smile and started hugging and kissing all of them. Julian said, "Go and look around your house."

She started running around the house like a big kid and G-Fly said, "And it even got a pool."

Her eyes got big and she ran to the backyard and said, "You guys is too much! I love you all so much and I'm so happy to be a part of you guys' lives. I don't know what to say!"

"Well, come on. We need to initiate you," G-Fly said, and she smiled in a seductive way and grabbed his hand as he escorted her into the family room. They all sat down on beige leather corner group set.

Julian said, "Baby, the same way you came into this world is the same way that you got to come into our lives."

She looked at them all confused. Ty said, "Baby, you don't need those clothes!"

She said, "Oh!" and started slowly undressing and said,

"You want me to take off my heels too?"

"Everything," G-Fly said. She stood before them in her divine beauty. Julian was sitting in the middle of Ty and G-Fly and said, "Come on and kneel down on your knees before the three men that you choose to devote your loyalty, devotion and life to."

She complied. Julian said, "In coming into our lives, you become our wife, sister, protector, companion, and soulmate. We become totally obligated to you the same as you would become to us. To satisfy us and keep us satisfied is your main objective and in return we will always be down for you and strive to keep you happy and satisfied as well. We will protect you, love you, and most of all trust you as that woman in our lives that we know and believe that we can depend on to keep it real. If you ever have sex with another man outside of us three, then it better be from our request. We expect you to recruit us a crew of down, real, and devoted ladies that will not only hustle their asses off to get our money right, but will also provide us with the best sex imaginable, not be scared of doing time, and will bust on anybody who pose a threat or oppose our family structure. Now you are our princess and from now on that's your new nickname, "Princess," because you are the young queen of this foundation of ours!"

"Now understand, our thoughts is law and isn't to be questioned at all. If we tell you to do something then strive to accomplish it. We would never deceive you or do anything to hurt you unless you betray us. If you or the girls violate our rules or laws, then we will hand down a punishment that we see fit, whether its an ass whoopin', dismissal or death, whatever we choose we expect you to honor our authority as law. Do you understand?"

"Yes."

"Do you accept these terms and conditions?"

"Yes."

"Do ya'll have anything that you want to add?"

"Yeah," Ty said. "Listen, this house is only for us, you, and any ladies that you choose to adopt into this family. It ain't for no brother, sister, friend, cousin or anyone else but us, and it's your duty to make sure that any lady you bring into this family know this too, because niggas and bitches get jealous easy and will run up in here and jack and possibly kill everybody in here. This house is home to us and we must try to maintain tight security. Do you understand?"

"Yes..!"

G-Fly said also, "We don't play that jealousy shit, so make sure that that's understood. Furthermore, we establish this house because you came to us with your proposal and promise of satisfaction and commitment. We got other lives and obligations that we hold strong to in this game, so our presence or actions ain't to be questioned. If we tell you something, then keep it to yourself. We vow silence and secrecy and death before dishonor. Do you know what this means?"

"Yes."

"Do you also vow to live by these codes and ethics in being down with us?"

"Yes."

"Anyone else want to add anything?"

"I think that we covered the laws pretty well. Any mistake on her part at this point would have to be intentional. Do you got her crown?"

G-Fly pulled out a box and said, from now on, every step you take would be for us and we expect for you to keep it real, fly, gangsta, and what we call GP—that ghetto pride. Stand up Princess."

She complied and G-Fly kneeled down and hooked the fat diamond ankle bracelet that Ty charged on that credit card on her right ankle. Always wear it on your right, okay?"

"Okay baby."

"Ty, do you got her birthday gift?"

Ty reached in his pocket and pulled out another box and grabbed her right hand and said, "Today is June 30, 1987, and it's considered the day that you gave birth into our lives and this day will always be considered your birthday to us."

He took the three-caret diamond ring and said, "Happy birthday Princess."

Janet was crying with happiness. Everyone gave her a hug and a kiss and told her happy birthday.

Julian said, "It's not over" and pulled out another box and said, "This present is so you would always remember what time it is with us" and opened the box and displayed a gold ladies Rolex watch. Julian took it and put it on her left wrist.

She just gave them a big hug and kiss and said, "I'll never let you down."

G-Fly hugged her and said, "I know you won't. I got a good gut feeling about you! Now get dressed. You're making me too horny with your sexy ass." She smiled and got dressed.

Julian said, "I'll be right back" and ran upstairs to grab the two pounds of weed that they already bagged up.

Princess said, "This is the best gift that anyone has ever gave me."

G-Fly said, "This is just the beginning Princess. We're about having the best in life, and now you have an opportunity to earn your keep. But know this, if you ever fail to live up to your obligations or our expectation, then we will replace you with someone who will appreciate and knows how to fulfill this position."

"You don't have to worry about that. I know my position!"

Ty said, "Can you cook?"

"Like a southern fat sista!"

"Well, you got my vote and I heard that you got that fire too and know how to work it."

Princess blushed and said, "I was told that, but you got to judge for yourself."

"Oh believe me, that's on my things to do list!"

They laughed as Julian walked back in carrying a duffle bag. "Have a seat Princess."

She sat in between Ty and G-Fly. Julian pulled up a leather footstool and sat in front of her and put the duffle bag down between them and unzipped it.

Princess saw all the bags of weed and said, "Damn, that's a lot of weed and it's that indo, huh?"

"Yep, it's all bagged up in twenty-dollar sacks for you.

Now it's $20,000 worth of weed here and all we want is $12,000 off of it. That leaves $8,000 for you and the girls that you recruit to work with. This is ya'll hustle. As long as our money is right, we're not going to dictate how you push it. It's your show. But we know that you'll be fair with the ladies so everybody will be happy and they won't be running around trying to do other things to get money because this leaves room for fuck-ups, or for another nigga to be able to slide under them and proposition them to betray us. We expect all our ladies to be happy and have money and nice things. You feel me?"

"Yeah."

"Now if you can drop a sack like this every week then we doing good. That would give you $32,000 a month that you and your sisters can split. Are you feeling me on this?"

"Hell yeah!"

"Now how many ladies do you plan on bringing home?"

"Anywhere from three to five."

"Please don't bring us ducks," G-Fly said, and everyone started rolling.

"You know that I'm only getting the best for my men."

"Now listen, this is my suggestion, but you can do it how you want. If I was you, I'll give the ladies a $2,000 packages and tell them to bring you $1,500 off each sack. That's a hundred bags. Therefore, the ladies can profit according to their determination and hustle. That will give the ladies $5,000 that they can split, and $3,000 that you would make automatically without having to side hustle. You can just supply them and they can push the hustle. If you had five ladies then they all can make a $1,000 a week and you will make $3,000 a week by just supplying them. If they can sell two of these sacks, then they can make $2,000 a week apiece and you will make $6,000 a week profit. This way you can never come short with our money because you have enough room to cover any losses. What you think?"

"I love it and I'ma do it your way!"

"It's far and beneficial for us all."

"Good! Now listen. We all got rooms in here so whatever room you select is up to you, and the ladies have the same option. Also, it is a fourth bedroom with two beds in it, so that's another choice.

"Hell, you can put two in my bed, you know I don't care," G-Fly said.

"Which one is your room?"

"The one in back with the red bedroom set."

"Well, that's the one that I'ma occupy too!"

"I knew you was a freak for pain."

Everybody started busting up. Julian said, "Here." He gave her an envelope with four sets of keys in it and $500, a piece of paper with all of their beeper numbers and the phone number to the house.

G-Fly said, "That's the number to the downstairs phone. The phone in our room has a different number that

I'll give you later. That $500 is for the house expenses so you can keep the needed necessities in order and if you need some money to hold you over until you get your hustle in full swing. The keys is to the two buckets outside in the garage. So you and the ladies can have transportation until ya'll start ballin' and flip ya'll some new shit."

Julian said, "G-Fly, why don't you take Princess and me and Ty will go and handle the other, and call us and we'll come by and get you when you done."

"Cool!" G-Fly said. "Go and put that money and weed up, and come on back so we can roll."

She said, "Okay."

Ty and Julian said, "We'll catch you later Princess."

She hugged them both and said, "How about I cook ya'll something for dinner tonight?"

Ty said, "Sounds good to me!"

Julian said, "How can we pass that up? Call us when ya'll get back 'rade! I got you!"

Ty and Julian left. Princess went to put the stuff up and then came back downstairs and said, "I'm ready. Where we going?"

"When you're with me it don't make a difference, and if I don't tell you then don't ask. You feel me?"

"Yes baby, I'm sorry!"

"Listen, don't ever refer to yourself as sorry. We don't fuck with sorry women, especially not one who supposed to be a reflection of us! It's alright to apologize if you're wrong, but never ever refer to yourself as being sorry! Do you understand?"

"Yes baby, I understand." Princess giggled and was so proud to have men who were so sharp, strong, and well-laced.

Chapter 9
Is It Trickin' or Boss Game?

G-Fly and Princess pulled up at the Fox Hills Mall at 2:30 p.m. and as they walked into the mall, Princess had her arm wrapped proudly around his arm letting the whole mall know that G-Fly was her man.

G-Fly walked into the popular ladies clothing store and said, "You know that we can't have our main lady looking hard up. We got to keep it fly!"

She looked at him confused and surprised, and G-Fly slapped her on her big butt and said, "Go on and do your thang."

The sales lady walked up and said, "May I help you?"

G-Fly said, "Yeah, take my lady and go hook her up fly."

The salesperson said, "So what would it be, Miss? Fila, Gucci, Guess, Nike, casual wear?"

G-Fly said, "Give her a little bit of everything!"

Princess smiled like a little girl and started doing her thing. G-Fly grabbed four nice hundred dollar dresses and said, "Try these on."

The saleslady took Princess the sexy dresses and G-Fly said, "Yeah, I like them!"

He spent $1,100 at that store and Princess was extremely happy.

"Thank you, baby!"

"You can thank me by getting that money right and show the world the true meaning of a down bitch." Then he lead her into the women's shoe store and said, "And by always keeping it fly!"

The saleslady walked up and said, "May I help you?" G-Fly looked at Princess and said, "You know what you like and need to go with your new wardrobe!"

Princess said, "I love you guys so much!" and gave G-Fly a big kiss.

G-Fly said, "Girl, you're making me feel like a trick.

Now take your ass over there and get what you want."

She smiled and said, "You're crazy!" and went to grab her some nice sandals and high heels. She bought five pairs and they left and went to J. C. Penney and she got some sexy underwear and bras. G-Fly picked out three sexy lingerie and five teddies. Then he grabbed some perfumes and bubble bath supplies and a bottle of Obsession perfume for a friend which he had gift-wrapped. On the way out, he stopped at a women's foot locker and brought her three pairs of different color Fila tennis and a couple of Fila tennis skirts and sports top and socks.

She said, "You sure know how to treat your ladies."

"Only my main one gets this type of love and respect! Like I said, I believe in you and my comrades trust my instincts, so the next move is on you!"

"Baby, you have showed me more love and respect than anyone in my life, and I would die striving to fulfill my obligation and promise to you."

"I hope so! And they left the mall."

It was 5:00 p.m. when G-Fly pulled up to the Touch of Class Beauty Salon. G-Fly said, "I know you don't think that I'm going to let you represent me looking all nappy-headed."

"What's wrong with my hair?" Princess had long pretty hair down past her shoulder.

G-Fly said, "Baby it's time for a change. You down with it?"

"If that's what you want baby, I'm down with it!"

"That's what I'm talking about Princess. Let's roll!"

They went into the beauty salon and the lady said, "Hi, may I help you?"

"Hi beautiful. Tell me who's the baddest stylist in this place?"

"That would probably be Lisa over there."

"Thank you, sweetheart." G-Fly walked over to Lisa's station with Princess and said, "What's up, Lisa?"

"Hi!"

"Baby, I hear that you're the baddest stylist in California."

"Oh yeah? Who told you that?"

"The wino on the corner!"

Everybody in hearing distance started laughing.

"You're crazy!"

"Listen baby, I want you to put one of those silky bobs on my lady. How much you charge me for that?"

"How short do you want it?"

"Whatever he says!"

"Chop-chop!" G-Fly said.

And the ladies started laughing. Lisa said, "Give me $60."

"How soon can you do it?"

"Well, my 5:30 appointment cancelled on me, so you're in luck."

"Good, and can you get someone to give my baby and manicure and pedicure?"

"Yes Mia-Mia, can you hook her up for me?"

"Of course!"

"Lisa, I'ma put her relaxer in and send her over to you."

"Who I pay?"

"You can pay me and I'll pay her."

"How much for everything?"

"Give me a hundred for everything."

"You got a deal."

"Who's your barber?"

"Josh over there."

"I'll see you later Princess. Lisa, take care of my girl and show her why they call you the best in California!"

They started laughing and Lisa said, "Girl, you got a good man."

Princess said, "You couldn't imagine."

G-Fly said, "Hey Joshua."

Josh turned around and put his hand on his hip and said, "It's Josh!" It was plain to see that Josh was gay.

"Damn Josh, don't get your panties in a bunch. I recognize that you're a sex symbol." Josh smiled and said, "How can I help you Fly Guy?"

"Listen, I need a cut."

"You got some pretty waves. I can really hook you up if you let me silk your waves out with a relaxer and then give you a nice cut."

"Oh yeah? What are you going to charge me?"

"Give me $20 and I'll hook you up!"

"Okay, let me see your work. Don't look at me like that. I mean my head. Nigga, you know what head I'm talking about!"

"You better be more specific, Fly Guy!"

Thirty minutes later, G-Fly was gazing in the mirror at his haircut, low with a nice silky wave shining all through it.

"You sure know your craft!"

"So I've been told."

"Good looking out Joshua," G-Fly said and gave him $30 dollars.

"I guess I'll let you call me that since you tip good, plus it sound kind of sexy when you say it!"

G-Fly smiled and said, "Is it a place to eat around here?"

"Yeah, it's a hamburger shop next door."

"You want something?"

"Yeah, grab me a cheeseburger, fries, and a strawberry soda. Here." Josh tried to hand G-Fly a $5 bill.

"I got this one. You get the next one."

"Deal!" G-Fly left out.

Thirty minutes later G-Fly walked back in the beauty shop with three big bags of food. He gave Josh his food and drink and Lisa and Princess the same. He smashed two cheeseburgers, fries, and a strawberry soda and had another burger and fry left in the bag that he gave to Mia. G-Fly went next door to the record store and bought three new CDs—Too Short, Keith Sweat, and Ice Cube—counted the rest of his money and realized that he already spent $2,400 on Princess. "Damn, this bitch better be worth it." He thought about the jewelry that they gave her and was glad that Ty put that lick down on that crazy white doctor for them credit cards because if he hadn't, Princess would not have no jewelry. But it was free, so hopefully it was a good investment because Princess was ready to sell her pussy on the corner if a nigga ordered her to.

G-Fly laughed as he walked back into the beauty salon and saw Lisa putting the finishing touches on now one of the finest bitches in the place.

Princess said, "Do you like it?"

G-Fly said, "Now that's the princess I want!"

She giggled as Lisa smiled and removed the silk smock from over Princess' clothes. Princess stood up and looked in the mirror. "Baby, I love it!"

"Me too!"

It was cut, flared and curled all in the right places. G-Fly gave Lisa $140 and said, "You're the best."

She said, "Thank you. When do you want your next appointment?"

G-Fly said, "Keep her on your weekly calendar for every Thursday at 10:30 a.m."

"Got you! What's your name anyway?"

"G-Fly baby."

"Yeah that fits you. Bye Princess."

"Bye Lisa."

"Bye Fly Guy."

"Take it easy Joshua."

G-Fly and Princess walked out the door. As they got in the car, Princess gave him a deep French kiss and said, "You're the realest nigga that I ever met."

"That's good to know."

"Also, I like your silky waves. That shit looks fly."

"Yeah baby, I got to keep it fly." They drove off.

It was 7:30 when they arrived back at the house and Princess said, "I'ma take a quick bath and slip on something more nicer before I start cooking. Do you want to join me?"

"Why not?"

They went upstairs and had a quick tense passionate fuck.

Princess took a nice quick bath and G-Fly settled for a quick shower then went and call his comrades at 8:30. Both Ty and Julian was working security and G-Fly told

Game to call him if they needed him. Princess came down in a red teddy and some sexy high heel slippers and was looking like a top ghetto model.

She said, "I'ma go and prepare dinner for Ty and Julian now."

"No need baby. They got caught up on some business. They might not make it until late. Come on and relax next to your man and let me enjoy the strength of your love."

She smiled and walked over to him and straddled his lap and they started kissing like lovers at a drive-in.

Chapter 10
No Fear, No Remorse

The next morning Julian and Ty came over to the new house at 8:10 a.m. When they got to G-Fly's room, G-Fly was sleeping with Princess cuddled in his arms. Ty and Julian laughed as they stood in the doorway and Julian said, "Look at the two lovebirds. Ain't that cute."

G-Fly and Princess looked up and saw Julian and Ty looking at them smiling. G-Fly said, "Yeah, ya'll crept up on me this time," and reached under his pillow and said, "I advise ya'll to knock next time."

Ty looked at him and said, "G-Red my nigga."

G-Fly instantly got up and said, "Give me five minutes."

Julian said, "Take ten minutes. We don't need you around us all day smelling Princess' exotic juices. You'll have our dicks hard all day!"

Everybody laughed as Princess blushed and got up and put on her silk robe. Both her and G-Fly was butt naked. Ty said, "Baby I knew that you was thick, but I didn't know that you were flawless."

She smiled and said, "Do ya'll want me to fix ya'll some breakfast before ya'll leave?"

Ty said, "Naw baby, maybe next time. Damn, I love that haircut. That's you all the way!"

Julian said, "Yeah, it brings out that beautiful face and sexy eyes that God blessed you with."

She said, "Thank you," and went to give Julian a hug.

Julian said, "Wait a minute sexy. I love my comrade, but I don't love him like that "hygiene."

She said, "Oh, I apologize" and walked into the bathroom as G-Fly was coming out and rushing to get dressed.

"What's up, my nigga? Game got a problem and is meeting us at the apartment at nine. He called a G-Red."

G-Fly slipped on his black Nike sweat-suit and black

Nike Cortes tennis shoes and grabbed his big 45 magnum, money, and joint from off the table and said, "Let's roll."

Princess was walking out of the bathroom as they were exiting and knew better than to say anything as they all three left without acknowledging her again.

They got into the Maxima and headed for the apartment. It was 8:50 when they arrived at the apartment, and Game and Lady-G were already there. Lady-G cooked a quick breakfast of bacon, eggs, and cheese sandwiches. Game greeted his comrades with a warm smile and Lady-G said, "Hey ya'll!" Everybody kissed her on the cheek.

Julian said, "I apologize for keeping ya'll waiting. We just swooped by the spots on the way and made the morning pick-ups and deliveries."

"Good," Game said as Julian handed him the money. "Just put it up until later. Listen ya'll, I got a very good friend up in Oakland who is having some major problems from a rival drug dealer, and he asked for my assistance. Now me and Julian is going to fly out there to find out the specifics, and Lady-G is going to drive with ya'll two up there to meet us. I'll put ya'll up on more when we get there."

Game looked at Julian and said, "Give them your guns to bring. They're going to meet us up there."

Julian went upstairs and grabbed his box Uzi and 9mm automatic and gave it to Ty. "Bring this for me."

Ty said, "Good choice!" Ty grabbed his 9mm and two extra clips and G-Fly grabbed his 45 automatic and they put it in their book-bags with extra clothes. Lady-G gave everybody two sandwiches and a soda, and they all left. Game and Julian jumped in the Maxima and headed for the airport. Lady-G, Ty, and G-Fly all jumped in Lady-G's new 300 Benz and jumped on the freeway.

"How long of a drive is it?" Ty asked Lady-G.

"About six hours."

"This Benz is like that," G-Fly said from the backseat.

"If you get tired of driving, little momma, let me know. I'll push this bad muthafucka!"

Ty said, "Sis, by any chance do you have any Ice

Cube in here?"

"Of course. Look in the tape box in the back seat."

"G-Fly grabbed the tape box and handed Ty the Ice Cube tape, and they bumped in silence.

Lady-G drove half the way then G-Fly drove the other half.

They met Game and Julian at the motel at 3:30. Game put everyone up on the carefully thought out plan that he and Julian came up with. Lady-G put on a red wig and Game put on a dred-locked wig, some dark shades, a dirty trench coat and old torn-up tennis shoes. His good friend rented them a white moving van and a rental car in an alias name. They went to the spot where the rival dope dealer and his worker hung out.

It was 5:30 Friday afternoon and Mac P and his crew were standing in the parking lot of the neighborhood liquor store in the 'hood and turf that they had taken over. Mac P had his convertible Cougar out there fixed up with the candy paint and Dayton wire rims bumping some Too Short. He was kicking it with six niggas out of his eight-man crew and as always he was the center of attraction. T Mac said, "Look at that crazy shit there."

Game was pushing a shopping cart full of junk and the three youngsters were walking on each side of him cursing him out, spitting on him, and Ty snuck up behind him and kicked him in the butt. The youngsters had their book bags on and looked like some young kids coming from school. Game said in a drunken voice, "Ya'll better leave me alone."

"Fuck you, you old dirty drunk muthafucka. Why don't you crawl your old miserable ass under a trash can and die?" Julian said.

"Or better yet, cut your damn wrist," G-Fly stated, as he pretended to spit on Game.

Mac P and his crew were caught up in laughter as the youngsters and game got within ten feet of them. T Mac said, "Ya'll leave that bum alone and take ya'll bad asses home."

Julian reached into his book bag and everybody saw

the signal and pulled out their guns simultaneously and started laying Mac P and his crew down. "Mind your own business,"

Julian said as he pulled out the Uzi. Ty and G-Fly already started busting their 9mm and 45 automatics before Julian started letting his Uzi loose on the six-man crew. Game came up out of the shopping cart full of junk with a modified 12-gauge pump shotgun, and it wasn't nowhere to run or hide as Mac P and his crew all lay in a puddle of blood. G-Fly and Ty ran over and shot Mac P and his crew in the head to make sure that they were all dead. Lady-G pulled up in the van and Game held the back door open as they all ran and jumped in the back and said, "Roll, baby," as he slammed the side door and Lady-G was gone.

Game said, "Is everybody cool?" as they were changing clothes in the back of the van.

Julian said, "We cool my nigga."

Game said, "How we look baby?"

"We look cool, and we're almost there."

Game put all of the guns in a big black duffle bag and put their clothes in a green plastic trash bag with his and Lady Fly's wigs and tied it in a knot. They pulled up in back of a Laundromat and Lady-G and the youngsters went and jumped in the rental car as Game walked over to a BMW and put the duffle bag full of guns in the trunk, then shook an older dark-skinned man's hand, jumped in the rental car and left. He drove around six blocks and pulled up to a liquor store and threw the green plastic bag with their clothes into a garbage container. He ran into the store and grabbed a bottle of Hennessey, cups, gum, and a cranapple juice for Lady-G, then he jumped back in the car and headed for the motel.

When they arrived at the motel, they all took a quick shower to wash away any gun powder residue and then had a cup of Hennessey and a joint to relax their blood pressure from all the excitement. Game said, "We got a turn around flight at 7:30 p.m., so we got to be going." He looked at Lady-G and said, "We'll meet you back at the main house."

She said, "Okay," and they kissed, then all departed.

Lady-G said, "I'll drive the first half and then one of ya'll take over. They smiled and agreed.

On the drive back from Oakland, Lady-G told Ty and G-Fly the story of how she met Game. "I met Game when I was 17 years old and working the street as a career prostitute. That was about five years ago, and he found me in an alley where I was beaten half to death by two Mexicans who raped and robbed me and left me there in the alley to die. When I woke up, I was lying in game's bed with his stepmother, Big Momma, taking care of me and nursing me back to life. Big Momma was an ex-veteran prostitute that took Game in off the street when he was 14 years old and laced him in the game. Game's mother was an ex-prostitute that worked the street with Big Momma back in the day. Unfortunately, she was brutally stabbed to death by a white trick who was a sick psychopath going around killing prostitutes back in the day. Big Momma told me how game found me in the alley and brought me to his place. Game was 24 years old when I met him and it was like love at first sight. He treated me so kind and respectful and asked me for nothing in return.

After I was healed, he gave me a couple of hundred dollars and told me that he hoped it could help me get on my feet. I gave it back to him and told him if he would accept me in his life, then I vowed to be devoted and loyal to him until the day I died.

Although he had four prostitutes working for him already, in a week's time I brung him four more and became his number one lady. Two years after Game saw opportunity in the dope game and took advantage of it, he never looked back. He wanted to provide his ladies with a more safe and secure working environment, so he gave us a pager number to give to our best tricks so we can build our own private clienteles to cater to in a more personal and private way. They would page me and make an appointment, and I'll send them the lady that they desired and kept the books.

He treated all his ladies with devoted respect and admiration, and he made sure that they all looked top-notch and had the best health plan and were paid well. They all make 40% of their weekly income and live rent free. So you can imagine how much they make! However, in return, they all are totally loyal, devoted, and down, and they will do anything at his request, regardless of the consequences. And he got 20 of them, not including me, and whether ya'll know it or not, all the girls have been given orders to cater to your every desire and request."

Ty looked over at Lady-G and said, "What about you?"

Lady-G smiled and said, "Even I."

Ty said, "Damn, Game must really be down for us."

Lady-G looked over at him and said, "More than you can ever imagine."

G-Fly said, "So you're our bitch too?"

Lady-G started laughing and said, "Yep, nigga I'm your bottom bitch for life."

"Now that's what I call a serious blessing!" Everyone laughed.

Lady-G, Ty, and G-Fly arrived at the main house in Hollywood Hills at 12:50 a.m. and Game and Julian both greeted them with an excited smile. Everybody gave each other a warm embrace. Game went and poured them all a double shot of Louise the XIII Hennessey as they all laughed, joked, and spoke about the lick that they put down. Lady-G said, "I was down the street watching ya'll put it down, and I must admit ya'll are some down ass gangsters! Ya'll made me want to jump out the van and bust my 3.80!"

Everybody laughed and Ty said, "Girl, you're not cut like that."

"Yeah right nigga, don't get it twisted. I'ma ride or die bitch. Tell them baby!"

"Yeah, she can be ya'll twin sister."

Julian looked at Lady-G, then at Game and said, "Like that?"

Game said, "Yep," and shook his head displaying his sincerity. G-Fly said, "I love a down bitch!"

Game said, "Yeah, I heard that you recruited you one."

"Yeah, she talk a good one and all that, but we've yet to see how well she can perform. Nevertheless, I got a pretty good vibe about her, and I believe with the right lacing she might prove to be a top-notch bitch."

"You want me to lace her?" Lady-G asked.

"Let me really feel her out first because if she ain't cut like I want her to be, then she won't be around long!"

Julian said, "We're putting together a crew of down bitches to push this weed operation that we're putting together, and we selected her as our bottom bitch to recruit the other down bitches and make sure that the operation is pushed and ran right."

G-Fly said, "I can tell that she's a cut above the rest, but she just never had a nigga who cared about her or laced her."

Lady-G said, "Baby, why don't you show them how to put locks on her just in case."

Game said, "Good idea!"

"What you mean by putting locks on her?" Julian asked.

Game said, "What she mean is you want to get something on her like a murder or something. That way if she ever get busted for anything or you tell her put down a vicious lick for you like trick a nigga in a motel and doom him, then she's obligated to you regardless and would never dream of crossing you."

"That's what I need right there," G-Fly said. "How can we do it?"

"There's a lot of ways, but I got a cool one that I know always works for me that I'll put ya'll up on."

"Yeah, good lookin-out 'rade," G-Fly said.

Julian looked over at Lady-G and said, "Girl, you always seem to amaze me!"

She smiled and said, "I told ya'll that I'm ya'll bottom lady as well, so that means that I'm obligated to ya'll in every way, especially in keeping a bitch in check!"

Ty said, "Game, do you got locks on Lady-G?"

"Of course, and her crazy ass probably got some on me too!" He looked over at Lady-G as she started giggling.

"Baby, you know that I don't need no locks on you. We're bounded for life!" She smiled and kissed Game with a deep passionate tongue kiss and said, "Baby, I'ma go take a bath and get some rest."

"Okay baby."

"Good night ya'll."

"All right sis, sleep tight," Julian said.

"I don't sleep, I rest…those who sleep never know what's going on."

"That's right baby. Correct his young ass," G-Fly said and everybody laughed as Lady-G walked out switching her big pretty ass and hips.

Julian said, "That's got to be one of the realest sista's in the world."

"The downest and realest as far as we know," G-Fly added.

Ty said, "You got that right!"

Game said, "Excuse me for a minute. Ya'll make ya'll self at home."

Ty said, "Pass me the weed box. Hell yeah, put it in the air!"

Game came back downstairs with three brown paper bags full of money and said, "My good friend really appreciates the good job that ya'll did and told me to give ya'll this." He smiled as he gave them all a bag.

They were shocked because they felt that that kind of work came with the game, and the thousand dollars a week that they got paid every week was surely enough to gain their loyalty and devotion to the game, and any problems that may exist.

Game said, "Listen, what we do is totally between us, and if you hear Lady-G running her mouth about it or anyone else, then you're obligated to blow their heads off. Our business or secrets ain't nobody else's business, you feel me?"

"Yea big bro, you know that we don't do no bragging or tripping like that. We abandon our conscience a long time ago!"

"I know, but I just felt obligated to speak on it, so we

could never have a misunderstanding."

Ty said, "Man, how much money is this?"

"If I told you, then that would take the fun out of counting it!" Game laughed and walked out of the family room.

Game opened the door to his bedroom and smiled at the beautiful sight of Lady-G lying on the silk sheets with a sexy see-through negligee and bumping Tina Marie on the stereo at a low mellow tone.

"I hoped that you didn't forget about me," she said and giggled.

"Not even on my death bed," Game stated as he slowly walked over to her unbuttoning his shirt.

As Lady-G crawled to the edge of the bed to meet him and started unbuckling his pants as they kissed and fall victim to the depths of their most deepest desire.

Julian, Ty, and G-Fly were all in the family room counting their money in excitement, contemplating how they were going to spend it. Julian said, "Man, I got nine g's saved already."

Ty said, "I got around nine to ten g's too."

G-Fly said, "I spent that $2,500 on Princess. That knocked me down to about $6,500 saved."

Julian said, "Don't trip. Me and Ty will give you $800 apiece to account for our half and we all will put another $1,000 apiece so we can make sure the bitches that Princess recruit got some nice clothes and hair fly."

"Yeah, we're going to nominate you the official fashion designer," Ty said as they smiled.

Julian said, "Yeah, cause Princess was looking way better than she ever looked to me. You took her from a low seven to a high ten on the player scale."

G-Fly said, "I can feel that, but ya'll need to give up $1,500 apiece because I take pride in my work!"

"Okay, you got that, here." Julian and Ty gave him $2,300 apiece.

"That's real," G-Fly stated. "I've been kind of looking out for mom with some food in the refrigerator and $20 a day."

Ty said, "Yeah, I drop moms off a couple of hundred last week too."

Julian said, "Shit, ya'll coming out cheap. I gave my moms about $700 already. Also you know that I gave smoked out ass Sam the shack.

Yeah, I went by there and he had Michelle's smoke out ass in there laying butt naked in the bed with him watching TV. He seen me and said, 'Yo Ty, Julian gave me the key yesterday and told me that I can have the spot.' I laughed and gave him my keys and $20 and he was happy and asked me did I want Michelle to hook me up. I just laughed and told him I was cool and left. Yeah, I forgot to tell ya'll that I gave him the spot."

"Listen man," G-Fly said, "it's about time to bust us some fly rides and shit. As long as we don't be fucking with no dope while we're in them, then we should be cool."

"I'm feeling that," Julian said.

"Me too," said Ty.

"Well it's official," G-Fly declared.

Game walked back into the family room an hour later and said, "Put it in the air my niggas." He started fixing him a drink and the three youngsters were smiling at him from ear to ear. "What you niggas smiling for?"

G-Fly said, "Man, just the smell of you when you walked by me made my dick hard."

Ty said, "Me too, and I'm about due for some pussy!"

Everybody laughed. Game said, "Nigga, ya'll got a whole stable of horny bitches waiting for ya'll wondering why ya'll ain't hit nothing. They think ya'll scared or something. Hell, I wasn't even scared of the boogie-man when I was young."

Ty said, "I was."

Julian said, "That nigga was big, swoll, and ugly as a muthafucka!" Everybody started busting up. "Anyway, fuck them bitches right now. We want to buss some new rides. It's the summer of '87 and we want to come correct."

Game looked at them and smiled and said, "Don't worry. I got a good friend who owns a car dealership on the west side. I'll call him in the morning and have Lady-G take you guys over there so you can get hooked up."

"Good looking out 'rade. You're the realest nigga we know," Ty admitted, "and we got mad love for you too!"

"And that's real," G-Fly added.

Julian said, "Let's give a toast to our god-brother and new comrade. It's us against the muthafucken' world!"

They all laughed and held up their drinks and downed it.

"Your good friend gave us "$50,000 apiece. That was good looking out," Ty said.

"Yeah, that's the benefits of being a real nigga and gangsta. Muthafuckas is going to always respect you and bless you in the game," Game stated. "Ya'll can stay here tonight and sleep in the guestrooms."

"Who's watching over the girls when we're not?" Ty asked.

"Well, Treasure's my second lady in charge, and she handles the books and sending the girls on dates when Lady-G is busy or away, and the girls just go and watch each other's back."

"Okay, I was wondering, Treasure's a beautiful sista, What is she anyway?"

"She's Cuban and just as down as Lady-G!"

"Yeah? Damn, I didn't see that in her, but I was captivated by her beautiful sex appeal. Five foot two with a dark bronze complexion and thick in all the right places, and that short wavy hairstyle is just making her features stand out," Ty stated.

"Yeah, my dick got instantly hard when I met her," Julian said, and everyone started rolling.

Chapter 11
Get Money

The next morning the three youngsters woke up at 7:30 a.m. pumped up and left early so they could go and make the deliveries and pick up then went back to their apartments to shower and get dressed in some proper sweat suits and they all took $15,000 out of their $50,000 and put $35,000 in a duffle bag that each one of them had, and grabbed their other guns and headed back to the main house. Now they had the majority of the day to themselves.

* * * *

Princess got up Saturday morning and went to go get her closest home-girls, Little Tish, Dee-Dee, and Gwen. They all was down for each other ever since elementary school and as always Janet a.k.a Princess was looked up to as their crew leader. Little Tish was short, light-skinned with a big hip, ass, and thighs, and she had sexy light brown eyes and long wavy hair. Dee-Dee was a pretty dark brown-skin sista who was 5’8” and weighed 135 pounds with a nice sexy well-built body. She wore braids that took away from her appearance but was a cold hustler that lived and was raised in the projects. Gwen was mixed with Mexican and was 5’4” with a nice sexy body. She was a pretty honey-coated complexion and had nice big firm titties.

All of Princess’ girls was down, devoted and loyal to the cause, and after they seen how much Princess came up and how fly she looked, they was seriously interested in being down.

Princess picked her home-girls up and said, “Bitch, this is where the game gets deep at. If you ain’t 100% down for the game and lifestyle that I’m going to kick to you, then ya’ll need to get the fuck on now and save yourself some problems, because if ya’ll try to manipulate, deceive, betray or violate these laws and rules that I’ma lay down to ya’ll, then I’m personally going to pop a cap in your ass! My new men took me in and gave me more than I ever had in my life, and told me to recruit some real and down bitches who knew how to be loyal and devoted to the game and who wanted to have something good in life. And it's my position and obligation to them to make sure that the ladies that I choose, and recruit, is down for the cause and deeply loyal and devoted to them and them only! That means all them good-for-nothing niggas and sugar daddies that you bitches got, got to get the boot. If you accept and choose to come home and become part of this sista'-hood, then satisfying our men is the only nigga that you will be sucking and fucking unless they tell you otherwise. Now they have set me up with a way so all of us can come up and have the flyest shit, and they got our backs to the fullest. My word is law in my crew, and I won't tolerate no type of betrayal. Ya'll been my sistas' since I can remember, and I know that all ya'll is down for whatever, so it's only right that I give ya'll the opportunity to be down for a real cause with some real niggas who's going to keep it real with you and provide you with an opportunity to have more than anything that you ever had. All that jealous shit stays at this table. Your obligations would be to protect, be down for, and satisfy all of them equally, and never question their thoughts or requests of you. And to make this money! Are ya'll down for this cause or opportunity or what?"

Dee-Dee said, "Janet, I mean Princess, we go way back and I've always looked up to you like my big sista and I know that you're down for me and us in every way. If you believe in it, then I'm down with you to the fullest. You know that I'll bust that thang too, so if it's real then I'm going to be real and loyal to it."

"Yeah me too," Gwen said. "Ain't no nigga down for us like that or trying to see a bitch with anything other than a pussy full of cum. We need some real niggas in our life and I'm down for the cause too."

"Bitch, you know that I'm down with you regardless of the game, and I ain't got no problem with poppin' that thang either, so whatever you got going on count me in,"

Little Tish said as they sat at the Mexican Restaurant.

Princess said, "Okay, now that we got a understanding, let's roll so I can put you up on the game more deeply."

Princess pulled up to the new house and said, "Come on."

Dee-Dee said, "This is a nice house. Your men must be doing big thangs."

Princess opened up the door to the big four-bedroom house and led the girls in and shut the door and said, "Welcome home, ladies!"

Dee-Dee said, "Girl, quit playing."

Everyone looked at Princess for confirmation. Princess said, "Listen, I'm dead serious about everything that I'm telling you! This shit is real and I expect ya'll to represent to the fullest. Now all three of our men got a bedroom in here and it's a fourth bedroom that got two twin beds in it. It's ya'll choice or ya'll can both share a bedroom. It's on ya'll.

I stay in the bedroom with the red bedroom set with G-Fly. I know that you all always had the hot's for Julian and now ya'll got him. He got the room with the black bedroom set and Ty got the room with the blue bedroom set. Go look around."

The girls ran around like little girls. Tish and Dee-Dee were both from different projects and never really had nothing more than a double-up hundred dollar sack of rock to hustle and survive on. Gwen was like Princess in a sense. She lived with her smoked-out auntie that was her father's sister, the black side of her family, and was a closet prostitute who lived month-to-month on Section 8. All the girls knew hard times and what it meant to be without. They even turned a trick here and there to survive or have more, but they would boost, rob a trick, fight, and shoot if ever needed to. They all was down and devoted to one another, and even though they really never had nice clothes or seen the inside of a beauty salon to many times, they was still clean and well kept up.

Little Tish and Gwen chose to share Julian's bed, and Dee-Dee hurried up and grabbed Ty's bed.

"This is the most beautifulest house that I ever been in," Dee-Dee said.

Little Tish said, "Yeah, I never been in a house this big, much less lived in one!"

Gwen said, "No more sleeping on that worn out couch or taking cold showers either. And I ain't seen that much food in a kitchen in my life. I thought that I was in a supermarket for a minute."

Princess said, "Don't worry sis. From now on we're going to have the best. Just stay real, loyal, and true to the cause and one another and we're going to always have the best. Our men promise me and I support and honor their thoughts and desires as law, and I expect ya'll to do the same. Did ya'll see the pool?"

"We got a pool to?" Little Tish said excitingly.

"Yep."

They all follow Princess to the backyard where a nine-foot pool with a diving board and a Jacuzzi were. Gwen said, "We got a Jacuzzi too! This place is like that, girl!"

Princess said, "When ya'll get finish fending, then meet me in the family room."

Princess went upstairs and grabbed the duffle bag full of weed and went back down into the family room where her girls were waiting.

"I know that ya'll wondering how we're going to hustle, and no Dee-Dee, we're not going to be selling pussy."

"How did you know that that's what I was thinking?"

"Because I know you like a sista!"

"Hell, I thought that too," Gwen said.

Little Tish said, "Me too," and gave Gwen dap as everyone laughed.

Princess said, "I hate to bust ya'll bubble but our pussies is strictly for our men only and that's law! Now peep this."

Princess unzipped the duffle bag and the girls all stared at the weed with lust.

"Damn it's on," Dee-Dee said.

"Yep, and we're going to push this shit like crack."

Little Tish said, "That's that indo, that shit's going to sell like alcohol!"

"Yeah, we can take over all of the weed spots because it ain't too many indo spots around, especially not in my project," Dee-Dee said.

"Mine either," Little Tish added.

Gwen said, "The Mexicans down the street from me got a weed house that sell stress and I know that I can take over majority of their clientele. They be short anyway. These bags is pretty cool for $20 sacks."

"Okay listen, our men is going to supply us and watch our backs to the fullest, so you ain't got to worry about problems because as you know, our niggas is true gangsta's! Now peeps!

I'm going to give each one of ya'll 100 bags apiece which is $2,000 worth of weed. Off that, you bring me $1,500 and keep $500 for yourself, and as quick as you can flip it determines how much money that you're trying to make. If you can drop a hundred sacks a day, then you will make $500 a day. Can ya'll feel this?"

"Hell yeah!" they all uttered. "A hundred sacks ain't shit once we get our clientele up, and once them wannabe baller ass niggas find out we got that indo, it's going to sell like crack," Dee-Dee said.

"We need to hit the clubs up tonight. We might can sell around a hundred bags tonight," Little Tish said.

"I'm feeling that, but peep, we got two cars too that our men brought for us to hustle in, so we got transpo," Princess stated.

"For real? We got cars that we can roll too?" Dee-Dee said with surprise.

"Yep, ya'll do know how to drive, don't ya'll?"

"Yeah girl, we all got our license. We just ain't got no cars." Little Tish said, and they all laughed.

"Gwen, your birthday's next month, huh?" Princess asked.

"Yep, I guess we will all be 17 and senior this year and having it in a major way."

"When is our men coming home?" Little Tish asked.

"This is just the house that they put together for us, and they just come in and out, but they got other places where they stay at too. Whatever you do, don't be nosy and all up in their business. If they don't tell you, don't ask. If they tell you to do something, then do it and don't ask any questions. And this place is off limits to everyone outside of us! In other words, don't even bring your mother over here. This place is for us and them and nobody else is to know about it either or get brung to this place. Do ya'll hear me?"

"Yeah."

"Now I'm going to give ya'll your first sacks, and Dee-Dee, you and Gwen go take the Toyota and get ya'll clothes and shit.

Here's $50 apiece so y'all can go get ya'll hygiene supplies together. And I'm taking all ya'll fast bitches to the free clinic tomorrow to get ya'll checked out and on birth control."

"We're clean girl!"

"Yeah, but I just want to make sure that them suckas' that ya'll been tricking with, did give ya'll something that ya'll don't know about. This is when it gets serious, so don't take this as no joke or silly game, because your actions reflects on all of us, and if ya'll try to fuck off what I'm trying to build for my down sistas' and my man, then I'ma bury you, so if you're not serious then you better walk away now."

"We feel you Princess, and we're down to the fullest. Ain't that right sista?" Little Tish said, and everyone agreed and embraced.

Now the ladies were up early in the morning enjoying each other's company. All the girls sold 50 sacks each as they hit up the clubs, parties, and located weed spots stealing their clientele.

"This is the bom hustle," Little Tish said.

"Yeah, I was mad that I only had 50 sacks on me!"

"Me too," added Gwen. "We're going to kill'em today!"

Princess said, "After we eat, I'm going to take ya'll to

the clinic and to go get ya'll some pagers and then we can go hustling."

"Sis you know we all weed heads, but do we got to quit smoking weed too?" Dee-Dee asked.

"Hell naw, we got our personal stash in that drawer over there."

Princess went and grabbed the Ziploc bag that had two ounces packed in it.

"Daaaaamn, now that's what I'm talking about," Dee-Dee said.

"Yeah, that would hold anyone for a while," Gwen added.

Princess handed the bag to Dee-Dee and Dee-Dee started rolling up some joints. "Just don't be high all the damn time and acting all stupid around our men. We got to act like ladies and mature. Also we got a cabinet full of liquor, so don't become no lush or be drinking and driving or drunk and acting no fool! All that childish shit end here. Now I'm going to go cook us something to eat so we can roll."

* * * *

As the youngsters arrived back at the main house, Game was sitting on the couch talking on the phone. Lady G was in the kitchen preparing breakfast. Game hung up the phone and picked up a joint out of the ashtray and lit it as Julian placed the briefcase on the couch next to Game, greeting him with a smile.

"What's up 'rade?"

Game opened the briefcase and said, "I see that you niggas is on point early this morning." He smiled as he hit the joint again and passed it to the three as they all gave a small laugh realizing why Game made the comment.

Julian said, "We picked up the chips from all the spots and delivered the work and the whole $20g's was accounted for plus I put the other $20g's that you left at the house yesterday, so that's the full $40g's."

Game said, "Cool, but peep. You guys been working for me for over two months now and since then the profit has doubled in weight and finances, therefore, it's only right that I double you guys' salary." He handed them all an envelope with $2,000 in each.

They all smiled with appreciation and gave Game a ghetto handshake displaying their appreciation and respect.

"Also, my associate who owns the dealership said for ya'll to come on down and he'll hook you up on whatever you guys what, and if he ain't got it, he'll get it. Now you can finance it from him and he'll carry the contract, or you can buy it. It's totally up to you guys. If you choose to buy it, then he'll fix the contracts like you're financing it for two years to cover his ass and yours, and then send you the pink slip at the end of the two years. If you sell it, then he'll give it to you sooner. This would keep the feds out of ya'll business. If it gets impounded for any reason within that two years, then he can go get it for you without the bullshit. Also, I advise you to put the cars in the new names that you guys use on your fake driver license, because in this game a car is nothing but a tool to be used for profit and gain, but sometime you got to accept your losses to gain. Can ya'll feel me?"

They all shook their heads in agreement, not knowing if it was the weed or the seeds that Game was dropping that put their thoughts in a daze. Lady G broke the silence by calling for breakfast and Ty said, "Man, I'm starving" as they all went to go get their grub on. After breakfast, Lady-G and the youngsters jumped in Game's new 560SEC convertible Benz and drove to the dealership.

Chapter 12
Ghetto Love Affair

As soon as they pulled up to the dealership, Ty saw exactly the car he wanted. It was a new convertible GT Mustang, black on black with gray leather interior. "That's her right there. That's black stallion."

They could see the desire in his eyes as he got out of the car and went to go meet his new lady. Lady-G was greeted by an older white man who introduced himself as Jim to the youngsters.

They introduced themselves and Jim told them to look around and see if they can find something that they liked. It was obvious that Lady-G and Jim knew each other well, and Jim had to be a trick that one of the girls cater to.

Julian and G-Fly went looking around on the big lot while Ty asked Jim, "How much for the black convertible Mustang?"

"$18,000."

Ty sat in the Mustang and asked for a test drive. Jim reached under the sun visor, grabbed the keys, and handed them to Ty. "She's all yours," he said, "but be careful. She got a lot of attitude with her."

Ty started the Mustang up and heard the roar of the 5.0 engine and smiled at Jim. "I wouldn't accept her no other way."

Then Ty put the stick shift in reverse and backed out. He drove to the edge of the driveway of the parking, dropped the top and punched out with precision on the main street burning rubber riding as if he was taming a wild horse. Jim looked over at Lady-G with a worrisome look, and Lady-G laughed and said, "Don't worry. Game's money sponsors their insurance plan!"

Jim smiled and said, "In that case, can I interest you in a new convertible BMW?"

Lady-G said, "No thanks, I just bought a new 300 Benz, but they might be interested!"

Jim looked over at Julian who was in a Nissan 300 ZX,

burgundy with T-tops and tan interior. G-Fly was in a convertible Iroc Camero, black on black on black. Both were pulling out and coming toward them by the exit to the parking lot. They both drove up and said they were going for a test drive, and Jim turned to Lady G with a smile and said, “I might just close early today. By any chance do you think that Star is busy tonight?”

Lady-G smiled and said, “For you, it can always be arranged.”

“Would you like a glass of champagne?”

“Why not?” Lady-G said as they went into the office.

Ty pulled back into the car lot with the 5.0 Mustang purring like a kitten and got out and walked into the offices.

"Jim, I'll give you $17,000 cash right now for it."

Jim saw the passion in his eyes and knew that he could probably go up on the price and the youngster would still get it, but he wouldn't do anything to ruin his friendship with Game, so he told Ty to come on with it.

Ty would have paid the full $18,000 for it but figured what good is game if you don't use it. "Deal!"

He got the keys from Lady-G to the Benz and went to get the money out from the trunk. He walked back in with his duffle bag and unzipped it, then started pulling out stacks of thousands. He counted out seventeen stacks and put it on the table. Then he reached over and picked up Lady-G's glass from the table and took a sip. He sat next to her with a big smile on his face.

She smiled back at him excitingly sharing in his joy, realizing that this is his first real car and true blessing from the game.

Jim finished counting the money and got Ty's driver's license and explained that his dealership would carry the insurance for the two years that they would be holding the contract, but it would cost Ty $150 per month. Ty reached into the duffle bag and grabbed two stacks and pulled two hundred dollar bills off one stack and gave Him $1,800.

G-Fly pulled up in the Iroc with the convertible top down and parked in back of the 5.0 Mustang and walked into the office. G-Fly saw the stacks of money on the table and smiled at Ty. "Is that you out there?"

Ty smiled with Lady-G and shook his head. "That's G.P., my nigga!"

"Big Jim, how much you want for that Iroc? Talk quick but don't talk slick now."

Everybody started busting up. Jim said, "Well, it's priced at $24,000, but you can give me $22,000 and I'll carry the insurance for you for the full year for an extra eighteen hundred."

"Deal." G-Fly walked outside to grab his duffle bag out of the Benz and before he closed the trunk, Julian pulled up and said "Grab my bag, too," then went to park the 300ZX in front of the Mustang.

G-Fly handed Julian his duffle bag and Julian said, "That's a done deal." They smiled and gave each other dap.

As they walked into the office, Julian said, "How much you want for that Z?"

Jim said, "Digital dash, leather seats, t-top. It's priced at $23,000, but for you I'll accept $21,000 cash and charge you an extra eighteen hundred to carry the insurance for the first year."

Julian smiled at Jim and said, "You got a deal." He started putting stacks of money on the table next to G-Fly's.

Jim called in two of his employees who started counting the money while Jim did the paperwork. After he finished, the youngsters gave Lady-G a big hug and kiss and told her that they would catch up with her later. She smiled and said, "Ya'll be careful, and take some of that money home."

"Don't worry baby, we're used to carrying large sums of money," G-Fly said and gestured toward his waistband where she knew that he carried his 45 automatic. She shook her head and said, "Nigga be careful!"

They smiled and jumped into their new cars and drove out caravanning behind one another.

Julian, Ty, and G-Fly pulled up at the audio sound system and rim shop on Crenshaw, parked and gave each other dap. G-Fly said, "Let's do this my niggas." They all were charged up. As they walked into the shop, a cute young female walked up and asked, "Can I help you with something?"

"If you promise that you'll make my dream come true," Julian said.

She blushed and Julian asked her, "Do you get commission on your sales?"

“Yes”

“Well today’s your lucky day.” She said in a sarcastic way.

"Oh really," and looked at them saying to herself that they can't be no more than 16 or 17 years old.

Julian said, "Really," with a player smile. "Listen baby, me and my brothers want three sets of Dayton rims with the new Yokahoma tires, three new Viper car alarms and also we would like three complete car audio systems complete with cassette amps, equalizers, woofers, and tweeters."

The store clerk looked at him in disbelief and said in a sarcastic way, "And what do you plan on putting it on? A ten speed?"

They laughed and Julian turned to his comrades and said, "See my niggas. No matter how real the game is there is always someone who looks down on you because of your race. It's a damn shame that it got to be one of your own." He turned back and looked at the clerk in her eyes.

Ty said, "Bitch, have you ever seen a ten-speed with Daytons, an alarm, and a booming system?" The three of them started busting up.

G-Fly said, "No, she just a part-time comedian. Tell us another joke." They laughed even harder.

The manager saw the commotion and walked over. "Excuse me gentlemen, is there a problem?

Julian said, "No, it ain't no problem." He glanced at the female's name tag and said, "Tracy was just about to help us find the best audio systems available for our cars."

The store manager said, "And what kind of cars do you want us to hook up?"

Julian said, "Well, I got a 300 ZX that I want major beats put in with crystal clear sound, and my comrade brought his convertible Iroc, and he pointed at Ty, and "he brought his convertible 5.0 Mustang, they want the same. Also, we all want Daytons on each one with the new Yokahoma tires and the new Viper alarm."

The manager said, "No problem, sir!"

Julian looked at Tracy and said, "Yes, Tracy told us that you were the best audio man around."

"Oh yes, the best," the manager said. "You know Tracy?"

"Of course. She's the one who referred us to you!"

The manager said, "Good, good," and looked at Tracy with appreciation. The manager called his two audio assistants and asked them to assist Julian, Ty, and G-Fly with pulling their cars into the garage. Julian, Ty, and G-Fly all went out and got their duffle bags out of the trunks and gave the two assistants the keys. When the youngsters walked back into the store, it was on. They started pointing out all the things they wanted. During the buying frenzy, Julian looked at the manager while they stood next to Tracy and said, "How about something to drink for me and my comrades?"

The manager said, "No problem, sir. Tracy, can you assist these gentlemen with some sodas out of the machine?"

Tracy looked at Julian and Julian smiled in a sneaky way to let her know that he did it on purpose. Tracy came back with the sodas and gave Julian his soda last along with an irritated look. Julian said, "Oh, I apologize. I should have told you before, but I'm allergic to Coke. Can you please get me a different kind?"

Tracy looked at him in shock and her tan, honey-coated complexion instantly reflected a light red tint. G-Fly was next to them and caught on to Julian's little game and started busting out laughing out loud. Tracy looked at G-Fly and shook her head, smiled and rolled her pretty hazel eyes. Right then and there, G-Fly knew that Julian had cracked her.

All three of them paid eight thousand apiece for the entire hook up with phones as well, and put the remainder of their money from the duffle bags into their pockets. The manager told them the cars wouldn't be ready for three to four hours, so the three youngsters decided to go to the mall, and do a little shopping to kill some time.

Julian walked over to the cash register where Tracy was, and said, "Baby, can you do me a favor and call me and my comrades a cab so we can kill some time at the mall while our cars is getting hooked up?"

Tracy smiled and said, "Sure, but first let me apologize for being so rude earlier. I was wrong for questioning your objective. Also, thank you for looking out for me on this commission. I really appreciate it!"

Julian said, "It ain't no big thang girl. Maybe someday you can find a way to pay a brother back" and he smiled.

"How about now?" Tracy said with a seductive smile. Julian looked at her curiously with a devilish grin and said, "Damn, you little freak!"

Tracy laughed and slapped him on the arm in a playful manner and said, "Boy! Get your thoughts out of the gutter!"

She reached in her pocket, pulled out her keys and said, "Here! You can use my car so you won't get stranded out at the mall."

Julian looked at her and said, "Shit, girl, I was about to take you down!"

Tracy laughed and gave him the keys to her car. "Boy, you're crazy!"

"You're really going to let me use your car?"

"Hell yeah, I need some gas anyway, and if you tear it up, then I'll have me a brand new 300 ZX.

"Shit girl, you ain't got to worry about a scratch."

Tracy walked Julian outside and pointed to a nice little '84 Nissan Sentra. Julian gave her his pager number and told her to call him when their cars were ready. She agreed as she smiled at him and turned to go back to work.

"Checkmate," Julian said to himself and walked over to the garage where Ty and G-Fly waited. As Julian walked in, he saw that the Dayton rims were already on their cars and they were all looking too cold. The Mustang and Iroc were sitting on chrome Daytons and his Burgundy 300ZX was sitting on gold and chrome Daytons with gold trim and gold knockoffs.

Julian said, "Now that's GP, my niggas." They all smiled in agreement.

"Did you call the cab?"

Julian said, "Better." He pulled out Tracy's car keys and said, "Let's ride."

"Who keys are them? Ty asked.

"Tracy's my nigga," and he smiled at Ty.

G-Fly said, "Ain't that a bitch! Game done created a monster!"

They all laughed and jumped in Tracy's car and left.

Julian stopped and filled up the gas tank while smoking a joint, and Ty and G-Fly each had a joint too. They were all enjoying the vibe as they visualized the pictures of their new rides looking pimped out with the captivating thoughts in their heads, and the beautiful feeling of having money in their smiles.

* * * *

Princess took all her girls to get checked out at the clinic and they were all clean and healthy. Then she went to get them all some pagers and treated them to lunch. After lunch, Dee-Dee and Little Tish took the Toyota and Dee-Dee dropped Little Tish off at her project so she can put her hustle down. Dee-Dee told her to page her if she needed her and Dee-Dee took the car and drove to her projects and sat out in front of the known weed spot and started serving like crazy.

Princess took Gwen to her block and watched her back as she sat out in front of the weed spot that the Mexicans served that stress out of, and started putting her hustle in. The indo was selling like crazy and within two hours Dee-Dee was paging Princess and putting in her re-up code.

Princess said, "Damn, Dee-Dee is sold out already."

Gwen said, "Shit girl, I only got 20 bags left myself. This shit's selling like crazy. Peep, put 50 bags away in my room drawer and bring me 50 back with you, okay?"

"Cool, but are you going to be all right out here alone?"

"Hell yeah girl, this is my block. These Mexicans is lucky that I let them even slang that bullshit over here. You feel me?"

"Yeah, I feel you sis!"

"Here's $600. Put this up for me okay?"

"I got you girl. I'll be back in an hour okay?"

"Cool, and bring me back a 7-Up okay?"

"Got you."

Princess left, and on her way back to the house, Little Tish paged her too and put her re-up code in. Princess was close to Little Tish's projects, so she swung by and picked her up.

Tish got in the car and said, "Princess, this shit is selling like crack. I need to re-up."

They drove to the new house. Tish gave Princess "$1,500, and Princess gave her another 100 sacks and grabbed 100 for Dee-Dee and 50 for Gwen and put her other 50 sacks in her bedroom drawer. They left back out and she dropped Tish back off at her projects, then went to deliver Dee-Dee her package too. Dee-Dee jumped in the car and said, "Here's $1,000. I got the other $500 at the house. This shit is selling like crack around here. The bitch that runs the weed spot over here is out, so I'm killing them over here."

"Shit girl, your sistas' is doing it big too!"

"Is that right? That's my girls."

"Here's 100 more. If you need me then just page. I'll be over on Gwen's block. Here, have a Millers."

"Thank you, sis. Let me go. I'll get at you later. Be careful girl."

"Always."

Princess went back to where Gwen was and Gwen said, "Girl, I was about to page you." She got in the car and gave Princess $400 more and said, "Girl, we're about to lock this town down with this indo. Guess what?"

"What?"

"I got Marcy right there across the street wanting to work for me. As you see, her spot's right across from the Mexican's spot and I told her that I'll pay her $200 a week to run her spot for me. She's a down older lady around 42 years old and on the County, so she ain't got no extras coming in and she don't smoke or use drugs. She just drink and don't get crazy drunk. I knew her for a while now. I even used to spend nights over her house sometimes when my auntie got her check and have her smoke fest."

"Well girl, it seem like you got it all figured out. No telling, you might be able to pump a hundred sacks a day out of there and if you get you three to four spots like that then you'll be balling. I tell you what, I sponsor you on this.

That means watch your back in case you take a loss, then I'll cover it, but your first $1,500 profit I want you to put to the side in case you take a loss with this project and only give her 50 sacks at a time until you build up your clientele, trust, and bank roll, you feel me?"

"Yeah, I got you sis."

"Come on, let's sit in her yard so I can make her spot known!"

"Cool, here's your 50 sacks. I put your other 50 in your top drawer."

"Thank you sis."

They got out of the car and sat in Marcy's yard while Gwen got her serve on.

* * * *

As Julian, Ty and G-Fly all walked through the doors of the Fox Hills Mall, it was obvious by the gleam in their eyes that they had a pocket full of money and they were coming to spend. Fila sweaters, pants, shoes and sweat-suits, Guess, Nike, Polo, Sergio - Takini, khakis, Levis, silk underwear, cologne, gold chains, bracelets, and watches.

Julian bought his mother a beautiful diamond ankle bracelet. "I had to get moms one of these after seeing how fly it looked on Lady-G and Princess."

"Yeah, I thought the same thing," G-Fly said. "We ought to make that our trademark for our girls. You know, have all our girls wear diamond ankle bracelets. We can get them $500 ones and I know that all our girls would feel that they will mean something special and floss them with a sense of pride."

Ty said, "Okay, since you're our fashion designer then we're going to embrace your desires to the fullest. I just hope that this project and investment is worth its weight in gold because we put a pretty good amount into it."

"Don't worry man. Believe in me if no one else!"

"You are the only one that I believe in," Ty told G-Fly and handed him $650. Julian gave him the same and he went back into the jewelry store and bought four diamond ankle bracelets of the same style and set. Julian said, "Let me get that Turkish bracelet and wrap it for me!"

G-Fly said, "I would like to buy my mother something nice, but it would probably just go up in smoke."

Julian said, "Man, why don't you put her in rehab to help her come out of that trance?"

"That's a good idea. I'ma check into that," Ty said.

"I'm going to just slide moms some extra paper and let her go and buy what she wants."

Julian's pager went off, and as he looked at his new Rolex watch he realized that three and a half hours had already passed. "I bet this is Tracy." He dialed the number on his new cell phone and heard a sexy familiar voice say, "Jim's Audio & Rim Shop. May I help you?"

"What's up pretty eyes?"

Tracy blushed on the other end and said, "Your cars are ready."

"Okay baby, I'll be there in 30 minutes."

"Julian, by any chance are you still at the mall?"

"Yes!"

"Can you do me a favor while you're there?"

"Sure, what's up?"

"Can you stop by the cookie shop and grab me a dozen of them chocolate chip and walnut cookies?"

"No problem baby."

"Thank you! I got you when you get back!"

"Yeah right. Promises, promises." He hung up and smiled.

"Yo my niggas, it's that time!" He walked out to where his two comrades stood talking to these two young girls. Julian smiled at the sight as he noticed how cute the two girls were. They looked around 16 or 17 years old and he could tell that the two girls were jockin' his comrades game real tough. Both of the girls were thick and high yellow and gave a pleasant smile as Ty introduced Julian as their big brother. G-Fly was talking to the girl named Kim and Ty was talking to the other girl named Robin. Julian greeted them with a smile and a nod and told his comrades that he had to run upstairs to grab some cookies before they left. Ty and G-Fly told the girls to page them that night so they could get together and go out. The girls agreed as they smiled and said their goodbyes. After grabbing the cookies, they headed to the car and when they went to put the last of their bags in the trunk, they all started laughing because the trunk was full to capacity. They were running back and forth so much during their shopping spree that they didn't realize they had so much stuff.

G-Fly jumped in the back seat of the Sentra with the majority of the bags, and Ty put the other ones between his legs in the passenger seat.

Ty said, "Man, I spent $4g's up in there."

Julian said, "You came out good because I spent a little over five."

G-Fly said, "I spent around four too. Well, one thing's for sure. We're cool on clothes for a while now. I can go a whole month without wearing the same thing twice and stay dressed to impress."

They all laughed and Ty blazed a joint as they headed back to the audio and rim shop.

As they drove up to the shop, their cars were parked out front sitting low to the ground and looking real fly on them deep dish Dayton rims and low profile tires. G-Fly and Ty pushed their way out of the car, giving each other dap as they walked over to their cars. Julian took the Turkish bracelet that he just bought and had wrapped at the jewelry store, and put it in Tracy's glove compartment before he stepped out of the car. He turned and was met by the store manager and the manager's two assistants.

Julian could tell by their eyes that they were very

proud of their work. They greeted each other and walked over to the cars. G-Fly was the first to jump into his Iroc and turn on the music. He put in that Ice Cube and when the bass from the 15" subwoofers hit, the ground vibrated and it was over.

Julian jumped into his 300 ZX and pulled his new Too Short tape from his Fila sweat jacket pocket and put it in the deck.

As soon as Tracy was walking up from the back of the 300 ZX, the music came on and said, "Say ho, do you like to fuck? Oh you don't want me to talk to you like that. Well, do you like to make love?"

The bass hit and it was all it took. Tracy looked at Julian and shook her head. "Julian, how old are you?"

"Well baby, I quit counting after I turned 15 years old because that's when I became a man."

Tracy looked at him with total respect, admiration and acceptance for she knew without a doubt that Julian was a lot wiser and sharper than average individuals she met within her age group.

Julian reached over and grabbed the bag of cookies that he bought her from the mall and gave it to her.

"Thank you. How much I owe you?"

"Nothing but a smile."

Tracy blushed and shook her head, not hiding the fact that she was really attracted to him.

The manager walked over to the passenger side of the 300 ZX and sat down and started telling Julian about all the functions of his new audio setup and Tracy went back into the shop. The manager's audio assistants were telling and explaining the same to Ty and G-Fly. After they finish explaining the details of all the functions, Julian, Ty and G-Fly all went over to the Sentra and popped the trunk and started getting their bags out.

Tracy walked back outside to her car where they were collecting their bags and stared with amazement at all of the stuff that they had bought at the mall.

Tracy said, "Man, you guys don't be playing when you say you're going shopping!"

G-Fly said, "Baby when you do something you might as well do it right."

"Amen to that my nigga," Ty said.

Julian handed Tracy back her keys, told her the gas tank was full and thanked her. After they'd finished loading their trunks with all the bags they'd bought, Julian got $20 each from Ty and G-Fly, went back into the shop, and gave a bill to each of the assistants and the manager and told them it was a tip for doing a fine job. They all thanked Julian and the manager said, "If you have any problems, just bring it on back and we'll hook you guys right on up."

"Will do."

Julian looked over at Tracy who was staring at him from a distance and made a gesture with his finger calling her over to him and mouthing the words "Come here."

Tracy was drawn like a magnet to him as she walked over.

Julian stared into Tracy's eyes and said in a romantic voice, "Hello pretty eyes, would you like to join me for dinner tonight when you get off work?"

Tracy said with no hesitation, "I would love to."

"Would 9 p.m. be all right? Page me at 8:30 and give me the directions, okay?"

Tracy smiled in agreement and Julian smiled as he turned and walked out of the shop.

Outside Ty and G-Fly were sitting in their cars fine-tuning their equalizers. When they looked up and saw Julian walking out of the shop to his 300 ZX parked right beside Ty's 5.0, Ty looked over and asked Julian with anticipation, "Are you ready to roll my nigga?"

"Let's do this," Julian said as he jumped into his car.

G-Fly said, "Where are we going first?"

"To the apartment so we can put these clothes up and handle our obligations so we can kick it tonight."

"Bet my nigga," Ty said. "We'll follow you."

They started pulling out of the parking lot, caravanning behind one another with the music bumping.

On the way to their apartment they couldn't believe all

the attention they were getting from other people. The ladies would wave, smile, blow their horns and kisses while the niggas and haters would just look at them crazy as they damn near broke their necks looking with envy as the caravan of youngsters passed by.

They arrived at their apartment and scattered all their shopping bags across the living room floor as they separated their clothes, laughing and joking about how much attention they'd gotten. Ty grabbed the cigar box that they kept full of weed and started rolling a couple of fat joints as G-Fly and Julian admired their new clothes and stuff. They were all full of excitement and acting like little kids celebrating the best Christmas of their lives.

Ty fired up a joint and passed it to G-Fly, then fired up another and gave it to Julian, then one for himself. G-Fly fixed them all a shot of Hennessey and they all kicked back and enjoyed the moment.

It was 5 p.m. already and they agreed that they needed to hurry up and get dressed so they could make the pickups and deliveries and have the rest of the night to themselves.

After they got all dressed to impress, Julian said, "Let's split up and take the buckets to handle this business. We'll meet up back here and make sure the money is right, then we can get in our new rides and go to the main house and show Game our ho catchers."

After taking care of their business and making sure all the money was accounted for, they put the money in the trunk of the Mustang and each jumped in their new rides and caravanned to the main house in Hollywood Hills to drop the money off and show off their new cars to Game.

It was 6:30 p.m. as Game was laid back in his easy chair watching the L.A. Lakers whip up on the Bulls when he heard this loud thundering sound and the foundation of his seven-bedroom baby mansion shook.

Game instantly jumped up and grabbed his chrome .357 revolver from beside him and rushed over to the window to see what was going on. When he saw the 300 ZX pull up with the convertible 5.0 and convertible Iroc right behind each other and Julian, Ty and G-Fly all jump out laughing to one another and giving each other dap, Game know that he had to open up the gates to hell when he adopted these three young demons as his soul-mates, then shook his head with a smile as he went outside to greet his little comrades in their glory.

As they gave Game the ghetto handshakes and slight embraces showing that brotherly love, Ty said, "So how do you like our new rides?"

Game walked around all three of the cars while glancing inside of each and said with a smile, "Now that's what I call GP my niggas."

They all laughed at the slang Game used to express his appreciation, realizing that he'd picked up on and used the slang that they made up as their fly saying to express something that they all liked, admired or found deeply attractive. GP stood for Ghetto Pride and this was something that was deeply rooted in all their hearts.

Ty went to the trunk of his Mustang and grabbed the duffle bag with the money from the pickup they'd just made from the dope spots and carried it into the house behind his comrades.

Once they were inside the house, Game fixed himself and his three young comrades a shot of Hennessey as they all sat around the dining room table. Ty sat the stacks of money on the table and started to give Game the rundown on what they delivered, to whom, and how much money they picked up from every spot.

Game noticed that he'd done a pretty good job of lacing his comrades and smiled with appreciation. G-Fly, Ty and Julian smiled back as if they knew what he was thinking, and G-Fly reached into his coat pocket and pulled out a diamond Italian bracelet that was full of diamonds that they all pitched in to buy for him. He handed it to Game with a smile and said, "This is from us to you!"

Game opened the jewelry box and smiled at the fine taste that his comrades displayed. "Man, this is a beautiful gift," he said and put it around his wrist, smiled, and lifted up his glass of Hennessey as he gave a toast to respect and appreciation.

Julian reached into his pocket and pulled out another jewelry box and put it on the table. "This one is for Lady-G!"

Game looked surprised as he realized his comrades loved and appreciated Lady-G as a part of them, and that they didn't possess selfish ways in their hearts and characteristics. He knew that money would never come between them.

"I'm sure that Lady-G would be very pleased to receive such a beautiful gift."

Game then looked at his comrades and said, "Listen here. Right now is where the game gets deep! You guys will make a lot of enemies in the jealous hearts of those who choose to envy you for what you have and possess within this game. Bitches will try to trap you, and use all of their scandalous tricks in hopes of receiving the financial gains that a nigga of your status and worth can bring. Therefore, you must always remember that a woman is only as good as her worth! And if she is not an asset, then she's nothing but a liability, so never accept a woman in your life if she can't contribute to your financial gain and success. For pussy is too easy to come by and if you allow it to trap you, then you will always be considered a trick in a bitch's eyes and she will never respect or appreciate you as nothing else other than that of a trick. It's cool to toss a cute bitch up here and there, but if that's all that she's worth, then remember a fuck is only a fuck and nothing more. But a bitch that's down for you is priceless, so find her true qualities in life, whether it's selling pussy, dope, or being business oriented and capitalize off it to the best of your benefits. Remember a real woman would always accept you for who you are and what you're about, so don't ever try to impress her with lies or give her a position that she's not worthy of. Either she's about you or she's not! There is no in-between or compromising to this. So keep your thoughts as law toward her desire to please you is her motivations in life. Now you guys is in a game that's very deep, and you should not ever let nothing or anyone, come between our love for one another or our devoted bound as blood brothers, not no bitches, jealousy or money! For together we are an unstoppable force that cannot ever be touched, not even by the death of one or two because spiritually we will be connected still, but if ever we should allow ourselves to be separated by petty differences, then we all will surely fall victim to the power of the curse that this game holds as a punishment for suckas', tricks, vics, and weaknesses.

Trust no one outside of this family and yourselves, and never betray one another for anything in this world. If ever your brother should call on you for your assistance in whatever, then regardless of the circumstance or situation, you make sure that you be there and be ready to die if that's what is called for. And if your brother should fall weak and violate the laws that we live by, then it's your duty to kill him, better cut off the hand that sins, than allow the whole body to fall. Now, if any one of you at this table cannot live by these standards, then let him leave this table now and take with him what he has already rightfully earned."

G-Fly, Ty and Julian looked around the table at one another and then looked at Game. Julian said, "I'm down with you to the end!"

G-Fly said, "I am too!"

Ty said, "It's us against the muthafucken' world!"

Game smiled and said, "A toast to the game, success, and the blood that we now accept, and that will forever and always bind us for life!"

They stood up and clicked their glasses together with one another's and downed the Hennessey as if it was water. Game looked at them and said, "Never mix business with pleasure, so when you're out there making your pickups and deliveries, never use your new cars because they're too flamboyant. Use the buckets instead for that's the purpose that they hold in this game. You feel me?"

The youngsters shook their heads in agreement.

* * * *

It was 8:00 p.m. and Princess was making her second

trip of the day back to the house to get all of her girls a hundred more sacks so they could re-up. All of the girls took over territory in the spots where weed was already known to be sold at, and they all established their own spots where they hired a worker to slang weed out of their apartments. Little Tish hired Mr. and Mrs. Franks, an old man and lady in her project who she was raised around and who sold dinners on the weekend for a hustle and were very real and game oriented. Tish already sold a hundred sacks from in front of their house and let everyone know that Mr. and Mrs. Franks would be on deck every day from then on. This spot was in the same complex as the Mexicans who sold the stress so the clientele was already pumping.

Princess pulled up and Tish gave her the full $2,000 and said, "That should cover me with the $1,000 I gave you earlier for the first two sacks and now I just owe you $1,000 for this one, right?"

"Yep, that's right. Listen, we're going to swoop by the clubs and parties at 10 p.m. so we can push our hustle to the max, so I'll have Dee-Dee pick you up, okay?"

"That sounds cool. I'll just leave some with Mr. Franks so he can keep this spot poppin' while I'm hitting the clubs."

"Cool, I'll holla at you later then, hear?"

Dee-Dee just hired Betty, the lady in her projects who sold the stress for the Mexicans, and offered to pay her $200 a week to just sell for her and cut them Mexicans off. Betty was only getting paid $150 a week from the Mexicans and was glad to accept Dee Dee's offer. They knew each other for years and all three of Betty's daughters loved Dee-Dee. Betty's daughters were 7, 8 and 11 years old, and Dee-Dee was someone they really looked up to, especially after they saw Dee-Dee beat up Troy, a smoker in the projects who used to try to act tough and snatch people's dope and run.

Dee-Dee dropped him with the first punch and kicked him until he lay on the ground out cold. Princess pulled up and Dee-Dee said, "What's up sis?"

"Girl, I see you doing it big around here."

"Well, you know that I'm a true hustler," Dee-Dee said as she handed Princess $2,000 and said, "now I just owe you for this sack because I gave you $1,000 earlier."

"Yep, you're on point. Listen, go get Tish at 10 o'clock and ya'll swing by some parties and clubs like last night. I'll catch up with you at the house, okay?"

"Okay, that's a good idea."

"Tish is at Mr. and Mrs. Franks' apartment. That's her new weed spot."

"Is that right?"

"Yep!"

"That's my girl."

"Let me go get this money girl. I'll see you tonight."

"Okay."

Dee-Dee got out the car with 100 more sacks and was putting her hustle down full force.

Princess was proud of her crew and knew that her men would be proud of her and her girls and the way they were putting their hustle down. Princess only had 100 sacks left after the girls sold the sacks she'd just dropped off and at the rate things were going, she'd be out tomorrow. She already had $9,000 put up that the girls already made and after they finished selling this next batch, she'd have $13,500 and a hundred more sacks of weed which she would profit another $1,500 and bring the total to $15,000 made. After giving her men their $12,000 that she owed them for the entire package, she would have $3,000 profit she made for herself, but she'd put her profit to the side just in case the girls take a loss so she'd be able to cover it. She'd promised herself that she would never come up short with their money and she meant it.

She pulled up at Gwen's new spot and Gwen said, "Girl, I got three niggas waiting to spend $100 each and I was hoping that you hurry up. Let me go get this money!"

Princess smiled as she saw the desire to hustle in her home-girl's eyes. It was about time they had a chance to come up and they owed it all to the three men who chose to give Princess a chance to be down and believe in her. There's no way that she would ever disappoint them. She smiled as she got out of the car and went to keep Gwen company.

* * * *

As the clock struck 8:10 p.m., G-Fly felt his pager vibrate. He picked up his cell phone and called the unfamiliar number back. As the person on the other end picked up, G-Fly asked, "Did someone page?"

A young soft voice on the other end said, "Yes, is this G-Fly?"

"Yes, who am I speaking to?"

"This is Kim."

G-Fly smiled and looked at Ty who was staring at him inquisitively and winked.

"Oh. What's up sweetheart? How are you doing?"

Kim said, "Fine!"

"I was anticipating your call baby. What's happening? We on tonight?"

"Of course. Ain't nothing changed. Also, Robin said what's up with your brother?"

"Oh, he's right here next to me getting his buzz on. Let me hit that my nigga?"

"Damn, ya'll doing too much! What time are ya'll coming to get us?"

"Give me the directions and we'll be there in about 30 to 40 minutes."

After Kim gave G-Fly the directions, Kim asked, "Where do ya'll want to go? If you want, my sister's girlfriend is having a birthday part at the Hyatt Hotel and it's supposed to be off the hook if ya'll want to go."

G-Fly said, "Yeah, that sounds cool. Check it out. Ty wants to speak with Robin for a minute, and we'll be there to pick you ladies up before 9."

Kim said, "I'll see you then," in a sexy voice.

G-Fly smiled and handed the phone to Ty. After Ty hung up, he smiled and said, "It's on my nigga."

G-Fly smiled back and looked over at Julian and said, "What's up my nigga? Whatcha' getting' into?"

"Most likely hooking up with Tracy and seeing what

she's about."

"She seems like she's cool people," G-Fly stated.

"Not to mention fine as hell with a nice fat ass," Ty added. Julian smiled at his comrades' brief descriptions of Tracy's most noticeable attribute. Tracy was indeed a beautiful and very well-shaped sista. With her honey tan complexion, hazel eyes, and sandy brown, long, wavy hair style, she stood around 5'5" and was thick in the hips and thighs with a nice chest on her and a small waist. Julian's pager went off and G-Fly looked at Julian and said, "Checkmate!"

Julian smiled as he dialed the number on his pager and when the voice on the other end answered, Julian said, "Hello, pretty eyes!"

"How did you know it was me?"

"Your beautiful presence entered my thoughts right before my pager went off."

Tracy said, "You're something else," with a blushful tone in her voice. "Are we still going out?"

"But of course. Where do you stay at?"

Tracy gave him the directions and Julian said, "I'll be there in about 30 minutes."

Tracy said, "Okay."

"Listen baby, I want you to do me a favor."

"What's up?"

"Go out to your car and look in the glove compartment. I left something there for you."

"Oh, no you didn't! What is it?"

"I'll see you soon baby." Julian gently hung up the phone.

Julian asked Game if he could use his VIP spot at Charlie Brown's in the Marina.

"Man that's our spot," Game said. "Yes, I'll call and make the reservations for you. What time do you want it for?"

"About 9:40 p.m. should be cool."

G-Fly looked at Ty and Julian and said, "Shit, that sounds too much like right! How about we all floss to the Marina and then we can roll to that little birthday party over at the Hyatt?"

Ty looked at Julian and said, "What's up my nigga? You want to roll with your 'rades or what?"

"Cool, let's roll."

"Ya'll enjoy yourselves. I got the girls tonight," Game said.

They all gave him some dap and Julian said, "If you need us, then just page us. If not, then we'll see you in the morning."

They smiled as Game shook his head with pride as his three young comrades left out the door.

Julian, Ty and G-Fly decided to pick up Tracy first and then swoop by and pick up Kim and Robin. As they approached Tracy's apartment, Julian picked up his phone and pressed redial and told her that he was out front. Tracy walked out looking fly with a sexy black silk mini-dress, a black suede coat, and some black suede high heel pumps with her hair whipped. Julian stepped out to open the door for her as Tracy walked up to him, put her arms around his neck and kissed him passionately. Their tongues slowly danced to a rhythm of their own. When they stopped, she looked in his eyes and said, "It's beautiful. Thank you"

"It can't even compare to the beauty that your smile possesses."

Tracy smiled and said, "Do you always find the right things to say?"

"Baby, I only believe in keeping it real."

Tracy smiled as she entered the car. Julian shut the passenger side door and went around the back of the 300 ZX and jumped behind the wheel. He beeped his horn and drove off with the Mustang leading the way, G-Fly behind in the Iroc and Julian bringing up the rear in the 300 ZX.

Julian looked at Tracy and said, "Damn, baby, you look fly!"

She blushed as she stared into his eyes. Julian gave her an admirable grin and turned up the music so that the mellow sounds of Keith Sweat began banging through the crystal clear sound system. "So what do you have planned for us tonight?" she asked.

"Well, first we're going to pick up Ty and G-Fly's dates and then we're going to get a little something to eat before we go to this little party that's supposed to be bumping over at the Hyatt by the airport. Tell me, do you have to be home at any specific time?"

Tracy shook her head and said, "No, I'm with you tonight!"

Julian blushed as he could not hold back his smile as he shook his head trying to disguise his feelings of delight.

Tracy smiled and asked him, "Can I ask you a question?"

Julian looked over at her and turned down his music because he knew that her curiosity was deep, and she had a lot of questions on her mind. "Sure beautiful, what's on your mind?"

"I would like to know more about you if you don't mind sharing your thoughts with me. I would like to know what type of man I am getting myself involved with."

Julian looked deep into her eyes and said, "Baby truthfully, I think that you are already aware of the type of man I am, for you have already had the pleasure of deciphering my character as the man that I am, and the real way that I can't help but to pride myself on being. And as for my struggle as a young black man, I guess that you can just regard me as a young street hustler who desires to have the best in life and will not settle for less."

"Tell me then, do you have a lady in your life or someone special that you go home to at night?"

Julian looked at her and said, "No baby, I have no commitments to any type of monogamous relationship for I don't believe in that kind of stuff. But I do got a commitment to the ladies who's down and devoted to me and that commitment is to always keep it real with them and be down to them!

Nevertheless, I haven't chose none of them as my main lady." He looked at Tracy and smiled as she blushed. "I guess that you can say it's hard to find that special woman who can relate to a hustler's lifestyle, and at the same time be strong enough to be down and devoted to me knowing the struggles that exist within my life. My life is very complicated, serious, and gets very hectic at times, and I can't allow myself to fall victim to the silly games that you know too many women be trying to play, or the jealousy that an insecure heart tends to possess. If a woman is about me 100% and her action reflects this, then she shouldn't question her position or my devotion to her in the midst of who I allow to be part of my life, because if another woman should come and prove herself worthy of playing a part in my life, and her devotion is true toward me in the way that I can tell, then I would accept her in my life also as long as we can progress and profit in this struggle together."

Tracy then asked Julian with an inquisitive look on her face, "so you're saying that you don't see yourself settling down with just one woman?"

"Julian looked at her with a serious look on his face and said, "No baby, marriage does not exist within my heart and mind in that way. But if I should ever find that special young lady who can relate to the man that I am, and the lifestyle that I live, and she proves herself worthy of being my main lady and being down with me to the fullest, knowing and understanding what it takes to love a man like me and stand by my side regardless of the circumstances that seem to exist within my life, then I'll truly give her my heart and the blessings that come with it. But as I said before, my life is very complicated and my beliefs are different, therefore, it would take a very rare and unique kind of woman to be able to deal with the type of struggle and expectations that exist within my life."

He looked at Tracy again as they pulled up and parked in front of an apartment complex in Inglewood and asked, "Tell me Pretty Eyes, do you know of any woman who may possess these profound qualities that I look for in a companion?"

Tracy blushed as she stared into his eyes with admiration and desire.

Julian's thoughts were distracted by G-Fly and Ty as they exited their cars and walked over to the 300 ZX. Julian rolled down his window as they walked up. "What's up my nigga?"

They smiled at one another and G-Fly looked in the car and said, "What's up Tracy? How are you doing?"

"Fine."

Ty bent down and waved as Tracy smiled and waved back. Kim and Robin walked out of the apartment building and were both dressed to impress with sexy mini-skirt outfits on and high heeled pumps, looking grown and sophisticated. Ty tapped G-Fly on the back to get his attention and when G-Fly looked up toward Kim and Robin and said, "Daaamn!" he looked back at Ty and Ty said, "I know! My thoughts exactly!" They both smiled.

G-Fly bent back down and said, "Our reservations at 9:40 p.m. so we got like 25 minutes to get there."

Julian said, "I'm following you my nigga."

G-Fly and Ty turned to meet their dates. As Kim and Robin saw the convertible 5.0 Mustang, convertible Iroc and the 300 ZX all parked out front squatted sitting on Daytons with their parking lights on, Kim and Robin paused for a moment and looked at one another with a shocked expression on their faces and then smiled. They had no idea that the two guys they met earlier at the mall were having it on this level.

G-Fly said, "What's up, ladies? How ya'll doing tonight?"

"Fine! Is that you guys' cars?"

Ty smiled and said, "Yeah, the 5.0 is mine, the Iroc is G-Fly's and the 300 ZX is Julian's, our brother that you met earlier at the mall."

Robin looked up at him and said, "They look real fly!"

Ty smiled as they all got into their cars and drove off on their way to Charlie Brown in the Marina.

Once on the freeway, Julian looked over at Tracy and said, "So tell me Pretty Eyes, what do you want out of a man and what do you want out of life?"

Tracy said, "Well, first of all, my man must be honest, strong-minded, motivated, real and must possess a good heart. I want a man who will be down for me like I will be down for him."

Julian cut her off and said, "How down would you be for him?"

Tracy said, "It's no limit as long as I know in my heart that he's real with me!"

Julian looked into her eyes and nodded that he understood what she was saying. "So what do you want out of life?"

"Really…to be able to own my own businesses and become a successful black woman in this capitalistic society that we live in."

"So tell me what steps are you taking to properly prepare yourself for the goals that you possess?"

"Well, right now I'm saving up to go to cosmetology school so I can learn how to do hair and then I want to open up my own business. I've already graduated from Wilshire School of Business, and I've learned everything from operating a computer to accounting and business management. So now I'm just trying to stack my money so it won't hurt me financially when I begin taking this cosmetology course. I don't want to be struggling too hard to maintain my rent and bills."

"Who do you live with?" Julian asked.

"I live alone," she replied, then looked down at the lights on the cassette and added, "unfortunately my mother died in a car accident when I was 14. A police car ran a red light chasing after someone and they didn't have their sirens on. My father sued the police department and settled for $250,000, took me over to my aunt's house, gave her $50,000 and I never saw him again. My aunt raised me till I was 18 and then she died of breast cancer. She left me $20,000 and I've been on my own since then. I'm 21 now, so I've been just trying to survive and do the best I can in life and making my dreams come true."

Julian looked at her with newfound respect for it was obvious that this young woman had been through a lot of pain and hardship yet it had obviously only made her a stronger person.

They pulled up at the restaurant in the Marina and Julian gently reached over and grabbed her hand, kissed it, and said, "Baby, my condolences and truthfully, I know that your mother and auntie are looking down from heaven together and smiling at the beautiful, strong, intelligent woman that you have become."

Tracy smiled and said, "Do you think so?"

"I know so baby girl."

They smiled at each other as Tracy leaned over and gently kissed him on the lips and said, "Thank you! Come on baby, let's go get something to eat."

They all exited their cars and hit their alarms. Tracy looked around the parking lot at all the fancy cars and said, "This place must be nice."

G-Fly and Ty were waiting for Julian and Tracy to catch up to them. G-Fly looked at Julian and his watch and said, "Right on time my nigga!"

"Like always," Julian replied. He looked at Kim and Robin and said, "Hello miss ladies."

They smiled and returned the greeting.

Julian said, "This is my beautiful friend and companion, Tracy. Tracy, this is Kim and Robin."

Chapter 13
Ghetto For Life

As they entered the restaurant, the ladies were intrigued by the expensive and elaborate setting. Tracy looked at Julian and said, "Baby, this is a very nice place."

G-Fly, Ty and Julian looked around and saw a lot of ballers they'd always seen in traffic but never really knew, they was there having dinner that night too. They'd been there on a couple of occasions before with Game but never when the restaurant was this packed.

A cute, thick, blonde-haired waitress approached them as they waited in line behind two couples.

"Gentlemen, how are you tonight? I've been expecting you guys. My name is Jane and I'm your host for tonight. I have your table waiting in the VIP area, so if you will follow me please, I'll show you to your table."

Kim and Robin glanced at one another out of the corners of their eyes, exchanging a shocked look of disbelief. Tracy looked at Julian with a confused smile. He smiled back and took her by the hand, then led her behind the waitress. G-Fly and Ty walked behind Julian and Tracy with their arms intertwined with their dates' arms. They all noticed that damn near the whole restaurant was staring at them with a surprised look, some whispering to the person next to them while others gestured toward the youngsters as they entered the VIP area where a $500 bottle of Dom Perignon Champagne sat chilling in a gold ice bucket. Wine glasses sat on a matching gold tray beside the bucket. Candles flickered all around the tinted glass booth.

As they sat down, the waitress grabbed the bottle of champagne and displayed the label to the group. "Compliments of your big brother."

Julian, Ty, and G-Fly all smiled nonchalantly at each other as the waitress poured the champagne and handed them menus. She looked at Julian and said, "Would you desire anything else at this moment?"

Julian looked around and said, "Not right now, thank

you."

"Okay, I'll be back to take your orders shortly."

Julian gave her an appreciative smile as she walked away.

Kim looked at G-Fly and said, "You guys must come here often."

"No, as a matter of fact sweetheart, this is only our second time."

Kim, Robin and Tracy all looked at one another, laughed quietly and shook their heads.

G-Fly looked around the table and made eye contact with each of the ladies. "Listen ladies, we came here to enjoy ourselves and to enjoy your beautiful smiles and company as well. Therefore, please don't allow the prices on the menu to discourage your appetites. If we couldn't afford it, we wouldn't be here, so please enjoy yourselves tonight with us.

Ty smiled and held up his glass of champagne. "I'll toast to that!"

Everyone complied by holding up their glasses as Ty said, "Let the party begin!"

Everyone laughed at his humor as they clicked their glasses together and started talking with each other.

After they ate like kings and queens, G-Fly looked at his watch and noticed it was 11:05 p.m. He looked around the table at his comrades and the ladies and said, "It's about that time.

Are ya'll ready to roll?" Everyone nodded. G-Fly signaled the waitress for the bill.

Tracy turned to Julian and said, "Thank you!"

"No, thank you," Julian said.

Tracy looked at him in confusion. "For what?"

"For introducing me to a very beautiful young lady."

Tracy blushed as Julian added, "I'm curious."

"Curious about what?"

"Everything!"

Tracy blushed with delight as she slowly shook her head.

G-Fly noticed a tall black man walking over to them

and stood up. The man gave a friendly smile as he approached, then reached out his hand. Ty and Julian also stood up to meet him and also to provide themselves with a better position in the event that he was bringing trouble. He smiled respectfully and said, “Hello, gentlemen. How are you guys doing today?”

Julian said, “Fine sir, and yourself?”

The man said, “Blessed, young bro. Blessed. Allow me to introduce myself. My name is Robert and I am a very good associate of Game, and also the owner of this place. Game has told me much about you all, and it’s truly a pleasure to make your acquaintances.”

G-Fly introduced himself and his comrades.

“I hope that the food and service was up to your expectations.”

Julian said, “Yes, it was delicious and the service was very hospitable.”

“Good, good, I’m glad to hear that. Anyway, gentlemen, I just came over to meet you all and tell you that this restaurant is open to your presence at anytime. I’ve informed my employees that your money is not accepted here for all your meals will always be on the house.”

G-Fly, Ty and Julian each expressed their appreciation and shook Robert’s hand. He smiled and gave a slight wave to everyone as he made his departure. Tracy, Kim and Robin excused themselves to go to the ladies room, freshen up and digest all the game that had just been exposed to them.

G-Fly looked at his comrades after the ladies walked away and said, “My niggas, I don’t know about ya’ll, but Game wasn’t lying when he said this shit was about to get deep.”

Julian said, “I know my nigga, but that’s what game is about. It’s real, and the deeper you get in the game, the realer the game gets.”

“That’s real,” Ty said. He pulled a hundred dollar bill out of a roll of money and put it on the table for the tip.

“Shit, it almost seems like yesterday we were starving looking for a lick to get a couple of dollars for something to eat and drink. Now we just got through drinking a $500 bottle of champagne and eating a thousand dollar meal for free, we're driving brand new cars fixed up to perfection, dressed in the best clothes that money can buy, with a pocket full of money, and bad bitches all on our jocks."

And my nigga just threw a hundred dollar bill on the table like it wasn't nothing," G-Fly said. "Yeah, my nigga, this shit is deep. Rags to riches my nigga!"

They all laughed. The girls walked back over to the table and they all exited the restaurant together.

Once they made it back on the freeway heading toward the party at the Hyatt, Tracy looked at Julian and said, "You know what Julian?"

Julian glanced at her and said, "What's up pretty eyes?"

Tracy said, "I can't lie or pretend with you in anyway,

I've never met a man like you before in my life. I'm confused as to what's required of me to become a part of your life."

Julian looked at her with confidence and said, "Baby, just be yourself and keep it real with me and if there is a position in my life that exists for you as the down and real woman you are, then it will surely be known in every way for your actions will always reflect your true feelings, qualifications, loyalty, devotion, and realness in everything to me, but only you can come to understand what's required out of you to fulfill your obligations to the man that you choose to be with within your life. If it's what I desire from a real lady then you would know! But also, know that I do have other down and devoted ladies in my life that will always be there, so never question their position in my life and always know, learn, and respect yours, for I don't allow jealous women in my life. Do you feel where I'm coming from?"

"Yes." Tracy was a bit spell bound as the soft sounds of Loose Ends caressed her thoughts and they pulled up and parked at the Hyatt.

"Come on baby, let's go get our party on!"

"Julian, can I ask you a question?"

"Yeah, what's up?"

"Can you dance?"

"No, but I know how to party!"

They laughed and exited the 300 ZX. G-Fly was standing next to his Iroc with his sounds still playing at a low tone, bumping the Isley Brothers' "Between the Sheets." Kim, Ty and Robin stood beside him. As Julian and Tracy walked up, G-Fly said, "I don't know about ya'll, but I'm trying to get buzzed before I go up in here."

Ty said, "I know that you got some kind of psychic powers now, because you're straight reading my mind!"

Everyone started busting up. Julian said, "I'll smoke to that!"

G-Fly passed Ty and Julian both a joint as they all lit up and smoked with their dates.

Kim said, "Damn, that's the bom" and she took a big hit like a professional.

Tracy took the joint from Julian and hit it, but it was obvious that she was new to it, as she blew the smoke right out.

Julian laughed and said, "Baby, you got to hit it hard and hold it in as long as you can."

Tracy tried it again, and took a big hit this time as she held it in, and five seconds later started choking and coughing as smoke came up out of her nose, mouth, and G-Fly swore that he saw some come out of her ears. Once Tracy regained her composure, everyone was cracking up and Ty said, "I know that she felt that!"

Julian grabbed Tracy in his arms and said, "Baby, are you all right?"

Tracy smiled as she looked up at him and said, "That shit's the bom!"

Everyone laughed again as Robin hit the joint and started coughing and choking. G-Fly, Ty and Julian finished off the joints as G-Fly hit his alarm and they began walking toward the hotel. Once inside, the clerk told Kim how to get to the lobby where the birthday party was being held.

As they entered the party, Kim saw her older sister

Gloria and called her over to introduce her new friends. Gloria greeted them all and led them to a table she'd reserved for them. As they sat down, G-Fly looked at Gloria and said, "Baby, I need something to drink!"

"Are you old enough to drink?" Gloria asked with a smile.

G-Fly smiled back as Kim said, "Of course, he's old enough to drink. He's with me, ain't he?"

Gloria smiled and said, "Kim, I'm just playing with him!"

Gloria turned and gestured to the waitress to come over. Ty and Julian looked at G-Fly and they all shook their heads as if they were reading each other's thoughts. The waitress walked up and said, "Hello sir, can I take your order?"

G-Fly looked at Ty and Julian and said, "I got a taste for some Hennessey, my niggas."

Julian said, "That will work."

G-Fly looked at the ladies and said, "What do you ladies want to drink tonight?"

Kim and Robin said, "We'll drink some Hen with ya'll tonight."

Tracy said, "I don't want nothing hard."

"We'll have two fifths of Hennessey and a bottle of Dom Perignon Champaign. Also, who's the birthday girl?" G-Fly ask.

Gloria said, "That's my girlfriend over there" and pointed two tables away.

G-Fly said, "And send the birthday girl a bottle of Don with our compliments."

The waitress looked at Gloria with surprise. G-Fly said, "Is there a problem miss?"

"No sir," the waitress said, and turned and left to fill the order.

Gloria looked at the three youngsters with a new understanding and gave G-Fly a surprised smile. "Mmmm, I'm scared of ya'll." She then looked at Ty and Julian and noticed that they had on about a thousand dollars worth of clothes and around $15,000 worth of jewelry.

The waitress came back with two more waitresses behind her to help her carry all of the drinks that G-Fly had ordered. They started setting down bottles and glasses all around them as almost everyone at the party looked on at the three waitresses catering to the youngsters as if they were royalty. The first waitress handed G-Fly the bill that came up to $350. He reached into his pocket and pulled out a big stack of money and pulled off four crispy hundred dollar bills, gave them to the waitress and said, "Can we also get a couple of Cokes, a couple of 7-Ups and a couple of cranberry juices to go along with this order?"

"Of course, sir," the waitress said.

"Keep the change."

The waitress' eyes lit up with appreciation as she said,

"Thank you, sir," and she filled everyone's glasses with precision.

Gloria smiled at her little sister as their eyes met and she said, "Well, it was nice to meet ya'll."

"Wait, give her a glass of that champagne!"

The waitress complied. "Thank you guys," Gloria said, "I hope ya'll have a good time."

Everyone smiled as she waved and left and the waitress left to go fill the rest of the order.

Robin looked at G-Fly, Julian and Ty and asked, "How are ya'll going to drive us home after drinking all this?"

Ty looked at her and said, "Easy! In the morning!"

G-Fly, Ty and Julian started rolling.

Robin said, "The party will probably end at 2:30 a.m.!"

"Well, we better enjoy it before it ends." Everyone started laughing but Robin.

Robin said, "Ya'll crazy! I'm serious. Ya'll ain't going to be able to drive after this."

"Shit, we know! That's why we ain't leaving until the morning!"

Kim and Tracy caught on and looked at G-Fly and Julian, shaking their heads and laughing at their comrades' game.

Robin said, "I don't get it."

Ty said, "Oh, you would!"

And everyone started busting up again except Robin.

Tracy said, "Girl, they're trying to tell you that they plan on staying at this hotel tonight."

"Oh, I see!" Robin said, then looked at Ty and said, "Damn, that's all you had to say. You know that weed got me trippin'! And oh, I'ma get it, huh?" She playfully punched him in the arm, and everyone laughed again.

The waitress walked up smiling and set the glasses of soda and juices on the table. She looked at G-Fly and said, "Would you like anything else at this time?"

"No thank you. We're cool for now."

"Well, let me go and fill that other order for you right now, but if you need anything then just wave my way and I'll be right over, okay?"

"Thank you," G-Fly said as the waitress went to tend to the birthday girl.

Kim looked at G-Fly and said, "I think she likes you."

"Oh yeah? What about you?"

Kim smiled and leaned over and gave G-Fly a quick, deep passionate kiss. "What do you think?"

G-Fly smiled at the thought knowing that Kim was jockin' his game. He looked deep into her eyes and saw nothing but dollar signs and reflected back to the conversation that Game had kicked to them earlier that day when he said, "Bitches will try to trap you and use all of their scandalous character traits in hopes of receiving the fundamental gains that a nigga of your status and worth can bring, so always remember that a woman is only as good as her worth. Remember, a fuck is only a fuck and nothing more."

Ty saw G-Fly in a daze and he broke G-Fly's trance by nudging him and asking him, 'What's on your mind, G?"

G-Fly looked up at Ty and started laughing. "Oh, I'm cool, my nigga. I was just reflecting on the previous game that Game had kicked to us at the house." He then looked casually over at Kim with a nonchalant smile as Ty and Julian caught onto G-Fly's thoughts. They all smiled at each other.

Tracy looked at Julian and said, "What's so funny

baby?"

Julian smiled at her and said, "Nothing pretty eyes. I'm just enjoying the vibes of this lovely scene that I'm caught up in."

Tracy just smiled but knew that Julian didn't reveal the truth about what he was laughing at, but knew that it wasn't something for her to know about so she abandoned her curiosity and leaned over to kiss him on the ear, whispering, "I enjoy being with you a lot."

Julian just smiled and took a sip of his Hennessey as her emotions deeply embraced his smooth character.

The birthday girl and Gloria walked over to the youngsters' table. Gloria introduced her as Jackie. Jackie was a short, thick-hipped sista with a nice fat butt, dark brown complexion, light brown eyes, and wore her hair in a fly bobbed hairstyle that complimented her beautiful features. Jackie just turned 23 years old. Gloria was already 23. They both had champagne glasses half-filled in their hands as they walked up. Ty noticed Jackie as she walked up beside him with that big butt of hers right in his face. He looked to his side and said, "Daaaaamn," then looked up at Jackie with a surprising lustful look in his eyes. Julian and G-Fly started busting up as Jackie looked down at Ty with a delightful smile. Robin looked over at Ty and gave him the evil eye, then looked up at Jackie and scandalously rolled her eyes and looked at Kim for support.

Jackie looked over the table at the youngsters with a flirtatious smile and said, "I just wanted to come over and thank you guys for the bottle of champagne that you sent to me for my birthday. I really appreciate it. Are you guys having a good time?" She looked down at Ty.

Ty said, "Yeah baby, it's a nice party you got going on here."

Robin looked up at Jackie and said, "Where's your boyfriend John at?"

Everyone at the table gave a small sound and verbal gesture of disappointment and disbelief for they clearly knew that Robin's statement was based purely on jealousy and insecurity.

Jackie smiled at Robin in a devilish way and said, "Oh girl, he's probably out there flirting with some bitches."

Then Jackie looked down at Ty and said, "Can I get a dance for my birthday?"

Everyone at the table looked at Ty as he stood up and looked Jackie deep in her eyes and said, "Listen baby, you're a very attractive young lady. I'm not sure of the kind of man that you're used to dealing with, but I'm not that type. You obviously got me confused with someone else for I don't play childish games and I'm not the type of man who's fond of a woman who possesses insecurity." He briefly looked back down at Robin who was looking and listening attentively. She slowly dropped her head in embarrassment. He looked back at Jackie who stared back at him in admiration and confusion for no man had ever checked her in this way. Ty continued, "Therefore, it may be best that you play these silly games with someone else."

At that time, John walked up and hugged her around her small waist and said, "What's up, baby girl?"

Jackie said, "Oh, nothing. I was just thanking Kim's friends for the champagne they sent to me for my birthday."

John smiled at Jackie as he looked around at everyone with no idea of the thing that just went down. "How's everyone doing tonight?"

Everyone greeted him as Ty looked at John, then at Jackie.

Jackie looked nervous and a lost for words. Ty looked back at John and said, "What's up man? My name is Ty." He smiled as they shook hands. "This is a nice party that you put down," Ty said.

John smiled and looked at Jackie, "Yeah, I had to throw something special for my lady."

Jackie smiled up at John. Ty looked at Jackie and she looked back at him curiously. "Jackie, where did you say the restroom was?"

She glanced at him with relief and said, "Oh, yeah, it's over there on the right side of the bar." She pointed toward the far end.

"Thank you," Ty said. He looked over at John and said,

"It was a pleasure."

John smiled and nodded. Ty looked back at his comrades with a smirk, then at Robin with a hard stare, and turned and walked toward the restroom.

G-Fly glanced at Julian and said, "Excuse me, you guys." He got up and followed Ty to the restroom. Ty walked into the restroom to the big mirror on the wall and smiled at himself.

The restroom door opened and G-Fly walked in with a big old grin on his face, looked in the mirror at Ty and said, "I must admit, I thought Julian was one of the coldest mac I knew until I saw your performance tonight."

"Ty turned to him with a modest grin and said, "Did I put it down like it was supposed to be put down?"

"Better." G-Fly gave his comrade some dap.

"Did you see the look on Jackie and Robin's face when I was spitting these P's at them?"

"Hell yeah. Truthfully I think Jackie got the hots for you my nigga, and Robin don't know if you're kicking her to the curb or what! What are you going to do?"

"It's only one thing to do, and that's keep it real!"

They both smiled and gave each other dap as the door opened and an older black man in his mid-thirties walked into the restroom. He nodded to G-Fly and Ty in a 'what's up' manner, walked over to the stall and started pissing.

G-Fly said, "Shit, I better release some of this alcohol out of my bladder, so I can enjoy filling it back up."

"Good idea!"

After washing their hands, Ty asked G-Fly, "My nigga are you heated?"

"Fo sho," G-Fly said, "and what about you?"

"You know I never leave home without it!"

"You ready my nigga?

"Let's roll." They exited the restroom.

Back at the table after G-Fly and Ty had left, Julian broke the ice and said, "So Jackie, how old is a young lady today?"

Jackie smiled and said, "23!"

"That's right." Then Julian glanced over at the man

who was walking up beside Gloria and recognized him from the liquor store the night that he and his comrades met Game. Game stepped to dude about some money that he owed Game before Game started pistol-whipping the mess out of him and they stomped him out. As the dude approached the table, Julian casually slid his hand up under his Fila sweater and touched the butt of his 3.80 that was hidden on his side, continuing to observe the man's actions as he approached.

The dude walked up to Gloria and hugged her around the waist. Gloria smiled up at him and greeted him with a big kiss.

The dude greeted John with dap and handed Jackie a gift-wrapped box. Jackie smiled and said, "Thank you, Mike."

He smiled back and said, "You know that I wouldn't forget your birthday girl." He then looked down at Kim and Robin, who smiled at him with familiarity. "What's up Big Mike?"

Mike then glanced at Tracy and Julian as Gloria said, "Baby, these are a couple of Kim and Robin's friends. That's Tracy and her man, Julian."

Tracy smiled at the introducing, loving the way Gloria expressed it, then glanced at Julian and caught an eerie vibe as Julian stared at Big Mike in a nonchalant manner.

Big Mike looked at Julian, stunned as he recognized him from the incident with Game a while back. He casually regained his composure and said, "What's up Julian?" He glanced at the table and noticed the bottles of Hennessey and Dom Perignon and knew that Julian had to be hooked up with Game.

Gloria noticed Big Mike's reaction and knew something was up.

"Do I know you?" Big Mike asked.

"Yeah, we kicked it before," Julian said bluntly.

"How's Game doing?"

Julian stood up from the table and said, "Nigga, do you really want to know?"

Big Mike changed his posture to stand more

defensively. It was obvious that Big Mike desired revenge and didn't care with whom for Big Mike hated everything that was affiliated with Game.

John and Gloria jumped in between them both as Julian pushed Tracy further away from him. Tracy complied with Julian's movement as Big Mike said, "Nigga, you got me fucked up!"

G-Fly and Ty were moving toward them swiftly as they saw the commotion, and when Big Mike made the statement, G-Fly and Ty were just a couple of steps away.

G-Fly stepped to him quickly and said, "Is that right?"

Big Mike turned to see who made the statement and when he saw G-Fly it was too late. G-Fly had his big black 45 automatic already in motion as G-Fly slapped the shit out of Big Mike across the mouth with the barrel of the gun. Big Mike fell to the ground and started spitting out his teeth with blood.

John said, "Hold up, man," as he saw his friend get slapped with the pistol and before John could get another word out, Ty socked him in the jaw, sending John to the floor next to his friend as G-Fly and Ty started stomping and kicking the shit out of Big Mike. Julian held the 3.80 to his side as he watched his comrades put in work. Jackie and Gloria reached for Julian, begging him to break it up. Tracy socked Gloria in the eye and said, "Bitch, get off my man," and Gloria hit the ground holding her eye.

Two buff security guards ran up and Julian raised the 3.80 at them as G-Fly spontaneously raised his 45 at them as well.

Julian said, "What's up niggas? Ya'll looking for problems?"

G-Fly said, "Nigga, take one more step and I'll knock the air up out of both you big muthafuckas!"

Ty reached down and took a snub-nosed 38 off Big Mike, kicked John in the face and said, "Fuck both you sorry muthafuckas."

Then he looked at Jackie and said, "I see the type of sorry niggas you fuck with." She stared at Ty in disbelief as Ty said, "Let's roll my niggas."

Julian looked down at Big Mike's bloody face and said, "You better watch who you disrespect, punk!"

G-Fly looked down at Big Mike and said, "Ah, my nigga, that's the same muthafucka we served at the liquor store that night!"

Ty looked down and said, "It sure in the fuck is!"

Julian glanced at Tracy standing by his side and said, "You ready to roll pretty eyes?"

"Yeah."

Julian took her by the hand and started walking toward the door. Ty grabbed the unopened fifth of Hennessey from the table, turned toward Jackie and said, "Nice party" as he walked out behind Julian and Tracy. G-Fly followed behind them with the 45 automatic held to his side.

The security guards helped Big Mike and John up from the ground. Big Mike yelled, "It ain't over nigga!"

G-Fly turned and lifted the 45 automatic, catching aim as everybody around Big Mike ducked for cover leaving him standing alone and staring into the eyes of G-Fly behind the barrel of death.

Ty touched G-Fly on the shoulder and said, "No my nigga. There's too many witnesses and that fool ain't worth it."

G-Fly slowly lowered his gun and they both turned and walked to the door where Julian waited with his 3.80 by his side, watching their backs. They all put their guns away and casually left the party and exited down the hall, through the lobby and to their cars without anyone outside the party looking in their direction or causing any suspicion.

"Follow me," Julian said as they jumped in their cars. They pulled up at Tracy's spot twenty minutes later.

Chapter 14
Choose, Loose, or Stay Confused

As they all entered Tracy's apartment, Julian told Ty to call Game and tell him what just went down. Ty went into the bathroom and made the call.

G-Fly held up the bottle of Hennessey and said, "We might as well finish this!"

Julian and Tracy laughed. Tracy said, "I'll go get the glasses. I think I could use a drink too."

G-Fly and Julian laughed as she went into the kitchen.

"Damn my nigga," G-Fly said, "where did that fool come from?"

"I'm pretty sure that he's Gloria's man because he walked up and kissed her and shook John's hand like they was homies or something. He gave Jackie a birthday present, then noticed me sitting there and recognized me from that incident. Then he started plexing like he had animosity, so I stepped to him to see what he had on his mind. When he started rearing up, that's when you guys walked up and kicked it off."

"Damn my nigga, I didn't know who that was or what was going on."

Tracy walked back in with the glasses as G-Fly said, "I just heard him say 'you got me fucked up' and the way that you was squared off with him I knew that it was going down, so I just kicked it off."

"Yeah, you kicked it off all right," Tracy said.

"What about you, Ms. Thing?" Julian said. "You sure put a cold hook on Gloria and laid her on the floor!"

Tracy blushed. "I'ma ride with my man regardless of the situation."

Julian smiled at her and said, "Your man, huh?"

Tracy looked at him and smiled as Julian walked over to her and put his arms around her waist. "Are you sure you can deal with that position?"

"I know that I can, or I'll die trying."

Julian gave her a long passionate kiss and when he

pulled back he smiled and said, “I hope so.” He pulled out his 3.80 and gave it to her. “Here. Do you know how to work that?”

“Yeah. My scandalous ass stepfather’s white ass was from the country and taught me and my mother how to shoot when I was younger.” Tracy checked to make sure the safety was on, pushed the button on the side to release the clip and ejected the bullet out of the chamber. “This is a 3.80 with an 8-shot clip and one in the chamber.”

G-Fly said, “Damn, not the Bonnie and Clyde thing!”

They all laughed as Ty opened the downstairs bathroom door and called for Julian to come to the phone. Ty handed him the phone as he walked out. “Game wants to talk to you.”

“What’s up rade?”

“What’s up young playa! I heard that you guys had a little run-in with Big Mike tonight.”

“Yeah man, that fool tried to disrespect you so we smashed his punk ass.”

Game laughed and said, “Is that right? Well, check it out. Are ya’ll coming by tonight?”

Julian said, “Well, we’ve been drinking a lot tonight, so I was thinking of laying low over here at Tracy’s until the morning.”

“Okay, cool, that’s a good idea, but after ya’ll get up I want to see ya’ll, so be here around 10 so we can talk and you guys can fill me in on the rest. Okay?”

“You got it.”

“What’s up with Tracy? Is she cool?”

“Yeah, from what I can tell, she’s a real down sista and she kind of proved herself tonight when she socked Big Mike’s girl in the eye for trying to get involved.”

Game laughed and said, “Is that right? Well, you make sure you let her know that nigga Big Mike ain’t to be trusted at all.

Can you feel me?”

“Yeah, I feel you ‘rade! I’ll kick it more with you tomorrow.”

“Okay, I’ll see you in the morning.”

They hung up and Julian walked out of the restroom and into the living room where his comrades and Tracy were. G-Fly and Ty were on the big couch talking and smoking a joint. Tracy sat on the loveseat listening to Freddy Jackson through her little boom box stereo. Julian sat next to her and she said, "I fixed you a drink."

"Thank you baby girl." Julian leaned over to her and whispered in her ear. "Listen baby, do you mind if me and my comrades kick it here tonight?"

Tracy gave Julian a seductive smile. "Did you think I'm going to let you leave tonight?"

"I hope that you don't think I'ma sleep on the couch then."

"Why would you do that, when you got a big bed upstairs?"

"Oh, so that's my bed?"

"Of course! Right next to me, that is, if you will accept me in your life?"

Julian looked into her eyes and said, "How can I ever resist someone as precious as you by my side?"

Tracy smiled with delight as she kissed him and said,

"Well, this will always be your home with me, as long as you desire." She then grabbed his hand and placed a key to the apartment in it. He looked down at the key as she said, "It's also the key to my heart, so please don't ever lose it!"

He smiled and gently kissed her lips, then turned and noticed his comrades staring at him. "Oh, that's so cute!" They said, and started busting up laughing.

Julian said, "Baby, would you grab some blankets for my rade's?"

"Sure baby."

Tracy got up and went upstairs.

"Let me hit that my nigga."

Ty passed Julian the joint. "Check this out. Game wants us to be at the main house at 10:00 in the morning so we can have a meeting. Ya'll can just kick back here and we can roll in the morning at 8, go do the deliveries before we head out there."

"Listen man, it's only 1:20, so me and Ty is going to roll over to the new house and have a little fun with Princess freaky ass. You obviously got your work cut out for you here!"

Tracy came back downstairs and said, "Here ya'll, if you get hungry help yourselves okay!"

"Good looking out, pretty eyes."

She looked at G-Fly and said, "Only my man can call me that!" Then she smiled and said, "Baby, I'ma go take a shower okay?"

"All right baby." She kissed him and turned to go upstairs.

"Aren't you forgetting something?" Julian asked and glanced over at the 3.80 lying on the table.

"Oh, I'm sorry baby." She walked over and picked it up. "Baby, I don't ever want to hear you use that word again in reference to yourself, because I don't affiliate myself with sorry people. Being a reflection of me, you can never be considered sorry in any way, you feel me?"

"Yes baby."

"Also from now on, it's mandatory that you keep that everywhere you go so you can always have your man's back, okay?"

"Okay baby."

"I'll be upstairs to join you in a minute."

She smiled and said, "Okay baby. Good night ya'll."

"Good night," Ty said.

G-Fly said, "I'll see you later sis!"

Tracy smiled as she went upstairs.

They all stood up and G-Fly said, "Peep, we'll meet you at the apartment at 8:00."

"Okay."

"Cool, ya'll drive carefully," Julian said, and gave them both a ghetto embrace.

Ty handed him the snub-nosed 38 he took off Big Mike and said, "Here's a house warming gift." They all laughed.

Julian finished the joint and downed his drink and made his way upstairs. As Julian walked into the bedroom he noticed how clean Tracy was. Then he heard the bathroom shower running. He quickly got undressed and walked into the bathroom. He noticed Tracy's sexy hour glass figure through the shower curtain, walked over and pulled the curtain back and said, "Daaaamn!"

She looked up and smiled as he stood there in the nude gazing lustfully at Tracy's sexy body.

"What took you so long?" she asked. She grabbed his hand and pulled him into the shower with her.

He stepped in and they embraced one another passionately. Their lips and tongues intertwined with a irresistible burning sensation.

It was 1:30 a.m. and Princess and the girls were all lounging in the family room, laughing, talking and enjoying each other's company. They'd each had a nice hot shower and were kicking back in the long t-shirts that they were used to sleeping in. They'd all sold the majority of their last sacks and paid Princess a thousand off the sack and owed her $500 more. All their weed spots were estimated to sell over a hundred sacks a day easy, so it was on and popping and the girls were just celebrating their new life and hustle together with a fat joint and some gin and juice.

The music was playing at a nice mellow level, and they talked excitedly about all the nice things they couldn't wait to buy. As Princess was telling her girls how proud she was of them, she looked up and saw G-Fly and Ty walking into the family room. G-Fly said, "So what do we have here?"

He looked at Ty and smiled as Princess ran over to them and kissed them both on the cheek with a hug and said, "Baby, I want to introduce ya'll to your girls! You probably already met them before, but it's only right that I properly introduce you guys.

That's my girl Little Tish."

Little Tish walked over and gave them both a hug and a kiss.

"That's Gwen, and that's Dee-Dee."

Gwen and Dee-Dee both smiled and walked over and gave Ty and G-Fly a hug and kiss.

"These are your devoted companions and loyal ride or die bitches! I took the time to lace them in your expectations and desires, and they have vowed to be all that and more."

G-Fly walked up to Dee-Dee and said, "Is that right?"

She nodded and said, "Yes, we all desire to be down and loyal to all of ya'll and strive to satisfy ya'll in every way."

G-Fly looked at Princess and said, "Come here sexy."

She blushed and walked over to him and put her arms around his neck. G-Fly said, "I'm proud of you baby." He kissed her passionately and said, "How about fixing me and Ty a shot of Hennessey so we can celebrate this lovely moment?"

"Okay baby." She walked into the kitchen to hook up their drinks.

Ty walked over to Dee-Dee and said, "Hello, beautiful! Something told me a while back that you would one day be part of my life."

She blushed as he pulled her to him and kissed her passionately.

G-Fly said, "Little Tish, how about rolling us a fat one?"

She said, "We already rolled up some." She went to get one off the table and lit it for him.

Princess came back and handed them drinks and said, "Baby, we got to re-up!"

G-Fly said, "You're bullshitting!"

"Nope, your girls is truly born hustlers."

Ty said, "Ya'll sold all that already?"

"Yep, they went right to work and sold all but a hundred, and that won't last us through the afternoon. They all cornered the market, opened up weed spots and all the spots is selling over a hundred sacks a day easy."

Ty and G-Fly looked at all the ladies with admiration and G-Fly said, "I'm proud of all ya'll. Tomorrow afternoon I'm taking you all to the mall and hooking ya'll up with some fly gear and shit. Also, we got to stop by the beauty salon because we want all our girls to look like ghetto superstars."

All the ladies smiled with excitement.

Ty said, "We need to properly lace them so they will know our expectations and our devotion to them."

"Cool man, let's do it." G-Fly looked at the girls and said, "Everything that we express includes our comrade Julian as well, so always know that it's three ghetto niggas that run this foundation and you are our structure. Now we need you all to be born into this family the same way that you came into this world."

Little Tish, Gwen and Dee-Dee watched as Princess took off her t-shirt and panties, looked at the girls and said, "That just means that you got to be naked."

They said, "Oh," and started getting undressed. After they finished, they saw Princess on her knees kneeling in front of G-Fly and Ty as they sat on the couch. G-Fly said, "Come and join your sister." They all complied, and G-Fly said, "This is a very unique and profound ceremony because tonight you ladies enter a bond with us and one another that will last forever.

You'll become our wives and soul-mates and we become the men in your lives who will always support you and be down for you to our dying day. As long as you choose to live by our laws and standards, you ladies will remain sisters and therefore nothing should ever separate you other than if you violate and get cast out of our family for doing some scandalous shit, which I hope would never occur.

"Now, Princess is our bottom lady," (and she tried to hold back her joy as he said those words,) "so she will have total authority over making sure that the house is run according to our expectations and laws, but if she should start fucking up and tripping, then it's your obligation to bring this to our attention so we can correct the situation before it becomes a problem. That goes for any of your sisters, because if not, then her mistake can also become your fate. Nevertheless, Princess' authority is law next to ours. Also, it's her obligation to make sure that you have what you need and to make sure that you're happy with what we're trying to accomplish and to provide for you.

That is the best that life has to offer. Your main obligation is to protect and satisfy us to the fullest, and our objective is the same. Secondly, to get that money so we all can enjoy the pleasures of life to the fullest. We know that niggas always tried to dog you and never wanted to see you with anything worth having. That's what suckas' do, try to misuse and dog people out because they got more or know that you're doing bad. So they make false promises to you and then take advantage of you as if you're not shit. Yeah, we know how it is and we come to bring you something real, so you can earn and have something worth having and at the same time provide you with three real niggas who's going to always be down for you, protect you, and keep it real with you to death do us part. But you got to be worthy of this opportunity and submit your loyalty, devotion, hearts and minds, to us and only us. If you can't do this, then we can never succeed."

"Damn, I left the crowns in the trunk of my car," G-Fly said to Ty. "Finish up as I run and get them." G-Fly ran out to his car to get the diamond ankle bracelets.

When G-Fly got back to his seat on the couch, Ty said, "So this is what's expected of you. If any one of you ladies do not desire to live by these rules and laws, then let her separate herself now."

Everyone looked around but none of the girls moved.

G-Fly said, "Good. Little Tish, do you accept these terms and conditions?"

"Yes!"

"Stand up and let me crown your sexy down ass then."

She stood as G-Fly pulled out a box, opened it and pulled out a diamond ankle bracelet. He clasped it around her ankle as she smiled with excitement, then he kissed her and she went over and kissed Ty.

After Dee-Dee and Gwen went through the same routine, it was official. G-Fly looked at Princess and said, "They are your responsibility now, and we expect for you to always be fair, loyal and treat them right."

"I will!"

G-Fly said, "Now how about ya'll come show us how good that lovin' is?"

Princess said, "They been waiting for the opportunity to show you that."

G-Fly and Ty stood as the girls undressed them, and they enjoyed a night of pure pleasure and ecstasy.

* * * *

Gloria, John, Kim, Robin and Jackie were all over at Big Mike's condo after coming from the hospital. Big Mike was lying on his couch holding a towel full of ice over his mouth as Gloria was tending to his wounds. Big Mike lost three top teeth, had two black eyes, a swollen jaw and two cracked ribs. John suffered a swollen jaw and black eye. Gloria's eye was swollen and a little red.

"Big Mike," John asked, "where do you know them young punks from?"

"Those are Game's people."

John said, "Man, you still haven't paid that crazy nigga his money?"

"Man, fuck that nigga. He ain't never going to get paid."

John said, "Man, you're trippin'. You know that nigga got damn-near the whole eastside on lock."

Jackie said, "You guys wouldn't be referring to that same Game who drives that dark blue convertible 560SEC Benz, would you?"

Big Mike looked up at Jackie and said, "What? You know that nigga?"

Jackie said, "I met him and heard a lot about him, but I really don't know him personally."

Big Mike snapped at Jackie and said, "Where you know that nigga from?"

Jackie jumped back and looked at him leery, then looked at John for assistance and realized he wasn't coming to her aid.

"It ain't like we kicked it or nothing."

"I didn't ask you if you fucked him. I asked you where you know him from," Big Mike said in an evil and hostile voice.

"You trippin'," Jackie said.

"Look at my face bitch. You got-damn right I'm trippin'!"

Jackie saw a side of Big Mike that she never saw before and it scared her. "This was way back around a couple of months before I met John. I was driving to work one day and my car broke down in the rain on the way. He was passing by and saw me stranded and stopped to help. He asked me what was wrong and I told him I didn't know. It just stopped on me. He asked me where I was headed and I told him I was headed to work. He said he had a friend that owns a car shop that owed him a favor, got on his cell phone and called him. Ten minutes later a tow truck pulled up. He told the tow truck driver to take my car, fix it, give it a nice tune-up for me and deliver it to my job before I get off, so I can have some transportation home. I told the tow truck driver where I worked and when I get off, and he said he'd deliver it before then. He gave me his business card. Game gave me a ride to work. I offered to pay him, but he just laughed and said it was his pleasure. He drove away like it wasn't nothin'."

Big Mike said, "And you expect us to believe he did all that and didn't want nothin' in return?"

Jackie looked at him with hatred and said, "I don't care what you believe. Shit, I ain't got no reason to lie to you!"

"Yeah, right bitch, you probably went out with him and fucked him after that."

Jackie got hot as fire and said, "Nigga, is that what you guys think of me as? A ho?" She looked at John with disgust and said, "For your information, I didn't kick it with him, but if he would've asked me to go out, like I wish that he would've, then hell yeah, I would have gave his fine ass some pussy!"

Big Mike jumped up and backhanded Jackie to the floor. "Bitch, who do you think you're talking to like that?"

Gloria said, "What you hit her for?"

Jackie looked up at Big Mike and said, "Oh, you're a big tough guy now, huh? You want to beat up on a woman, but your big ass was curled up like a bitch on the floor when those youngsters was whoop'in your ass tonight."

Big Mike leaped at her again as John caught him just in time and said, "Nigga, you trippin'. That's my lady."

Big Mike said, "That ain't your bitch. That's Game's bitch."

Gloria helped Jackie up and said, "Come on girl, we ain't go to take this kind of shit."

Big Mike swung at Gloria and missed as John held him back.

"You need to find you a bitch who you can put your hands on cause I ain't going for it! I'm out of here."

Gloria started walking with Jackie toward the front door, then turned and looked at Kim and Robin and said, "Come on ya'll, let's get the fuck up out of here."

Jackie looked at John in a pathetic way and shook her head as she walked out the front door.

"Fuck all you bitches," Big Mike said. "Get the fuck up out of my house!" Then he looked at John and said, "Nigga, you can roll too!"

John shook his head and said again, "Nigga you trippin'."

"You ain't seen me trip yet nigga. Get your square ass up out my house before I shoot all you muthafuckas."

"All right man, I thought we were better than this," John said.

"Well, you thought wrong nigga. It's Big Mike against the muthafucken' world nigga." He slammed the door behind John. "I don't know who these niggas think they're fucking with, but I guarantee I'll get my revenge!"

Chapter 15
Sip From The Game Of Life

The youngsters all met up at the apartment at 8:00 that morning. They quickly showered and dressed and were off to make their morning deliveries. They got back to the apartment at 9:10 a.m., counted the money to make sure that it was all accounted for and grabbed the brown paper bag full of the weed that was already sacked up, counted and separated, awaiting and ready for delivery. Then they jumped into their cars, dropped the tops and Julian took off his T-Tops, and they caravanned to the new house to drop off the weed.

As they pulled up at 9:30, the girls were just waking up after a long night of enjoyable sex with G-Fly and Ty. G-Fly and Ty had sex with every one of the girls and passed out at 5:30, only wake back up at 7:45 to go meet Julian at the apartment.

G-Fly walked in the house and saw Little Tish. "Hey, little good and plenty, where's Princess?"

She blushed at the compliment and said, "She's in the kitchen. Princess, Daddy's looking for you."

G-Fly said, "Damn girl, I could've yelled for her."

She smiled, kissed him and followed him toward the kitchen where Princess walked out to meet him. She kissed him with a sexy smack on the lips and he handed her the bag. "Here baby, I'm in a hurry and got to go." He started walking back toward the door and said, "I'll be back to take ya'll shopping at 12."

Gwen and Dee-Dee were walking down the stairs.

"Hi baby!"

"What's up girls? Got to go." He walked out the door and to his car in the driveway.

Princess and the girls looked out the door and saw the 5.0 with Ty sitting behind the wheel, Julian and his 300, and G-Fly jumping into the Iroc. Princess waved and said, "Baby, who cars are them?"

"What? Ya'll think we're faking?" G-Fly said.

Julian waved at the girls as he pulled off with Ty trailing behind. G-Fly pulled out of the driveway and cut his music up.

Roger & Zapp's "Computer Love" came over the sound system as he smiled and waved at the girls staring in amazement before he pulled off.

Princess closed the door and Gwen said, "They are doing the most! Girl, that 5.0 and Iroc was like that."

Dee-Dee said, "Hell yeah, but that 300 ZX was looking fly as hell too. They was looking so good in them."

Princess said, "Girl, I told ya'll that our men was doing big things, but whatever you do, don't ask them about their business! They don't like that nosy shit. I don't know about ya'll, but Ty wore this pussy out last night, and he's strapped too and knows how to work it."

"You ain't lying, girl," Dee-Dee said. "I had to let him hit this thang from the back and I was coming like a nympho."

Gwen said, "Yeah, he was good, but my G-Fly knows how to fuck his ass off."

"You're not lying about that, sis, he be hitting this pussy in all kinds of angles and positions."

Little Tish giggled and gave Gwen dap. "Yeah, girl, I looked over and seen that you was bent up like a pretzel," Gwen joked.

"Let's eat and go get our money and spots right so we can be back by 12:00."

"Yeah girl, I can't wait to ride in that Iroc! That thing was bumping too."

Princess started counting out sacks and said, "I'ma give ya'll this next sack, but I want the $500 as soon as ya'll pick up from ya'll spots."

"Girl, don't trip, we'll just give you the $500 that we already got put up, so we will be even and just owe you for this here sack."

"Now that's what I'm talking about. Let's keep the books right."

They laughed as they all ran upstairs to get the money they owed.

At 9:45 G-Fly, Ty and Julian pulled up at the main house in Hollywood Hills. They jumped out of their cars and walked up to the front door as it opened and Lady-G greeted them with a big smile, hug and kiss. Lady-G grabbed the brown paper bag with the pick-up money inside and said, “I’ll put this up. Game is in the dining room with company waiting for ya’ll.”

G-Fly said, “Thank you sis,” and they walked into the dining room to meet Game. Game was sitting at the table with an older black man who was wearing an expensive double-breasted suit. As the three youngsters walked over to the table, Game stood and greeted them.

“Ron, these are my three god-brothers. This is Xavier, that’s Tyquoine, and this is Bryan. Gentlemen, this is my good friend and loyal attorney Ron Johnson.”

The youngsters each shook Ron’s hand. “It’s a pleasure to meet you.”

Julian said, “No, the pleasure is ours.”

Game said, “Please, gentlemen, have a seat.”

They sat down and Game said, “Ron here has been with me for a very long time. He handles all of my legal business as well as a majority of my financial investments. I asked him to join us this morning to better acquaint you with him and vice versa.

There will come a time when your financial interests will be in need of his professional assistance. He has friends in high places who can assist you in securing your money in bank accounts overseas. This will cost you 10% of the amount that you choose to place in the account you open. So, say that you take Ron $100,000 to be placed in your account. You will also need to provide him with an additional $10,000 so he can properly make the transaction or you will only be depositing $90,000 in your account as the 10% will be deducted from the $100,000 if you do not bring the extra $10,000 to cover the 10% processing fee.

“Now, I have taken the initiative of opening this account for you all and depositing a little something in it for each one of ya’ll as a token of my love, respect and loyalty to ya’ll.”

Game passed the youngsters a bank book inscribed with London International Bank. They opened the book and noticed their real names imprinted on the inside of the bank book. On the next page was inscribed a deposit of $100,000. Game noticed the smile in the youngsters' eyes and said, "That number at the top of your bank book is your account number. The access code is right underneath it."

They looked at their account number in the bank book. Underneath it read "Ghetto Pride." They looked up at Game and smiled.

"Yes," he said, "you all got the same access code but different numbers, so if something ever happens to one of ya'll, his money would not be lost as long as you have his account number. I gave Ron an envelope with all your account numbers, but he doesn't have your code. Therefore, he can only put money in your account, not withdraw it, since it takes both your account number and your access code for any withdrawal from your bank account. This procedure can be performed from any bank around the world. All you have to do, for instance, if you're in Jamaica and you want to withdraw some money from your account, you go to the nearest bank and tell them you want to open an account with them and transfer some money from this account into your new account. They will call your overseas bank to set up the transfer and give you the phone so you can provide the proper information, which will be your account number and access code. Then tell them the account that you wish to transfer to and it's a done deal. You can either close your new account and pay the small interest rate for doing business with this bank or you can keep the account open and request some prepaid credit cards for the amount you choose to satisfy your spending desire. Any questions?"

The youngsters shook their heads no.

"If ever you get in trouble with the law, don't say nothin' to try to justify your actions. Just tell them you wish to call your attorney and Ron will be there to assist you in every way needed. Do you guys understand?"

All three said, "Yes."

Game turned to Ron and said, "I think that should cover all bases for now. I understand that you're a very busy man, and I don't think it would be necessary to take up anymore of your precious time."

Ron smiled and stood as everyone else stood as well.

"Gentlemen," Ron said, "again it was a pleasure. If ever my assistance is needed, my loyalty and devotion is here for you."

Game shook Ron's hand and embraced him like an old friend.

"Thank you for providing us with your time."

"No problem at all my friend. When you need me, just call."

Ron turned to the youngsters, gave them each a quick handshake, then followed Game to the door.

As Game walked back into the dining room, the youngsters all stood to greet him with a warm smile and embrace.

"Man," Julian said, "we don't know what to say!"

"Sometimes it ain't necessary to try to find the words to define realness," Game said, "therefore, it's no need to try to waste your time."

"Damn, that was deep!" G-Fly said.

"Yeah, I need to write that down," Ty said and everyone laughed.

"Not as deep as this $100gs that Game just blessed us with," Julian said. "You're not lying my nigga, cause all them zeroes gave me a head rush."

They all laughed. Game took out a pre-rolled fat joint out of his weed box and lit it. He asked the youngsters to have a seat around the table. He let out a cloud of smoke and hit the joint again, passed it to G-Fly on his left. After letting out the second cloud of smoke, Game looked at Julian and said, "So what went down last night?"

Julian began telling Game in detail what went down.

* * * *

Back at Big Mike's condo, Big Mike was sitting on the couch across from two of his most scandalous comrades. He always hooked up with them when he put together or came up with a lick of some sort. One of the guys was short and was known as Psycho for his rowdy characteristics. The other guy was Gangsta Dan, known for his affiliation with Gangster Disciples. He had a big-boned heavy weight built with a rough look about himself. A native of Chi-town, he'd been in L.A. ever since he got out of the pen 15 months ago. They'd all become good friends back in the pen when they all spent time in Old Folsom together. They hooked up when they all got out, and had been pulling robberies and jack moves with each other ever since.

Big Mike said, "Now listen man. I've been scoping this lick out for a month now and it's sweet. It's an inside job, and we can all walk away with about $200,000 apiece or better, but that's as long as both of y'all can play your part to the fullest."

Big Mike had a rough draft sketch of the floor plan of the bank laid out on the table before them.

Gangsta Dan said, "Nigga, you're brilliant. This shit is a master mind."

Psycho said, "Yeah man, I'm feeling it too. My only question is can we trust the inside connection to keep her mouth shut?"

"Let me deal with all that, Big Mike said, "and if she do break weak, later on in the game when the cops come to get me, you guys just make sure that bitch don't get a chance to testify on me. You feel me?"

"Don't worry about nothing," Gangsta Dan said.

"I feel ya!" Psycho said.

"Good," Big Mike said. "We move on this thing tomorrow!

Let's roll by it so I can put you guys up on the neighborhood in case things flip and it gets ugly."

Gangsta Dan said, "Man, I'm holding court in the street."

"So if it gets ugly, then you better get away or die

trying because it's going to be a hell-lu-va price to pay if you let those crackers get you. You know what I'm saying?"

"Man, it's going to be as easy as getting a nut on the ho-stroll," Big Mike said, and they all laughed.

* * * *

After Julian finished relaying to Game what happened at the party last night, Game looked at his three comrades with pride.

He shook his head with a big smile and said, "Boy, I hate to run into the three of you in a dark alley!" They all laughed.

Game said, "Listen, Big Mike is not to be underestimated at all, for if he ever gets the opportunity to see you again, then you best believe that he will try to lay you down. So if you ever see him again, then don't hesitate to take him out because if you don't, then you will allow him the chance to kill you next time or maybe your brother. Do you feel me?"

His eyes met his comrades' as they all shook their heads yes. Game said, "I'm trying to get a trace on Big Mike's location so we can bring it to him first."

G-Fly said, "I can hit Kim up and see if she will provide me with the information that we need."

"No, that probably will be a bad idea," Game said, "because even if she do give him up then she automatically becomes a threat that can put you in jail for life. Therefore, it's best that you guys just leave them alone, because we don't need no one else involved who may end up getting caught up in the end."

"Now check it out," Game said. "It's time to take this game to another level! You guys seem as though you're ready for it, therefore, I might as well give it all to you and see what you really can do. Now listen, as you already know I get a hundred birds from Hector for a mill ticket. That's 10g's a bird that I pay for them. They go on the street for $15,500 to $16,000 a bird all day, and if a person is buying 10 or better, then he can get them for $13,500 from me with no problem. But what I'm going to do is give them to you for $12,000 apiece, so you guys can make as much money as you can slang. It's entirely up to the clientele that you build and how quick you can slang them. But remember this, all money ain't good money, and all niggas ain't to be trusted, so choose your clientele wisely. And always count the money and try to get the money before you give or show any product. If a nigga won't let you count the money, then he ain't got it, and if a nigga won't give you the money after you count it, then make sure that you set up the transaction somewhere that you know more about, and you set up security around you to not only make sure that he don't try to jack you, but also to make sure that he's not trying to set you up with the police. If you're meeting him for the first time to negotiate the transaction, then don't hesitate to take one of the girls with you and have her search his ass to make sure that he ain't wearing a wire. If he is wired, then he won't let her search him, and you watch your back and get the hell on! Any one of the ladies will assist you, so use them accordingly, and make sure that you always bless them for their assistance to you in this game. Because a woman will always be down for you as long as she knows that you're down for her, and got her back to the fullest. And never underestimate a woman's perception and intuition, for they tend to see things that we don't, therefore, don't ignore their gift for this is a blessing that they seem to possess."

"Now, I've already had another apartment set up for ya'll different from the other safe house that we use to store our product at. I want you to take the majority of the product to this new house, and leave 25 birds at the old house that you use for storage now, and when you run out, then go get 25 more birds, so we would never have all of our eggs in one basket. You dig?"

They all shook their heads in compliance.

"Good, now you guys will still get paid $2,000 a week apiece to maintain the deliveries and pick-ups, at the other spots, and I expect these spots to be maintained and taken care of as your first priority. Do you guys have any questions?"

G-Fly said, "It sounds good to me!" Everyone started laughing.

Game said, "How many birds do we have left at the spot?"

Julian said, "Seventy, not including the 50 ounces that we got already cooked up and cut down waiting for delivery."

"Okay, when you get down to your last ten birds, let me know so we can re-up. And always keep the cooked portions of the dope with the 25 birds at the old house. I'll also introduce ya'll to some of my elite clientele. They cop from me once a month on a regular, so ya'll can come up quicker. You guys may want to consider investing in you a nice house somewhere, or just maybe a place where you can keep the bulk of the money that you will be making at. So you won't get caught slipping if a jacker finds out where you stay, or if the police decide to kick in your door one day. And remember; don't ever keep your money over a broad's house."

Game turned to look Julian dead in the eyes, "Or let a broad know where you keep your money, dope, or business at. Let her play her part and never your part. Our business is our business, nobody else's. The only reason why I trust Lady-G with the game and the things that she knows is, because she stood by my side through thick and thin and helped me build this empire, as we both wiped the same blood from our hands. But even now as we sit here and converse, she's out of the way and minding her own business for she knows her part and plays it to the fullest.

She's a reflection of me, just like ya'll and I represent the best, so always remember this."

"I know that you guys got a lot to do, and a lot of business is waiting on ya'll so I won't take up no more of your time. Here's the keys and address to the new apartment. It's on the west side in a cool neighborhood, so be discreet when you go there. After you guys transport the work and take care of the other spots, give me a call."

The youngsters agreed as they all got up from the table

and walked out of the dining room headed for the door. Before they walked out, they gave Game dap. Lady-G walked up and said, "I love this bracelet. Thank you!"

Julian said, "And we love you baby!"

She smiled with devoted appreciation and gave them all a big hug and kiss on the lips.

"Bye-bye," Ty said as they walked out.

“Check this out,” Julian said, “let’s head over to the apartment and change cars, and go transport the work to the new apartment, then we can go relax at the spot and kick it and digest all of this game and get our heads right.”

G-Fly and Ty agreed and they jumped in their cars and left.

Game was standing in his doorway with Lady-G listening to Julian give the plan and instructions to G-Fly and Ty. He smiled with pride.

Lady-G said, “You laced them well baby. I believe they can handle the power and obligation, and I know that they’re totally loyal and devoted to you and would kill or die for you at your request.”

“You think so?”

“I know so!”

“Well, what about you?”

“At a drop of a dime!”

“You know that I get horny when you talk like that.”

“I’m glad, because I got just the cure for that!”

Lady-G led him into the family room to his favorite chair and stripped naked while doing her exotic dance number. Five minutes later they were making love like two animals in heat.

Chapter 16
Perceive, Prosper, Profit, and Ball

After G-Fly, Ty and Julian arrived back at their apartment; Julian called Game to let him know that everything went well. Ty got some steaks from the freezer and started cooking, and G-Fly rolled some joints. After Julian got off the phone with Game, he took a deep breath and said, "Damn my niggas. It's about to go down now!"

G-Fly looked over at him, tossed him a joint and said, "You ain't lying. I was sitting up here calculating how much money we're going to start making and my head started throbbing! If we made two to three G's off every bird and flipped 100 birds a month, that's like a $200,000 a month profit that we would make at the least."

"Shit, that's like $70g's apiece, my nigga," Ty added.

"That's what I'm trying to tell ya'll!"

"That's all good, but first we got to establish our clientele," Julian said.

"Do ya'll remember my cousin Killa?" Ty asked.

"Hell yeah!" G-Fly said.

"That crazy nigga who used to always chase us and sock us out when we were younger?"

"Yeah, we remember that nigga. What about him?"

"Well, last I knew, he was ballin' and having big paper a while back. I haven't seen him in about eight months or so, but if he's still ballin' I'm sure that he'll be interested in hooking up."

"Can you call him?"

"I ain't got his number, but I know where he be hangin' at. He be over there on the west side. He's from Raymond Crip 120th!"

"G-Fly said, "Well, shit, after we eat we'll roll over there and see if we can catch him."

"Oh shit, I forgot I promised Princess and the girls that I was going to pick them up at noon. What time is it?"

"It's one o'clock."

"I'm just going to swoop by there on our way and drop

Princess off the money and let her go and take them for me. Hand me the phone."

"Hey Princess."

"Hi baby."

"Listen, something came up that's pretty important, so I'm going to stop by there and give you the money so you can take the girls shopping and get them new haircuts. You know how I like it. Sexy, classy and sophisticated."

"I got you baby."

"Okay, I'll see you in about 30 to 40 minutes."

"Okay, bye baby."

G-Fly smiled. "Bye-bye, Princess."

Princess blushed as they hung up.

Julian said, "Check this out 'rades. I've been thinking and I think that it will be best if we all just put all of the profit that we make off selling these birds away, and at the end of the week, we split up all the profit three ways just like we do everything else. That way, everybody will get a mutual cut and nobody will make more than the next."

Ty said, "I can feel that."

"I wouldn't want it any other way my niggas. We're going to keep this thing real until death do us part. We come into the game together and, like Game said, together we can only win, but apart we will surely lose. So let's put this thing down like it's supposed to be put down and ball together. Can ya'll feel me?"

"That's right my nigga. Keep it GP and for life!" Everyone started rolling at Julian's statement.

Ty said, "Let's eat so we can get this thang crackin' on a full stomach."

"Man, that's what I'm saying!"

After they ate and freshened up, they jumped in their new cars and rolled to the new house where the girls were patiently waiting. As they walked in, they were greeted with hugs and kisses.

Julian said, "Daaaaamn, I like this kind of love," and the girls laughed as Little Tish said, "Julian, me and Gwen both chose to share your bed together. I hope that you don't mind!"

Julian smiled and said, "I guess I better come kick it there more often then!"

Little Tish and Gwen hugged each side of Julian and giggled. G-Fly looked at Princess and said, "Let me holla at you baby." He took her upstairs to the bedroom to talk to her in private. "Baby listen, the reason why I pulled you up here is because a lot of our conversation would be held in private away from our girls. This way you will be able to maintain your position as our bottom lady. If we spoke freely in front of them on every issue, they would become equal to you and we don't want that yet. They got to prove themselves with time, just like you got to as well, but you're given the benefit of the doubt right now until you prove us wrong about you.

"Now listen, here's 7g's for you so you can get the girls right. Spend $2,000 apiece on their clothes and take the other $1,000 and take them to get a manicure, pedicure and their nappy ass heads hooked up. I want them to be the flyest young bitches in the city."

"I got you baby."

"Okay, I got to go. I'll catch up with you later."

"Wait!" Princess grabbed him and started passionately kissing him. "I'm so much in love with you it's crazy!"

G-Fly smiled and said, "You supposed to, but listen, don't buy nothing for yourself. When you're at the mall, cater to the girls and deprive yourself. The girls will respect and appreciate your leadership more. But if you started shopping for yourself too, they might secretly embrace envious ways. So show them that you're there for them and not for yourself. You can always go back and shop for yourself later."

"Okay baby, I feel you on that! You're so wise and game conscious. I never knew that you was cut like this or I would have been chose you in school."

"You did! You just didn't know!" G-Fly said as he walked out.

Ty and Julian were being entertained and spoiled by the girls as G-Fly and Princess walked into the living-room. G-Fly accepted the joint from Ty as he sat on the loveseat with Dee-Dee cuddled up next to them. Julian was sitting in between Little Tish and Gwen on the long leather couch, and it was obvious that the girls were serious about their commitment and feelings toward them.

G-Fly looked at his comrades and said, "Ya'll ready to go?"

Julian and Ty stood up and said, "We'll catch up with you ladies later, okay?"

They all agreed as G-Fly, Ty and Julian made their exits.

As they pulled up on the block, Ty saw his cousin Killa standing outside by a black convertible 'Vette talking to a thick dark-skinned girl with a big round ass. As Ty pulled up on the Vette and stopped, his cousin Killa' pulled out a big black 357 Magnum and Ty said, "Slow down my nigga, before you kill your own cousin!"

Killa looked and said, "I'll be damn. Is that you Ty?"

Ty jumped out of the Mustang and said, "What's up my nigga?" They hugged and Killa felt the butt of Ty's 9mm through his Fila jacket.

"Look at you little nigga. You look like you're doing big things around here!"

"Did you expect anything less?"

Killa just smiled as he noticed G-Fly and Julian both exiting their cars which were double-parked in the middle of the street behind each other. Killa looked at G-Fly and Julian excitedly and said, "Oh shit! Look at my three niggas! They all ballin' out of control!"

G-Fly and Julian walked over to Killa with a big smile and embraced him with respect. Killa said, "Damn my nigga, what ya'll doing? Robbing banks or something?" He looked at Ty for a reply.

"Hell naw nigga, we ain't no damn fools. Them crackers is washing niggas up for that type of shit! We're more like ghetto businessmen. We came through to see if we can improve your investments."

"What? Ya'll got work?"

"Fo sho. You still in the game?"

"Hell yeah."

"Are you interested?" Ty asked.

"Hell yeah if the price is right!"

Ty looked over at the girl standing to the side that Killa had been talking with and said, "Well, check it out. We're going to park these cars and why don't you shake thickness so we can talk a little business."

"Cool."

The youngsters all went to park their cars. G-Fly parked the Iroc across the street, Ty parked the Mustang behind the black Vette, and Julian parked his 300 ZX in front of the 'Vette. G-Fly noticed six niggas at the end of the block and four niggas outside five houses from the end of the block. He had on a Fila sweat-suit like Ty, but Ty's was white with red and blue stripes. G-Fly's was dark blue with white and red stripes. Julian had on a white and green Gucci sweat-suit and they were all fully strapped. G-Fly carried a 45 automatic and Ty and Julian both had 9mm.

As they got out of their cars, the thick sista walked past

Ty. "Hello beautiful," he said as she passed. Ty noticed how fat her ass was in her Guess jeans and said, "Damn girl, like that?"

"Like what?"

"You know what I'm talking about girl. Quit playing."

She just laughed and walked away with a little more sway in her hips. Ty smiled and shook his head and said, "Witchcraft!"

He walked over to his cousin and said, "Damn nigga, is that your girl?"

"Naw man, that's just one of the home-girls who stay down the street. She just wanted to buy a sack of this Indo that I been selling to the homies around here."

"She must be fuckin' with one of your homeboys then?"

"Naw, that's the homeboy Nut, rest in peace, little sister."

Ty said, "You ain't talking about the Nut that used to kick it with you back in the day?"

"Yeah, you remember my nigga Nut?"

"Yeah, of course. I remember him. He used to give me

$5 damn-near every time he seen me."

"Yeah, he did, huh. He got took out the game a couple of years back in a jewelry store robbery. The police shot him 28 times, but my nigga smoked one and shot two before he went out."

Ty said, "Damn, he was a good nigga too."

"Yeah I know," Killa said. "Come on, let's go in my spot so we can talk."

They all turned and started walking toward the front door of Killa's house and G-Fly said, "Is that your Vette?"

"Yeah, I just got it a couple of months back."

"That muthafucka's proper!" G-Fly stated.

Killa' smiled. "Shiiiit, look like ya'll doing the most too!"

They all laughed as they entered the house. "Check this out," Julian said as they all sat down at the kitchen table.

"What are you buying your birds for?"

"I'm getting them for $14,500 to $15,000 depending on how many I'm buying."

"Is that right? Well, check it. We'll give them to you for $14,000 all day and it's the bomb."

Killa looked at all three youngsters and smiled. "Ya'll bull-shittin'!"

Julian said, "Nigga, you know business ain't to be played with!"

Killa looked at Julian. "Well, if it's like that then I'll take five of them right now."

"Cool, bring us $70g's to the table and we'll have them here before you can bust a nut."

"Is that right?"

He got up and walked into the back room. When he came out he was carrying a black duffle bag. He put it on the table unzipped it and poured the money out on the kitchen table. "Nigga, that's a hundred G's all in stacks of five thousand."

Julian looked at his comrades and said, "I'll go get the work and ya'll do the math!"

G-Fly and Ty said, "Cool!"

Julian looked at Killa and said, "I'll be back in a

minute my nigga!"

"A'ight," Killa said as he walked Julian to the front door and let him out.

Julian jumped into his 300 ZX and drove off.

Killa walked over to the table and picked up six stacks and said, "That's 70g's right there."

G-Fly and Ty began counting the stacks professionally as if they worked at a bank. Killa laughed and said, "You niggas is something else. What y'all do? Jack a truck full of birds or something?"

G-Fly and Ty laughed. Ty said, "Naw my nigga, you can just say that we fuck with a real nigga who's doing big things."

"Is that right? Well, if this shit is as good as y'all say, then I know a gang of niggas who would want to hook up with ya'll."

"Cool."

Thirty minutes later after Ty and G-Fly had finished counting the money, Julian knocked at the door. Killa' let him in and Julian walked in with a big brown paper bag and his hand inside his pocket where Killa noticed he was gripping the butt of a 9mm. Killa laughed and said, "You little niggas sure did grow up fast!"

Julian said, "Shiiiit, in this scandalous world you got to. It's either learn quick, struggle, strive, or die."

"I heard that."

Killa shut the door and followed Julian over to the table. Julian set the bag next to the money G-Fly and Ty had counted out. "That's 70g's right there," Killa' said.

Julian pushed the brown paper bag over to Killa and said, "I'm sure your clientele is going to love this shit!"

Killa reached in the bag and pulled the birds out one at a time. He noticed the symbol on each bird indicating 'First Class.' "Oh yeah, these are those First Class. I know this is the bom! I had a hook-up on this brand a year and a half ago from these Mexicans I used to fuck with. My clientele went crazy over it. I've been trying to find this brand for the longest."

Killa went over to the kitchen cabinet and grabbed a

big mayonnaise jar, set it on the counter and grabbed a cooking pot, put some water in it and placed it on the stove to boil.

"Check it out my nigga," Julian said. "I don't mean to get in your business, but if you're cooking your work up like that then you're going to cut your profit by at least 6 G's."

Killa looked at Julian and said, "What you mean?"

"You don't know how to dry cook?"

"What's that?"

Julian looked at his comrades with confusion at Killa's lack of knowledge in the game, then looked back at Killa' and said, "Check it out my nigga. I can bring you back 47 to 48 ounces on each bird, and the shit would still be the bomb, but I'ma charge you $1,500 on each bird, and you got to buy the supplies I need which will run you about $250 and you'll be in the game."

Killa looked at Julian. "Is that right?"

Ty said, "All day!"

"Young nigga you got a deal!"

He reached in his pocket and pulled out three hundred dollar bills and said, "Here, make it happen."

Julian took the money, smiled at his comrades and said, "Killa must think we're faking with this game!"

They laughed as Killa said, "Naw, I don't think that. I'm just glad you ain't!"

Julian laughed as he looked at G-Fly. "I'ma go put this money up and buy the supplies we need to make this thing happen.

Why don't you run to the store and get me a two-liter bottle of 7-Up, a fifth of Hennessey, and a fifth of Bacardi 151 Light."

"Cool, I got you."

Julian then put the stacks of money in the bag and said,

"I'll be back in about 20 minutes."

Ty nodded as G-Fly and Julian walked out the door. He watched them from the porch to provide added protection as they jumped into their cars and drove off. Ty noticed that Julian was driving one of the undercover buckets and smiled, realizing that his comrade was on top of his game.

Ty and Killa went back in the house and kicked it at the table. Ty said, "Damn my nigga, you've been playing yourself kind of short on your profit."

"Yeah, it seems that way, especially when you're talking about bringing back an extra 6g's off a bird! Shit, that's like 30g's more off every sack I cop, not including the extra profit that I make off my two rock houses. I get a thousand dollars off every ounce and push a ounce a day out of each one of them."

Ty said, 'Well shit, you're going to elevate your game to a whole 'nother level. Just think, it's like you're only paying $9,500 a bird now, and making over a $10,000 profit off each one."

"You know what. You're right. I haven't thought about it like that. You young niggas sure came a long way fast. Whoever laced ya'll did a damn good job!" And they both laughed.

* * * *

Little Tish, Gwen and Dee-Dee were all full of excitement as Princess took them store to store in the Fox Hills Mall and spoiled them with a gang of fly clothes, shoes, perfumes and lingerie. They all had bags of stuff like; Fila sweat suits, sweaters, Guess outfits, miniskirt outfits, sexy dresses and short set outfits, high heel shoes and sandals, four pair of tennis shoes and tennis outfits, five sexy lingerie outfits each, panties and bra sets, and a couple of bomber jackets each.

Little Tish said, "Princess you're not going to get nothing for yourself?"

Princess smiled and said, "Listen sis, I'm here to make sure that my girls is a'ight, my obligation is to ya'll, I want my girls to have what they need and want, so they can keep it fly."

The girls looked at Princess with the utmost respect and appreciation, and Dee Dee said, "We love and respect you so much Princess." Then they all gave Princess a big hugs as Princess said, "Ya'll ready to roll – we got a beauty appointment set up for 5 o'clock.

"A beauty appointment Gwen said?"

"Yep, your man especially requested that all of his girls have the flyest hair cuts around."

"What's wrong with my hair?" Gwen said, trying to protest…!

Princess looked at her and said, "Chop, chop!" And everyone started busting up, except Gwen.

Princess said, "That's what G-Fly requested and you know, daddies request and thoughts is law!"

They all shook their heads "yes" in agreement, as they walked out of the mall with the arms full of shopping bags.

* * * *

G-Fly knocked on the door and Killa opened it and let him in. G-Fly had a bag with the liquor in it and a bucket fried chicken.

Ty said, "You must've been reading my mind because I was just thinking about some fried chicken too."

Killa grabbed some plates and they started punishing the chicken. After eating Ty poured everybody some Hennessey and Julian knocked on the door.

Killa opened it as Julian walked in with a big box and looked at Ty and said, "go grab that bag out of the bucket!"

Ty, went outside to grab the bag, and when he came back Julian and G-Fly was taking the microwave out of the box. Ty took out three flat glass microwavable bowls from the bag and eight boxes of baking soda with a bag of ice, and put it all on the counter. Killa pulled out the birds from the cabinet and put them on the counter. G-Fly pulled out a big gumbo pot from underneath the counter and asked Killa to get the triple beam scale.

Killa went into the bedroom and came back out with the scale, and set it on the counter next to the dope. G-Fly cut open a bird and put it in the big pot and started crashing it up into a powder substance. G-Fly was weighing out the baking soda and put 12 ½ ounces of baking soda in the big pot and grinded and stirring in all up together with the cocaine real good.

Killa was sitting at the table with Ty sippin on his cup of Hennessey as they watched G-Fly and Julian put in work. Killa looked at Ty and asked him, “Do you know how to cook like that?”

“Yea, we all can get down, but Julian’s the best!”

G-Fly grabbed the big pot and poured all the dope into the long 2 inch high glass microwave bowl and smoothed it all out. Then Julian grabbed the 2 liter bottle of 7-up and poured a top full of soda into the soda top, and poured it into the dope.

Then Julian grabbed the Bacardi 151 light from the table, and poured 3 tops full into the dope and mixed it all together real good before putting it into the microwave for 10 seconds and pulled it out and mixed it up again real good, before pulling it back into the microwave again for another 10 seconds, and pulled it back out and repeated the process 5 more times before pulling it out mixing it up like a cake and smoothing it back out before placing it in the sink full of ice, and a little water so it can cool off and harden. Killa walked over and looked at the dope as it started getting hard before his eyes.

G-Fly was finish breaking down another bird and Julian was mixing up the baking soda with the dope and then poured it in the other glass microwave bowl and started repeating the cooking process.

After Julian finished cooking the second bird, he pulled the first one out of the ice and put the second one in the sink with the ice, and then got a butter knife and cut around the edges of the first glass bowl and turned it over on a brown paper bag and tapped the bottom as the dope fell out of the glass cooking bowl like a layer of cake, but hard and white with diamond flakes showing all over it.

Killa said, “Damn ya’ll good.” As he went over and observed the long brick of dope.

Julian took the butter knife and broke the dope down in four large pieces and weighted it. It all weighed 48 ounces.

Killa picked up the phone and called the lady next door.

When she answered the phone Killa told her to come

over. Two minutes later the lady from next door was knocking at the door.

It was obvious by her appearance that she was a smoker, and as she came in Killa said, “Do you got your pipe?”

She pulled out a pipe from her pocket rapped up in a face towel. Killa gave her a $20 dollar piece of dope and said, “Try this out, and tell me what your think?”

She hurried up and broke a piece from it and put it on her pipe, then pulled out her cigarette lighter and put the fire to the tip of her pipe as the smoke appeared through the glass pipe and was inhaled into her mouth, as she took a big hit of the smoke. She held it in for thirty seconds and then blow out a cloud of smoke and said, “damn that shit’s the bom”.! As sweat started appearing on her nose and forehead.

She said, “Damn that shit got me hot!”

And started taking off her blouse as she stood there with her chest exposed and said, “That shit is better then all the stuff you ever gave me!”

Killa began laughing and said to the girl, “put back on your damn clothes and go finish smoking that shit at your own house.”

“Okay, but can you first give me something for this $40 dollars I got?”

Killa took the $40 dollars and walked into the kitchen and got two fat $40 dollar rocks from the brick and handed it to her.

“Here girl, he said, “now put your damn clothes on and take your ass back home and get naked at your own house and smoke.”

Ty and Julian started busting up laughing…..! As the girl lift.

“You’re still crazy nigga.”

Killa started putting the dope in a big zip lock bag and said, “Ya’ll going to make a killin with this shit.”

“Ya’ll want me to call a couple of my homeboys who might be interested?”

Ty said, “Yea, go ahead..!”

Killa jumped on the phone as Julian was finishing up cooking the 3rd bird.

Killa hung up the phone and said, "I got two of my homeboys on their way over here."

15 minutes later one of Killa's homeboy knocked on the door. Killa walked over and open the door to let him in.

"Hey ya'll, this is my homeboy Blue……!"

"Blue, these are my little cousins' that's G-Fly, and Ty, and that's Julian over there cooking.

Blue seen the three bricks of dope sitting on the counter, "Damn, how much is one of these?"

Killa said, "My young niggas here is bringing back 47 to 48 ounces off a bird."

"Is that right….!"

"How good is it?" Blue asked.

"Better then anything that we ever came across, it's the bom."

"Is that right….!"

"How much are you guys sellin' them for?"

Ty said, "as long as ya'll buying 5 or better, then we'll give them to you for 14 g's a piece.

"Is that right!"

"How much do ya'll charge to cook'em?"

"We'll cook them up for 15 hundred a piece, Ty said."

Blue looked at his homie Killa and said, "Let me get a piece to go take to someone to try, before I buy. If it's like you say then I'll be looking to buy 5 of them."

Ty said, "Bring us 70 g's plus $7,500 dollars if you want us to cook it and it's on."

Killa gave him a fat hundred dollar rock and Ty gave him his pager number.

Blue said, "I'll get at ya'll within the hour."

Five minutes after Blue walked out Killa's other homie Insane knocked on the door and Killa let him in.

Insane said, "What's crackin Loc?"

Killa' said, "My little cousin got these birds for sale and it's the bom shit! I thought maybe you might be interested in getting something."

"Hey ya'll, this is my homeboy Insane, Insane that's

G-Fly, Ty and Julian over there putting the twist down."

Insane greeted them with a hand shake, and then walked over to the dope on the counter.

"Damn these young niggas know there work….!"

Killa said, "Ya, they're bringing back 47 to 48 ounces off every bird."

"Your bull shitting!"

"Hell naw, and it's the bom – I had Cindy next door try it out and she started getting naked on me. She said it was the best shit that she ever had!"

"Is that right?" Insane looked over on the side of the counter and notice a first class symbol on the paper that the bird was wrapped in.

"O'shit, I see why this shits the bom – ya'll working with the first class shot."

Killa said, "What are you trying to do my nigga?"

Insane looked at Ty and said, "What are they going for?"

"If you're buying 5 or better we'll give them to you for 14g's a piece and if you want us to cook them up for you we'll charge you 15 hundred for each bird and guarantee you 47 to 48 ounces on each."

Insane looked over at Killa and said, "is that right?" And Killa shook his head yes…..

Insane, looked back over at Ty and said, "Well if it's like that then I want 10 of them and I'll pay for ya'll to put the cook down too!"

"You holla at me with $155.000 g's and that's it!" Ty said.

"I'll be back in 30 minutes."

"What about a place to cook at?" Ty asked.

"What's wrong with here? Killa don't mine, and plus it's convenient for both of us."

Ty looked at Killa, and Killa said,

"Get your money nigga? Cool, we'll be kicking it here waiting for you then!"

"I'll be back in a few." With that Insane gave Killa dap and left out.

Ty looked at Killa and said, "I hope them niggas

straight up, cause if they try to come with some shady shit, then I'ma lay them down….!"

Killa looked at his little cousin with admiration and said, "you suppose to, but you ain't got to worry bout that my nigga.

My name means more to these niggas then these birds. I put those niggas in the game when they was young and broke, and they respect my word as law! Nigga I'm the triple O.G. around here, and those niggas is my young soldiers – you feel me?"

Ty laughed and said, "Ya my nigga I feel you!"

"I always knew you was a raw nigga, cause you got my blood in you" and they started laughing as Julian pulled the last brick out of the glass microwave bowl and made it drop out on the counter like a professional baker.

"Here you go my nigga it's all good!"

Killa broke it down and weighed it at 47½ ounces and started grinning at Julian as Killa said, "You know your work!"

Then Killa pulled out $7,500 dollars and handed it to Julian.

Julian counted it and gave him back $1,500, "That for allowing us to use your spot and introducing us to your homies.

"Good look-in playa'

Julian said, "When ever your ready to do it again, then just holla my nigga. Here's our pager number."

"O'Yeah I'll be hollering at ya'll soon, cause it's going down!"

Killa put the dope in a big zip lock bag. "If ya'll tryin' to smoke some of that Indo, then help yourself, it's under the couch. I got to go and take this dope to my safe house, but I'll be back in bout 30 or 40 minutes."

"Remember Insane should be back soon, but if anybody else comes by, just tell them that I'll be back in an hour."

With that Killa put the dope in a duffle bag and left out the door.

Ty walked over and grabbed the cigar box from

underneath the couch and walked back over to the table and opened it and seen the light green staring him in the face.

"It's something about the color green that just turn me on" Ty said.

"Put it in the air" said G-Fly, as he poured everyone some Hennessey.

Julian finished washing out the bowls that he used to cook the dope in, and cleaned up the evidence then went to kick it at the table with his comrades.

G-Fly said, "Check it out rades, we can make just as much money cooking the dope as we can selling it."

"I was just vibing of those same thought my nigga", said Julian. "We made 10g's off selling the dope and $7,500 dollars off cooking it – minus the $1,500 I gave Killa for letting us use his spot and hooking us up with his Homie's. Other then that, we made a $17,500 dollars profit off 5 birds."

Ty let out a cloud of smoke, and as he exhaled reminded Julian and G-Fly that Insane was coming through for 10 birds, which would allow them to make another 35g's profit with the cook. "And if that nigga Blue comes through for them with the other 5 birds, that would be another $17,500 dollars profit with the cook, allowing us to make a $70,000 dollars profit for just today", Ty brought to their attention.

"Damn, no wonder why Game gave us them bank accounts…!

And everyone began busting up at Julian sense of humor.

"No…! for real, these niggas is sleep on the dry cook game, so we got to keep them sleep! Once we establish their trust, then we'll cook the dope after they pay us and bring it to them already hard."

Ty agreed with Julian, "Yea, that will be the lick, that way they won't be all in our mix and catch on to the game."

"Exactly," Julian said.

"Peep this out, we can cook up a bird or two and let Princess and them sell ounces for us" said G-Fly.

"Now feel me out….! G-Fly broke it down for them,

"An ounce goes for 5 to 6 hundred on the street. We can give them to Princess for $400 an ounce and she can turn around and give it to the girls for $450 dollars an ounce. Off a bird we're bringing 48 ounces so that $19,200 dollars off a bird that we will make selling them for $400 dollars an ounce, that's a $7,200 dollars profit off each bird, and the girls is natural born hustlers, so they're probably would sell one to two birds a day. Princess would make $2,400 dollars off each bird and the girls would split $2,400 to $4,800 dollars off a bird depending on what they selling them for."

"Man I'm feeling that", said Ty.

"Yea, you're a genius for coming up with that one. Since you like dealing with them girls on the business level and Princess nick-name should've been called 'Lady Fly' instead of Princess – because it obvious that she is your number one," said Julian.

And Ty smiled and said, "so it's only right that you be in charge of them bitches….! I got faith that all them ladies will be vicious when you're through lacing them."

"Yea, don't worry…!" Said G-Fly, "I'll have them all on point, and just because Princess has chose to give her soul to me, doesn't mean that ya'll shouldn't fuck her!"

"I prefer it, because it will keep that bitch in her place and let her know that her obligation is always to all of us."

"Feel Me?"

"G Fly your one of a kind," Ty said.

Just then there was a knock on the door. Ty went to the door and seen that it was Insane. Ty opened the door and Insane walked in and put a duffle bag on the table and said, "that's a $155,000g's."

Julian looked in the bag and poured it out on the table and said, "I'ma go and get your order while they do the math." "Cool..! Julian said, "I'll be back in 20 minutes and left. "There's some Hennessey on the top of the counter and some fried chicken help yourself, said Ty.

"The weed box is over there too" and him and G-Fly started counting.

Chapter 17
Born To Mac

While Julian and G-Fly was cooking Insane's dope, Blue called and order 5 birds too. He brought the money and Ty counted it and then went to get the dope for Blue. When he got back with the dope and needed supplies, Isane was leaving and Julian and G-Fly cooked up Blue's dope while he waited and kicked it with Killa.

The youngster made it home at 6:30 p.m. and was exhausted. Ty took the bucket and made the pick ups and deliveries while his comrades took a shower and relaxed.

Ty made it back at 7:30 that evening and went to go jump in the shower and get dressed for the night as Julian and G-Fly made sure the money was right and added it to the $240,000 dollars that they made today by sellin' 20 birds, which made it $260,000 dollars totaled, and they went to jumped into their new cars and caravan to the main house to deliver the money and tell Game about how they came up.

Game was kickin' back watching a movie when the youngsters pulled up. Lady-G opened up the door and embraced them with a big hug and kiss and told them that she had cook some Mexican food and would heat them up a plate. They walked in the family room where Game was at and walked in and greeted their comrade with a loving ghetto embrace. G-Fly dropped a big heavy brief case at Game's feet, and Game looked up with surprise and opened it and seen all of the money and said, "Damn how much is this?"

"Julian said, "20g's from the spots and 240g's from the 20 birds that we sold today. Game smiled and said, "I'm glad to see that ya'll was truly ready for this aspect of the game."

"I'm proud of ya'll......!"

"I got a friend, Game said, 'who's looking to but 30 birds tomorrow. I'll set up the transaction for 10:00 o'clock in the morning. He's out of Seattle, Washington and I've been dealing with him every month for a year and a half now. He's always been straight up. In the past I've charged him $13,500 per. Bird and from now on you will be dealing with him. Just bring me the $12,000 dollars off each bird and the extra $1,500 hundred is yours."

"Good looking out big bro." Julian said.

"That would leave us down to our last 20 birds and that can go just as quick!"

"Okay, I'll give Hector a call and set up a purchase so keep your schedules open," said Game.

"Cool…!"

Lady-G said, "Ya'll food is on the table!"

"We can talk at the table", said Game as they went to go eat Lady G's delicious Mexican food.

It was 10:30 in the evening and the girls just came back from making their pick-up and deliveries from their weed spots.

They all sold out while the girls was preoccupied at the beauty salon and they were laughing and joking while putting away all their new clothes.

A new hair style can turn a cute woman into a dime piece and this was surely the issues here. Princess smiled with pride as she seen her girls looking more beautiful and sexy then ever.

Dee-Dee and little Tish both had their short silky styled Bob's hair cut. While Gwen's was short on one side and medium on the other and feathered in layers, passed her shoulder, with curls in a unique style at the ends.

Princess was taking a quick bubble bath as little Tish and Gwen patiently waited their turn.

Princess was glad that her girls was in the game with a nice wardrobe now, so now she won't have to dress down so as not to offend them.

Princess had her burgundy Teddy laid out and was happy that she could also get rid of that T-shirt trip. She wanted all her girls to always look sexy while they lounged around the house. Just in case their men came home. Although G-Fly was her heart and soul, she knew that she had to love them all and cater to them all equally. Princess knew that she had to go buy her and the girls some vibrators, because that once and the blue moon dick, or fuck, will be hard to get use too. But it was worth it and if she can do it, then she knew that her girls can do it too. Maybe they may have to resort to satisfying one another with vibrators. That might not be so bad considering that they all are deeply down and devoted to one another anyway.

Little Tish walked into the bathroom and interrupted

Princess thoughts, Tish said, "are you going to be all day? I would like to wash my pussy too. My man might come home tonight."

Princess said, "Girl if you're in that much of a hurry, then get in, it's big enough for both of us."

"Girl quit playing; don't think I won't……!"

"It ain't like I haven't seen your little ass."

Little Tish smiled and said, "Okay move over as she got naked and got into the bathtub between princess legs. Princess set up and put her arms around Tish and said, "Girl we're going to have a lot of nice things."

Tish said, "I believe you Princess I already got $2,000 dollars and it only been a few days."

"Do you think that they really love us and are down for us like that…..?" Tish asked.

"I know that they are, and as long as we stay loyal, devoted, down, real and faithful to them, then they will always bless us with an opportunity to have the best."

"But we can't fuck around with no other men?"

"I can understand that, damn they don't come around enough to satisfy my sexual desires either!" Said Tish.

Princess rubbed Tish pussy and said, "That pussy is hot huh?"

Little Tish let out a soft moan and said, "That feels good."

Princess said, "listen I was thinking, we might have to buy us some vibrator and use them on each other so we can stay sexually satisfied while our men are away."

"I'm down with that!" Said Little Tish.

"I rather satisfy you'll then to see ya'll fall weak to

another man and loose everything that we got going for ourselves."

"I'm feeling that," Little Tish said, as she turned and tongue kissed Princess.

Princess said, "Have you ever did this before?"

"No, but I fantasized about making love to you a lot", and Tish started giggled.

Dee-Dee and Gwen walk in and Dee-Dee said, "What's going on in here?"

Princess said, "Me and Little Tish was talking and decided that it might be in our best interest to buy some vibrators and satisfy one nother while our man's away, that way we won't start fending for no dick and mess off our blessing…..!"

Princess looked over at the girls and continued explaining, "this dick diet can become hectic and since we all are down and devoted to one nother we shouldn't have no gripes about satisfying each other."

Dee-Dee said, "that's a smart move because I don't know how long I'll be able to go without….!" and they all started laughing.

Gwen said, "You know that I'm down for whatever! I tasted Dee-Dee pussy already when I was suckin on Ty."

"How did it taste……?" Dee-Dee asked!

"The bom…..!" And they started laughing as Dee-Dee pulled Gwen to her and said, "Let's go practice….." and Gwen smiled as they walked out.

"We need to practice too," said Tish….as she turned around and started kissing Princess.

Princess said, "Let's go get in the bed"?

"Give me a couple of minutes so I can finish washing up," said Little Tish.

Princess smiled as she got out and said, "Don't make me wait to long" and grabbed a towel and dried off as she left out of the bathroom.

Little Tish smile and started washing up good.

* * * *

After the three youngster left the main house Ty said

that he was going to take them out to celebrate and for Julian and G-Fly to follow them.

He stopped at a 7-11 and ran in, and came back out then he jumped back in his car as he lead-the-way to his secret designation. He pulled up at the mansion in Altadena where their ladies worked the escort service lived. As they got out of their cars, Julian said, "what's up, Lady-G asked you to drop something off?"

"You can say that!" Then he handed Julian and G-Fly both a 12 pack of condoms.

"It's time to show and prove!"

"We're going to go up in here and fuck everything in her with a pussy!"

G-Fly said, "I'm most certainly down for this."

"You ain't said nothing but a word," said Julian, and they all laughed and headed in the house.

G-Fly opened up the door with his key as they walked into the plush mansion. Me-Me' and China walked up and said, "Hey ya'll what's up?"

G-Fly asked with a serious face, "how many girls is here?"

"Everyone except Nina – she's on a date," said China.

"Well gather all of the other girls up and have them all meet us in the family room……!"

Me-Me' went up stairs and China followed the youngsters in the family room. Julian and Ty knew better then to interrupt their comrade performance. He was in a zone and about to go after his oscar.

All six of the girls quickly arrived in the family room as China handed them all a glass of Hennessey. The ladies looked on as Julian and Ty sat down and gave G-Fly the stage.

G-Fly begin by saying, "it's been said that a couple of ladies in this house has been dishonest and disloyal..!"

The ladies all looked around as Me-Me' said, "we don't understand, who are you…?"

"Silence….!"

"It don't matter who, if one of you ladies is in violation, then all of you are."

"But!"

"I said, silence woman….!"

"Look at you; you're being disloyal now by talking when I said not to. I hate disobedient ladies."

"But we…..!"

"Woman did I say silence….!"

Me-Me' shook her head yes….

G-Fly said, "well you better learn how to obey my orders woman, you're not to good to get dismissed do you hear me…?"

"YES….!"

"Now take off your clothes all of you!"

Every one of them took off their clothes and stood posing with their hour glass figures.

"Now I want you all to bow down in front of us." And he sat in between Ty and Julian on the leather couch as the ladies all bow down on their knees around them.

"G-Fly said, don't you ladies know that Game has given us power and authority over you? DON'T YOU?"

"Yes….!"

"Therefore, what we say is law in this house and every house that's under this family!"

"Now Me-Me' tell me why we got the finest ladies in California and, who allegedly got the best pussy, but got us starving on minimum wage?"

G-Fly kept talking, "Now maybe this big O' mansion and all those nice fancy cars out there got ya'll on some conceit trip but, is that what it's all about, Huh?"

"No…"

"I can't hear you?"

"NO…..!"

"Would you rather me go rent some rooms at the motel down in Hollywood and we start back from scratch.. Huh?"

"NO…..!"

"Then why do I come here and only one of my ladies is out trimming a sucka….? Huh!"

"Well I'll tell you what, after tonight I want to see you bitches out and about…. At the executive and Elite functions, at the Five Star restaurants, basketball games and anywhere you can make money.

It's time to get this money while you're still young and fly, so you can live like a queen when you get old. And me and my comrades want you ladies to consider starting businesses that you may want to own and we'll meet you half way on what ever you chose. We'll be partners 50/50 but, you got to run it…..!"

"For instance, say that China and Africa (Africa a beautiful exotic dark skinned girl with long silky black haired, five feet, eleven inches tall who blushed at her new name that G-Fly just gave her) they wanted to start a production company and do concert promotion. If they did the research it might cost them $300,000 dollars to start, ya'll put up $150,000 dollars and we'll put up the rest to get you started. But, you got to run it yourself. We'll just be your silent partner. See we believe in you, and is totally down for you, but you got to believe in yourself and show us that you're down for us too."

Ty and Julian looked over at each other, then at the girls setting at their feet and motioned with their head, yes! Agreeing with what G-Fly was telling them.

G-Fly made it clear telling the girls, "Your not hoe's or prostitutes. You're exotic and erotic entrepreneurs! Your sexy bodies is just a stepping stone that your smart enough to use to get a head in life, but it's just temporary so you got to make other investment that all of us can become wealthy on, so you can kick back like 'this'….. not trippin' off no sucka' for your independence."

"Do you feel me…?"

"Yes……!"

Me-Me' said, "I always wanted to own a woman's clothing store."

"Well go find a vendor that you like, find out how much it cost and find a good location and we can make it happen!"

Africa looked up at G-Fly with her big baby doll eyes and said, "Baby, I was thinking about trying to do the concert promotion once before, but I know that I didn't have the money for it."

Right then China spoke and said, “Africa I’ll invest with you……!”

“For real…?”

“Yea girl, that sound like fun and profitable.”

“It is girl..! We can make millions, and have fun doing it!”

Africa looked at the youngster and said, “ya’ll really gonna invest with us?”

“Of course beautiful, you are our ladies and we are devoted and obligated to all of ya’ll,” G-Fly told them.

“But you ladies got to do your part and work hard in making our investment successful,” Julian said.

“We promise!”

“We never had anyone who cared about us like that, other then Game,” Diamond said.

“Baby it’s us against the world.” G-Fly stated.

“You’re a part of us now. These sucka’s don’t care about none of ya’ll, or us, that’s why we play them out of their life savings to enjoy your bom sex!” Ty said.

Julian added, “But, it’s time to pump this game to a whole nother level, I want to see ya’ll getting money and stacking, so we can turn our dreams into a reality and have it on a major level. It’s to early in the game to just want to kick back and except the simple things in life, we are a royal family in this game and we desired the best in life. Are ya’ll down for the hustle or what?”

“Hell yea, we’re down with ya’ll…..!” All the ladies shouted.”

“Well let’s celebrate this new struggle in our life, with a night of pleasure,” said Julian.

“Yes indeed,” said G-Fly, “for to satisfy us must become your biggest ambition and motivation in accepting us as your men and, you must desire to satisfy us sexually like no other man has ever been satisfied by you before, for you are ours for life! This is like a marriage that no one other then us can understand and everything that you ladies will possess is ours, especially your bodies, for we will love you until your dying days and this you would never be able to deny.”

"Now come and show us how good your loving is and how much you appreciate us." And G-Fly, Ty, and Julian all stood up and the ladies gave them what they came for and more.

The youngsters was back at their apartment the next day after doing the transaction for 30 birds with Game's clientele from Seattle name Paper. G-Fly was in the kitchen cooking up 5 birds, and Julian was putting the $45,000 dollars profit that they just made with the $70,000 that they made from yesterday hustle. "Peep man, we made a $115,000 dollar profit in two days, not including the $24,000 dollars that we would have after we pick up the money form Princess for the weed. Yea, she paged me an hour ago and said that she had our money, and that they would probably run out of work by 2:00p.m. it's 12:40p.m. now!

So after I finish cooking this shit up, then I'm going to take 96 ounces that's 2 birds over there with the weed and put Princess up on game! If they sell these ounces, any thing like they sell that weed, then it's on and poppin". G-Fly said, as he finished cooking the 5th bird, and put it in the ice to cool off.

Ty said, "I'ma roll over there and kick it with you today, but I hope that they ain't to horny and shit, because I don't know if my dick can even get hard after last night. I think that I hit everything in that house twice."

"You ain't lying", Julian said. "That was the most fun that I ever had in my life. Them women's is truly professionals! I don't think that my dick every got soft and that sista China's a monster, the muscles in her pussy is so powerful, it felt like she was jackin me off with her hand using hot baby oil"

"Yea, but Me-Me wasn't nothing nice either," said Julian.

"They all get a standing ovation from me, G-Fly said; I can't wait to do it again and you know that we got to hit the other houses too!"

Hell yea; you right..! I'm down with that, said Ty. But tell me rade – where did you come up with the business idea from?"

"Yea, that was a brilliant idea," said Julian.

"Well I know that we got to make some nice business investments somehow, so I figure why not capitalize off our ladies who I now is intelligent and need something solid to fall back on. Think about it, if we don't provide them an outlet then pretty soon we might end up having to take care of them!

The pussy's good, but don't no one wants to buy an old bitch, when they can buy a younger bitch for the same amount. So all we doing is providing them with an opportunity to elevate their game and circumstances in a more secure way. And at the same time, we can make millions! Think about it, we got 20 ladies who all got business dreams and idea's that's waiting to be put down and all we got to do is back them, and we will profit off all of them. We became a small investment corporation that profit off multiple business investment that our women own, and operate. We can't really loose."

"I'm feeling that", Julian said.

"Me too", said Ty.

The phone rang and Julian pick it up and said, "Oh, what's up sis?" It's Lady-G he told his comrades.

Lady-G said, "Hey Julian, I just called to commend you'll on you performance last night."

"O' yea?"

"Yea, ya'll got all the ladies talking about how ya'll put it down, and how ya'll going to support them in their business investments. That was a very wise idea that you guys come up with and I'm confidant that it would become a big success!"

"You really think so?"

"Yes, I know so, and so do Game! He loves the idea too and proud of ya'll for taking interest and advantage in your opportunities, and believing in the ladies like that. You got a couple of ladies who got bachelor degrees in business and accounting in your stable, but it's no better money then hoe money, so they quit there 9 to 5 to capitalize off a bigger hustle, but now that you guys has brung this opportunity to the table, they are motivated to start their own businesses and provide you'll with the needed assistance to support their sister efforts. But they want to know whether you just meant the Altadena ladies or all of the ladies?

Oh it's for them all….!

Well, I'll let you guys tell them that! Also, Game said that he will help financially sponsor you guys motivation, because he knows that you've probably bite off more then you can chew. Because you do have 20 ladies who all have an interest in owning their own business, and that might become pretty expensive for you guys at this stage of your hustle. But with his support, you shouldn't have a problem. And O', one more thing, your ladies at your two other houses heard about how you guys put it down, and they can't wait for you guys to stop by and enjoy their bodies too." Lady-G started laughing and said, "I heard that ya'll put it down like porno stars!" And she started giggling over the phone.

"You just let them know that when we show up that they better be ready, because we come to put in work," and he started laughing.

"OK, I'll pass on you message and we'll see ya'll soon, bye…. Julian hung up the phone and looked at his comrades who was all in his grill and said, "Man It's on and poppin! You wouldn't believe what Lady-G said….?

"What nigga," Ty said.

Julian started telling his comrades what Lady-G said in full detail.

Chapter 18
Scandalous Games, Locks, and Deception

"New accounts, how may I help you gentlemen?"

"Yes Ms, We would like to open up a new account with your bank", Psyco said, as he sat next to Gangsta Dam wearing a nice double breasted suit and sophisticated glasses. Psyco opened up his black brief case and turned it so the lady behind the desk can see the contents, and what she saw brought instant fear to her eyes, because what she saw in the brief case looked like a bomb! Big Mike took some flairs and wrapped them up like sticks of dynamite, and placed wires into the ends coming out running to the insides of a portable radio that displayed just the circuit panel with a red light attached to a small battery pack that made the light blink off and on randomly, and everything was glued down so it wouldn't move.

Psyco said, "Don't be afraid, I want you to smile for me and please don't do nothing stupid or you will never have a chance to correct it. Now listen, this is a professional bank robbery and you need to do exactly as I tell you to do, or this will be your very last day on earth, now smile. O'kay now….. who's the manager?

"Jackie…!"

"Well, I need you to smile and act like nothing's wrong! Call the manager over here, but don't give no signals because if the police get wind of this party, then it will be your last dance-do you understand?"

"YES….!"

"Now call the manager!"

The lady wave for the manager, and as the manager came up the lady said "Jackie these gentlemen is requesting your assistance."

"Hello how may I help you?"

Psyco opened up the brief case and showed the Manager the gadget that resemble a bomb, and she said "O my god!"

"Yes, you will see god very soon if you do not do exactly as I tell you to do. Now I want you to remember that we got two other people in the bank who is watching for any suspicious signals or movements. So please do us all a favor and don't try to do nothing stupid."

"I won't sir, just please don't hurt nobody."

"You will not have to worry about that if you do what I tell you. I want you to take my associate in the volt and assist him in getting the unmark bills. If you try to give us any dye packs, sensors, or bait money, then we will make you pay dearly. And make sure that you have your assist with the other key with you so; you can eliminate any unwanted delay's."

Gangsta Dam placed a fake police badge hanging out of his front suit coat pocket, so everyone can see and picked up the other brief case with the big duffle bags in it, and took it with him as they walked into the volt. The lady looked around the bank and notice a man with a baseball hat on and dark glasses over at the counter with the withdraw slips and filling out some papers, but now everyone look suspicious.

"Your doing to much looking, I want you to act like your filling out that piece of paper and the lady complied."

Gangsta Dam was in the volt and stacking stacks of hundred, fifties, and twenty dollar bills in the big duffle bag, and then he filled up the brief case with some more bills. He stood up and looked at the manager and assistant manager and said, "the other brief case with the boom will be left behind, you are to wait five minutes before you evacuate the bank and get everyone a hundred yards away and then contact the boom squad. If you notify any police before the five minutes is up or before you evacuate the bank, then the bank would go up. You go out and notify your cashier to not push any buttons or alarms so when I walk out, they won't do nothing stupid and get everybody killed."

"Okay", and the manager walked out of the volt.

Gangsta Dam said, "it was nice doing business with you and grabbed the duffle bag and brief case and walked out."

Psyco seen his homie walking out of the volt and

looked at the lady and said, "if you try to move this brief case, then it will explode, if any alarms is hit, then I'll set it off from inside my car. So go and consult with your manager before doing something stupid," and Psyco got up and left and the man that was at the counter was gone too.

Twenty minutes later Big Mike, Psyco, and Gangsta Dam was in the Travel Lodge Motel counting stacks of money and watching the news. It was a clean get away and the biggest lick that they every hit. An hour later they was all smiling and laughing with joy as they realize that they hit for $670,000 dollars.

Big Mike said we're going to give our inside connect the 70g's and we all can walk away with $200,000 a piece. Psyco and Gangsta Dam knew that Big Mike had some shit with him, but they didn't trip because they knew that it would lead to some blood shed, and they was satisfied with the $200,000 dollars that they came up with.

Gansta Dam said, "just give me my $200,000 whatever you decide to give the bitch is on you."

"Yea, I ain't trippin either," Psyco said.

Big Mike said "man, we need to put up $120,000 a piece and hook up with this Mexican that I know and order 30 birds from him, and get our paper in a major way."

"Man, that's a lot of money to be putting up," Psyco said. "Damn nigga, I ain't talking about buying no damn dope, all we need is the money so we can show it to him, and once he bring the dope, then we lay his ass down and take the fuckin dope! Ain't nothing change because we came up."

Gangsta Dam said, "you know I'm down for that. But after the lick I want my money and 10 birds off the lick."

"Yea, me too," Psyco said.

"Yea man, I ain't trippin' that! I just want ya'll to be there with me to get down with those Amegos,' because you know that they can get rowdy too!"

"Yea, I hate them muthafucka's too" Gangsta Dam said.

"Well it's on, I'ma hook it up for tomorrow so be ready and have your half of the buy, because you know that they like counting the money before they bring the dope!"

"Yea, nobody trust a nigger – we got it hard," Gangsta Dam said as they all laughed.

"I'm out, I got some celebrating to do and some pussy to reck!"

"Yea, I'm out too! Get at us tomorrow Mike, and let us know what time you set it up for," Psyco said, as him and Gansta Dam left the room.

* * * *

The youngsters walked in to the new house at 1:50p.m. and heard the girls out back by the pool. G-Fly, Julian and Ty looked out the sliding glass door and seen the girls sitting out by the pool in their sexy two piece bathing suits.

Ty said, "Do you see what I see?"

Julian said "those don't look like the young ladies that we adopted!"

"What ya'll mean," G-Fly said.

"I told ya'll that I was going to hook them up, what you thought that I was joking?"

"Man, they look as fine as our other ladies that work our escort service now," Ty stated.

"Yea, but with a ghetto twist," G-Fly said, as he smiled and walked outside and said daddies home, and the girls looked up and smiled as they jumped up and ran over to greet their men.

"Look at my ladies looking all sexy, sophisticated, and fly!" Princess, hugged him and gave him a big kiss, and then hugged and kissed Ty and Julian, as all the girls did the same, then Princess said, "how do you like them?"

G-Fly said, "They look super fly" and the girls blushed, as Ty said, "yea ya'll looking real good.

Julian said, "I always though that ya'll was beautiful but now ya'll look to good!"

"Thank you!"

We came to kick it with ya'll today and enjoy all that quality time that we've been missing out on," Ty said.

"Good baby, because we've been missing ya'll," Dee-Dee said, and gave Ty a deep passionate kiss.

Julian rubbed little Tish big pretty fat butt and said, "how about fixing me some Hennessey and grabbing me a fat joint."

"Okay baby," and she gave Julian a deep kiss and walked away. He looked at Gwen who was in his other arms and said, "how's my sexy exotic lady doing?" She blushed and said, "just trying to hustle and keep my men happy."

"Every time I look at you I get happy" and they kissed.

G-Fly said, "let me holla at you Princess," and he took her in the house and went to the up stairs bedroom of theirs.

When they got in the room he shut the door, and she walked up on him and started passionately kissing him and said, "I've missed you baby!"

"I missed you too, and you look sexy in that two piece."

"You like it?"

"Yea, that's nice! But listen we got something special for you and girls to help elevate your game to an whole nother level."

"For real? What's up baby?"

"Now listen, we put together another kind of sack for you ladies to be able to work and come up on. Look…!" And he took the duffle bag off his shoulder and opened it up and pulled out two zip lock bags full of ounces. She said, "damn y'all doing it big!"

"O' Yea, but now ya'll going to be ballin too!"

"Now peep. We're gonna give them to you for $400 dollars an ounce (and her eyes lite up) and you give it to the girls for $450 an ounce. Now here's 96 ounces, which will allow you to make 5g's off the sack and the girls will be able to split 5g's among themselves. And you will bring us back 38g's off each sack. So, what do you think about that?"

"That's love, and I know that the girls would be very happy too. We know a gang of nigga's who buy ounces, and we can kill'em by selling ounces for $500 a pop, because niggas is paying $550 and ounce and $300 dollars for a half of ounce."

"Well, all you need to do is supply your girls, watch their back, and make sure that our money right, and you're gonna make 5g's on each sack! Yea, imagine if you sell a sack a week then that 5g's a week that you will profit not including the weed."

"Man, I love you so much daddy!"

"Your suppose too – I'm your man! And they smiled.

"Here this is for you and the girls too," and he give her four 3.80 automatic pistols.

"Do ya'll know how to use them?"

"Of course, we're ghetto baby!"

"O'kay now listen, I need a favor from you tonight!"

"What's up daddy?"

"I got a client that's coming in town to buy some work and he's a cold trick for a big butt and smile. He wants me to set him up with a date, so he can get this freak on. Are you down?"

She looked at him and said, "if that's what you want me to do, I'm down!"

"That's what I like – my woman to be down for whatever!"

And they smiled. "But listen you ain't got to fuck him just tease him and I got something that my pharmacist partner gave me that would knock him right out, and all you got to do is slide it into his drink, and stall him until he pass out, and call me up on this cell phone and I'm going to come in and jack him for his cope money. You feel me?"

"Yea, I feel you baby!"

"Are you down or should I get one of the other girls?"

"Why you do that? You know that I'll always be the one and only that you can always depend on!"

"O'kay put on something tight and sexy and it's set up for 8:30p.m."

"I'll be ready, Now can I have some of that bom dick?" Don't you want to give the girls their weed sacks, and introduce them to this new game first?"

"They can wait better then me!" And G-Fly said, laughing as they started making wild passionate love.

An hour later G-Fly and princess emerged out of the

bedroom feeling good, and as they walked back outside they looked surprised as everyone was butt naked having sex. Ty and Dee-Dee was in the pool locked in ecstasy and Julian had Little Tish and Gwen in the Jacuzzi as he preparing for round two.

Ty said, "what took ya'll so long? And G-Fly and Princess got naked and got in the Jacuzzi with Julian, Little Tish and Gwen. G-Fly said, "I need a drink and Little Tish said, "I'll grab you one," and got out of the pool naked.

"Damn Little Tish you got it good baby," G-Fly said, "Bring the hole bottle and the weed too!" Ty and Dee-Dee got out of the pool and went to get in the Jacuzzi with everyone else. Tish came back with the 5th of Hennessey and some plastic cups with the bag of weed that the girls kept pre-rolled. She got back in the Jacuzzi and sat on G-Fly lap, and G-Fly dick got instantly hard. She smiled and slid it up in her and rode him like a professional as G-Fly laid back and smoke a joint with her and Dee-Dee. Julian was lying back as Gwen got her sex on and Princess was getting hit from the back from Ty.

G-Fly said, "now this the life!" And everyone started laughing.

The party went on until 6:30 and princess put the girls up on the new game and gave them their new guns and the girls was really happy now. They never imagine making money like that and they were totally excited about putting it down in a major way.

They grabbed their weed sacks and was gone. Julian took a shower and got dress and went to spend some time with Tracy.

G-Fly told Princess that he'll be back to pick her up at 8:00p.m. and him and Ty went to do the pick up's and deliveries.

* * * *

Big Mike was in his motel room having the best sex of his life as he got finish releasing his orgasm, and him and his lover just laid in bed, breathing hard. Jackie said, "baby you got the best dick that I ever had and, I'm glad that you excepted me as your lady!" Big Mike got up and went to go flush his condom and wash his dick off and took Jackie a worm wet towel. He said, "you just glad that you got a real and down man by your-side now." And he lite a fat joint and laid next to her on the bed. She said, "Yea, John was to square for me, I know when I first met you that I had to have you."

"Yea, what about your home-girl Gloria?"

"Fuck Gloria! She didn't know how to treat a man like you, she fucking Ken on the side anyway, she don't know how to be down for a man like you. "Yea, but she was a cold freak – she got the bomb head, and she loves it in the butt."

"You mean anal sex?"

"Yep, I love a woman who got a big fat tight ass.

"I ain't never did that before!"

"Damn, I know that that ass hole got to be tight then and you got a fat pretty ass to. "

"I know that your going to let me break it in for you!"

"No, I ain't into that."

"No, what you mean no bitch, how are going to be my lady and your telling me no"? I just risk my life robbing your fuckin job, and you can't satisfy me, what if I took that 50g's back and tell you No!

"Wait a minute baby, you know that I was only playing if you want my virgin ass, then you know that you're the only man who can have!"

"That's more like it, now get this dick hard with some of that boom head of yours." Jackie know that she didn't have a choice, she was in to deep and she had to at least play it off until she secured her 50g's that Big Mike just gave her for her part in setting up the bank robbery. She know that he got away with $670,000 thousand dollars from the bank report, and 50g's was an insult. But, it was better then nothing, and if she ever get a chance to find his stash while he's slippin, then she already had it in her mind to run off with it. She smiled as she sucked him to his second erection.

Big Mike said, "I got something special for you and he went to the closet and grabbed some cloth strips and said

I'ma tie you up and suck and fuck you to death. She smiled thinking about having Big Mike sucking on her pussy, and she know that he was getting sprung because he wanted to suck her off. He tied her up on her belly with her legs spread wide apart, then blind folded her and gagged her. She was getting soaking wet thinking about it. Big Mike lubed up her ass hole and she know what was coming next. He went over to the table and mixed up a speed ball, which was a mixture of heroin and cocaine melted down with a couple of drops of water in a spoon, and drown up into a syringe so it could be shot into the vein. The excitement hand him rock hard. He placed a cloth strip tightly around her arm and when he seen the vein appear on her arm he place the needle into the vein and injected the substance out of the syringe.

Jackie was wiggling as Big Mike said don't be scared baby, you'll love it! He straddled her and slid deep into her rectum with half of his nine inch dick. She let out a muffled scream as he thrust his dick all of the way up in her. She was screaming in pain as Big Mike laughed and said, "relax and it won't hurt" and she tried, but it was to painful. Big Mike just kept on fuckin her little tight ass and when he started feeling her relaxing more, he unwrapped the cloth that was tied from around her arm as he was coming close to his orgasm, and as the warm substance was release though her body, her whole body tense and Big Mike felt her ass hole put a death grip around his dick, and he busted his nut as Jackie body shook like she was having a seizure, and she died in his clutches.

Big Mike checked her pause but knew that she was dead. He laughed and said damn baby, I wish that we can do that again. And pulled up out of her and went to go flush his rubber and washed up. He came back and took some bleach out of the closet and wiped her body down, and then put some in a douche and shot it up in her pussy and butt hole. He cleaned up the motel room and grabbed his 50g's and said bye baby, it's been fun, but, I just can't trust you and laughed as he walked out of the motel room.

* * * *

Princess knock on the motel room door and a older black man answered it, and when he seen Princess he said, "hey beautiful you must be princess, G-Fly sent you right?"

"Yea"!

"O, come on in, come on in – I've been expecting you!"

"Damn your everything a man could every desire." Princess smiled nervously, but knew that she had to represent for her man.

Jack was caught off guard by Princess beauty and sexy body, and wanted to play her out her pussy bad, but then shook the thought and said, "can I offer you a drink to ease the mood."

"Yes, that would be nice."

"Please have a seat." Princess went and sat on the couch.

Jack said, "My name is Cash and handed Princess a drink.

Princess said, "Please to meet you Cash, are you from around this way? "No, I'm from Organ! I'm just here on business, and a little pleasure while I wait, and he smiled as he sat his drink down and said, "excuse me for a second sweetheart while I go release my bladder," and got up and went into the restroom and closed the door.

Princess hurried up and put the powder substance into his drink, and stirred it up with her finger. A couple minutes later he came back and said, "so tell me Princess, how long have you been working in an escort services?" After saying that Cash downed his drink and lite a cigarette.

Princess said, "O I'm new, I'm trying to pay for my college education.

"Yea, what are you going for?" and his eyes started dozing off.

Princess smiled, and said, "for business do you mine if I used the restroom?"

"No please, go ahead." And Princess got up and left. Cash, smiled and shook his head.

Princess came out of the restroom three minutes later

and seen Cash laying on the floor out cold. She pulled out the cell phone and paged G-Fly and left her code.

G-Fly pager went off as he was in the parking lot at the motel where Princess just went into. He looked and seen that it was Princess code and smiled, and said to him self, “that’s my girl.” He looked up and seen a familiar face go over to the car five parking stalls in-front of him, and said Damn that’s that muthafucka Big Mike, and G-Fly pulled out his 45 automatic.

Another couple just pulled up next to Big Mikes car as Big Mike throws his duffle bags in his trunk and went and jumped into his car and drove off.

G-Fly said, “Shit! My fuckin luck.” Then he got out of his car and went and knocked on the motel room door that Princess was in.

Princess heard a knock and looked out of the peek hole and seen that it was G-Fly and opened it up. G-Fly walked in and princess said, “he’s out cold baby.” G-Fly looked and smiled and went to look at Cash and bent down and checked his pulse and said, “Damn this muthafuckas dead!”

“What?”

“Yea, how much of that shit did you give him?”

“I gave it all to him……”

“Damn, that was probably too much!”

“Don’t trip! Did you touch anything?”

“Yea, the glass and I used the restroom.”

“Okay here, take this towel and wipe down everything in the bathroom that you think that you could’ve touched, and don’t touch nothing else.”

“Okay baby…!”

G-Fly put on his brownies and pulled out a brief case and opened it up in-front of Princess, and she seen all of the money and was surprised. G-Fly took the towel and wiped down the table and took the glass that Princess had and put it in a bag that was on the table next to the drinks.

Then G-Fly got on the his cell phone and said’ “peep this out rade, I got a code G red at the Travel Lodge Motel on Crenshaw. I need you to come and clean it up for me and bring your large shit case. Yea, its room 187, the door would be unlocked. Cool, call me when you're done. Later!"

"Come on baby let's roll" and G-Fly wiped off the door knobs and they left."

Once they got in the car and pulled away G-Fly said, "listen this is our secret you hear me?"

"Yes, baby I won't tell no one."

"You represented for your man like a thoroughbred and I like that. I guess that you're really my main lady for life now, Huh?"

"Of course baby, you know that I'm down with you to the grave, and see I'll even kill for you too!"

G-Fly laughed and said, "Yea, you're my ride or die bitch, and lend over and kissed her deeply at the stop light. Then he said, "lets go and get some sea food at the Red Lobster, would you like to go out to dinner with me tonight? And when we get back home I'll let you ride this dick until you fall asleep."

"That would be nice Princes said," as she blushed with delight.

Cash got up from the floor and laughed as he called Game up on the phone and said, "yea man everything worked out sweet!,

She brought it like a free dinner at the dog pound", then they both laughed.

Game said, "Good, good! I knew that I could count on you Jack. Your next sack's on the house"!

"Man, I'm cool! I owed him one for saving me from the Jack move that them sucka's tried to put down, and from my lady Missy getting raped. If it wasn't for him, I probably wouldn't be here today."

"Okay", Game said, "I'll respect that, and I'll let him know about your appreciation and respect for him."

"A'ight man, I'll catch up with you later" and Game hung up the phone.

G-Fly and Princess made it back from dinner at 11:00p.m. and when they walked through the door of the new house Dee-Dee, Little Tish, and Gwen met them walking in and said, "Princess I hope that you don't be mad at us!"

"Why Dee-Dee?"

"Because we had to go in your stash and get some more dope."

"What ya'll sold the ten ounces that I gave each of you?"

"Yep!, I sold 28 ounces, Little Tish sold 24 ounces, and Gwen sold 22 ounces and it's only 22 ounces left and Gwen just got paged for nine of them. They love that shit!"

Princess smiled and said, "You girls is going to be rich in a month if ya'll keep hustling like this."

"Yea, I made $2,400.00 dollars today with my profit for my weed and the ounces," Dee-Dee said proudly.

"I made $1,800 hundred total," Tish said with a big grin on her face, "after I sell this nine ounces I'll have $2,550.00 dollars for today."

"You know that I'm proud of ya'll. But I always had faith in ya'll because you ladies come up like me and my comrades from the ghetto, and all ya'll needed was an opportunity to grind and shine and it's was on. I'm just glad that I was able to adopt ya'll and provide ya'll the opportunity. As long as ya'll stay down for one another and loyal to us, this family and the cause, then it's on! We got your back from the pen to the grave. If you ever get popped then don't try to justify your actions just call home, and we will have an attorney and bail bonds man on the way."

"You mean we got an attorney and bail bonds man too?" Dee-Dee said. As all the girls looked surprised even Princess tried to hide her curiosity.

"Of course baby! Ya'll fuckin with the real. We won't never leave ya'll hanging or without? We love ya'll, because we know that ya'll love and loyalty is true to us." They all gave him a hug and a big kiss and Gwen said, "Come on Little Tish and watch my back.

"I'll roll with ya'll too," said Dee-Dee and they left.

Princess said, "Remember your promises," and smiled.

Chapter 19
Pirates, Thieves, Gangstas, and Cut Throats

Ty took the girls another 96 ounces that night and spent the night cuddled with Dee-Dee and Gwen, and G-Fly was cuddled with Princess and Little Tish. They woke up at 7:30 the next morning and took the $37,000.00 dollars that the girls made minus the thousand spent on food and house hold necessities.

When Ty and G-Fly got to the apartment they left a brief note for Julian as they went to make the morning deliveries and pick-ups. When they made it back, Julian was home and freshly showered. G-Fly hit the shower as Ty cooked breakfast and then G-Fly told Julian and Ty about the locks that he put on Princess and how he did it, and they laughed.

Julian said, “Them girls be hustling there ass off, and

G-Fly said, “And they’re down and freaky as fuck, ‘a good combination.’”

Julian said, “man I know that you wanted to gun that nigga Big Mike down when you seen him?

“Hell yea, my dick got hard, but it was too many witnesses, so he survived that one by luck”.

Ty said,” Did you say that you was at the Travel Lodge Motel on Crenshaw?”

“Yep….! Look”, then he cut up the news and Jackie face flashed across the TV screen.

“Hell naw, ain’t this a bitch G-Fly said, that muthafucka’ killed her.”

“Man, I know it!”

“Listen, listen……!”

The news reporter said, “Investigators have reason to believe the 23 year old Jackie Johnson was involved with yesterday bank robbery of the First Hood Bank of Trust, where it’s reported that 2 to 4 men got away with $670,000 dollars in a professional bank robbery. Twenty-three year old Ms. Jackie Johnson was a manager at the bank during the robbery. Investigators are calling this a case of eliminating a key witness and crime partner. Ms. Jackie Johnson was hideously raped and assaulted and then injected with lethal amounts of heroin and cocaine mixed, that viciously busted her heart. The investigators say that this hideous act was inflicted during the time that the victim was being sexually assaulted and then thereafter, the murderer used a comical compound to wash the body down and injected it into her virginal and rectum with a douche like object to try to cover up his DNA. This is one of the most devious crimes that anyone could of committed and the police is asking anyone with leads to call 1-800-2-SNITCH that's

1-800-2-S.N.I.T.C.H.

"Man that's a sick muthafucka", Ty said angrily.

"Yea, I kind of wish that I would've blown his fuckin' head off now", G-Fly said.

"Listen man, he'll get his soon," Julian said, "but for now we need to get ready so we can go and re-cope, I told Game to order us 40 pounds of weed, so we got to get the money together too!"

Then they all got dressed in old clothes and waited for Game to arrive.

* * * *

Game, Lady-G and the youngsters was all at the safe house after coming back from re-coping. Julian and G-Fly had two microwaves going at the same time as both was showing their advanced expertise in cooking up the dope. Ty was helping them by breaking down the dope in the big gum bowl pots and measuring and mixing up the baking soda, and then Ty would cut the slab of dope out of the glass microwave bowl and put them over on the table stacked next to each other.

Game looked over at Lady-G in amazement and Lady-G started laughing and said, "I told you that they where natural hustlers!" Then she started laughing as Game just shook his head.

They cooked up 20 birds in a little over an hour and

after they used 3 scales and weighed the dope into ounces and sacked up over 890 ounces. It took two hours to complete the whole process.

Game said, "I'm really impressed, it seems like ya'll mastering the game, just always keep your wits about everything and stay focus. Come on let go have a drink and I got some jewels that I want to drop on you."

They sat down in the living room and Lady-G fixed everybody a glass of Hennessey as she sat down next to Game.

Game blazed a fat joint and looked at Lady-G and said, "Baby you got the envelopes?" Lady-G reached inside her purse and pulled out two envelopes. Game opened up the first one and took out some documents and a bank book. He handed it to Julian who was sitting on the left side of him and said, I took the liberty of establishing a Corporation for you guys and opening up a Corporate Account to assist ya'll in helping the ladies establish there businesses and dreams.

Your corporation is an Investment Corporation that's established as a fictitious over sea's corporation, but is doing business over here under the name 'Ghetto Pride'! Ya'll are silent partners but own and have total control over the corporate ventures. The money that I placed to get you'll establish, you can just pay me back in installments as your profit and game progress. Julian opened up the bank book and it displayed One million dollars.

Julian said, "Daaammn….! It's a bullet ya'll."

Let me see said Ty, "Man this is the second best day of my life!"

"O' yea, what was the first Lady-G asked?"

"When we first met Game," Ty admitted and everyone smiled, but knew that he was speaking from the heart.

G-Fly said, "Now this shit is getting real deep! Puff-puff pass Julian, Puff-puff pass nigga!" And every one started rollin' as Julian handed him the joint.

Game said, "That ought to get you started on your business investment with the ladies. I placed Lady-G as your secretary over your corporation, and she would over see the ladies research and make sure that the financial assessments is accurate and on point. Lady-G has a bachelor degree in business, she graduated from the Wilshire School of Business two years ago in 1985, and she's gifted and blessed in everyway".

"Baby I know that you was a cut way above the rest, but this puts you in a class that's untouchable, G-Fly said.

Julian, did you say that Tracy have a business degree too, G-Fly asked?"

"Yep, and she graduated from the same place that Lady-G did".

"Is that right Game asked, and Julian shook his head."

"Game said, well you might as well bring her home then, because she got to be a beautiful and real sista' to captivate your attention beyond all these other beautiful sista' that you got jockin you. Just let Lady-G lace her, and she can become Lady-G's assistance if that's what you guys want?"

Julian looked at Ty and G-Fly and Ty said, "I love the idea."

G-Fly knew that Julian really cared for Tracy and knew how they was spiritually connected and said, "I would have bung it up if I did want her to come home!" Everyone smiled as Game said, "Oh your planting seeds now Huh?"

I didn't believe that I taught you that aspect of the game yet!"

"Some things just come natural when the real is exposed to the real."

"Lady-G laughed and said, "We got a Socrates in the family."

"Soc-ra- Who?"

"SOCRATES...... he was a wise prophet back in ancient history."

"Did he sell dope too", G-Fly asked?

"No, I don't think so," Lady-G said.

"Well we can't be related then" then everyone started busting up.

"You're crazy boy!"

Game said, "Listen ya'll, me and Lady-G went out and

found ya'll a more better spot for y'all to kick it at. It's purchased up under my Corporate Real-Estate Firm, so you guys would just have to pay your monthly mortgage to Lady-G, she'll give you the specifics. Your mortgage is $3,000 dollars a month, but I'm sure that you'll find it well worth it's mortgage price. Plus, as much money that you guys make, this is just a penny to a dollar. However, you guys choose to enjoy your living arrangement there, is totally at you own discretion.

Just don't have no dope in it, or the bulk of your money, that's my advise. When you come up in the world, then you can purchase it if you desire, it's totally up to you.

It's located in Altadena Hills, so you shouldn't be bothered with nosy neighbors. Here is the address, keys, and security codes and all that I can say is ball until you die, and enjoy the beautiful blessing that life holds."

G-Fly said, "you know that we love ya'll right?"

"Yea, of course we know. And everyone embraced one another, then Game said, "if ya'll need any assistance then you know where I'm at…!"

"Now go and get the money." And everybody smiled.

Lady-G said, "G-Fly here's the address to the drug rehab center that I've enrolled your mother into, she was kind of pissed-off for a minute, but I set her straight with a little ass woopen, I hope you don't mind."

"No baby, I love you for it! I've been wanting to kick her ass for the longest now, but just couldn't muster up the heart too. I'll go and see her in a couple of days and grab her some things."

"Oh, I took care of that too. I took her shoppin for some clothes and necessities. Nothing fly, but something that she can stay warm and comfortable in. Give her a couple of weeks, then go and check on her. That way she could have overcome the initial withdraws."

"Thank you sis…..!"

"You know I got your back don't you?"

"Yep and you're the realest and downest of them all, and I got 24 of them." Everyone laughed as they all left out of the safe house.

The youngster beeper was going off like crazy. Kill, Blue, and Insane all started selling birds already cooked up for 36 ounces for $14,000 dollars a bird. And a bird of powder for $15,500 dollars, and they was sellin 10 birds a piece everyday, like clock work. They will get the money up front and the youngsters would bring what they request. When they sold a bird already cooked up, the youngsters would give them 48 ounces for $13,500 dollars, and they would give their clients 36 ounces and they would keep the extra 12 ounce for themselves. So they will make 12 ounces and $500 dollars on each bird. And on the bird soft, they will just make a $2,000 dollars profit off each bird and they was sellin' them like crazy.

After the second package, the youngsters started giving Princess an ounce for $300.00, instead of $400 hundred dollars an ounce, and told her to give it to the girls, so they could make a hundred dollar profit off each ounce that they sold for $400 hundred dollars.

The girls was sellin' 2 birds a day which was equivalent to 96 ounces on each sack so the girls all was splitting a $9,600 dollars profit each day and Princess was still making a $4,800 dollar profit herself. Not including the profit that they made off of sellin' their weed.

* * * *

Big Mike was at the motel room with Psyco, and Gangsta Dan putting down the lick for the 30 birds. Tito the Mexican baller who was light weight supplying 40% of the weighed being purchase in Los Angeles was with two out of his three worker-body guards.

Two of his workers was counting the money, and the other one was outside in the Mini Blazer with the 30 Birds and a Mac 10.

Big Mike looked at Tito and said, "Yea Tito, we was coping from Game, but he tried to go up on his prices on us to $14,000 thousand dollars a bird, and we was already paying $13,500 dollars a bird, and only getting 25 birds so he was already getting over on us. Now we're able to get 30 birds for damn near the same price by fuckin with you, and we be coping this every week. Me and my homeboys be hard on the grind."

Tito knew that Game was considered one of the major players in L.A. and was glad to be able to steal a piece of his action.

Tito said, "Just call me, I got you! We do good business together and my product is the best, you'll see!"

Tito's worker said, "It's all here boss."

"Go and help Juan bring in the Yayo, Vominos!" His worker went outside and told Juan to bring the dope. Psyco and Gangsta Dam was posted up in the motel room on point, and when the worker's and Juan bung in the dope, and Psyco closed the door behind them. Gangsta Dam seen Juan walk in with a small suit case in one hand and the Mac 10 in the other and when Juan looked at Tito for directions, Gangsta Dam pulled out his 380 with a silencer attached to the end of it, and in one motion shot Juan in the temples and blow his brains out the side of his face. Then pointed the guns at the other worker who was in shock. Then Psyco and Big Mike drew down on Tito and the other worker.

Tito said, "man don't shoot, don't shoot, take the fuckin dope!'

Big Mike said, "put your damn hands up muthafucka!" Tito and his worker complied as Gansta Dam removed their guns and handcuffed them. Big Mike reach down and pick up the Mac 10 out of Juan hand and said," I always wanted one of these and he grabbed the suit case and opened it and said, "that's what I'm talking about as he seen the 30 kilos of cocaine. Gangsta Dam started gathering up the money and Big Mike said, "Listen Tito, I'ma give you and ultimatum, and you can decide what's best for you and your people. You can take me to you safe house and give me the rest of the dope and I'll let you and your boys live, and you take your ass back to Mexico and lived like kings off the money that you already stashed away. Or we can just kill you all now and be happy with just coming up on these 30 birds."

Tito said, "Do I really have a fuckin choice?"

Big Mike laughed and said, "Hell yea you have a

fuckin choice, because if you try something stupid, then you and your boys is dead. I'ma leave my homeboy behind with your two associates, and he looked at Gangsta Dan, then said, " and if you do what's right then he's going to let them live and leave, and you can come back and get them later and ya'll go back across that boarder and don't bring your bean eating ass back out here! But if you do something stupid, then he will kill them and if we don't call him back at the appointed time, then he'll kill them as well. So what you gonna do?"

"I'll take you to the spot……!"

"Where is the spot located at?"

"In eagle rock….!"

"Is any one living there?"

"Just my girls, but it's my safe house."

"Okay listen, 'G', keep the dope, and money with you and once we get the rest of the dope then we will call you on your cell phone and you just take the dope and leave them here."

"Listen, will-call-YOU, let me tell you the time in your ear," and Gangsta Dam walked over as Big Mike said, "Kill them when we leave, and we'll page you and meet up later."

"You understand, and if you don't hear from us during that times that I told you, or within five minute of that time, then kill them and get on. Because that would mean Tito pulled a fast one on us, and is probably on his way back with his pose'!"

Big Mike laughed and said, "Get up Tito we're going to take your truck."

Big Mike and Psyco escorted Tito out to the Blazer and Psyco drove as Big Mike sat with Tito handcuffed in the back seat. The mini Blazer was tinted dark so it wasn't obvious.

After they left the worker looked up at Gangsta Dam and said, "You're going to kill us huh?"

"Yep…..! So if you want to say a prayer I'll give you a minute."

"The other worker said, "Hey Amego? I go money and

Yayo at my house, and if you let me go you can have it all. I got over $200,000 thousand dollars and 25 kilos at my apartment. Gangsta Dam eyes got big and he shot the first worker in the head twice and said you should've been smart like your friend here, instead you want to pray when you know that your doing wrong. If you do something stupid I'ma kill you and if you're lying to me then I'ma kill you."

"Who lives in the apartment?"

"Just me girl….!"

"Where is it?"

"On the Westside."

"Come on," and Gansta Dam went and put the dope and money in the truck of the 79 Cadillac coup and came and placed a coat around the worker handcuffs and escorted him to the Cadillac and made him sit on the floor on the passenger side and he jumped behind the wheel and headed toward the workers spot.

* * * *

Big Mike and Psyco escorted Tito into his plushed out safe house in Eagle Rock, and as they walked in with Tito's keys they was greeted by Tito's two young beautiful mistresses. Both was young about 17 and 18 years old and extremely gorgeous with well develop bodies. Big Mike pointed the big 357 magnum at them and said, "I want both of you to lay down on the floor and don't move. Who else is in here?"

"No body," said the taller one.

Big Mike looked at Psyco and said, "Go and make sure!"

Psyco went looking through the house with his 9mm drawn. He came back two minutes later and said, "It's clear."

Big Mike looked at Tito and said, "Where is the dope at?"

Tito said, "Go look in the second bedroom on the right in the closet." Then Big Mike said, "Lay down," and pushed Tito on the ground and looked at Psyco and said, "Watch them."

Then Big Mike went to look in the closet for the dope and when he opened it, his eyes opened with shock as he gazed at the stacks of kilos that was neatly stacked in the corner. He seen a suit case and opened it and it was filled with money. He grabbed a sheet and walked back into the living room tearing long strips and said, "How many keys is that?"

Tito said, "it should be a 150…..!"

"How much money is that?"

"About $800,000 thousand dollars."

Psyco smiled and Big Mike said, "tie these bitches up and Psyco took the strips of sheets and tied the girl's wrist and ankles.

"Now back the truck up to he door and pop the back of it, we got some loading to do." Psyco smiled as he did just what Big Mike told him to do.

After Psyco loaded the dope and money into the Mini Blazer, Psyco looked at Big Mike, and then Big Mike took a pillow off the bed and drug Tito in the bedroom and shot him in the head using the pillow to muffle the sound. But, it was obvious to the girls what just happened. Tito was crying and pleading and then they heard two muffled pop and didn't here Tito voice no more.

Big Mike came out and Psyco said, "What about them?"

"You want some of that Big Mike asked and Psyco smiled and said hell yea!"

Big Mike said, "Either we can kill you or you can fuck the shit out of us, and I'll let you ladies live. What would it be?"

They looked at each other and said, "we rather have sex with ya'll."

"Good choice!"

Psyco untied the short ones legs and pulled his pants down and stared fuckin the mess out of her like a true pervert and two minutes later he bust his nut and rolled off and said this young bitch got that fire and looked up at Big Mike and Big Mike had a pillow in his hand and shot Psyco twice in the chest. The sound was muffled but the girls screamed was pretty loud. Big Mike said, "shut the fuck up before I kill both you bitches!"

"Now listen, he was the one that escorted Tito into the house and tied ya'll up, and then he took some money that Tito had stashed in the house, and when Tito wouldn't tell him where the dope was, he took Tito in the bedroom and shot him. Then he came into the living room and was raping your friend, when you got your hands loose, and grabbed his gun and shot him three times."

"Do you understand?"

"Yes", both the girls said.

"Now, I'ma give you both 10g's and a key a piece so ya'll can keep you mouth shut and do what I tell you to do. If you bitches tell the police any thing else, then I'ma find you both and Kill you, do you understand?"

"Yes, we understand, and don't worry we know what time it is."

Big Mike went out to the Mini Blazer and took out 4 birds and 30g's, he gave the girls a bird and 10g's a piece, stash the other 2 birds in the bedroom closet under some clothes, and then put 10g's in Psyco pocket's.

He looked at the girls and said, "When I leave go and stash your money and dope outside some where, and then call the police. Do you understand?"

The girls said, "Yea we understand."

Big Mike said, "Since I'm letting you live and giving you some money, then I might as well hit that pussy too. The tall one said, "I'm down with that, and Big Mike untied her legs and wrist and made her get doggie style and started fucking her hard from the back. Her pussy was so tight, hot, and wet and he knew why Tito had this hoes locked up in his safe house. The Mexican girl was moaning and talking to him nasty as she tightened up her pussy muscles and Big Mike could hold out and bust his load.

He pulled out and said, "Damn senorita, you got that chili pepper pussy, and he pulled up his pants as she smiled up at him. Big Mike said, "if we meet again, then we can really go somewhere, where we can get wild and crazy….!"

"You too, little lady. You owe me one-you hear me?"

"Anytime baby," she said and giggled.

Big Mike took the 357 magnum and went over and put Psyco finger prints all over it and said, "come here calling the tall one and said, "this gun got 5 shots – Tito got shot twice and he got shot twice. Now I want you to take the gun and shot him again, so you can have the gun powder residue on you hands and he would be considered shot by you three times do you understand?"

"Yes, she said.

Big Mike pulled out the 9mm that he took off Psyco and said, "if you try something stupid then I'ma kill you and her."

Then he got behind her and put the 9mm in her back and handed her the 357 magnum and she didn't hesitate and shot Psyco dead off in the face.

Big Mike said, "Damn Bitch, you didn't have to shoot his face off.

She said, "I didn't Know…..!"

Big Mike said, "I'm gone, if you girls try to change you story up, then the police is going to book ya'll for murder, so stick to the story and ya'll will be cool."

Big Mike left in the Mini Blazer full of dope and money.

The tall Mexican girl name, Lupe went to untie her friend Martha and said, "go and pack your clothes, and wash yourself up. We're getting the fuck up out of here girl. We ain't going to tell the police shit".

Lupe ran in the master bedroom and said, hey Martha he didn't get the other two suit cases. We're rich girl!" Then she ran and put them in the trunk of her Nissan Senta, and ran back and pack all of her clothes and washed her pussy up and grabbed her chrome 38 that Tito gave her and said, "Martha you get your gun?"

"Yes Lupe, and I'm ready when you are."

"Look at Tito!"

"Poor Tito, He was no good anyway meha' – we will have all kinds of men begging us to suck our pussies, we're rich now let's go!" And they jump in the Sentra with the $1,600,000.00 dollars and left.

They pulled up at the liquor store and grabbed some zums and wams, and when Lupe got back in the car she seen two young black boy around 15, and 16 years old and said, "hey, come here!"

"Us"?

"Yea, both of ya'll come here, the two boys walked up looking all bummy and broke.

She said, "What's your names?"

"I'm Keith and this is my brother little Ken!"

"We're your guardian angels and we come to bless you both with a new life."

"How's that", little Ken said?

"Here"……! And Lupe gave them a bag with the two kilo's of dope and said, "Do you know what that is?"

"Hell yea we know".

"Don't every use it, or tell no body where you got it from, and don't trust no-one, because a person will jack you and kill you for it if you get caught slippin!"

"Here!" and she gave them 10g' and Tito's 9mm and said, "Good luck and watch each other's back"

"We will thank you". Lupe waved good-bye and pulled off.

Keith said, "we ballin now Ken – you can't tell nobody.

Here, go and buy us some zum and wams and let go to our secret hide out and stash it".

* * * *

Gangsta Dam took the other worker who name was Joe back to Joe's apartment where Joe had his money and dope stashed. Also, Joe had his baby momma and 2 year old child living there too.

Gansta Dam tied up Joe's girl and grabbed the suit case full of money and 25 birds. He looked at Joe girl tied up crying with tears in her eyes, as she laid next to Joe on the floor with their little 2 year old daughter sitting between them.

Gangsta Dam said, "Listen, Tito is died and as you know, your other friends is died too. You know who Big

Mike is right?" Joe shook his head yes. "And you know the other one name Psyco the short stock built one." Joe shook his head again. Gangsta Dam pulled out 10g's and a kilo of cocaine and said, "I'ma let you live and pay you this – but you got to kill them both or I can kill you and your family, keep the dope and money and kill'em both myself.

"You call it?"

"You let me live, then I'll promise you I'll kill them both within a month" Joe said.

"If you don't, then I'll be back and I know both of ya'll real name's, so I will find you," said Gangsta Dam.

"Don't worry you got my word!"

"Okay, Hodios amigo"……. And Gangsta Dam, left.

Gansta Dam went back to his apartment and grabbed his clothes and the other 80g's that he robbed the bank for, and was on the freeway headed to Colorado to start a new life of pleasure. He had over $600,000.00 thousand dollars and 55 birds and said to himself, 'fuck Big Mike and Psyco punk ass. They'll fuck around and get a nigga killed or life in the pen. But not me….. Not the kid!' Gangsta Dam laughed out loud as he left his problem behind him.

Chapter 20
Rotten To The Core

The youngsters pulled up to their new seven bedroom baby mansion in Altadena Hills, and was full of excitement as Julian pushed the code to the front gates and the big black steal front gates started to open. Ty said, "Can you believe this shit?"

As Julian drove up the brick circular drive way to the front stair, that had two statues of a lion on both sides of the front stairs leading to the big double front door. In the front yard was a nice size pond that was full of big carps, and to the side was a six car garage. The youngster went up the stair and opened up the front door and step into another world.

Julian hit the security code and the alarm cut off. It was a three story baby mansion with three master bedrooms located on the third floor equipped with fireplace, big Jacuzzi bath tubs, see through showers and his and hers toilets and sinks.

The second floor had four bedrooms with connecting bathrooms shared between two bedrooms a piece, and a little study room in-between two of the bedrooms. It was a big circular stair case and the foyer was paved with burgundy marble floor tile.

There was a living room, dinning room , big family room and a big kitchen customize with black marble floors, and counter tops with cherry mahogany cabinets.

Also, they had a inside pool that went up to twelve feet with a big Jacuzzi next to it, and two more room attached to the pool, which was a gym with weight machines and tread mills and a big tinted window looking out toward the backyard. The other room was a sauna. The back yard was gated with a sixteen foot fence, and a beautiful view of the mountain that surrounded their area.

It had a full length basket ball court and a picnic area with beautiful patio furniture, surround with a custom brick Bar-B-Q pit area. There was another grassed area that had a full tennis court.

G-Fly said, “man this shit is too deep now! Game must me filthy rich man…..! Look at this place, man it’s bigger and badder then all of his houses. I love that nigga ya’ll!”

“I feel you ‘rade – he’s my heart too! Look on the fireplace what’s that?”

“It’s an envelope with a letter inside,” Ty said.

“What do it say,” ask Julian?

“It say’s, “me and Lady-G left ya’ll a present in the garage”.

This must be the remote control,” and G-Fly reach up on the fireplace and grabbed the remote control and they almost ran outside to see what was in the garage. G-Fly hit the button and all of the garage doors opened, and in three of the garages was three brand new 300 E Benz’s. A black one, Burgundy one, and a Dark Blue one, and all of them was trimmed with the gold pack and sitting on chrome and gold Dayton’s. On the windshield were all their names written in lip stick. The black one was Julian’s, the Dark Blue one was Ty’s and the Burgundy one was G-Fly’s. Then they grabbed the keys that was under the windshield wipers, hit the alarms and jumped in and started them up. G-Fly pulled out, and Ty and Julian followed him as they parked in the circular drive way, and got out and just sat on the pouch and stared at their cars.

Ty said, “man I can’t believe this….!”

“Listen ‘rades,” Julian said, “It’s ain’t hard to figure out, Game is retiring and he’s passing down the game to us.

It’s like he’s the Godfather and we’re his appointed Dons! He’s just letting us know that money ain’t no problem, and as long as we stay down we’re going to be blessed with the best. He’s down for us in everyway, and as you see, he got more money then he can ever spend and we are his adopted brothers, so he wants us to understand our position in life, and what he has blessed us with and handle it like it suppose to be handled. It’s our time to ball and we got to prove that we’re worthy of this position.”

G-Fly said, “I’m feeling that and I’m ready to pump

this game up to a whole nother level. We can't allow this small shit to blind us from our primary focus. It's 5:30p.m. now, lets put these cars back up in the garage, and go and handle our clients that's on hold, and let's take the girls out to dinner like we promised and then drop their asses off and go to the mansion in Westwood and lay down the law and get our major freak on. Then tomorrow we will hit the furniture store and pimp this spot out and once that's done we can floss like we got money. Ya'll feeling that?"

"Hell yea!"

"Well let's get back with Killa' and them and make the necessary pick ups and deliveries, then we can shoot by the main house and show our love and appreciation before we take the girls out to dinner and then drop their ass off and do it like only we can….!"

They all laughed and gave each other dap as they parked their new Benz's back and left.

When they made it back to the apartment they all split-up. G Fly took Blue 3 Birds hard and 3 birds soft, and Blue had $81,000 thousand dollars that he picked up from his client for their orders. Insane wanted 4 birds hard and 3 birds' soft, and Julian took him his order and picked up $94,500 dollars from him. Ty went to do the pack ups and deliveries to the spots and Killa' paged him requesting 5 birds hard and 3 birds soft, so after Ty finished his pick up and deliveries to the spots, he went to go take Killa' his order and left with $108,000 thousand dollars.

They all got dress to impress and put the $282,000 thousand dollars that they made for Game in a suit case and caravanned to the main house.

When they pulled up to the main house Game and Lady-G was watching a good movie and when they heard the vibration of the music they know exactly who it was. Lady-G got up and went to let them in, and the youngster walked in and all gave her a big hugs and kiss to express their profound love and appreciation.

They walked in the family room and Julian looked at Game and said, "Stand up and give us a big hug my nigga," and Game smiled as they all gave him a big hug and a mafia kiss on each side of his cheeks. Game blushed because he never had been kissed by another man, but knew how much love that his young comrades had so it filled his heart with joy.

Ty said, "this is $282,000g's, we sold 21 birds and 20g's from the spots."

Game said, "I see that ya'll went right to work. I thought that ya'll might be out joy riding tonight".

"You know it's always business before pleasure, we got an obligation first and foremost," said G-Fly.

Lady-G smiled and Game said, " I'm very proud of you guys, ya'll don't let materialistic things over-rule your judgments and responsibility."

Ty smiled and looked at G-Fly with admiration.

Julian said, "Man that mansion is like paradise."

"I'm glad that you liked it! Lady-G picked it out for ya'll, she thought, that ya'll need something that compliments your personality. Lady-G started blushing as Ty stood on the side of her and gave her a loving kiss.

"And them Benz's really complimented our characters too, especially with them Daytons! Who's idea was that?"

Game said, "Well truthfully, your bottom Lady brought ya'll them, she said that it was her obligation to cater to her men."

And everyone looked at Lady-G and she was blushing like crazy as all the youngsters stared kissing her all over her face. She began playfully fighting them off.

G-Fly said, "You got paper like that girl?"

"Of course! I'm married to the Game, both of them." And everyone started busting up laughing.

"Well get your fine ass up and fix your men a drink so we can smoke and toast to the good life." And she got up and did it without any hesitation.

"G-Fly said, "I love that girl" and everybody smiled and felt the same way.

"Game we need reservations at Charlie Browns."

"At what time?"

"It's 8:30p.m. now, so how about at 9:45p.m."

"You got it."

Lady-G gave them all a drink and a joint and she had herself a drink and a joint too!

G-Fly said, “Okay first everyone light you’re joint.” And they all complied.

G-Fly said, “A toast to us, love, loyalty and devotion, and may we always enjoy the best of life together and they hit glasses and took a drink of the Louis the XIII Brandy and a big hit of their joints, as all of them started choking and coughing at the same time.

The young men arrived to pick-up the girls at 9:10p.m. and was off to the restaurant. All the girls was dressed to impress and madly in love with their men, and it showed in their eyes.

As they got to the restaurant the girls was all floating on cloud nine, they never ever been to a restaurant this nice before, and as they walked in and was escorted to VIP section, their thoughts was racing. All eyes was on them, and they enjoyed all of the good and jealous stares. As they sat down the waitress displayed the $500 dollar a bottle Dom Perignon Champagne, and poured everybody a glass. Then he smile and said, “I’ll be your waiter for tonight, my name is Roberto can I get you an appetizer to start off with.”

“Yes said G-Fly, “shrimp and crab cocktail to begin and some raw oyster on the side.”

“Coming right up”……! And here is our menu and I’ll be right back to take your order.”

Princess said, “This place is the bom….!”

“You ladies is a part of us now, and we only except the best and strive to have the best in our life, said G-Fly. “What ever ya’ll desire to eat, then order it. Money is no object when it comes to us and ours, a toast to us, and the loyalty, devotion and principles that we live by. May we enjoy the best of life together,” and everyone clicked glasses and sipped the pleasures of ballin.

Everyone ate good and was full. Ty said, “ladies we was going to spend the night with ya’ll tonight, but something important came up, and we got to handle some business later on.

So we're going to have to make it up to ya'll some other time.

The girls was disappointed but knew better then to show it.

Ty put a $150.00 tip on the table and said, "Are ya'll ready?"

"Yea, it's about that time," Julian said as his Rolex watch displayed 11:00p.m. they got up and left and the waitress asked, "did ya'll enjoy your meal?"

"Yes, it was spectacular," G-Fly said.

"Well come again soon now!"

"Okay bye Jan," and they left out of the restaurant.

Little Tish whispered to Julian and said, "We forgot to pay for the dinner!"

"They don't accept our money here," said Julian and the girls looked puzzle.

G-Fly said, "every body loves you when you got money, but nobody can't stand you when your broke, so let this be a lesson to you. Never be broke!"

The girls started laughing, then Gwen said, "and that's for real."

They dropped the girls off with a kiss and words of departure, and headed straight to the mansion in Westwood. When they walked in star and Peaches came from the living room to see who it was, and G-Fly said, "Honey I'm home." Then the ladies started smiling with excitement, because they had been waiting for this moment for almost a week, and was glad that it finally came.

"How many girls is here?"

"All of us Precious and Unique just came in a couple of hours ago."

"Go and get the ladies and meet us I the family room," and Star ran up stair.

"Peaches fix your men some Hennessey!"

"Okay baby."

Two minutes later all of the ladies was assembled in the family room. G-Fly said, "first and foremost I want to see my ladies in their sexy birthday suits. And they quickly got undressed and stood before them in the best of their beauty.

G-Fly told them all to kneel down in front of them as the three youngsters sat on the couch next to each other. Ty blazed 3 joints, and passed 2 to the ladies, and they smoked one as G-Fly and Julian laid down the laws and business plans. All the ladies was captivated and excited by the ideas, and expressed their interested. Julian told them to research it and write up a brief business plan, and submit it to Lady-G, so she could make sure everything is estimated right and then they would put it together. G-Fly express the need for the ladies to campaign more and put their hustle in full effect, and the girls agreed and promised to hustle harder.

After the motivational speech was over, it was on and poppin'. The youngsters got naked and enjoyed the pleasures of the sexiest and freakiest ladies alive.

G-Fly and Julian fell asleep at 5:00a.m. and woke back up at 7:30a.m. and Ty was still putting in work. G-Fly went into Star's room for an early morning nut. And Julian went to hit Peaches again. At 8:30a.m. they was on the freeway back to their apartment and Julian received a page from Blue and he wanted 2 birds hard and 3 birds soft.

Julian said, "Damn, it seems like niggas in the game don't rest!"

They made it back to the apartment and Julian took a quick showered and left. G-Fly left right behind him and went to make the morning deliveries and pick ups. Ty got a few hours of sleep. Julian and G-Fly got back at 10:00a.m. and laid down and got some rest for a couple of hours. They got up at 12:30p.m. feeling rejuvenated and Ty left a note saying, "Went to see Killa', be back at 1:00 o'clock." Julian fixed them some breakfast and Ty walked in at 12:50 and said, "Killa' needed 5 of them things. After we go shopping for furniture today we got to go and cook some more dope up. We're down to our last 3 birds hard.

They got dressed and was off to the exotic furniture store that's known to have all of the fly shit. They took 60g's and had intentions of spending it all. They spent $3,000 dollars on each one of their bedroom set and $1,000 dollars on each of the other ones. They paid $4,000 dollars a piece for the off white leather corner group family room set, and for the butter taffy leather living room set. They put 8 dark blue leather chairs in the pool area with 2 nice exotic tables that cost $3,000 dollars for the set. Then brought a big beautiful black 12 chair dinning room set that cost $2,000 dollars and then went to Circuit City and brought 4 big screen TV's for $20,000 dollars 6 19" TV's and 6 nice stereo system and 8 DVD's that came up to 6g's and a nice black stove, refrigerated and microwave that came up to 3g's and a washer and dryer that cost $800 dollars.

G-Fly went to the mall to buy the blankets, sheets, towels, pots, dishes and glasses and spent $3,500 dollars at J.C. Penny's, and had them deliver it. He got a page from the girls and went to take them their sacks of ounces and weed. And then went back to the safe house and started cooking.

Ty came in forty minutes later and said, "Smart move! I need 3 birds hard and 2 soft."

He started bagging up the ounces as G-Fly was cooking. He bagged up 3 birds and grabbed 2 soft and said, "I'll be back in an hour."

Ty got back a hour later and started helping G Fly cook.

They cooked 30 birds and bagged them all up and got pages from Insane wanting 3 more birds. Then Paper called and wanted 30 more. Paper gave them his motel room and they told him that they will see him in an hour. They hit Insane off then went to go take care of Paper, and when they was finished it was ten o'clock at night when they drove to the new mansion.

They walked into their new mansion and it was plush.

Julian was smiling and said, "how do ya'll like it?"

Ty said, "its paradise!"

G-Fly said, "I know, we're ballers now…….!"

"You're damn right we are," said Julian. After that they drove to get some thing to eat at a hamburger joint and then returned to their new mansion to spend the night.

They was hustling for two weeks straight, and had to re-cope from Hector 6 times in that two weeks. Games was amazed at how much their clientele picked up and decided to start buying two hundred birds at a time, instead of just the hundred. He was proud of his comrades but didn't know that Tito wasn't around no more, so a lot of his clientele is coming to the youngsters and they are enjoying every bit of it.

Game got a call from one of his old associate and when he hung up he paged Julian.

Julian, G-Fly and Ty was at the apartment counting their profit up when Julian got the page. He called Game back immediately when he seen the code and after speaking briefly he hung up and phone and looked over at his comrades. Then he said, "We got a code G-Red!"

G-Fly and Ty looked up with excitement and Julian said, "We got a trace of Big Mikes spot. Game is on his way and he said for us to be ready to ride." They quickly put the money up and got dressed in dark clothes and grabbed their desired heats.

They pulled up at Big Mikes apartment at 9:30p.m. Julian said, "listen, Ty I want you to stay out in the car just in case we have unexpected visitors, that way we won't get caught slippin. Game, I want you to use the crow bar on the door – me and G-Fly's going in and you come up at the rear and watch our backs. Any question? Let's roll then!"

Julian, G-Fly, and Game was out the car and on a mission.

When they got to the apartment Julian peeped though the crack in the curtain and it was quiet and dark, with just a deem light coming from the hall-way.

Julian said, "either he's sleep, fuckin, or gone."

"Game hit the door," Julian ordered.

Game took the crow bar and placed it in between the crack of the door and frame of the door, and used his shoulder with his arm strength at the same time and knock their door open.

Julian was in the apartment first and running full speed into the bedroom with his 9mm drawn and G-Fly was right in back of him and they reached into the bedroom together with the arms only and gun in hand, and then looked and seen that it was empty and hit the bathroom and said, "Clear…!"

Game said, "Kitchen's clear too."

They looked around as Julian looked in the closet and seen a gang of dope and grabbed a suit case and opened it and it was filled with money.

Julian said, "Game, Fly, Come here," and they both walked in with guns in hand and seen the suit case full of money and dope, "jack pot….!"

Julian yelled, "G-Fly go stand outside and make sure papa bear don't show up while our backs is turned."

"Gotcha….!"

Game grabbed that bed spread off so they could tie the dope up in it.

They put all the dope in the blanket and tied it up. Then they took the dope and the money and left. They went straight back to the apartment and started counting what they came up on.

They took 120 birds and $600,000 dollars from Big Mike's apartment. And they was laughing their asses off.

G-Fly said, "I wish that I could see the look on his face when he finds out he just got robbed..! He'll probably start crying."

"I know I would," said Ty.

"Yea, that's a vicious lost….. Payback a bitch!"

"Damn Game, how much money did he owe you anyway?" asked Julian.

"Only 7g's.

"Wow……! That was a wicked 7g's." and they all started laughing.

"He got his ass whooped twice and get hit for 120 birds and 600g's. That's crazy.!"

Game said, "Since we all hit this lick together then we split it 4 ways that's a $150,000 dollars each and 30 birds a piece."

"Wait a minute Game!" said Julian, we owe you a meal ticket for the money that you put up for the corporate account so why don't you just keep the money and when we sell our portion of the dope then we will pay you the rest!"

Game laughed and said, "man I ain't trippin' – just pay me when ya'll become millionaires, which would probably be sooner then later if I may add, especially at the rate ya'll going."

"Are you sure man, because we're not trippin' at all about this sit, it was free anyway."

"Yea I'm sure…!"

"Now put it in your damn over sea's accounts, when ya'll balling out of control then I'll let ya'll pay me back!"

"Much respect 'rade," Ty said and they all gave him dap."

The youngsters pagers has been blowing up for the last hour, but they put every thing on hold.

Ty said, "Do you want us to go and sit on Big Mike's apartment and catch him when he comes home?"

"Naw, we'll catch him another time."

"Ya'll go and handle ya'll business and just bring me 12g's off each one of my birds. We got you 'rade, and good looking out. You know that I got to look out for my young comrades.

I'll catch up with ya'll tomorrow!"

"Cool, Oh Game here! This is the money we made earlier.

We sold 35 birds, that's $440,000 – $420,000 thousand dollars for the 35 birds and 20g's for the dope spot!"

"Damn, ya'll going to get me jacked with all this money on me."

"Do you want one of us to follow you?" Ty asked.

"Naw, I'm just joking I got it….!" Then Game smiled at his comrades with respect and appreciation and left.

G-Fly said, " I got about $380,000 dollars now and not including this weeks hustle."

"Yea, I got close to $400,000 dollars too," said Julian.

"Me too," said Ty.

"Listen man, I'ma call Ron and give him $330,000 dollars so he can put in my over sea's account G-Fly said.

"Good idea"

"Yea, count me in for $300g's too!"

"Cool, I'ma go call him now at his home, so we can just meet him tomorrow".

"Yea, let me call these nigga's back on the cell phone so we can get this money," said Ty.

"Hey don't forget tomorrow we got to take the girls and hook them up for being down and real with us," said Julian.

"That's right, we got to keep it real with our girls," said Ty.

"Listen ya'll, let's wait until after we sell these last 30 birds from our last batch, and then sell these other birds before we re-cope again. That way we can keep our profit separate from our normal hustle," said G-Fly.

"Cool, I'll tell Game so he will know the reason why we're delaying the re-cope," said Julian.

* * * *

Big Mike seen his door to his apartment door looking like someone kicked it in and shut it back, and he pulled his 9mm and ran in with his gun drawn. He made his way to his bedroom and looked in the closet and said, "ain't this a bitch…! I can't believe this shit! No body knew about the lick but one person – that muthafucka Gangsta Dam! I'll kill him if I ever see his big fat ass again. Something told me to move it to my condo too. Damn, I should have listened to my first mind. Let me get my clothes and leave this jinxy ass place. I'm glad that I kept some of my money with me. I still got about $600,000 dollars!"

Big Mike grabbed his good clothes and was on his way out the door, and fat Nell freaky ass was coming down the stairs.

"Hi Mike, why you don't come and see me no more baby, you know that I miss you!"

"I miss you to baby – check it out, since you always did me right I'ma do you right. You can have everything in my apartment here's the keys. Bye……!"

Chapter 21
The Big Payback

The youngsters spent the night with the ladies at the Marina Del Rey Mansion and the law was laid down. The ladies wasn't use to a man putting down the full court press on them, and they were loving every bit of it! They promised to go out and play more tricks, and they couldn't wait to invest in their own business. They all enjoyed a night of pleasure, and it was obvious that Ty was Jewels' love interest; because after the orgy was over, she made sure that he came and laid in her bed to get his rest. When he woke up at 7:00a.m. she made sure that he left fully satisfied.

It was one o'clock that afternoon when the youngsters pulled up in front of the house where the girls live, and all the girls was inside anticipating their men arrival. G-Fly had called Princess and told her that they wanted to spend some quality time with them today, and for the ladies to be dressed fly and ready to roll.

The youngsters walked into the house and were greeted with the deepest of affection. Everyone kissed and hugged and all the girls looked beautiful and sexy.

Ty looked over at Julian and said, "These ain't the same girls that we went to school with!" The girls all giggled at he indirect compliment.

"Yea I know!" Julian said, "Because I wouldn't be able to get any work done with any of them in my class, and everyone started laughing. "Come on ya'll let's go," and as they was leaving out of the house, the girls saw the three brand new Benz's and little Tish said, "Ya'll are clowning in a major way now!"

"You ain't lying girl," Gwen excitedly added.

G-Fly said, "Now, how are ya'll going to love us and not know us? Baby you better recognize the type of men that ya'll down with, because it's about having the best! That's why we adore ya'll because ya'll is truly considered the best, now let's ride." Princess took her place next to G-

Fly in his new Benz, Little Tish and Gwen jumped in the car with Julian, and Dee-Dee was full of joy sitting next to her Ty. G-Fly was leading the caravan, and everybody that they passed was all eyes, smiles, and frowns. They pulled up at Jim's Choice Cars and Dealership and G-Fly said, "Come on," and jumped out as Ty and Julian all pulled behind him and everybody got out of the cars.

G-Fly said, "Come over here ya'll," and the ladies surrounded them. "Listen ladies, this is our gift to ya'll for your loyal, devotion and realness to us, and to this game.

We're going to put a down payment on whatever you want, but you have to pay your monthly payment yourself, so whatever ya'll desire to have, then go and get it….We got your back!" And the girls all looked around in excitement as they started hugging and kissing all of their men.

Julian saw Jim walking-up, and Jim said, "How's my favorite playa's doing? I've been expecting ya'll!"

"What's up Big Jim, listen man, these are our devoted companions, please make them happy for us!"

Jim said, "Ladies, whatever you want, just grab it, the keys is under the sun visor."

And the girls looked at G-Fly stagnated and G-Fly said, "What are ya'll waiting for? Vominos meha's" and they all laughed and started running around the lot.

Julian looked at Jim and said, "We got the down payment to whatever they chose, and they will carry their own monthly payment. We just ask that you carry the insurance for a couple of years and make the monthly payments about three to five hundred with insurance so they can pay it off quick. Nine times out of ten, they will pay it off within a year or two, so don't worry about the number that you put down."

"I got you," Jim said, as Little Tish, Gwen and Dee-Dee all drove by smiling in three brand new convertible 5.0 Mustangs.

Ty looked at his comrades and said, "The girls got good taste!" And they all started laughing.

Princess excitingly ran back up to G-Fly, Ty and

Julian, and said "Baby I like that red and gold 190 Benz over there!"

G-Fly said, "I like it to, and I think that you would look fly in it, because it compliments your character. But why you ain't test driving it?"

She laughed excitedly and said, "I love ya'll so much!"

"We know girl, now go and see if you like the way it rides," Julian said. Princess smiled and was in the car and out the parking lot in no time.

Ty said, "So if the girls get the three 5.0 Mustangs and the 190 Benz, then what are we looking at for the total down payment?"

Jim said, "Just give me 5g's a piece for each 5.0 Mustang and I can put their payments at $550.00 a month and carry the insurance. For the Benz you can give me 9g's, and I'll put her payments at about $650.00 a month, and carry the insurance."

"That sound's pretty good," Ty said.

"Yea I can deal with that too," Julian said.

"Well how about some champagne gentlemen?"

"Sounds good!" And they all followed Jim into his office.

All the girls came back, and it was a done deal! Little Tish, Gwen, and Dee-Dee all got convertible 5.0 Mustangs and Princess got her Red 190 Benz with the gold package and chrome 19" Lorenzo Rims. Julian gave Jim the 24 G's, and Jim and his associates hooked the necessary paperwork up. G-Fly explained the specifics to the girls, and told the girls to give them a call when they got back home.

G-Fly, Ty, and Julian all left to go take care of their business while the girls waited for Jim to finish their contracts.

Jim looked at Princess and the girls and said with a lustful desire in his eyes, "Are ya'll some of the girls that work for their escort service?"

Princess looked at the girls with a smile on her face and said, "No Jim that's their other business."

"O' excuse me, I didn't mean no disrespect!"

"It's okay, it was a compliment," Princess said. And

thought to herself no wonder why they don't be jockin no pussy like that. They always said that they had other ladies in their life and this kind-of explains the void.

Princess saw the suspiciously look on the girls faces and said, "Every lady got to play their position and play it to the fullest."

And the girls all smiled and gave each other dap and Little Tish said, "A woman like me can never be replaced, because I play my part viciously."

"That's right girl!"

Jim said, "Ladies here's your paper and enjoy your new cars."

"Thank you Jim! Bye!" And all of the girls walked out.

Princess said, "Let's go and take care of our business and cook our men a nice home cook meal."

"Cool, we'll follow you Princess," Gwen said. It was the best day of the girls life, as they caravanned together catching every bodies attention and flossin' in their new whips.

* * * *

"I fixed it sir! It was just a minor problem, the wind must've knocked down your antenna last night. That's why your cable went out.

"Is it working now?"

"Yes, everything is working good now!"

"You know I got to have my sports channels."

"I feel you sir, and if you have anymore problems, then just give the cable office a call and they'll send someone right out."

"Good looking out young bro, here's something for your time," and Game gave the cable man a $20 bill.

"Thank you sir, I really appreciate it! The cable man walked out and got into his truck; he picked up his cell phone and dialed a number.

A man picked up the phone on the other line and the cable man said, "What's up Big Mike, this is your boy J-Cat, you know that nigga Game that you've been looking for?"

"Yea, what's up?"

"Well I just left his Mansion!"

"Is that right, where he lives at?"

"Not so fast nigga, what is it worth to you?"

"Man I'll give you two ounces, right now!"

"Cool, where do you want to meet?"

"Meet me at the Ralph's parking lot on Vernon Ave., in 20 minutes."

"See you then," J-Cat said, as he smiled and hung up his cell phone.

G-Fly pulled up on 53 and Hoover in his 300 Benz, and he seen who he was looking for sitting on the porch of his mother's house. G-Fly said, "What's up Big Max, you act like you don't know your young playa partner no more!"

"Well I'll be damn, is that you G-Fly?"

"Of course my nigga, what's up?" The two men gave each other a ghetto embrace.

"Look at you man, you're doing big thangs, it's only been a few months and you look like you just hit the lottery!"

G-Fly smiled and said, "You know us black folks don't hit lotteries," and they laughed.

"So what you been doing since school's been out?" G-Fly asked.

"I've been just trying to sell some of this weed to stay alive."

"What kind you got?"

"Just some of this good Mexican sess, you want a joint or two?"

"Naw man, but I got some Indo if you want to smoke some," G-Fly said.

"Hell yea blaze it! Your mom ain't going to get mad?"

"Hell naw, she might want to hit it too.

"O yea, well let me roll a joint and ya'll can have this sack."

"Damn thanks man, that's like a $100 worth of weed."

"Yea, I been selling that too!"

"You must be selling an awful lot, because you looking good."

G-Fly smiled and said, "Peep this, I came to see if you want a job?"

"I don't know if I'm ready for the type of job you're talking about."

"Naw man it's strictly legal in a sense," G-Fly said.

"In a sense like what?" and G-Fly seen Big Max's mother staring out the dark screen door and said, "Hello ma'am," and she just looked at him with a plain face.

G-Fly said, "Listen I own an escort service, and I need a down and strong man to watch their back and manage my security over them."

"O yea, I'm down for that – that's a legit job."

"But you can't have sex with the girls and you must be professional in dealing with them. If a client tries to hurt them or disrespect them, then I expect you to do what is necessary to deal with the matter. For instance, this is an incident that happened a while back with one of the girls," and G-Fly told him about the incident with Jewel and Ty! And Big Max laughed and said, "Young Ty's a fool for that one, but he's lucky, I probably would've just beat the mess out of him and got on!" And G-Fly said, "What do you get paid at the school for doing security?"

"They pay me $500.00 every two weeks," he said proudly.

"Well I'ma make you my head man, and let you manage the employees that I want you to hire. Someone who you can trust and be professional with dealing with the ladies. Do you know anyone who you can hire that fit these qualifications?"

"Yea, I got two cousins that's older but thuggish nigga's, and they will do what I say and be trustworthy.

"O'kay, do you got transportation?"

"Naw, my shit broke down last month and I need a whole new engine and transmission."

"Don't worry about it! I'ma supply you with three cars, and 3 pagers so you can be their when the ladies need you. They may call you at 2 a.m. in the morning or 7 a.m.

in the morning, whatever time they call I need you guys to be on point! Now peep, I'ma pay you $500.00 a week and your two employee's $250.00 a piece."

"You feeling that?"

"Hell yea!"

"But if you slip up once and leave my girls hangin, then I'ma fire you and hire some crackers. And if something happens to my girl's and you didn't prevent it when you could've, then we're going to get on some ghetto shit!"

"Man I won't let you down!"

"O'kay now my security company is called GP Security and everything is legit, so I'm looking for some professional employees."

"Got you boss," Big Max said.

"O'kay here," and G-Fly reached in his pocket and pulled out a thousand dollars and said, "Here, you go and get you some nice clothes, so you can look presentable, and get a good shave and hair cut or curl. I'll see you tomorrow morning at 11:00 a.m.!

"Good looking out young bro. Don't worry, I wont let you down."

"I know you won't, that's why I came to get you!" Big Max mother said, "Would you like something to eat young man?"

"No thank you ma'am, maybe some other time okay?

"Okay son, you're always welcome here!"

"Thank you Ma'am! I got to go Big Max, but I'll come and pick you up tomorrow Okay."

"I'll be here Fly and thanks a lot!"

G-Fly smiled and gave Big Max his pager number and left.

Big Mike finally had the location to Games main house and knew that his day of revenge was drawing near. But not only that, "Game was sitting on millions!" So if it's done right, it can be a beautiful come up. Big Mike laughed to himself as he drove his brand new 87' Cadillac Fleetwood through the L.A. streets.

* * * *

The youngsters was at the girls house relaxing after a nice home cooked meal that Princess and the girls cooked for them. G-Fly told them about his conversation with Big Max and how optimistic he felt about the whole business that he established.

Lady-G and Game was also glad and fond of the idea. Lady-G got the business licenses and the $20.00 an hour for escorting the ladies would go to the security business. And the way the escort business has picked up since the youngsters motivational speech, Big Max and his two employees would surely have their jobs cut out for them.

Julian said, “Lady-G went over to meet Tracy today. I wonder how they clicked?”

Ty said, “Man, as long as Lady-G is on the job, then Tracy’s going to be laced to the fullest.”

“If Lady-G came back and told me to dump her, then I would without a doubt,” Julian stated.

“I feel that,” G-Fly said, “Because if she don’t meet the standards for Lady-G, then she ain’t worthy of my acceptance!”

And Princess walked in and said, “Hey ya’ll, can I holla at ya’ll for a minute?”

“Sure Princess, what’s up?” said Julian, as she stood before her men as a devoted Lieutenant. “It’s nothing really, but I thought maybe I should bring it to ya’ll attention today, Jim asked us was we part of your escort service and I told him naw, that those are your other girls! Then I told the girls to don’t worry about the next lady position, but make sure that they know there’s and play it to the fullest. The girls agreed, but you know how women’s are when competition is in the picture. So if they try to please ya’ll too hard, then you know why! Also, we share each others bed too, when you guys ain’t around. Because it helps us to be sexually devoted to only ya’ll, and not running around horny all day when ya’ll be away for to long!

“Well we truly respect and appreciate your honesty and realness, and we admire you for being loyal to us and informing us of the girls possible feelings and thoughts," Julian said.

"Your not upset at us, or think bad of us for being sexually involved with one another like this, I hope?"

"Hell naw baby," Ty said, we glad that ya'll was smart enough to find an outlet, as oppose to allowing another to infiltrate your mind, heart, and body." Princess smiled.

G-Fly said, "I only got one question?"

"What's that honey?"

"Can we watch?"

"Are you serious?"

"Hell yea I'm serious, I want ya'll to put some blankets and pillows right here on the family room floor and get it crackin for us, and if it's hot enough, then we will join ya'll.

"If that's what you want then I'll go and tell the girls." Princess walked out of the family room and Ty said, "Boy this is going to be a night to remember."

"Ain't they all been like that?" Julian asked as he lit the joint and passed Ty and G-Fly one. Ten minutes later the girls walked back in with three big quilt blankets, and butt naked carrying vibrators. Princess said, "Ya'll just sit back and enjoy the party and whenever you want to join in, then just jump right in! Princess laid on top of little Tish and they started passionately tongue kissing and Gwen was on top of Dee-Dee kissing and sucking. Ty said, "I don't know how much of this I can stand," and hit his joint. Princess started licking little Tish pussy and put her big pretty round ass up in a doggy style position, and then started fucking little Tish with the dildo while licking and sucking on her clit.

Julian said, "I got to learn how to do that!" As he seen how little Tish was going crazy. Gwen and Dee-Dee was in a 69 position and licking each other while using the dildos to fuck one another. The youngsters watched for about ten minutes and G-Fly looked at Ty and said, "I don't know about you, but I can't handle it know more!"

Ty said, "Me either," as they all laughed and got undressed and jumped in. G-Fly got behind Princess and

Princess smiled as she seen her man choose her first, and moaned as he slid into her. Ty got behind Gwen and started hitting her doggy style too and at the same time Dee-Dee was licking his balls and driving him crazy. Julian called little Tish over to him and she straddled his lap while he sat on the couch, and she rode him like a true nympho. The party went on all night and everyone just fell asleep on the family room floor all cuddled up.

Chapter 22
The Rise Of The Dons

Two months has passed and business couldn't get no better. The youngsters was selling 200 birds every week and 20 pounds of weed. The escort service was moving in full swing and the ladies was doing triple the amount of dates then as before.

Game cut the youngsters in for 50% of the profit that was being made through the escort service. Lady-G opened up an office and made Tracy her assistant manager over the accounting department and research. The Asian lady name Zan who also work's for the escort service, handle's the accounting and book keeping side, and Jewel and Peaches are over the research and planning department.

They help the ladies research and write up the business plans, then Tracy would oversee the business plan and make sure that the numbers are accurate, and Lady-G would present it to the youngsters as a finished plan, and the youngsters would cut a check.

Then Lady-G would have the business attorney write up the contract and then put both of the checks in a business account to establish it's business purpose.

The corporation provides accounting services and business management advise to all of the ladies, and all of the businesses must pay the corporation 20% from there gross profit yearly for the services that the corporation renders.

All three of the youngsters have their own office in the corporation with their names in gold writing on the doors as CEO's/Executives.

Lady-G and Zan have their own office and Tracy desk is out front with Jewel's and Peaches' desk. They all fell in love with Tracy skills, and Lady-G embraced her like a little sister.

Game even admired her and told Julian that she reminded him of Lady-G when Lady-G was younger. Julian embraced this opinion as his fate and moved her in the mansion with him and his comrades. G-Fly and Ty gave their approval and was happy to have a good woman around them.

China, Africa, and Nina all put their money together, 80g's a piece and started their concert promotion and production company. The youngsters put up the other $240,000.00 to give the ladies $480,000.00 to start off with.

This sent the other ladies over the top with excitement and it was on in a real way. Me-Me' hooked up with Precious and they opened up two nice lady clothing stores that sold the expensive and popular name brand clothes and sandals. They both put up 100g's and the youngsters gave them another $200,000.00 to give them a total of 400g's to start with.

Diamond and Treasure started a night club that headlined live entertainment and hired China, Africa, and Nina production and Promotion Company to find and hire good comedians, entertainers and singers. They both put up 100g's and the youngsters put up $200,000.00 to give them $400,000.00 to start with considering that Game already had a liquor license.

Diamond and Treasure's grand opening had Keith Sweat perform and a special appearance by Robin Harris. The club was an instant hit! The name of the club was "Ballers Only" and the grand opening admission was $100.00 at the door.

The club held 1300 people at capacity and the club was packed wall to wall.

Plus the club sold baby back ribs and buffalo wing dinners for $16.00 dollars a plate, it was poppin in a major way.

There was two exclusive VIP area's one for Game and the youngsters with their family and associates, and the other one for whoever else could afford to live like a baller for one night.

All the girls showed-up and Princess and the girls learned the truth of how large and loved the youngsters was by all of their ladies. But once introduced, Princess and the girls was embraced as family, especially after everybody seen Lady-G hug them and introduce them as her god sisters.

All of the youngsters was over a million and a half strong and life couldn't be sweeter.

* * * *

Big Mike on the other hand had established a down young crew out of the Eastside of Los Angeles that was selling ounces and managing Big Mike 3 rock houses.

Big Mike was buying 20 birds from his Compton connection for $12,000 a piece, and giving ounces to his crew for $450.00 an ounce and making $16,200.00 off a bird of straight 36 ounces. He was making a $4,200.00 profit off a bird and his six man crew was getting off the whole 20 birds every two weeks allowing Big Mike to make $80,000.00 profit every two weeks, not including the $800.00 a day profit he make of each one of his rock spots.

Big Mike crew was a crazy and scandalous bunch of Niggas, who was as dangerous as they come, but loyal to Big Mike! Big Mike gave them a chance and they was out to prove their appreciation. Big Mike was outside one of his rock spot when this smoked out lady walked up to Big Mike with her young thirteen year old daughter tagging behind her, after coming back from the supermarket with her mom.

The lady said, "Hey Big Mike, do me something for this $8.00 dollars that I got."

Mike said, "Bitch I don't even know what a eight dollar rock look like!"

"Just give me a dime piece and I'll owe you two dollars.

"Bitch I don't sell no shit that small!"

"Listen, just give me something and I'll suck your dick and give you some pussy."

"Look at you girl, your sexy days is over," Big Mike said and laughed.

"I still got the best head in town," the smoker said.

"No, I'll pass, but I tell you what, I'll give you a $50.00 dollar rock if you let me fuck her!"

you do it anyway!"

"No that's not it Kim, he wants to have sex with you and he's going to get us some food and give me some dope, please!"

"I can't believe that your asking me this, you know I'm a virgin."

"Baby it will be real quick and once he's in you, then it will start feeling good. You got to do it sooner or later might as well try to benefit from it! Do it for me – you know that I'm sick and I need something baby or I'ma go crazy."

Kim was crying tears of anger and hate. "Just this one time baby – for me," Sandy pleaded.

"Big Mike, come here," and Big Mike walked in smiling like a true pervert. The tears from Kim's eyes only excited him.

Sandy said, "Give me my shit first!"

Mike said, "I put it on the kitchen table," and Sandy said, "Be gentle with my baby she's still a virgin," and Sandy walked out and closed the door behind her.

Big Mike started getting undressed while Kim just stood there in a trans. Big Mike said, "Don't worry baby I won't hurt you, I'ma take care of you and look out for you."

After he got naked he walked over to her and lifted her head and said, "Don't you want a man who's going to take care of you and keep you fly all the time," and she gently shook her head and Mike kissed her and started undressing her. As he kissed on her neck and ear he laid her down on the bed and pulled her old dirty jeans and panties off at the same time.

And her young fat pussy was enticing his desires. He un-did her old dirty bra and laid on top of her as he started kissing her chest and rubbing her pussy and once he touch her clit, her body became alive to his every touch and when Big Mike went to kiss her again she responded by allowing their tongues to dance erotically. Mike said, "Yea baby show me that you want to be my down ass bitch."

She knew that Mike had the hood on locked and had a

lot of money, and if anybody can save her from this misery and pain it had to be him. She would do anything to be able to leave her mother's horror and if this is what she had to suffer then so be it!

She said, "Just don't hurt me, I'm a virgin!"

Mike's dick was rock hard, but he knew that he had to take his time, "Don't worry baby I'ma make you love it, and he kissed down her body and once he got to her pussy lips he started kissing and heard her moan and he stuck his tongue deep off in to her pussy and her ass bucked, and Big Mike parted her pussy and started licking away at her fat clit. She was moaning and humping like crazy and when she cummed he stuck his tongue deep off into her juicy pussy and enjoyed the taste of her purity.

Mike kissed back up her body and said, "Did you like that?"

"Yes, it made me feel so good!"

"Now it won't hurt as bad," and Mike put the head of his dick between her pussy lips and slid in deep in one full thrust, she screamed and Mike let her adjust and then started gently fucking her with ¾ of his dick up in her and once he felt her adjust a little he rammed it all in her and said, "That was the hard part, now it's time to enjoy the pleasure of having your virginity took." And he started pumping his dick more and more as she moaned and cried in pleasure and pain. And Mike knew that he had to break her in good and he said, "Just fuck me baby, fuck the pain away, come on you're a big girl now, and you got to do it if you want to be able to satisfy your man." And she struggled through the pain as she started responding to his thrust. Kim's pussy was so tight that it was driving him crazy and he started deep stroking her and the pain started to fade and Kim's pussy was on fire as her orgasm started to build. She was moaning hard and humping back like a nympho. Mike knew that he couldn't hold back much longer and she said, "I think I'm coming," and her tight pussy clamped around his dick and he came with her as their bodies locked up in pure ecstasy. She looked at him as he laid on top of her and she kissed him deeply and said,

"Would you take me with you so I can be your lady for real, and only have sexy with you?"

Mike thought about the possibility and said, "Let me see what I can do."

Mike put on his clothes and left the blood on his dick as he got dressed. He said, "Take a shower," and she got up and did what he said. Mike walked into the living room where Sandy was smoking at and Sandy said, "Did you like it?"

"Hell naw and I want my damn dope back"

"Wait a minute, we had a deal!"

"Yeah but I didn't get a nut so the deals off."

Sandy clenched the dope in her hand and said, "That's not fair!"

"Okay I tell you what then," Mike said, "You come and finish off what she didn't and we'll be even!"

"I ain't got a problem with that," and Mike said, "Let's go in your room."

Mike shut her door and said, "Get undressed bitch," and she complied but stashed her dope in her shoe. Mike got undressed and seen that Sandy wasn't all that bad naked, especially that fat butt on her!

Mike said, "Suck it and you better suck it good."

She started sucking and tasted a bitter taste and looked and said, "You still got blood on it!"

"So what, are you refusing to do it?"

"No, but!"

"But my ass, it's your little girls blood so you shouldn't care, now suck it good or give me my shit back!"

"Okay don't get mad, blood ain't never hurt nobody."

Sandy started sucking it like it wasn't nothing and she was good too. Mike said, "Damn girl, now I know why they call you headquarters," and she smiled at her nickname.

Mike said, "Wait a minute I want some of that ass of yours."

She looked at him and said, "Wait," and went to get some grease and put it in her butthole and said, "Okay, now," and she got in a doggy position and Mike slid up in her butt with no problem and she started working her butt muscles like a vet hoe and Mike busted his second nut in her butt and then he pulled his dick out and "Said suck it clean." She looked up at him about to argue and then just started sucking him again but this time throwing up and Mike laughed and said "Go get me a towel out of the bathroom and clean me up right bitch!" and she complied.

Mike got dressed and pulled out the ounce of crack and said, "Listen," and broke off half of it, and her eyes was big and full of desire.

Mike said, "I'ma take Kim and let her live with me and raise her like my wife. I'ma pay you this half a ounce and give you the same amount every month, but nothing more! If you try to report it, then I'll tell them that you sold her to me and they'll take your ass to prison with me and as you know, them crackers will give you more time then me, so keep your mouth shut and we all can be happy!"

"What you say?

"As long as you take care of her and treat her good then I'm cool with it, you're going to give me this every month?"

"Yep!"

"Deal!"

Big Mike laughed as he walked out and went to Kim's room.

Kim was dressed and sitting on the bed. Mike said, "Do you really want to roll with me?" And her eyes got big and she said, "Yeah if you promise to treat me right and be down for me!"

"Of course I will, but if you betray me then I will kill you, and understand my word is law, you understand?"

"Yes!"

"Let's go then."

"I got to pack my clothes."

"Don't worry about that. I'ma buy you some new shit."

And she jumped up full of excitement and gave big Mike a big hug and a deep kiss and said, "Thank you baby, I'ma make you happy I promise!"

"You better," Mike said. They walked out the door

and Kim didn't even look at her mother.

Big Mike took her to the Slauson Swat Meet and grabbed her a gang of jeans, and shirts, mini dresses outfit, underwear and bras, lingerie outfits, socks and four pairs of nice tennis shoes and three pairs of sandals. Then he brought her a nice Turkish rope chain, and bracelet, and two pairs of Bamboo earrings. Then he took her to the Fox Hill mall and grabbed her some nice Guess jeans and a skirts, Fila sweat suits, and shirts and 3 pairs of Fila shoes. Some nice sexy summer dresses and bubble bath supplies, sexy underwear and bra sets and a few baby doll lingerie outfits.

Then he dropped her off at the beauty salon to get a fly Bob and a manicure and pedicure. He picked her up at 8:30 from the beauty salon and she looked every bit of 17 years old and cute and sexy in everyway.

Big Mike took her to Sizzlers and then they went to the Supermarket to buy some food and Kim's woman hygiene products. He was happy to find out that Kim was an excellent cook and when they got to Big Mike's new two bedroom condo, Big Mike said, "Welcome home Young

Tender!" Kim looked around the plush laid out condo and was in shock. She has never seen a apartment that looked this plush before in her life.

Big Mike said, "This is your new home now, as long as you know how to take care and satisfy your man and stay loyal and devoted to only me."

She looked at him and said, "I will, I promise!"

"Okay, but you can't let no one know where we live, or bring on one here and the other bedroom upstairs is off limits.

I got a lock on it and that's my personal room, do you understand?"

"Yea!"

"I put your clothes upstairs in our bedroom, so why don't you get settled in and take a nice bubble bath and put on something sexy for your man so we can celebrate our new life together.

"Okay baby," and Kim gave Big Mike a big deep

tongue kiss and said “You make me so happy and I’ma do my best to love you and satisfy you right, Okay?”

“I know you will baby.” Kim smiled and ran upstairs.

Later on that night Big Mike and Kim fucked all night and although it hurt a little bit, Kim ignored the pain and gave him all of her love.

For three weeks straight, Big Mike took his Young Tender everywhere and they had a lot of fun together. They went to Magic Mountain, Sea World, Knott Berry Farm, Disney Land, Universal Studio and the movies. Big Mike never had anyone who he loved or appreciated in his life until now, and Kim fulfilled a void in him that he never allowed anyone to fulfill. She was his young tender and his ghetto chosen wife. And he was her night in shinning armor and she deeply came to love him as well.

He gave her a nice diamond ring, a chrome 25 automatic and 2g’s and told her that he would buy her a car soon. He taught her how to drive and how to shoot and she loved Big Mike’s dirty drawers.

Big Mike enjoyed the best three weeks of his life, kicking it with Kim, but he had to get back hard on his grind and to the business at hand. His workers was complaining about how long it’s been taking Big Mike to get back at them and they’ve been loosing a lot of business and money.

One day Big Mike swooped by to take O.G.V his sack, after Mike and Kim came back from the movies and O.G.V seen Mike pull up two hours late with Kim in the car and O.G.V. started talking shit to Big Mike while three more of Mike’s workers was present.

O.G.V was a big tall muscle built nigga who was a cold killer and had a vicious reputation around the hood. O.G.V said, “Nigga I just lost out on about $2,000.00 in the last two weeks because you’ve been around her bullshitting. What, do that young bitch got your nose open like that? I don’t like the thought of loosing money like this.”

Then everybody heard three loud shots as O.G.V looked down at his chest and looked at Big Mike and said,

“That little bitch shot me!” Then another loud shot popped and a hole appeared in O.G.V’s forehead right before he fell to the concrete head first and dead to the world.

Everyone looked back at Kim holding her 25 automatic in her hand and she said, “Do anybody else got any complaints?” And looked at the other three workers. “If you don’t want to be apart of this hustle, then get the fuck on, either you down with us, or against us, and if anyone of ya’ll every disrespect me or my man again, then I’ll kill you too! Now take this piece of trash and get rid of him and after you finish, then we can resume our business dealing. Now get his punk ass up out of here!”

Everyone seen death in Kim’s eyes and Big Mike laughed and said, “Go put his ass by the railroad tracks over there in blood hood, when you get back give me a call. I’ma give each one of you guys 2 ounces a piece for your pass losses and we can get back on track then. “Any questions or problems?”

“Naw big homie, he brought that shit on himself. You know we still down with you!”

“Cool I’ll see ya’ll in a couple of hours then.”

And Big Mike and Kim got back in the Fleetwood and left. Big Mike kissed his young tender and just smiled. He took her to the Santa Monica pier and had her throw her 25 automatic in the ocean and then he took her home and went to check on his crew.

Chapter 23
Behold A Pale Horse

Game, Lady G, G-Fly, Julian, and Tracy was all secretly planning Ty a surprise birthday party at the club.

Ty's birthday was September 19th and Ty was turning 15 years old, nobody really knew Ty's real age but Princess and the girls and his comrades. All the other ladies that worked the escort would've guessed Ty's real age if it was a million dollar prize for anyone who could. They knew that he was somewhat young, but could never imagine him being anywhere near 15 years old. For he was truly considered a real, true, strong, and intelligent man within their eyes, and even if they found out that he was this young, it really wouldn't make much of a difference.

The party was scheduled for Saturday night and Lady-G was out Wednesday evening making the last minute arrangements, while Game was kicking back watching the Lakers get their ass whooped by the sorry ass New York Knicks.

"Come on Magic, just pass the damn ball right – fuck all that fancy shit," Game shouted at the T.V. as he coached his team in a subliminal manner.

"That's right, take his ass to the hoop then," Game uttered as he got up out of his big leather Lazy Boy chair to go fix him a drink at his bar.

As he was pouring himself a shot of Crown Royal to go with his indo joint he caught an eerie vibe and the sliding glass door that was next to him shattered as he felt a sharp pain in his right leg and fell to the ground as he grabbed his right thigh, as he looked up he seen Big Mike and two other niggas walk through the broken sliding glass door with their guns drawn.

Big Mike had a 9mm with a silencer on the end of the barrel and it was obvious that he shot Game through the sliding glass door.

"What's up Game! Long time no see," said Big Mike as he smiled down at the Game on the floor.

Game said, "I hope you brung my got damn money with you nigga."

Big Mike laughed and said, "You always was a stupid muthafucka! Pick him up and handcuff his ass," he told one of his crew members. T-Loc reach down to handcuff Game and Game socked T-Loc in the eye and tried to grab T-Loc gun from his waste band. Big Flip kicked Game in the face and knocked Game back down and Big Flip slapped Game twice with the big 357 Magnum that he had and knocked Game semi unconscious. T-Loc kicked Game in between the legs and Game grabbed his groining and curled up in a fetal position and T-Loc grabbed his arms and handcuffed Game with his hands cuffed behind his back.

Game laid on the ground and started laughing.

"What the fuck are you laughing at nigga?"

And Game looked up at Big Mike and said, "I'll buy you a drink in hell nigga."

Mike looked at Big Flip and said, "Go and make sure that ain't no one else here." And Big Flip went to go search the other room in the house.

"Bring me that dinning room chair over there," and T-Loc went to grab the chair. Big Mike sat Game in the chair and snatched the phone cord out of the wall and tied game to the chair as Big Flip said, "I checked all the rooms and they're empty, also there's a big safe in the master bedroom closet."

Big Mike said, "Okay nigga you know what time it is, we can do this the easy way or the hard way – it's your choice!"

"Nigga you might as well kill me now and save yourself the time, because you ain't got nothing coming from me!"

"O yea, well we'll see about that, Big Flip see what you can do," Big Mike ordered.

Big Flip said, "My pleasure," and pulled out his buck knife and said, "I spent ten years in Solidad State Prison and all I did was study books on how to torture muthafuckas!"

Game spit in his face a big nasty glob of spit that was

mixed with blood and Big Flip slapped Game four times like a bitch and took the buck knife and stuck it deep off in Games left thigh, and Game hollered in pain. Big Flip said, "I knew that you had bitch in you," and T-Loc started laughing.

Big Flip said, "Give us the combination and we will just go ahead and kill you and get it over with."

Game said, "I'm addicted to pain bitch, so all you're doing is making me horny!"

Big Flip started twisting the knife and said, "I'm getting horny too and if you want to keep your virginity then I advise you to tell me the combination."

Game was gritting his teeth and started laughing out loud. Big Flip got mad and started socking Game in face and after hitting Game eight good times and breaking Games jaw in two places. Game just giggled as blood ran down his chin from his twisted mouth.

T-Loc said, "Damn man, you broke the nigga jaw, he couldn't tell us the combination if he wanted to now!"

Big Flip said, "Shut up man, I got this," and pulled his knife out of Game's left leg and stabbed it deep off in Game's right shoulder by his trap and Game's bladder gave out to the excruciating pain as he clenched his teeth and screamed madly through the agonizing pain.

T-Loc said, "Man this nigga done pissed on his self," and Game giggled out loud.

Big Mike said, "Man you're making this harder then it has to be."

Game giggled again. Mike said, "Ya'll watch him while I go and check out the rooms. Game was sitting there drenched in blood and T-Loc started taking off Game's jewelry.

Big Flip said, "Man let me get that Rolex watch!"

"Hell naw, I got it first."

T-Loc stated as he put it in his pocket and took off Games two diamond rings and put them in his pocket too.

"Man let me get something," Big Flip argued.

"You can have the diamond bracelet and chain," T-Loc said. "Man I don't want that bullshit, you take it and give me the rings," Big Flip protested.

Lady-G pulled up to the main house and seen the dark blue Cadillac Fleetwood parked to the side of the road where no cars ever park at. Either they go up the road to one of the Mansions in the spaced out area or park in the drive way of whoever they're visiting, but never park at the bottom of the two car road.

Lady-G received that eerie feeling that's connected to a woman's intuition and parked out front on the out skirts of the main house, and crept in through the back way with her 3.80 in hand. When she got around back, she seen the sliding glass door shattered, and when she gazed into the side of the door she seen T-Loc and Big Flip standing next to Game arguing over something.

Game whole face was swollen and transformed and he was drenched in blood. All Lady-G seen was death in her eyes, as she stepped around the corner of the sliding glass door with her gun in hand, and as T-Loc looked up Lady-G hit him twice in the chest with the hollo points, and T-loc grabbed his chest and fell down backwards on the carpet.

Big Flip reached for his 357 in vain as Lady-G shot him twice in the face, blowing the back of his brains out. T-Loc was on the ground holding his chest and coughing as Lady-G walked up and stood over him and as his eyes got big, she shot him in the forehead.

She bent down by Game and said, "O' baby are you alright. Please baby don't die on me," and Game tried to say something but couldn't say it clear because of his jaw being broke.

Lady-G said, "What baby, say it again for me!" As Game was mumbling something, Lady-G heard two soft pops and looked up and seen the side of Game's head blown away. She looked up and seen Big Mike coming from the living room with his gun in hand and she jumped back and let off two of her shots as Big Mike's bullet just missed her head. Her two shots barely missed Big Mike's head and his gun jammed as he had her dead bang in his sights. He dived to the side over the couch as Lady-G jumped up and grabbed Big Flip's 357 Magnum, and emptied the rest of her bullets from her 3.80 into the couch and the area where Big Mike dove too.

Big Mike jumped to his feet and ran and jumped out of the big picture window as Lady-G opened fire with the big 357 magnum. Big Mike fell two stories out of the big picture window and rolled when he hit the ground to break his fall. He quickly got to his feet and limped down the driveway, as Lady-G let off her last two shots at him.

Lady-G ran back and looked at Game and said, “I'm sorry I didn't make it back sooner baby, I didn't mean to let you down.”

Tears ran down her soft pretty brown cheeks. She looked back at the two dead niggas and said, “Don't worry baby I'll get the other nigga too, I know who he is,” and she pulled out her cell phone and paged Julian and left her cell phone number and emergency code.

Julian, Ty, and G-Fly was counting up the money that they made today and separating their profit when Julian pager went off. He looked down at the number and dropped the stack of hundred dollar bills that he was counting and picked up his cell phone and immediately called Lady-G back.

Ty and G-Fly noticed Julian's quick reaction to the pager and just paused and stared at Julian to try to figure out what was going down.

Julian said, “What's up baby?”

As Lady-G picked up the phone, she said, “I need ya'll at the main house now!”

“What's up sis?”

“Just come now it's an emergency!”

“We're on our way.” Julian hung up the phone and said, “Something is wrong at the main house,” he threw a blanket over the money and said, “Let's roll.” And they all jumped in the 79 Cutlass and hit the freeway rolling in and out of traffic and trying to avoid the highway patrol.

They pulled up to the main house and Julian said, “We're going to play it as a G-Red.” Me and G-Fly would go in first and Ty you wait for three minutes and then creep.

They all got out and Julian and G-Fly crept around back and noticed the sliding glass door broke, and peeped in with their guns drawn and seen Lady-G sitting at the bar sipping a cup of Crown Royal and Game was still tied to the chair and the other two Niggas was just laying there dead as well. G-Fly walked up to Lady-G and hugged her and said, "Are you Okay baby?"

"Yea, I'll be okay!"

Ty walked in with his gun drawn and froze when he saw Game with his face blown off and the other two bodies.

Julian said, "What happened Lady-G?" and Lady-G told them everything. After she finished she said, "Look I have to call the police and explain this, so I'll probably be at the police station all night. I'ma call Ron in a minute and have him come so he can be here when the police come. Them two suit cases is full of the money that was in the safe in here, take it with you to the house and I call ya'll from the mansion in Westwood when I get back."

"Girl when you get finished you come to our mansion in Altadena and stay with us, you hear me?" G-Fly ordered.

"Are you sure?"

"Don't ask silly questions now! Our home is always your home." And she gave G-Fly a big hug.

G-Fly said, "Now go and pack you some clothes so we can have at the house for you, you don't need to be coming back here.

"Okay and she ran upstairs."

Ty looked at T-Loc and Big Flip's tattoos and said, "Both of these Niggas is from the Low Bottom. One got T-Loc on his arm and the other got Big Flip across his chest. These nigga's from the same hood that nigga Wheels is from. As a matter of fact Julian ain't this that nigga that you took off on at Princess party that night we kicked Wheel and his hommie ass?"

"It kinda' look like him, but it's hard to tell with half his face gone."

G-Fly said, "Don't worry comrades, vengeance is ours!" and Lady-G walked in and said, "Here, now take this stuff and go, I'll come right over once I'm finish with the police okay? Don't trip I got this, just leave!" G-Fly walked passed her with the two suit cases and kissed her on the cheek and left as Ty and Julian followed him.

The attorney Ron showed up and they called the police. Lady-G's 3.80 was legally registered to her, so it was all justified as self defense. Lady-G told them that she didn't get a good look at the third robber. And after the police found Game's jewelry in T-Loc and Big Flip's pocket it was obvious that it was a robbery. They asked Lady-G why it took so long to call them, she said that she was praying and leading her man to the doors of heaven. Her religious purpose could not be disputed, so the police just had the bodies removed and left.

Ron stayed until Lady-G finished packing some clothes and they had someone come and board up the windows and left.

G-Fly went to go do the early morning deliveries and pick ups and when he got back to the mansion, Lady-G was there already having coffee with Julian and Tracy. Tracy went to work and had orders to not tell the ladies that Game was dead. Julian told Lady-G that they would start combing the streets for Big Mike and see if they can find a location on him.

Lady-G said, "If possible, I would like to do the honors." And Julian, Ty, and G-Fly saw the death in her eyes and Julian said, "If we can take him alive, then we'll call you, okay!"

G-Fly said, "Listen our house is yours, pick you any bedroom and call it home. You're our bottom lady and we will appreciate it if you continue to play your roll in our lives.

Game gave us his all and told us to always honor and appreciate it, and you have always been our most admired gift of all.

Lady-G looked at them and smiled and said, "You guys really don't understand huh?" "What do you mean?" G-Fly asked.

"You guys was his chosen predecessors and he left ya'll his whole estate.

"Listen Lady-G, you can keep his belongings we're not tripping off his wealth," Julian stated.

Lady-G laughed and said, "Let me put this another way, Game was one of the biggest baller in L.A. he own businesses and real estate all over. He was fading back from the dope game when he met you guys and you was the joy of his heart and soul. Game had no family and couldn't have no kids! Also, he was dying from a rare kind of cancer and knew that he wouldn't be around long. The streets was his high and he couldn't walk away, so he vowed to play until his dying day. Everything that he owned he left to ya'll, now ya'll are the Game of the streets! And this is where the game gets ugly, because once niggas find out that Game is gone, then they will come for his territory. And just like Game had to kill to take it, ya'll will have to kill to keep it. That little money that he had in the mansion is nothing. He only laundered his money five million at a time and got a safe house where he kept the bulk of his money at in Inglewood. All that belongs to ya'll too! He had a Will that he left behind that Ron will read after the funeral. And I'm sure that you will enjoy your inheritance.

"What about you and the ladies at the escort service?" Julian asked.

"Well truth be told, we're apart of your inheritance as well! He made me promise on my life, to submit to you guy's as will to be your bottom Lady, and the only way that I won't is if I die, or you won't except me, or honor me with the position!"

G-Fly looked at his comrades and then at Lady-G and said, "Baby we all love you and of course we want you to continue to hold your position in our lives, but what type of bottom lady are you referring too?

"Well in order for me to be your bottom lady then either one or all of you must except me as your main lady." G-Fly said, "Baby can you go make us a drink and grab me a joint, I got to consult with my comrades for a minute on this one!"

"Sure," she laughed and walked away.

Ty said, “Man I love her but more like a sister! I was too close to Game to accept Lady-G as my lover.”

“Yeah that is kind of awkward,” Julian stated.

“Listen here,” G-Fly said, “Lady-G is bred as a thorough and veteran hoe. Her position is constantly threatened by rival hoes who want to become the number one. If she gets rejected by us now, then she would probably go crazy. Have it even occurred to you that she could have easily took the money and walked away rich without us even knowing about it. Her loyalty and love for us is her chosen fee, so to speak. She was always ours, but we just didn’t notice it in that sense, I love her and I love Game and if that’s his last present to me, then I’m glad to be able to receive her.”

“Well its final then, you accept her as your lover and we will respect that and just honor her as our bottom lady,” Julian said.

“I’m down with that,” G-Fly stated.

“What about you Ty?” Julian asked.

“I can respect that too, somebody got to except her like that, she’s the back bone to this organization, and she knows what Game never had a chance to teach us.”

“What about Princess,” Ty asked and looked at G-Fly for a reply.

“Man, FUCK Princess! She’s a down bitch, but she can’t even compare to Lady-G.” And they all started to laugh.

“Princess knows her position and I’m sure that she won’t try to over step her boundaries either”.

“Lady-G,” G-Fly called.

Lady-G walked in carrying four glasses of Hennessy and three joints on a gold serving tray. She handed them all a glass and a joint and lit the joint for them.

“Thank you baby, listen Lady-G, we sat back and considered your position in our lives, and all of us want you as our bottom lady, but would you share my bed!”

She looked and smiled and gave G-Fly a big hug and kiss and said, “Thank you for accepting me, I’ll always be devoted to only you, I promise!”

"I know that you would and I know that Game would never forgive me if I didn't accept one of his most precious and devoted gifts."

Julian said, "Now that that's resolved, are you going to be okay?"

"Yeah, I knew that Game would be leaving me soon, but I didn't know that he'll go like this."

"Listen baby, we want you to put down one of the flyest funerals money can buy. I want the world to know that Game was the prince of the ghetto, and make the world respect and envy the Game!" G-Fly stated.

"Okay baby, I'll get right on it."

Julian said also, "Call a meeting tonight at 6 p.m. and have all of the ladies meet up here so we can notify them all and assure them that the Game is still alive in us and that we will always be down and devoted to there needs."

"Got you baby! Oh and before I forget, here is the key and address to the other safe house. Also, this is the combination to the safe."

Ty said, "Lady-G, why didn't you just take the money and leave?"

"Baby I got money! I got a couple of million saved, so money isn't a big issue. I'm married to the game and I gave my word that I'll watch over and love ya'll. Whenever ya'll choose to get out of the game, then I will too, and if you guys choose to die in the game, then I will too!

The money that Game had put up in the safe at the main house was $1,300,000.00 and Game had another $3,400,000.00 stashed away in his safe house. The youngsters had $350,000.00 that they was about to take to Game and had 140 birds that they hadn't sold yet.

They broke the news to the ladies and after overcoming all of the tears, the youngsters reassured the ladies that they had their best interests at hand, and their number one priority to fulfill it. The ladies all vowed their loyalty to the youngsters and had confident in their abilities to satisfy their obligations. They knew that Lady-G was still considered the bottom lady and her authority was still law, and not to be compromised by the ladies at all.

Ty cancelled his birthday party and ordered everyone to fast for 24 hrs and only drink water from 8 p.m. tonight to 8 p.m. tomorrow. This was in commemoration to the respect that they shared for Game. The youngsters had a caterer bring some Mexican food and everyone ate before 8 p.m. and they started their fast together.

Chapter 24
Am I My Brother's Keeper?

It was a day after the funeral and everybody felt much better now that Game was laid to rest properly. The youngster's and all of the family members was told to wear all red during the funeral at Game's special request. The youngsters rented six beige Mercedes Benz limousines and put chrome and gold Dayton wire rims on all of them.

Then they rented a beige and gold carriage chauffeured by four beautiful white bouquets of red and gold painted roses. Big Max and his eight assistants was dressed in all black and walked along the caravan as they drove slowly down Crenshaw for a two mile radius. On lookers knew whoever funeral it was they had to be very rich and important, and the news was all over it.

After the funeral was over, Diamond and Treasure gave a big going away party at the club. It was suppose to be for Ty's birthday, but when Ty heard about it he changed it to a going away party for his God brother and devoted comrade Game. The party was off the hook, it was $100.00 at the door and all entrance proceeds was given to the Cancer Research Study. So the party got big news reviews as well. They had special performances by Guy and Tina Marie, and the party was off the hook. They took in every bit of $130,000 at the door and donated it all to charity.

Big Mike and Kim was laying back watching everything on T.V. and Kim said he must've been a very important person. Big Mike said, "Yea I think that he played basketball or football or something," and started laughing.

A baller named Little Creep from Compton looked over at his two right hand mans and said, "Listen up, now that Game ass is out the game, it's time to go out there and take over some territory. Go out there and set me up five crack houses. Have Crime and Felony go out there and start moving birds for $13,500.00 a pop! I'ma put fifty of them to the side for them and tell them to just bring me $12,500.00 of each bird."

"Gotcha boss"

"And tell them that I expect the body count to go up by next week."

"Gotcha boss" and Monster walked out.

G-Fly woke up on side of his new soulmate and knew that he had one of the downiest bitches in the world. She cut her hair into a sexy short Toni Braxton hair cut at G-Fly's request, and looked like a super model. G-Fly told her, "with every end there is a new beginning, and he desired his Bottom Lady to come a new." And as always she complied. She rolled over and seen him laying there staring at her as she woke up and smiled and said, "What's on your mind baby?"

"I'm just enjoying my blessings" G-Fly stated.

She said, "Our soulmate Game is in heaven flirting with the angels by now."

G-Fly said, "Or in hell pimpin up on some beautiful she devil, shit he might have a whole stable by now!" and they both started laughing.

Lady-G said, "Well I'm glad he blessed me with three of the downiest niggas alive! But tell me, since I'm all of ya'll bottom lady, am I obligated to please all of you guys sexually or just you?"

"Well we kind of had that conversation and both of them love you and respect you more like a sister, but I love you and desire you in everyway! So basically, they probably would never come at you on that level because of their feelings, but if they do then you are also obligated to satisfy them as well! Similar to how me and Ty feel about Tracy, we can fuck her if we ever desired to, but we won't unless we lost our brother to the game and chose to except her to fulfill his obligations to her. Just like if I was to die then one of them is obligated to fulfill my obligations to you and you to them as well, Do you understand?"

"Yep! Similar to the bible teachings when it said a brother should marry his other brother wife if his brother should die," Lady-G said.

"I guess! I don't know much about the bible, but it was a lot of fucking going on in there." And they started laughing.

G-Fly said, "You welcome to wait until you feel more comfortable with me, before we start enjoying sex together. I'm not tripping," G-Fly stated.

Lady-G laughed and said, "we could've been sexually active with one another when Game was alive. He told me if ya'll ever desired to have sex with me, then I was obligated to satisfying ya'll just like I was obligated to him. Ya'll just never showed a desire to!"

"Is that right?"

"Yep, one thing about Game you can believe is that he was totally down with ya'll and loved ya'll to death!"

"I guess he had to be to allow us the blessing of sharing his most prized possession!"

"And what's that?" Lady-G asked.

"You baby."

She blushed and rubbed his dick and said, "Well are you ready to enjoy your favorite gift?"

"More than you can imagine, but first let's do this in a special way." He reached over and grabbed a fat indo joint and lit it and him and Lady-G laid there and got a good nice deep high, and then he put two jolly rancher cherry candies in his mouth and gave her two strawberries and it was on in a exotic way. Princess showed him how to give oral pleasure to a woman and he mastered the art, and Lady-G was instantly sprung.

Game was from the old school and didn't believe in giving oral satisfaction to a woman, so Lady-G would have to go and kick it with one of her ladies to enjoy it, but something about a man serving his lady brings a different kind of satisfaction into play, and made a woman what to just do everything to satisfy him in return, and Lady-G was a professional in the art of sex and prided herself on being able to control her pussy muscles to make them wrap around a dick like a hand and make a man moan in pleasure. G-Fly thought that he had enjoyed some of the best sex with his long breath taking episodes with all of the women in his life. But Lady-G was by far the best of all!

After his second orgasm he rolled over drenched in sweat and said, "No wonder why you was his bottom lady, I had them all and nothing comes close to the loving you give." And Lady-G started giggling and said "You're the bomb too! I hate to admit it, but no man has ever made me feel that good!" And G-Fly blushed and gave her a deep passionate kiss and said, "Well you better get use to it because I'ma keep you full of my love juices!"

"I hope so!" and they both laughed and went to take a bath together as they enjoyed another fulfilling episode of intense pleasure.

* * * *

Ron read the Will that afternoon and Game left them all Julian, Ty, G-Fly and Lady-G ten million dollars a piece. He left the youngsters the five mansions, six houses and three apartment complexes worth twenty-six million dollars. He owned half of Charlie Brown's and two beauty salons and half of a trucking company that's all worth eighteen million dollars. And he had another fictitious corporation set up that had ten million dollars in it's corporate account. He left Ron five million dollars to take care of his family for life and the youngster's mind was blown. Lady-G said, "I told ya'll!"

Chapter 25
Friend or Foe

"Hey Wheel's long time no see!"

"Hey Janet, damn girl look at you, looking all fly and shit. What have you been up to girl?"

"O' nothing much I just been working and shit trying not to struggle to much."

"Well look like you've been kind of successful! What kind do work you do girl?"

"Well as quiet as kept – I'm doing escort and exotic dancing!"

"For real, now I know why you living good, because you got it good like that!"

"Thank You."

"So what you doing tonight?" Wheel's said as he looked lustfully at Princess hour glass figure hiding little in the tight sexy mini dress outfit and high heels.

"Well I was just laying back at this motel that I rented for the night. I had a date lined up, but he stood me up, so I'm just about to go and relax in the Jacuzzi and kick back. I might as well, I paid for the room!"

"Well baby you want some company?" Wheel's asked.

"Well I don't usually kick it with niggas for free, but since I always had a crush on your sexy ass, I might make an exception tonight. I tell you what, go and grab a pint of Hennessy and some rubbers and let's go and enjoy a night of pleasure together.

"I'll be right back," Wheels said, as he ran into the liquor store to buy the Hennessy and condoms.

Wheels came back out of the store and said I'ma follow you baby and he jumped in his V W Rabbit and followed Janet to the Comfort Inn on Crenshaw. Wheels smiled to his self knowing that he always wanted to hit that. Janet was known as a cold freak around school too, and now she looks fly as a muthafucka and her body had filled out viciously. She got to be getting paid a helleva lot with a body and looks like that, Wheels thought as he grabbed his dick and said we gonna put in some work tonight big guy, and he started laughing as he pulled up at the motel room.

Come on playboy, and Princess walked with her big pretty ass switching seductively in front of him as he walked behind her staring at her big ass like he was hypnotized. They walked into the dark motel room and as Princess shut the door. Wheels felt a hard punch to his eye and seen a flash of light as he hit the ground and said, "What the fuck!"

And G-Fly cut on the light and Wheels looked up and seen Ty standing over him and said, "What's up bitch? long time no see," and he pulled out his 9mm and said "Nigga lay down on your stomach and put your damn hands behind your back," and Ty handcuffed him.

"Wheels said, "Man I ain't beefing with ya'll like that no more – I excepted the lost man," and Julian knocked on the door, and Princess peeped out and let him in.

Julian smiled and said, "What's up nigga? I know you was a sucka for a big butt and a smile," and slapped Princess on the ass and said now I see why Adam got caught up," and everyone started laughing except Wheels.

"Put him in the chair and tie his damn legs up. They don't call him Wheels for nothing; this nigga can run like a dog."

"Listen man, why ya'll tripping on me like this – I ain't even did nothing to ya'll! Every time we fought I came up short, and I ain't trying to rec. no more!"

"Who was them two niggas with you that night at the party?" G-Fly asked.

"Oh that was Big Flip and Kato, but Kato ain't tripping and Big Flip got himself killed last week, so I know that ya'll ain't got to worry about him."

"How did he die?" Ty asked.

"Well I heard him and T Loc got killed during a lick."

"What happened to Big Mike?"

"Oh his ass is still rolling around with that crazy young bitch of his acting like nothing happened."

"Who's his bitch?"

"Some young 13 year old crazy bitch name Kim that he got turned out, and got her thinking that she's Foxy Brown or some muthafucken body. The bitch killed one of the Big Hommies from the hood for calling her a bitch and talking shit to Big Mike, and after that niggas bow down to her. Her mom was a cold base-head and rumor has it, that her mother sold her little virgin ass to Big Mike for some crack and Big Mike took her and spoiled her with the best and she will ride or die for him! And that nigga got the hood on lock with the Big dope sack so niggas basically kiss his ass. He got like eight of the homeboys slinging big dope for him, so niggas ain't about to jump out there and fuck off the hommies hustle. You know niggas kill for less, and all these niggas was broke and starving before Big Mike came and put them down with the hustle, so they all are devoted to him and got his back to the fullest."

"Is that right?" said Julian, "Tell me where he live at."

"Nobody knows, him and his young bitch Kim live together and he brought that little bitch a Suzuki Jeep, so you know that little bitch ain't giving nobody a second look, she totally devoted and loyal to only him! You know a bitch would sell her soul to a nigga for some new clothes, so you can imagine what a crazy bitch would do for a new Suzuki Jeep!"

"Where do his crew hang out at?

"Them niggas be posted at Fred's liquor store in the bottoms.

"Listen man," Wheels said, "It took me a minute to recognize, but I know who ya'll are now. Ya'll them three youngsters that everybody's talking about, ya'll was that baller nigga's who Mike just killed young Don's."

"You're a very smart nigga," Julian uttered.

"Listen man, I know we had our differences, but I can't stand Big Mike or that punk bitch that he got. They killed my Big homeboy O.G.V. for nothing, and O.G.V was the nigga that put me on the set when I was twelve years old and he taught me how to run and play football. He was like a big brother to me!

When I spoke on the subject, them punk niggas from

my hood started siding with Big Mike, and said if I ever spoke on it again, then they would have to deal with me. I wanted to get at those niggas but they're too deep, and all of them would kill!

So if I didn't take them all down, then I know that they would end up laying me down. They got the man power and the money so you know that you can't try to recruit no other hommies, because they might try to sell me out for a sack. But now if you put me on your team, then I'll help ya'll kill them Niggas, and we can take over the hood. All I ask is that you help me move my grandmother somewhere safe, and we can start laying these sucka's down, then I guarantee you that I'll be able to sell ten to twenty birds a week, not including the three rock spots that Big Mike got. I know that ya'll are some real and thorough niggas, and I know for a fact that ya'll are gangsta's. And if ya'll embrace me then I'll ride or die for ya'll and the cause."

"If we except you, then you got to show your loyalty by dropping two of your sell-out ass homeboys that work for Big Mike, and we want it done tonight."

"No problem my nigga – I ain't got no problem with handling my business. I just worry about my grandmother!"

"If you be down and loyal to us, then we will make sure that you have the best," Ty stated, and walked over and unhand cuffed Wheels and said, "Consider this your reincarnation nigga, and the beginning of your new life of happiness. But if you ever try to betray us, deceive us, or beat us, then you won't live to tell about it."

"Excuse us for a minute Ty," Julian said. "G-Fly, let me holla at you!" Julian took G-Fly in the bathroom and said what do you think?"

"I think that is a brilliant idea," said G-Fly. "The law says, if you turn your enemy into your friend, then he will be eternally loyal to you!"

"My thoughts exactly! Now have Princess drive him and I'll watch them, and have Princess drive to the alley in back of Jack in the Box on Vernon and Central after he put it down, I'll take him to the house on 54th and 2nd Ave.

and let him move his grandmother there, so she can be secure and have something nice, and I'll give him that 79 Cadillac Coup that's there and some change so he know that he's fucking with the real! Have Princess give him the gun in the car, so if he tries to go against the grain then all he would be able to get is her."

G-Fly said, "Cool!"

Julian walked out and said, "Princess go and holla at G-Fly," and she went to the bathroom to receive her instructions.

Julian said, "Listen Wheels Princess will take you to go and put down the lick, after you do it, then she would bring you to meet up with me. I'll be watching you to see if you're real or not. If you stand on your word, then we will recruit you as one of our lieutenants. If not, then you will really find out who we really are!"

"Don't worry cuzz, I got you."

Wheels knew that this was an opportunity of a life time and he wanted to become the man, and run his hood like it was suppose to be ran. Princess pulled the bucket in the cut a half block away from where three of Big Mikes crew members was standing smoking weed and sipping on some Gin and Juice.

Princess gave Wheels the 9mm and Wheels said, "Princess was you going to really kill me?"

"Of course, and once you come into the family, then you would know why."

Wheel's smiled at the thought and said, "Time to retire these suck ass niggas!"

And he got out of the car and started walking up to this homeboys. And Crip said, "Who's this nigga walking up?"

Gangsta stood up and looked and said, "Man that's that young busta ass nigga Wheels."

Sam cut back up the sound on his 63 Low Rider and said, "man if that nigga come over here crying about that O.G.V incident, I'ma knock his sorry little ass out!"

Wheels walked up and said, "What's up cuzz?"

"Nothing, just crippin, smoking and sipping, you know how we do it Loc," Gangsta said.

"How can ya'll let a busta with a sack and a thirteen year old bitch take over and regulate ya'll hood?"

Sam said, "Bitch ass nigga I'm tired of this shit, and put his drink down and started walking up and Wheels pulled out the 9mm. and shot him twice in the head and then hit Gangsta five times in the chest and looked at Crip and said, "Tell my nigga O.G.V. that I'ma ride for him," and shot Crip three times in the head and then emptied the clip in Gangsta and said, "I never liked your bitch ass anyway." And ran and jumped in the car with Princess.

Princess laughed and said, "Welcome home nigga!" She pulled up in the meeting spot and said give me the gun and go get in the car with Julian!" Wheels did it with no hesitation.

Princess started to laugh as she put the gun in a zip lock bag and said, "We got to have a strong insurance policy!" and drove away to meet G-Fly.

Julian pulled up at the nice three bedroom house on 54th and 2nd Ave. and took Wheels inside and said, "I hope that your grandma will like it here!" and Wheels looked around and seen the plushed out three bedroom house that was already furnished with the black leather couches and nice bedroom and dining room set. The back yard was big and had nice fruit trees and a flower gardens. It had a single car garage and in the driveway was a nice gray and black 79 Cadillac Coup.

Julian said, "That car is for you too!"

"How much do I got to pay each month for rent?" Wheels asked.

"As long as you apart of our family then she can live here rent free, and if you go to prison for a bid or die in the line of duty, then we will still pay her rent until she goes to heaven!"

Wheels embraced Julian and said man much love. Don't worry, my loyalty is for life!"

"We know, also, we put that 9mm in a safe place so we can make sure we can trust your loyalty and devotion to this family and this game, here's a couple of thousand, move grandma tomorrow morning and make sure that she got what she needs.

There's a clean 9mm for you in the second bedroom under the mattress, and you should find some clothes that will fit in the closet. Take a shower and throw away them clothes that you're wearing and here's my pager number. When that little bitch Kim comes to the hood I want to know immediately! And if you got any Niggas that's down for you, then keep them around you and out the hood, don't tell them why, but take them to a motel and get drunk and get an ounce of weed and party with some bitches.

Here are the keys to the house and the car, and when we get rid of Big Mike and his crew, then get ready to ball! Also if you get a trace on Big Mike or where he hangs out, then page me immediately! Your code is 888! I'll get at you later!" And Julian left.

Chapter 26
Fools Revenge

It was 6:00 p.m. the following day and Julian and Ty was at the apartment counting money from the forty birds that they sold that day. G-Fly went to sell fifty birds to Paper from Seattle and he took Princess with him to watch his back.

Julian pager went off and it displayed the code 888 after the phone number. Julian picked up his cell number and called, and Wheels answered and said, "What's up cuzz?"

"Peep, that busta that you've been looking for is having a meeting with his crew on the block, it's about four of them out there and they smoking and drinking, so it might be a good opportunity."

"Good looking out, stay low and out of the way."

"Gotcha"

Julian looked at Ty and said it's a G-Red, we got a trace on Big Mike he's on the block smoking and drinking. Then Julian picked up the phone and called the girls house and Little Tish answered.

"What's up little momma?"

"Hey baby, how ya'll doing?"

"Bad..!"

"Is Princess around?"

"No she left with G-Fly just me and Dee-Dee's here, why baby, you need some help? You know that we're down for whatever!"

"This is kind of ugly baby!"

"Listen baby whatever you want or need we got you! You're our heart and soul, don't you know that?" Little Tish said.

"Peep baby, I need a driver!"

"No problem I'm down baby!"

"O'kay meet me at Ralph's parking lot on Central and dress for the occasion."

"I'll be there in five minutes," Little Tish said, and she

hung up as Julian changed his clothes and grabbed his Mac 10 and 9mm. Ty grabbed his 12 gauge with the pistol grip and his 357 magnum.

They pulled up in the 76 Nova with the tinted windows and told Tish to follow them, they parked her bucket three blocks away in the alley and smiled when they seen Little Tish put on the blond wig. Julian said, "Girl you look kind of sexy in that wig, remind me to buy you another one later!" And she smiled.

"Listen baby, this is the nigga who killed our comrade, so we're very serious about this move. We need you there on point O'kay?"

"I will baby."

Little Tish parked down the street after she let Julian and Ty out around the block, the car was registered to a deceased person and nobody ever drove it or touched it. Julian gave Tish some latex gloves and she had on her wig and sunglasses.

Julian and Ty went around the back way and was creeping like two alley cats. Big Mike was out front of his dope house with three of his now five man crew members.

Big Mike said, "Hey Mick what time did Cat and Seven say that they was coming by?"

"They said that they had to go deliver some work or pick up some money or something. They ought to be by in another twenty minutes or so," Mick said as he turned back to the thick sista who just recently started smoking crack and ran out of money looking for some credit. "Listen baby I'll give you a fat $30 rock, but you got to let me and all my niggas's hit!"

"It's too many of ya'll for just a $30 dollars worth of dope. I can get more then that on the hoe stroll for this bom pussy," the smoker said.

"Well bitch go and get the money and come back, I can give Sandy a $10 rock and she'll fuck and suck me all night," Mick stated.

"Come on Mick you tripping! I'll do just you for that $30 rock and you can have as much as you like for three hours."

"Fuck that bitch, you ain't no muthafucken Halle Berry with your super high ass prices! Either me and my crew hit for the $30 rock or you go and sell it and bring me the money!"

Julian and Ty came from around the vacant house with ski masks on bussin like Navy Seals. Big Mike seen them first and dove behind his Fleetwood and grabbed his 9mm Mick turned around right in time to catch ten shots from Julian's Mac 10, and Ty hit Lip three times with the 12 gauge, and the third shot blow half his face off! One Punch tried to out run the Mac 10 as Julian hit him with six shots to the back. Big Mike reached his 9mm over the hood of the car and fired seven shots in Julian and Ty's direction. Ty seen the door to the dope spot open up and he pushed Julian down, right when old Man Pat started letting off his 45 automatic. Ty emptied his 12 gauge into the door of the dope spot and old man Pat jumped back just in time to miss the second wave of buck shots. Pat got hit with a few and he knew that it was enough to keep him out of the gun fight.

Seven pulled up and skidded next to where Big Mike was and started bussin his 9mm at Julian, and Julian jumped up and emptied his Mac 10 in Seven's 82 Cutless, Seven barely escaped through the passenger door. Seven was behind his car and Big Mike jumped up and made a run for it across the street as Ty and Julian was bussin viciously at Big Mike's every step, and Big Mike dove over a brick fence right in time. Seven seen that Ty and Julian was out of bullets and while Julian was trying to reload Seven was walking out in the street to get a good aim on Ty, Seven turned around a second to late and Little Tish ran him over in the Nova and stopped ten feet away. Julian seen Big Mike and shot five more shots at him in vain. Julian ran over to Seven, as Seven was trying to crawl away and he shot him five times.

Ty said, "Come on nigga," and Julian ran and jumped in the car and Little Tish pushed out.

Little Tish said, "Are ya'll a'ight?" as she seen the police hit the corner right before she turned at the other end.

Julian said, “We cool.”

Ty said, “Damn man, I ran out of bullets.”

Tish said, “We got company,” as she hit the alley to try to shake the police that was a couple of blocks in back of them.

She hit another street and turned down a back street doing a 110 mph. She hit another alley and pulled under a carport and said come on, and they all jumped out and followed her as she hopped a fence and ran around the back of some apartments and hopped another fence and said, “Take off your ski masks and give them to me!” and they complied and they turned into more apartments, and she knocked on the door. An older woman answered and Tish said, “Hi Auntee Sonia.”

“Hi Tish, how’s my favorite niece doing?” and Tish stepped in and pulled Julian and Ty in. “Let me speak to you auntee,” and Tish said, “Ya’ll have a seat and go wash your hands in the bathroom.” Julian and Ty went in the bathroom to wash there hands and Julian said, “I love that little down bitch!”

“Me too, she saved my life back there, because dude had me dead bang right before she hit him.

Julian and Ty walked out of the bathroom and Tish gave them both two men shirts. My auntee said that you guys can have these, and Dee-Dee is on her way to pick us up.

Sonia walked back in the front door and said, “Yea the ghetto bird is out there, but it’s like four blocks over. Ya’ll cool! Would ya’ll like a beer or a glass of E & J?” Julian and Ty said “E & J please!” and Tish and Sonia started laughing as Tish said, “I’ll take a glass too!” and Julian and Ty started busting up. Ty said, “Tish come here! Peep, would your auntee mind if we smoked a joint?”

“Naw she might want to hit it too!” and Ty laughed and said, “Give me a kiss,” and she kissed him and he said, “Thank you baby!”

“You know that I got ya’ll back, ya’ll all I got and love!” And they hugged and kissed again. Dee-Dee knocked on the door and Sonia let her in and she hugged

Tish, Ty and Julian and said, 'I'll pull the car to the front door and ya'll can just get in," and she left back out the door.

Julian went over and kissed Sonia on the cheek and gave her a wad of $3,000.00 and said, "We really appreciate it, and if you ever need anything then call Tish and she will let me know."

Sonia eyes were big and Ty kissed her on the cheek too and then Little Tish said, "Bye Auntee," and gave her a big hug and kiss and said, "If you need me call me okay?"

"Okay, thank you guys so much."

"No thank you," Julian said as they left.

* * * *

Tish was the life of the party and everybody showed their gratitude. Julian brought her a gold Rolex watch. Ty brought all the girls diamond bracelets and brought Little Tish a beautiful 4 carat diamond ring. G-Fly just brought them all a round trip ticket to Hawaii, four days and three nights in one of the best hotels and gave them five thousand to spend. The girls was excited and left two days after.

While they was gone the youngsters took the money that they got from selling the mansion in Hollywood Hills and brought another mansion for them and the girls to live in, in Anaheim Hill, it was eight bedrooms with a pool, Jacuzzi, sauna and tennis court with a basketball court, gym and six car garage with circular stairs and driveway, marble floors and cabinets. It cost four million and it was worth all that and more.

G-Fly and Lady-G did all of the shopping and it was laid out proper. Lady-G had Jim order all of the youngsters 560 SEC convertible Benz's and had them delivered to their Altadena Hills mansion along with Tracy's 300E Benz. G-Fly's Benz was egg shell white all over and trimmed in gold with the AMG kit,

Julian's was a burgundy and beige with gold trimming and the AMG kit, Ty's was all black and trimmed in gold with the AMG kit, and Tracy's 300E was dark blue and white with the AMG kit. All of them was wrapped in a big bow and had everyone's name written in lip stick on the wind shield.

As the youngsters pulled up at their mansion and noticed the four Benz's parked out front in the circular driveway.

G-Fly looked over at Julian and said, "I love that bitch man!"

"We know," said Julian, "We love her down ass too." And they got out and went to look at their new Benz's and they were just like the one that Game had. Lady-G said from the doorway, "My men only drive the best!" and G-Fly said, "Come here bitch," and she laughed and walked over and they gave each other a big hug and she said, "I got another surprise for you too!"

"What?" and she whispered in his ear and he looked at her with excitement in his eyes and said, "Guess what ya'll?" and Ty and Julian said "What Nigga?"

"We're going to have a little Gangsta running around!"

"What!" said Ty.

"For real" Julian stated, and Lady-G said, "Yep!" And they ran up and gave her a big hug and kiss. G-Fly said, "We have to go out to celebrate tonight, call the restaurant baby it's party time.

Tracy pulled up and seen all of the Benz's and got out of her new 5.0 Mustang that Julian brought her. "Ya'll doing to much!"

"Lady G brought us these."

"Those are nice," and she seen the name on the 300E and looked at Lady-G full of excitement and ran over and gave her a hug and kiss on the lips and said, "It's beautiful sis, thank you, thank you, thank you!" G-Fly said, "Guess what else?"

"What?"

"We're going to have a baby!" G-Fly said.

"For real!"

"Yes" Lady-G said.

Tracy looked at Julian and said baby, I'm pregnant too! And everybody eyes got big and started hollering and screaming with joy.

Julian pager went off and he looked at it and after the number it had 888! Julian pulled out his cell phone and called and when he hung up he said we got a G-Red. Big Mike's bitch is in the hood waiting to pick up some money, we got to move. And they ran and jumped in the Iroc and G-Fly was rolling.

They arrived in Wheels hood just as she was pulling off.

She pulled up in the liquor store and G-Fly said, "Should we follow her?"

"She might spot us and fuck everything up," Ty said, "I got a better idea, Julian follow me – G-Fly watch our back and we're going to the spot on 47th and Broadway through the alley!"

Ty and Julian got out of the Iroc and when Kim walked out of the liquor store Ty walked up to her and when she turned around he hit her right on the chin and knocked her out cold, then picked her up and put her in the back seat of her Jeep and drove off while Julian sat in the back seat with her. Julian looked in her Fendi purse and took her 380 and put it in his pocket and grabbed a wad of money that she just picked up from Big Mike's spot and her little stack.

They pulled up in the back of one of their old safe houses that they don't use no more and carried Kim in and handcuffed her and tied her ass up. They put on hat's and T-shirts tied around their mouths.

G-Fly said, "I got this," and Julian and Ty shook their heads. G-Fly walked up and threw a cold glass of water in her face and when she awoke from the initial shock, G-Fly slapped her hard enough to let her know that it was the real deal.

She looked up and he said, "Bitch wake your stupid ass up we ain't got all day. We know who you are and we know who your man is, he's that nigga name Big Mike who got the bottom on lock. That nigga fucked my bitch a couple of weeks ago cuz, I ought to fuck his bitch now that we got her! Teach that nigga about running around fucking everybody bitches. You know what I'm saying cuz!"

"I feel you cuz we all should fuck that young bitch,"

Ty said. “Listen bitch we going to sell you back to that nigga for 100g’s and if he don’t want to pay, then we’re going to fuck you and then kill you and then fuck you some mo!” and G-Fly, Ty, and Julian all started to laugh. If that nigga really loves you he’ll pay up the little money. He’ll make that in a couple of weeks. Hell he gave that bitch Lisa 5g’s, a fat diamond ring and that new 5.0 Mustang and all she do is fuck him and suck him every now and then. You should be worth way more then her.

Now what’s your number so I can call him and get this money and let your dumb ass go back home and play hoe to his desires

HA, HA! What’s the number?”

“777-9311.”

G-Fly faked like he really called. Kim knew that Big Mike would pay that little money easily for her, especially all the money he got in that room of his.

G-Fly said, “Is this Big Mike? What’s up cuz, listen we got your little young bitch here – what’s your name bitch?”

“Kim?”

“Yea, her name is Kim and either you’re going to give us a 100 g’s or we’re going to kill her. What you don’t care? What you mean you don’t care if we kill her? Okay man listen just give us 50 g’s, okay 25 g’s then! Man you think that we won’t kill her. What you mean you got three more waiting to take her place? Man she loves you!”

“Let me talk to him,” Kim said nervously.

“Listen man, just give us 10g’s and a bird! Okay just a bird then! What-you-mean, kill her? Man you’re a cold nigga!

Hello, Hello, Hello! Cuz, this muthafucka hung up, and told us to kill the bitch, because he’s tired of her!” He said that he got three more waiting to take her place and that he’ll pay us an ounce to kill the bitch.”

“Damn cuz, that’s a dirty nigga! He probably thinking about moving Lisa in after this bitch is gone. I don’t know who this fool think that he is fucking with cuz – since he won’t give us the money for this bitch and we don’t know where he lives, then we might as well kill this bitch and teach that nigga a lesson."

"I know where he lives," Kim said.

"What bitch?"

" I said I know where he lives if you let me go, then I'll tell you!"

"If you tell us then we don't have no reason to kill you."

"He lives in Inglewood on 113th and Crenshaw."

"How we know you're not lying?"

"Because I'm not going to give my life for a nigga who don't give a damn about me! Just give me the little money you took out of my purse and let me go and I'll tell you or take you if you want me too!"

"What's the address?"

"357 apartment 4!

G-Fly pulled Julian and Ty to the side and said, "What do ya'll think?"

"Man she knows too much! We got to kill her or she can kill us," Julian said.

G-Fly said, "Did you check her purse good?"

"I took her money and gun out!"

"Where is it at?"

"Right there!" G-Fly picked up the purse and looked through it and said Jackpot. Her ID says that she's 21 years old, and also says that her address is 113th and Crenshaw 357 apartment 3 not 4. Also her bank book got the same address.

G-Fly said, "Bitch why did you tell us apartment 4 when its apartment 3!"

"Don't worry, I got this!" Ty said. "Listen we're going to blindfold you and take you to a undisclosed location. But we're going to leave you tied up, so when you get out, then you can go about your business."

"Okay thank you!" Ty blind folded Kim and put her in the back seat of her Jeep tied up and drove ten blocks away and parked in a alley and put his silencer on his 380 and shot her twice in the heart and said, "Game will look out for you now!" And he walked around the front and jumped in the Iroc and said let's finish it.

Chapter 27
Pay Back's A Bitch

Big Mike was laying back on the soft butter taffy leather couch watching the Lakers and Houston Rockets square off when he heard his young tender walk in the door. Big Mike said, "Damn baby what took you so long". He looked-up and seen his worst nightmare staring at him from behind the barrel of a 9mm.

Lady-G said, "Oh, it just took me a minute to find your punk ass! Now ease off the couch slowly and keep your hands where I can see them".

Big Mike said, "Okay baby take it easy!" and Ty shot him in the knee cap with the 380 automatic with the silencer on the end and Big Mike cried out in pain as Julian grabbed him by his curl and drug Big Mike to the floor and went to handcuff him behind his back. Big Mike tried to snatch his hand back and was kicked in the face by a foot and knocked unconscious.

When he woke up he was tied to a chair and handcuffed with a gag in his mouth. G-Fly was sitting on the couch playing with the big chrome 44 bulldog that Big Mike had under the pillows of the couch. And the N.W.A tape was bumping at a nice loud volume to drown out any sound that big Mike could make. Julian and Ty came from upstairs carrying two suit cases full of money and one duffle bag with 15 keys in it.

Lady-G said, "I'm glad that ya'll made it back in time to witness the fun".

Ty and Julian looked over on the table and seen a hammer, 2 big butcher knives, and an iron. The microwave bell went off and she came back with a cup and set it on the table and Ty said, "What's that?"

"Oh, just some hot grits!"

Ty looked at Big Mike and said, "You fucked up." Big Mike started trying to say something and Lady-G stabbed him in the thigh with the big butcher knife and he hollered like it was the worst pain in the world and then Lady-G slapped him across the face with the hammer and broke his jaw instantly and knocked him smooth out. Lady-G threw the cup of hot grease and grits in his face and he woke up screaming as his whole face started blistering up. G-Fly looked at his comrades and knew that it had to end before they all have nightmares behind this shit.

He walked over to Lady-G and said, "Let me finish his bitch ass off for killing our comrade!" She stepped back and said, "Be my guest."

Thinking G-Fly was going to torture him some more, G-Fly then went over and grabbed Ty's 380 with the silencer and shot Big Mike six times in the heart. And he seen the disappointment in Lady-G's eyes and he grabbed a pillow off the couch and shot Big Mike in the face with the 44 bulldog and it took half of Big Mike's face and all of the back of his head off.

He looked at Lady-G and she was smiling now, and Julian said you two is meant for one another because both of you guys is crazy! Lady-G said, "We ain't going to ever let anyone disrespect the family."

And she took a bird from the duffle bag and placed it under the kitchen sink. Julian said, "Why you do that?"

"So it can be considered drug related and the police won't investigate that much, basically an open and shut case!"

Ty said, "Yea ya'll are meant for each other and I can imagine how much game that little baby boy is going to have!" And every one laughed and Lady-G said, "What if it's a girl?"

"That would be even worse!" and they all walked out carrying the suitcase full of money and duffle bag full of dope.

Lady G said, "Now our soul mate can rest in peace."

* * * *

Wheels said, "Hey Cat, what you been up to man?"

"Cuz, I'm just trying to stay low pro while this little war is going down."

"Yea I feel that! But peep this out cuz, I got some of

this indo man, you want to smoke a joint?"

"Yea blaze that shit up Loc! Bump that cut, you still got them four 12" woofers in the truck?

"Yea, listen." And J-Cat cut up his car stereo system and the car was beating as Wheels pulled out the 9mm and shot J-Cat eight times and no one heard a gun shot. Wheels cut down the music and got out the car and ran around the block to his G ride and rode out. He changed cars and went home to shower and then he paged Julian.

Julian heard his pager go off and looked at the number then seen the code 888. He looked at his watch it was 10 p.m. and he called back. Wheels said, "It's over, cuz!"

"Cool, I'll meet you at your house in thirty minutes."

"I'll be waiting!"

Julian and Ty pulled up to Wheels new house on 2nd Ave and Wheels came and jumped in the passenger seat of the mini blazer.

"I just dropped J-Cat punk ass, so we should be ready to put it down."

"Cool man, peep! This is 144 ounces and all I want from is $350 a ounce, that's $54,400 that you owe for your first sack, and when you finish that, I got another one for you! If you sold them all for $450.00 a ounce, and only made a hundred dollar for every ounce, then you will make $14,400.00 off each sack. The object of the game is to be able to drop one to two sacks a day! Not trying to make a thousand off every ounce and taking two weeks to move a sack. You feel me?"

"Hell yea, I feel you, and good looking out! I ain't never seen this much dope."

"Don't trip, you a part of us now and we got your back to the fullest! Here's a present from us to you to let you know that we keep it real." And Ty gave him a bag with 36 ounces in it.

"Now go get the money hustler and always keep it real to the game.

This is just the Beginning!

www.ingramcontent.com/pod-product-compliance
Lightning Source LLC
LaVergne TN
LVHW020703110826
845149LV00012B/2097

* 9 7 8 0 9 8 9 7 4 8 6 0 5 *